W9-ASE-558

THE MEASURE OF THE YEARS

Also by Alice Ross Colver

THE PARSON

KINGSRIDGE

DREAM WITHIN HER HAND *(A Biography)*

UNCERTAIN HEART

THE MERRIVALES

HOMECOMING

FOURWAYS

and others

THE
Measure
OF THE
Years

BY

Alice Ross Colver

PEOPLES BOOK CLUB
CHICAGO

Copyright 1954 by Alice Ross Colver

All rights reserved

No part of this book may be reproduced in any form
without permission in writing from the publisher

This is a special edition published exclusively for
members of the Peoples Book Club, P.O. Box 6570A,
Chicago 80, Illinois. It was originally published by
Dodd, Mead & Company.

Library of Congress Catalog Card Number: 54-11718

Printed in the United States of America

For
my two small grandsons
JEFFREY ROBERT BRINK
and
PETER WYCKOFF BRINK
who provided constant
enchanting interruptions
during the writing of this book

Author's Note

THIS IS THE STORY of a place born of an idea—an ideal—a dream. It is the history of Stockbridge, Massachusetts from its early beginnings to 1785. I have chosen to tell it through the happenings in the lives of a wholly imaginary family. Indian Town (as Stockbridge was originally called) is, however, as real as research and my limited ability can make it. And the well-known figures who move in and out of these pages, together with the historical happenings that occur, are based on town, church and family records and the records of established historians. It should be added, however, that the exigencies of the plot have required certain minor deviations from established facts. For example, there was no fifth white family living in Stockbridge as early as 1739. Nor was the land on the hill that Mark Martin bought from Ephraim Williams in his possession at that time. It still belonged to the Indians. And the little boy who was carried off by the Schagiticoke was actually killed before they reached the woods. Nor, in my reading, have I discovered any mixing of Indian blood with white. These and other differences that may be discovered by my readers will, I hope, be understood to be necessitated by story requirements and not due to careless-ness on the part of the author. I believe this tale is worth the telling, for Stockbridge is important and unusual. Its way of life, forever changing, yet forever the same, is impressive. And it has given and is still giving to America and the world great gifts to be remembered and cherished.

Acknowledgment

THIS BOOK could not have been written without the friendly co-operation and assistance of Mrs. Grace Wilcox, custodian of the Historical Room of the Stockbridge Library. For her generous help in unearthing and making available to me old records, books, maps, pictures and letters, I am deeply grateful. I am also indebted to Mr. and Mrs. John Palmer * whose forbears were early settlers in Stockbridge and who have contributed a number of suggestions together with family anecdotes and some factual material which I have their permission to use. I would also like to express my appreciation of the aid rendered me by the Tenafly librarians, especially that of Miss Margaret Doyle, who has unfailingly and tirelessly sought out background material for me whenever I have asked for it.

For the historical background given in the Prologue, I freely used two books, viz:—

Stockbridge, Past and Present. Records of an old Mission Station. By Miss Electa Jones. Samuel Bowles and Company, Springfield, 1854.

Stockbridge, 1739-1939. By Sarah Cabot Sedgwick and Christine Sedgwick Marquand. Berkshire Courier, Great Barrington, Massachusetts, 1939.

* Captain Roswell Palmer moved from Stonington, Connecticut to Stockbridge in 1803 and in 1822 bought the farm on the hill—holdings of more than four hundred acres and the setting for this story.

Prologue

WHEN THE PILGRIMS LANDED at Plymouth Rock the area all around the present village of Stockbridge was a vast forest wilderness. At that time the Indians owned the land from the Hudson River to the Connecticut and used the Berkshires only for hunting. But by the year 1680, decimated by plagues and endless warfare, the Mahicans who remained had been pushed east by the Dutch along the Hudson and west by the English along the Connecticut and had retreated to the Housatonic Valley.

In 1722 the first land grant in Berkshire County was made to the whites. For four hundred and sixty pounds of legal tender, three barrels of cider and thirty quarts of rum, the whites secured possession of an area stretching from the Connecticut border west to the New York line (then undetermined), east to the Housatonic River and north to Rattlesnake Hill in Stockbridge. This transaction completed, one hundred and seventy intrepid souls ventured to settle there.

It was an interim of quiet between wars. King Philip, who had led the violent and bloody opposition to the white man's presence, was dead. In the north at Springfield, Hatfield, Northampton and Hadley, there were outposts to protect against danger from the French, and to the British it seemed an opportune time for them to push further development of their rich new colony.

The domain they acquired presently became two contiguous towns known as the Upper and Lower Housatonic Townships. The Indians kept for themselves only two small reservations—Skatacook, on the northern boundary of the Lower Township, and Wnahtukook, beyond the "Great Mountain" (probably Monument Mountain in Great Barrington). Wnahtukook was later named Indian Town and, still later, Stockbridge.

About a dozen years after this land grant, there occurred in 1734 a great religious revival led by Jonathan Edwards in Northampton. And as part of the vigorous push toward a more fruitful Christianity, several ministers in Connecticut joined in an appeal to Colonel John Stoddard, a prominent member of the Massachusetts Board of Commissioners for Indian Affairs, urging that a mission be established to convert the Housatonic Indians who were known not to be hostile to the white man's faith.

The appeal was approved and Colonel Stoddard went to Boston with the proposal and returned from there with funds for the mission given by the British Society for the Propagation of the Gospel in Foreign Parts.

But the Christian faith could not be proffered where it was not wanted. The Indians must first give their consent to the establishment of a mission among them. Accordingly Konkapot, the chief of the tribe who dwelt in Wnahtukook, and Umpachenee, who was next in importance, were invited to Springfield with an interpreter, a Dutchman named Van Valkenberg, who lived in a cabin near Konkapot on land the Indian had given him.

Ostensibly the visit was for the purpose of bestowing a reward on the two Indian leaders in recognition of the services rendered by the Mahicans to the English during King Philip's War. But it was also to be an opportunity for sounding out the idea of sending a minister to them who would, in addition to converting them, freely educate them. Present at the meeting were the Reverend Stephen Williams, of the powerful Williams clan, the Reverend Nehemiah Bull and Colonel Stoddard.

With due ceremony Konkapot was named a captain in the British Army and Umpachenee a lieutenant, and these impressive military titles were accompanied by gifts of the appropriate scarlet and gold uniforms. Not until then was the subject of the mission broached. It must have furrowed Konkapot's brow, for, considering the increasingly wealthy settlement of English in the

Lower Housatonic Township (now Sheffield) south of Wnahtu-kook, with its trim houses, its church, its school and its prosperous farms, as contrasted with the steady depletion in numbers of his own people and their poor estate, he probably felt that the white man had something in his religion it might be wise for the Indian to embrace. But he could not answer for them without consulting them. He therefore invited the Reverend Williams and the Reverend Bull to come to the Great Wigwam (in what is now Great Barrington) in July, at which time, after consultation with his people, his answer would be given.

While waiting for the time to pass, John Sergeant was selected by the Boston commissioners as the person best fitted for the difficult and important work of minister. He was then a tutor at Yale College, but it was decided that he should go with the Reverend Bull to the Great Wigwam that July, and if, after seeing him and hearing him, the Indians wanted him, he would live with them through the summer as an experiment. Should this prove successful, he would finish his commitments at Yale the following winter and then return as a missionary to make his home among the savages.

July came. And through the deep wilderness across forty miles of mountains, following a faintly marked trail, rode the Reverend Bull and John Sergeant. The younger man, with his flashing dark eyes, his sensitive face, his moving voice and his manner of utmost sincerity, appealed to the Indians. After four days of deliberation, he was requested to remain among them.

By October he had his first convert, and when he returned to his duties at Yale in the late fall, he took with him the eldest sons of Konkapot and Umpachenee. These lads, willingly and trustingly sent by their fathers, lived with Sergeant at the college learning English ways while at the same time helping him to learn their language. Left behind to take the minister's place was Timothy Woodbridge, a teacher, who had been appointed by the Boston commissioners.

John Sergeant was possessed of the true missionary spirit. His concern over the wretched conditions of the Indians in his charge was genuine. His single-minded desire and most earnest prayer was to help them. He had no thought of personal aggrandizement or of possible political gain for the British.

He was ordained in Deerfield, in August 1735. A meeting had been arranged there between Governor Jonathan Belcher, together with an imposing number of His Majesty's Council and House of Representatives, and a delegation of the Six Nations, for the signing of another treaty. For six days the Indians and the British officials gathered "in solemn conclave" before the council fire. Beaver skins were exchanged for blankets, knives and ammunition. Wampum was passed, the peace pipe was smoked and finally the treaty was signed, after which a salute was fired by the British guard. Then the Indians were invited to the Deerfield meetinghouse to witness—as a fine climax—the ordination of the minister who, because of the friendliness and interest of the British government, was to live with the "River Indians" and give to them—freely—the white man's religion and the white man's knowledge.

It was an unforgettable spectacle. For during that hour the plain meetinghouse was brilliant with the red and gold regimentals of the British, with their wigs and ruffles and silver-mounted swords. No less vivid were the gay blankets and brightly feathered headdresses and beads and paint of the delegation of the Six Nations all decked out in their best regalia. In sharp contrast to all this richness of coloring was the sober black and white garb of the ministers present and the fluttering rags and tatters of the half-clad Mahicans among whom John Sergeant was to live.

"But the Lord said unto him—Go thy way; for he is a Chosen Vessel unto me to bear my name before the Gentiles."

In every corner of the room the solemnly read text was heard. A lengthy sermon followed. Then the moderator, the Reverend William Williams—another of that immense family—rose and addressed the governor, Jonathan Belcher. Was it is his pleasure that John Sergeant be set aside for this work? His approval signified by a nod, John Sergeant was asked if he was certain he wished to consecrate his life to the mission as a minister to the Indians. Clearly, quietly and firmly fell the answer in the still room: "I do." Finally, through an interpreter, the Reverend

Stephen Williams, of Longmeadow, questioned the Mahicans. Was it their wish to have this white man—this John Sergeant—come among them to teach and to preach? If so, would they "give some sign or manifestation thereof?"

In a body the ragged little group rose and "with grave as well as cheerful countenances signified their full and hearty acceptance of him."

Thus was founded the mission in Indian Town, the church that first brought fame to Stockbridge.

Contents

PART FOUR: THE FAMILY
1760—1775

PART FIVE: PA AND PRUE
1775—1785

Captain Mark Martin (b. 1705) married Esther Richardson (b.1710), daughter of Boston merchant. Mark retired from the sea (1739) and with wife and family moved to Indian Town (Stockbridge) that same year. Esther died 1747, leaving him six children—viz:—

Prudence
b. 1726
m. 1748
to Lt. David Reynolds

Mathew
b. 1728
d. 1780
m. Myrtle Avery 1760

Andrew
b. 1731
m. 1755
to Hannah Smith
Both killed
by Indians 1760

Luke
b. 1734
Killed in
battle
1755

Mary
b. 1734
m. 1760
to
Alec MacDonald

John
b. 1789
m. 1781
to
Myrtle Avery Martin
(Matt's widow)

Keith
b. 1761
and
Kim
b. 1761
Phoebe
b. 1763

Lived with
Marie 1746

Aaron
b. 1747
m. Sara Haskell

Ben
b. 1766

Rebecca
b. 1773

Luke
b. 1760

Lucy
b. 1761

Mary-Etta
b. 1763

Mark
b. 1749

Esther
b. 1751
d. 1753
(Killed
by Indians)

Faith
b. 1753
m. 1773
to
James Humphrey

Dulcie
b. 1773

William
b. 1775

CHAPTER I

The Arrival

THE MAN IN THE LEAD of the little cavalcade hunched his shoulders, adjusted his powerfully built frame more comfortably in the saddle and spoke sharply to his big black horse. "C'mon, Bess. C'mon! Be a good girl now. Step along!" The tone held sharp impatience as well as command, for he was tired to the bone.

Ten days and more he'd been hacking and slashing and hewing and chopping his way through this forest wilderness and still there was no end to it. The farther you went, the farther it went before you. Look around you and all you could see was green walls. They closed up ahead of you and closed up behind you. The thin twisting thread of trail they were following was swallowed up fore and aft. It was enough to drive a man crazy.

"C'mon! Step along!" he urged.

He was dressed in an odd outfit. Buckskin trousers, a wool shirt, a sea captain's cap and high sea boots. His great hands on the reins were hard hands, thick and calloused. His face, darkened by wind and weather, and gaunt from strain now, was

1

square in shape and bearded. Above his beard his black eyes shone with a piercing, bright, unquenchable light. A musket lay handy across his horn and all the time they were in the woods he kept it primed and ready.

He peered ahead trying to see through the green gloom. They'd all be blind as moles before they got out of here, he was thinking. Was that just a curtain of vines that had growed up across the trace ahead or had he mistook his way again? Abruptly he drew rein and looked about. There on his left was a darkened blaze on a tree. He was all right, then. Dismounting, he went forward and began tearing at the obstructing vines. By the tarnal! Now in front of him, directly across the path, lay the giant corpse of a windfall.

Rage stormed up in him like a tornado. Another! And this one a good six feet in diameter. Take all afternoon and then some to cut through that butt and they hadn't that much time. They'd ought to get there before dark. Well, they'd have to go around.

He looked to where the roots stood up in a mass of dirt. That would be the end to skirt, he decided. The top stretched too far into the tangle. Likely in falling, the underbrush had torn loose around a ways and he might open a path fair easy. Well, get to it.

He came back to his horse and stood for a moment looking at his following—the loaded mules, the dun-colored ox with his low-swinging head, the lumbering two-wheeled cart piled high with their possessions, the children frozen into waiting statues of suspense, unconsciously reproachful, and his anger that he could rightly vent on none of them for this new fix, came out in a roar.

"Matt! Bring the ax!"

He turned then to his wife. She sat sidewise directly behind his horse on Daisy, a brown and white mare. A long maroon cloak concealed her figure but she appeared to be tall and her shoulders were slender. Her head was bare. Her hair that might once have been bright, was faded now to a dull sand color and was fastened in a knot on her neck. The bones of her face were built for a beauty which was not lessened by her look of deep fatigue or by the tracery of fine lines all over her tanned skin or by a mouth that had learned to set firm and narrow through lonely and difficult times. Her clear gray eyes met those of her husband's with a look that, in spite of her weariness, had in them a gleam of wonder still, for she had thought he could not surprise her about anything after all these years, and he had.

"You all right?" he asked. His tone gentled when he spoke to her.

She nodded. The next moment uncertainty took her and she turned thoughtful. He did not notice the slight change of her expression as Matt came up then with the ax and she was glad. No use to speak yet. Could be just her imaginings.

He handed Matt his musket and took the ax and went forward again to the fallen tree. All the time he worked at cutting a clearing his thoughts were busy.

They had told him, back in Springfield, that he couldn't get an ox cart over Hoosac Mountain. They had warned him, but he had refused to listen. He was one made for combat and conquest, and what seemed impossible to others, was to him the invariable spur to achievement. If horses could follow the trail, he had reasoned, an ox could. And if an ox could, a cart could—provided it was narrow enough and sturdy enough. So he had had one built to his order. It had meant a delay, of course, and he had disliked that. However, the tavern where they waited was comfortable, and they'd have had to stop over, anyway, until Andy's foot healed.

But the men at Springfield had been right when they'd said he would need to chop down half the forest to get his cart through. That he'd done, all right! This trail was only a footpath made by Indians and difficult even of discernment. To ride over it was a feat. To draw a wagon through it was a miracle. The trace not only turned and dodged and looped to miss the monster trees, it plunged up and down steep rises and declivities. It crossed bogs and brooks. It went over boulders. Once they'd lost a wheel. Once they'd near mired in mud. Once the chest had tipped out and rolled over and over down a bank and the devil's job it had been to get it up again. They had slipped and slid

and climbed and plunged and pushed and hauled, sometimes
making less than three miles a day, and the week's journey,
which he had thought allowed him ample time, had already
stretched to nearly three. Only forty miles over this mountain
but it might have been four hundred.

He'd had to bring the cart. The cart held his ship chest—and
the ship chest contained all Esther's most treasured possessions.
And she'd given up enough. The ship chest must go through.
The ship chest was the home that had been and the home that
was to be.

Esther sat quietly holding her horse with one hand and the
reins of Mark's Bess with the other. She was hot. The leafy roof
high above her head was matted so thick that no air could get
through at all, seemed like. It made a green daylight underneath
so you couldn't tell morning from afternoon. No sun ever came
down. There were only pale thin beams sometimes by which they
knew it was time to pause and eat the midday snack.

She turned her glance to a scene grown too familiar. Her husband, bare to the waist, violently attacking the tangled growing
wall that obstructed their progress. Eleven-year-old Matt, silent
and sullen, on guard with the gun while his father worked. Eight-
year-old Andy pushing cautiously through the bushes, peering
and squinting, trying to discover a nearby spring. Prue, her first
born, patiently minding the little ones. The ox blowing out great
noisy breaths, his sides heaving. The mules foraging for grass,
their tails switching against the flies. And all around them the
deep, dark forest, the endless forest, the forest that defied Mark
and frightened her and was tiring them all to death. How far
back now was the white square house at Stonington with its big
kitchen and wide-throated fireplace, its shaded "best parlor" and
airy curtained bedrooms looking off to sea! Like something un-
real. Something she had dreamed. And all the weeks and months
and years lived there a storybook of other people. Well, so it was,
then.

The ax rang out. Where did Mark get his strength? You could
believe it would be used up long ago the way he'd had to work.

Sometimes lifting the cart himself over a fallen log to save the time it would take to saw it. Each day she'd watched the flesh dwindle off him. Yet now his great arms swung up and down in a steady rhythm as in the beginning. Oh, he'd get them there in the end—and safely. She'd always known that. Only would he get her there in time? But she would not startle him yet.

She pressed her lips together and watched the chips fly. Squirrels scattered, chattering their wrath. Birds flew up in flurried flight. The mules flapped their ears and edged farther and farther away.

"Andy! The mules!" she called.

Andrew came running, still limping a little. The mule with the feather bed on his back was all tangled in a brambly bush. Andy freed them both and a few feathers floated through the air to the ground. He turned his earnest face to his mother, his near-sighted eyes anxious.

"I couldn't help it, Ma."

The muscles of her face, long tensed to anxiety, felt stiff to her smile. "I know you couldn't. Never mind. 'Twill mend. Did you find a spring?"

He nodded. "A good one."

"Fill the pail, then."

He got it from the cart and disappeared. Matt sat silent as the rock beneath him, his dark face brooding, the gun across his knees. Prudence had found some wild berries and was helping the twins fill their little buckets, her soft voice encouraging them, keeping them forgetful of gnats and mosquitoes, and hunger and blisters and scratches. Esther's eyes rested on her with an anguished tenderness. For Prue was young to have to do what she might be called on to do this day.

The ax rang out again and again and there was a ripping and crashing and stamping. Mark never stopped. He was a hard one to stop at anything, she thought. She could see sweat streaming down his body, great drops of it glistening on the dark hair of his chest, dripping off his forehead, pouring down his cheeks and getting lost in his beard. Presently he went out of sight around the wall of roots. How much longer would it take?

Her glance moved to young Matthew again and her look grew troubled. A red-tailed hawk screeched high out of sight above her. Andy came back with a full pail and joined Prue, who had discovered something of interest—a tree worn smooth where deer had rubbed against it and bits of the soft horns they had discarded lying like little gray stones in a heap on the ground. For a long time the children examined these.

The sudden silence startled her. Thankful heart, Mark had finished! He came back around the way he had cleared and stood breathing heavily, his tired muscles jumping. After a while he spoke.

"Where's your spring, Andy? I could drink it dry. Prue, give the children some water. And your mother, too, if she wants it. Then water the animals, you and Matt."

He went away with Andy. In a moment they both returned. Mark had washed off his dirt and was wet to the waist. He picked up his shirt, shook it for spiders, rubbed himself half dry with it and pulled it on. Matt, still silent, returned the ax to its place in the cart. Andy and Prue lifted the twins to the back of one of the mules where they rode in panniers on either side. Presently they were on their way once more.

An hour had gone by.

Mark, in the lead again, glanced up to see where the sun was in the sky. But the wild creeper vines and branches above him were so thickly interwoven that he could not tell and a frenzy of madness seized him. It suddenly seemed as if he'd spent half his life in this forest wilderness. Day after day of sweat and toil and struggle like this. Day after day! And always the woods crowding close around him. Always—always—the woods. He wasn't used to them. He didn't like them. They were a prison. He liked the open. The sea was none too wide. And shut in the way he had been by these green walls, he'd grown uneasy and doubts had beset him. They beset him now and he thought maybe he'd been daft to make this move. It had been sudden—and it might have been a mistake. But what with his arm that would never be right again and the state of affairs in the economic world and Matt's hankerin'. . . .

It had been Matt that had settled his mind for him and drove him to the decision. And now between him and his oldest son there was a hard and bitter estrangement.

He jogged along, fatigue heavy on his body, his thoughts a cobweb in his head, and right and wrong, and wise and foolish, and worry and anger snared in it like so many flies.

All afternoon they plodded ahead, each absorbed in his own thoughts.

Prudence walked lightly in a half-dream of muted excitement. No matter how tired she was there was always this excitement. It was made up of myriad things. The leaves an emerald sea above her. The cushiony, starry moss soft as a bed when she lay on it at night. The long marks on some great brown trunk where an animal—a wild cat, mebbe—had sharpened its claws. The butternut tree that all five of them could not reach around holding hands. The water in the brooks running cold as ice and black as tobacco. The smell of the pines and the hemlocks after a rain. The surprise in a doe's eyes before it took startled flight. And always the darkness and stillness.

It was so still that when they stopped a spell to rest you could hear the fall of a leaf, and so dark, even in the daytime, you could scarce be sure whether yonder crouching shape was beast or bush. Only their own pack train made any noise. But that made a plenty and no mistake. Could be, Prue mused, her young face tiptilted to the canopy above her, that all their racket was what silenced the wild critters. The breathing and blowing of the horses, the rustle and thump and slide of the mules' feet as they scrambled for a sure foothold on slippery pine needles or damp matted earth, the rattle and creak of the ox cart and the repeated banging of the big wooden washtub hanging against its rear end. But still and dark or not, it was part and parcel of this adventure. It was a piece of the excitement and nothing to fash you. It was one with the business of living which had recently widened out to something tremendously big and passing strange. And that was all it was, but that was enough.

Her eyes came down and moved quickly over the cart checking

to be sure nothing had slid off and no rope was loosened. That was her responsibility. Matt's was the ox. He had to guide and goad Star to keep him moving so he didn't get too far behind the mules. And he had to be quick with a stone under the wheels on the steep places. Andy was to watch the packs the mules bore, see that the quilts and Ma's feather bed didn't drag on the ground and that the twins were all right as they rode. Sometimes he rode, too, on the second mule.

At night when they camped they each had their tasks also. Matt and Andy got wood and built the fire and found a spring. Prue unpacked the pots and grub and helped her Ma with supper. Pa tended the stock and then rigged up a tarpaulin for their night's shelter while the twins ran about looking for berries, Mary running the farthest always and giving them many a startle by reason of her curiosity and fearlessness.

Camping wasn't too bad, Prue's thoughts went on, but it was cold high up on a mountain like this even in early August, no matter how hot the day. And one time at dusk she'd laid her bedroll over a nest of rattlesnakes and didn't know it till the next morning when she'd picked it up. The snakes had been warmed some through the night but they had still been sluggish so no harm had come. She'd kept a sharp eye after that, though.

But could be they'd had their last night of camping. Could be they'd get there before dark. She hoped so but she didn't know. It all depended.

Reassured now that everything was still secure on the cart, she lifted her face once again and let her mind say over the words that were in her head. Come a day, mebbe, and she'd get those words runnin' right so they'd make a kind of music. Sometimes she got the swing and sometimes the sound but never both together.

Matt moved along in silence, his eyes seldom lifting from the ground beneath his bare feet, the whip he held dragging behind him, an angered puzzlement souring his young face.

Some things you knew the way you knew how to breathe, without ever thinking, and that was the way he'd knowed he wanted to go to sea. Soon's he was big enough. An' now he was. He'd hardly been able to wait till Pa got home from his last voyage to tell him that this year was the time. Wasn't he as old as Pa had been when he went? Older. Pa'd just turned ten and he was way past that. He was most eleven.

Oh, it was time, all right! And when Pa'd seen him waiting out there on the wharf in the wind and whirling snow and had stared at him as if he couldn't believe his eyes and then had laid a hand on his head and said, "Is this my son, Matt? Well, by the Great Horned Spoon! You're all growed up in three short years since I last clapped eyes on you, ain't you!"—then Matt had known everything would be all right. His Pa saw he was a man. He'd take him as cabin boy next time he went off. That was for sure.

Instead—

He kicked at a stone in his path, remembered anguish bringing back all the sharp and awful bewilderment, the unbelief, the ensuing searing pain and the futile flare of rebellion—for there was to be no next time. His Pa—Captain Mark Martin, the best whaling captain out of Stonington Harbor—had given up the sea. He had sold everything, his ship, his house, his share in the yards there, and was going to buy a farm in western Massachusetts, a hundred miles or more from the coast. A *farm!*

For a wild moment Matt had told himself he'd run away, sneak aboard some ship and hide till it was too late to send him back. But his Pa had read his mind, for he'd lifted his arm that had been smashed in a gale this last trip and had had to mend itself and now wouldn't straighten out any more, and he'd said, "I'll need you, Matt, for my right hand."

But it wasn't just that. Matt knew. His Pa had decided Matt shouldn't go to sea. He was determined on it and was taking him away on purpose. He was crossing Matt's will with his own and his own was older and stronger and had in it the duty a son owed his father that made it seem right. So Matt was helpless.

Only—why? Why?

To Esther riding along with her mind first stretching ahead to the future, then reaching back to the past, and sometimes spear-pointed to the immediate present by the recurring dull ache, no longer imagined, in the small of her back, the sounds they made as they traveled were all homely, reassuring ones. They were a promise that somewhere not far ahead in time or distance, a permanent abode would be theirs once more.

How thankful she'd be to reach their destination! She'd held out this far, all right, but the journey had taken longer than they'd figured, and she didn't know as she could hold out much longer. She waited a moment for the pain to pass and then spoke her husband's name quietly. "Mark."

He reined up with a jerk and swung about in his saddle. Under his captain's cap she saw the fear that sprang to his face and she hastened to reassure him.

"I just want to know how much further you reckon."

"Not ten mile."

She made swift calculation. Not ten miles. That meant four hours, likely enough, at the ox's plodding gait and if Mark didn't have to chop down any more trees.

His black eyes were on her watchfully. "I figure to be there by sundown."

She gave a soft little laugh. "Better make it sooner."

"You mean—?"

She nodded. "It's starting."

He stared at her. Laugh! She could *laugh*. For a second there was room for only one thought in his head and that was that God had favored him better than he deserved the day this woman had consented to join her life to his. Not a many would pull up roots the way she had, leaving behind comfort and safety, friends and possessions, all without a grumble, to go into the wilderness with her man. And his heart was cramped with the love that was always in it for her and for which he could seldom find the words. Then, swept again by the import of what she had told him, his face came alive to instant command and his big voice resounded through the woods.

"Matt!"

Matt, who had dropped behind to walk with Prudence, reared up his head in a rebellious attention.

"Yes, sir?"

"Stop your gamming back there! Get on up with the ox! Step lively!"

Esther half-turned in her saddle, too, for she always felt she must interpose her spirit between Matt and his father. They were too much alike was the trouble. Even from here she could see the boy's face blaze with the same fire that lay in Mark's and though he sprang to obey, there was noticeable resentment in the set of his solidly built shoulders and in the way he cracked his whip above Star's head.

Their pace quickened slightly. Mark, in the lead, sat forward in the saddle, his massive body bent, as though by thus holding himself his frantic desire for haste would be communicated to the horse under him and from the horse to the mules and from the mules to the ox. Blast that critter's slowness!

Behind him, Esther drew her cloak closer about her and tried not to think of Matt. It was because of him that this migration was being made. He knew it though he did not understand it and he hated it with all the passionate helpless hatred of childhood. And what would come of it she didn't know. She only knew you could not change nature and Matt was Mark's son with the same sea blood in his veins. Yet though her heart ached for the boy in his bitterness and frustration, she could not help but exult in the decision taken by the man.

She had never thought he would make such a one. Not in this world or the next would she have asked it of him herself. But it had been made and of his own free will. That was the surprise he'd given her.

She lived the scene again. Matt standing there in the Stonington kitchen that night last January, the night of his father's return, the firelight ruddy on his rough dark hair, his eyes anguished with the desire which she, long before then, had read in them. Yet hopeful, too.

"Pa, when you go off again, where are you goin'?"

"Can't rightly say."

"Well, when you go, will you take the same crew? Or—or will you be needin' a—a new man?"

It was then that Mark had sensed the direction of Matt's questions, for he made no reply. And when Esther had looked up from her mending it was to see him holding himself rigid in a curious way as if lightning had suddenly struck him. At last he had stirred.

"Why?" he'd asked, measuring off each word. "You know somebody would like to ship with me?"

"Yes! Me!" Matt had blazed into the speech held banked within him too long. "Take me, Pa! Please! I can do everythin' a cabin boy has to do! I won't get seasick! You went when you was only ten an' I'm goin' on 'leven. Please, Pa! Say you—"

He had stopped, for his words had dropped into a cavernous silence. It was a silence that stretched on and on in which her heart as well as Matt's had been held in a vise, for how could she live fearing for the two of them?

She knew well enough what Mark was thinking. She could see it on his face. He was thinking back to that first trip of his about which he'd told her once. He had been a stowaway. And the captain under whom he had sailed had been a rare cruel man. The wonder was that he had ever wanted to sail again. She could see it all coming clear to him—too clear—in that moment. The kickings and the beatings and the work beyond his small strength. The foulness of the ship and the foulness of men about which he'd learned for the first time. The seasickness and the cursing and the stench. The freezing and the sweating and the starving. And the danger. Always the danger. He'd lived it again with his eyes like live coals burning on Matt's face.

And then had come Mark's answer, slow and heavy, as if it weren't he himself giving it but somebody else. Somebody he couldn't stop from speaking and to whom he had to listen, too.

"No. I'll not take you."

"Wh—what?" It was a squeak, the astonished squeak of a small creature unexpectedly trapped. But the hurt of his reply was eating into Mark, too, and now he roared at his son.

"I said no! I'll not take you because I ain't a-goin'! I've made my last trip! I'm through with the sea. Hear me? Through with it! And I've got better things in mind for you. Now get out!"

She could hear him even now. Both her men folks trapped,
she had thought. The one by his youth, the other by his remembered youth. The one by his dream, the other by his knowledge.
Oh, Matt! Oh, Mark!

The pain came again. How long since the last one? She had no
notion. Ten minutes, mebbe. Mebbe longer. Mebbe not so long.
There was no way of telling. She'd best live in the present, not
the past, and think what to do if the child within her should
decide to get itself born like a little animal here in the woods.

If it did, it would be the first birthing Mark had ever attended.
Always he'd been away. But from now he'd be with her through
everything. Through all the days and all the nights. That was the
thought she'd kept close when it came to partings back there in
Stonington. Anything, even a log cabin in the wilderness, was
better than being alone for years at a stretch. Waiting and watching and praying as the time drew near for his return. Growing
tense and fearful as the weeks slipped by and still he did not
come. What if he never did? What if his ship had been wrecked?
Or burned? Or just was mysteriously lost forever in some unknown distant place?

Suddenly she drew a short, startled breath. "Mark!"

He was off his horse in a trice and back beside her, his face
protesting what he did not want to believe.

She nodded. "It's coming quick now. Quick and hard."

He stood there trying to think and not able to, trying to decide
something and not knowing what to decide. Never in the worst
that had ever happened at sea had he felt like this, with his bones
all gone to water and his muscles awash inside his skin like so
much seaweed.

"You're—early," was all he could manage.

"Six weeks. The riding did it."

"You won't last?" He was still hesitant, still uncertain, and the
knowledge galled him. He spoke with sudden resolution. "I'll fix
up a bed for you in the cart. Then we'll push on."

"No."

She was staring straight before her, her gray eyes dark, her mouth setting into a straight line. He put his big hand up and laid it gently over hers, by the gesture relinquishing his command to her surer knowledge of what was best.

"We'll stop," she said. "Prue can help me. She knows what to do."

His voice was hoarse. "Whatever you want."

She looked down at him and smiled faintly. Then she lifted her head, turned her horse about and let her eyes go over the little group that had come to a halt when they had. Directly behind her in the panniers hung across one mule's back rode the five-year-old twins, Mary and Luke. Luke had fallen asleep, his baby face placid, but Mary was wide awake, her bright brown eyes peering out between the tangled locks of her brown hair. She minded Esther of a pixy. As quick in her motions and as fearless. She had only an anger for fear. She waved a small hand now in airy detachment at variance with her fixed, watchful gaze. But she said nothing.

Esther's glance moved to Prue where she stood in a shaft of sunlight, her slim, adolescent body in its straight-hung frock giving only a hint of the lovely curves and grace that would some day be hers. But already her lifted face, framed to a heart shape by the peak of her goldy hair in the middle of her forehead and her two braids swinging down, held a grave translucent beauty. Meeting Esther's strained look now, awareness sprang into the deep blue of her dark-lashed eyes, and she ran forward. Reaching her mother, she laid a firm capable hand on the horse's bridle and said, "Get down, Ma. I'll help you. Bear all your weight on my shoulder and slide down."

Matt was already throwing stuff out of the ox cart, his face wild-looking, and Andy was off his mule working at the feather bed wrapped around with quilts. Mark, stung by their competence and his own ineptness, yelled at his daughter.

"I'll help your Ma down! You—you do what else you have to do!"

On the ground Esther left her hands on his shoulders a moment. She could feel surging through him all his furious shame at his helplessness, mingled with a masculine abhorrence and dread of what was to come, and there was both pity and forgiveness in her touch. Fleetingly she thought how terrible a thing it was to be only a man at a time like this. To have to wait beyond the pale of knowledge and service.

"Don't fash yourself, Mark. You know other things," she said. "And here's something you can do. Get the ship chest out of the cart, then take the twins for a walk. I won't be long. Likely only an hour—"

She swayed toward him, her eyes closing, and he felt her fingers dig deep into his flesh and saw big beads of perspiration spring out on her forehead. The next moment she was erect again and giving him a small smile.

"We'll still be there by sundown—or leastways soon after," she whispered.

Her name came from him in a half-groan. "Esther—Esther—"

She stood away and took hold of Prudence, urgently gesturing him with her free hand toward the twins in the panniers. "Hurry. But keep an eye on Mary."

He nodded and turned.

She waited till he had heaved the chest to the ground, lifted the twins from the panniers and gone with them out of sight, then, leaning heavily on Prue, she made her way back to the ox cart.

"Better unhitch Star," she told Matt. "I don't want he should take it into his head to carry me along till I'm ready to go." She gave a little gasp. "Help me up there. Prue—Matt—"

She lay under her maroon cloak on top of the oldest quilt, concealed from her children's eyes, all but Prue's, by the billowing folds of the feather bed beneath her. Between her pains she issued orders she had thought out as she rode:

"Tell the boys to build a fire and put some water on't. Plenty. And keep the fire going for burning things after. . . . You'll find a heap of old rags in the panniers where the twins were riding. They made it soft for them and 'twas the handiest place. . . . You remember that little old blanket I always had for wrapping each and every one of—"

Her eyes clouded and through the haze that enveloped her she heard Prue's steady voice.

"I have it, Ma. I found it."

Presently she looked up at her daughter. "You sure you're able, Prue?"

"I'm able."

"You're mighty young for this."

"I'm past thirteen. You weren't much older when you had me."

Esther nodded and set her mouth against her mounting agony. Through it there came to her ears the sound of the boys moving around on the ground below her, the whinny of a horse, the slow heavy feet of the ox, the snap of wood being broken and soon after that the crackle of mounting flames. There came to her nostrils the fragrance of sweet fern mixed with the pungency of pine and the fecund scent of wet earth and leaf mold, and then the odor of woodsmoke. And above her, through the interlacing green, she glimpsed, in the fractions of time when she knew respite from labor, the bright, brief flash of blue or red wings, the tawny stripes of a chipmunk whisking along a branch, the round bright eyes of a squirrel and—marvel of marvels—golden motes whirling silently in a beam of sunlight. Seeing it, a strange and unexpected thought came to her.

"A baby born beneath God's sky is mebbe specially marked for some good thing."

She went through her ordeal silently. Only Prue heard her low-spoken, "Now—*now*—" But the boys' ears caught the sound of a sharp slap on bare flesh and Mark, coming back up the trail with the twins, heard the tiny angry wail that followed.

There was a silence while they all stood waiting, then Prue called softly, "It's a boy, Pa!"

Mark reached the ox cart just as Prue slid from it holding the wooden washtub. He caught her shoulder, his eyes burning on her face.

"Your Ma—?"

"She's fine. You can look at her now." And she went forward toward the fire with her burden.

Mark peered over the quilts. Esther lay white and still beneath her maroon cloak. But her eyes were open and against her side he saw a small wrapped bundle.

"His name is John," she said, her voice slow and tired yet holding a faint note of triumph, too. "You wanted an Andrew for your brother after he was drowned. But I always wanted a Matthew, Mark, Luke and John. And now I have them."

A short while later they were on their way. Esther was still in the cart, her baby, washed clean, close against her breast. She lay content, glad it was over and proud—so proud—of Prue. And then, for the first time since Mark had told her of his plan, misgiving smote her.

What was she getting into? What kind of life lay ahead for her children with them going to school with savages? It was Prue that came most to mind. Would Prue ever know, as Esther had known, what it was like to be the belle of a ball? To dress in silks and crinolines? To coquet with a fan and dance all night? In Boston, Esther had done these things when she was no older than Prue. Then one day Captain Mark Martin, dark, handsome, impetuous, had sailed into Boston Harbor with a hold full of oil for her father, John Richardson, and not long after that he had carried her away as his bride to the little village of Stonington. It had certainly not been like Boston! But it had had a church and a school and a mill when she went there. And the people had been fine people. And even if there had been no governor's balls, at least there had been quilting bees and corn huskings and all the excitement that goes with a seaport town.

Yet surely there would be, in time, quilting bees and corn huskings and such as that in Indian Town (which was what the place was named where they were going), she told herself. Doubt came only when she thought of Prue and wondered who there would ever be there for her to marry? For she was nigh fourteen now and 'twas time to think about it.

Well, leave it to the Lord whose ways were inscrutable.

She drew her baby closer. The chill of evening could already be felt though the sun was not yet gone down.

A singing came to her ears. That was Prue. And now Andy's

uncertain voice—he had no ear for music—joined the rollicking tune. And then Luke's and Mary's high treble.

> *"The Devil came to the farmer one day.*
> *Fol-lol-fol-li-dee-i-lee!"*

The twins must be walking. They always asked for a song when they walked. Probably they'd have to walk the rest of the way since the mule they had been on now carried some of the things that had been in the ox cart. Her horse bore the remainder. It had all worked out—this birthing—better than she'd thought and they'd had to leave nothing behind except Mark's great ship chest. It was packed with goodness knew what all. Her whole garnish of pewter, the silk-embroidered shawl Mark had brought her from one of his voyages, the little ivory carvings and the family's best clothes. Well, no wild animal could make off with it, that was certain. And Mark would go back for it as soon as ever he got them settled somewhere. And if some stranger followed the way they had come she could only hope he'd be honest. Leastways, there was a lock on the lid.

> *"And now, says the farmer, It's I am undone,*
> *Fol-lol-fol-li-dee-i-lee,*
> *For the Devil has come for my oldest son—"*

She did not hear Matt's voice in that young chorus. How long would he be this way? No other child of theirs bore anger so long. But ever since that night last winter in the kitchen his dark eyes had smoldered and his mouth had set in a down-pulling line and his words had come out short. He had his father's good looks and boldness and determination. But so far he showed little of the tenderness that underlay and overlay Mark's great strength. Today, in her hour, was the first time in months she'd seen any of it in him. Was he going to grow up a hard man? Perhaps, she told herself, tenderness came only with the later years. In the push of a lad's need to establish himself in a harsh and combative world there was little room for gentleness.

> *"Oh, no! said the Devil. It's not your oldest son!*
> *Fol-lol-fol-li—"*

"Land! Ho!"

Esther lifted herself up and looked over the edge of the ox cart at Mark's jubilant shout. Light was visible through the trees ahead. She saw her husband's horse break into a trot and the twins race after him with Prue and Andy not far behind. Only Matt maintained his stolid pace behind the ox. Indifferent, belike, to whatever awaited them all. But even his manner could not now check the rise of Esther's heart. She watched breathlessly as the open space widened before her eyes.

She could see a broad verdant meadow with a stream winding through it. She could see wigwams and gleaming fires and dark moving shapes around them. A little beyond, on an elevated plain that had been partially cleared, were two or three simple log cabins and more wigwams, while rising behind these in an easy slope stood a wooded hill where she could just make out through the trees the roofs of a few more pretentious houses.

This was Indian Town. This was to be Mark's and Esther's new abode. It was remote from all they had ever known. It was rough. It was primitive. There were no streets, and the Indians outnumbered the whites. But it had been born of a man's fine dream. And in the fading light of that summer's day, peace lay over the land and it was beautiful.

CHAPTER 2

The Welcome

MARK GESTURED for his family to wait, then he rode slowly toward the lower clearing. Before him was a scattering of tents, one bark-covered house and a single log cabin somewhat removed from the tents. Women in deerskin skirts bordered with scarlet and topped by varicolored blouses, were crouched over little fires preparing their evening meal. Half-naked children were running about in play. Men clad in deerskins also, but bare from the waist up and with their long black hair tied back or braided, were tending their horses or lolling beneath the trees. No one paid any attention to him, but as Mark came closer, in the opening of the central and largest wigwam which stood next to the bark-covered house an elderly Indian appeared and regarded him in silence.

He, too, was dressed in deerskin and around his shoulders he wore a dingy blanket with faded red, yellow and blue stripes. For a moment he studied Mark and the halted procession behind him, then he emerged and moved forward, the beads and shells that decorated his costume making a small tinkling noise; his bearing as he advanced, dignified and calm.

Mark put up his open hand in friendly salutation and drew rein. But years of command and his present tension and fatigue made him terse of speech.

"I'm looking for Mr. Sergeant."

The door of the log cabin opened now and a white man stood there. The Indian turned his face toward him and nodded and the white man came forward, too. He was thick-set and slow-moving, his crafty little eyes nearly lost in the heaviness of his pock-marked face, his bullet head sunk on a short neck, his mouth loose-lipped and cruel looking. A Dutchman, Mark told himself, and did not like the cut of his jib.

"Vot you vant?"

"I'm looking for Mr. Sergeant. Or Mr. Williams. We're new settlers."

"New settlers!" The Dutchman repeated it, scowling. Then he jerked his head backward. It was clear that Mark's answer, which had surprised him, was not to his liking.

"Meester Sergeant leeves on de plain yonder to de vest. Villiams leeves oop on de hill. You talk to dis Injun. He iss der chief. Chief Konkapot."

Konkapot bent his head gravely as his name was spoken. His dark glance was wise and bright and there was intelligence and strength and kindness on his lean, deeply lined face.

"You come long way. Over mountain. You tired," he said slowly in his limited English and, turning, he raised an arm in a signal to some one in the rear. At once a tall, well set-up brave came running and Konkapot spoke to him in the gutteral language of his tribe. The Dutchman stood by listening in a scarcely veiled unfriendliness that mystified Mark but he translated readily enough as the younger Indian nodded and glided away.

"Konkapot tells dot you are velcome here," he said, his words carrying easily to the ox cart through the stillness of the dusk. "He say you eat vit' heem. Ven you haf rested und eaten vill Mr. Sergeant den coom."

Mark shook his head, his voice rising as his control snapped.

"Tell him we don't want anything to eat! Tell him all we want is to see Mr. Sergeant and find out where we're to camp tonight! Tell him to send some one at once! Lord, man! We've been on the trail nigh onto a month. My wife's just—"

He stopped abruptly as Prue's hand fell lightly on his sea boot and, frowning, he looked down at her.

"Pa, Ma says we're very grateful for the chief's invitation." She pressed her hand down warningly on his foot and sent a smile

straight into the unsmiling face of the watching Sachem. "Ma
says the chief is most thoughtful and we'll take it kindly to have
some supper with him." She looked up now at the Dutchman.
"Will you tell him that for us, please, Mister?"

How had Esther known this was the thing to do, Mark wondered. But that was the woman of it. He, himself, possessed of a
purpose, never saw on either side of it but was driven by it toward his goal, suffering interruptions with poor grace. Even now,
though he realized she was right, he chafed at the delay of this
required ceremonial and rode back toward the ox cart in a fume.

"Esther! You're not fit!"

"I am all right," she said quietly. "Drive as close as you can
and then help me. This is the chief's town as well as Mr. Sergeant's. And it will be our home. We will all be friends together.
Never forget."

The cart lumbered into motion again behind the mules. At
the chief's wigwam Mark dismounted and spoke in a low tone to
Matt. "Stand by. It's your watch." Then he lifted Esther to the
ground and, with the babe held close and Mark's arm supporting
her, she made her way slowly into the tent. Prue and the twins
and Andy followed close but Matt, after tying the animals to
trees, stopped just over the threshold where he squatted down
cross-legged facing out.

The tent was empty save for a few stools and a rude pallet on
one side. A fire burned on the hard earth floor at one end and the
smoke went out through a hole in the roof. Before the fire a
woman was bending over a pot suspended above the flames. She
neither looked around nor spoke.

Konkapot stood in the center and as his glance touched Esther
and the bundle against her breast, it seemed to her the fixed inscrutability of his countenance relaxed slightly, then he grunted
and nodded imperatively toward his bed.

Esther smiled her thanks. She was fearful of picking up lice but
she was too exhausted to sit upright. To her pleased surprise, the
bowl of soup that the squaw presently brought her in an earthen
bowl, had a savory odor and taste. She told herself she would not
think about vermin. Perhaps in the two years since the mission

had started the Indians had learned to be clean. Surely it would be one of the first things taught.

She lay quiet, resting and watching the others in the flickering light of the fire. Prue was helping the twins drink from the bowl that had served her and would later go to Andy. Andy was looking with a shrinking horrified interest at a tomahawk and some bows and arrows piled in a heap near him. A girl of perhaps ten was peering shyly through the open doorflap at all of them and finally gathered courage enough to venture inside where she dropped down on the ground next to Matt. She was rather pretty, Esther thought, with large, softly bright, black eyes in the sensitive oval of her pale brown face. And she was neat. Her raven hair was brushed smooth, her deerskin dress was unspotted and her hands were clean.

"Me spik Ingliss," she murmured, after a moment.

Matt looked at her in surprise. "Where'd you learn that?"

"Me go Ingliss school in bark house." She nodded toward the outside. "To Mister Woodbridge. You go school here mebbe?"

Matt shrugged. She contemplated him for a moment, then spoke again.

"One day me show you where Great Eagle put his claw on rock."

He gave her another glance, and, encouraged, she went on.

"Me show you where is ice all summer. Me show you beeg cave on mountain. Me show you spring. Me show you shining pond water—"

"You can keep 'em," Matt said rudely, and turned his back on her. Presently he rose and went outside. The little girl rose then, too, and moved over to Prudence.

"You go school here mebbe?"

"I think so."

"Me like school. School good place. School in beeg bark house." She nodded again toward the outside. "Meetinghouse in beeg bark house also. Nudder new meetinghouse finish soon." She paused. "Some day you come school mebbe. Mister Woodbridge good man. He teach. Mister Sergeant good man. He preach. Konkapot good man for Indians. Umpachenee good man for Indians." She was plainly proud of herself, Esther thought, and well she might be. "My named Marie," she concluded. And she came to Esther's side and peeped over the edge of the blanket. When she saw the baby she clasped her two hands together in silent delight. "A papoose! A leetle white papoose!"

Esther nodded. The child looked a moment longer, then she sat down quietly nearby and presently Esther's glance went to Mark and the chief and the big Dutchman who stood near the fire. Konkapot was speaking, his words coming slowly and with difficulty.

"Indian here all friend to white man. White man help Indian. White man teach Indian white man's ways. Give Indian white man's God. But Indian stumbled to find white man not all times good Christian like he preach to be."

The Dutchman spoke. His voice held a sneering bitterness. "Sure! Dot's de stumble all right. Ven de vhite man say von t'ing und doos anudder. Dot's ven you vatch out, Konkapot." He turned to Mark, his belligerence finding expression at last. "Ven dis township set up, dere vas to be joost four vhite famblies here. Now you coom und dere are five." His eyes held a hard animosity. "Vere you vill get de lan' you settle, hein? You t'ink de Injuns sell to you? It all belong dem 'ceptin' vot vas set aside vor dose vurst famblies und de teacher und de minister. Von sixtieth to each. No more."

"Mr. Williams wrote—"

"Ach! Dot Villiams! Hear me!" He leaned toward Mark, his pig eyes gleaming, one fist pounding into the thick palm of the other. "Iss dis Villiams de law? I know de law! I know de Indians' right und I know yours." He pointed a thick finger at Mark's face and finished angrily, "You haf none. Nod here."

A stir at the doorway interrupted them and Umpachenee, the young brave whom Konkapot had sent away earlier, entered, followed immediately by a short stocky man in a black steeple-crowned hat and long black coat with white lappets showing under it. Beneath the coat he wore riding breeches and leggings. He looked to be about twenty-four.

Esther liked him at once. As he swept off his hat she saw thick,

dark wavy hair cresting a finely shaped head, a slender aristo-
cratic face in which were large, brilliant black eyes that held a
lively and sympathetic intelligence, and a mouth of unusual
sweetness. With one glance he took in the scene, sensing at once
the animosity between the two men, Esther's anxiety and the uncertainty of the children.

"Captain Martin!" He came forward briskly, his whole bearing
conveying a graciousness and sincerity. "How glad we are to see
you here at last! We looked for you days ago and were growing
alarmed. I had thoughts of sending out a scouting party. You had
no trouble, I hope?"

Without waiting for an answer, he came over to Esther on the
pallet and bent above her hand with easy grace. "Ah," he said
gently, as he saw the baby against her. "So this was your delay."

"Yes."

He straightened. "We must make you comfortable at once."

He turned and it was then that Esther noticed his left arm
hanging shorter than the other and quite withered.

By now the Dutchman was gone and Umpachenee and little
Marie, too. The squaw, after gathering up the bowls, followed
them silently. Only Konkapot remained.

Mark, reassured by Sergeant's presence, spoke with more ease
and courtesy than he had so far shown. "Chief Konkapot has
been kind enough to extend us his hospitality while we waited
for you."

The minister smiled at the old Sachem. "Of course. He never
fails us. I only hope we will never fail him. Or his people."

Mark nodded. "By the way, that Dutchman— What is his
name?"

"Van Valkenburgh."

"He seemed to think we'd have trouble getting title to some
land."

A faint shadow touched the minister's sensitive face. "I believe
that is already taken care of," he said quietly. "Colonel Ephraim
Williams has arranged it." He fell silent for a moment. Then—
"I will take you to his house now. He has offered to give you
shelter until you can build." He touched Konkapot's shoulder

and spoke to him at some length in his own language, then he smiled at the children. "Quite a family you have, Captain."

"This is Prudence, Mr. Sergeant. And Andrew. And Mary and Luke are the twins. Matt! Where are you! Come in here! Mr. Sergeant, this is my oldest son, Matthew."

The girls, taught by Esther, dropped curtsies. The boys came forward and extended their hands. John Sergeant shook them gravely.

"Now let me see," he said. He seemed to be turning something over in his mind. "I wonder— Well, to speak the truth, Captain, Mr. Williams has a sizable brood of his own, so I think we may have to divide you up. I keep bachelor quarters at the moment but I always have room for nine or ten boys in my house, so suppose Matt and Andrew come to me? And Prudence might take care of the little ones at Mrs. Timothy Woodbridge's place. She is our teacher's wife and will be happy to have them, I know. That will, I think, be the best arrangement if it is agreeable to you, sir, and to you, madam?"

"We are in your hands, Mr. Sergeant," Esther said.

Mark went to help her to her feet and seeing her weakness, John Sergeant said with ineffable kindness, "You will be glad of a woman's companionship, Mrs. Martin. Abigail—that is Mr. Williams' daughter—will take good care of you." He paused and his sweet smile slipped over his face lighting it to happiness. "As," he finished, "she threatens to do of me after we are married."

Esther's heart, which had lain heavy and mortal tired within her ever since her entrance into Konkapot's tent, lifted a little. A wedding! A wedding in the wilderness! It was the last thing she had expected.

Indian Town was originally settled on three levels—the great meadow which Mark and his family first saw, the plain north of that and the hill beyond.

Rumbling up from the meadow in the twilight of their arrival, Esther noticed that on the plain, in addition to the orderly circle of wigwams there were several log cabins, neat in appearance, with smoke coming from their chimneys, and a few bark-covered frame houses that had glassed windows. Behind and beyond these there were fields, some of them already fenced, and to the west she could just make out the dim shape of the incompleted log meetinghouse and John Sergeant's own cabin nearby, which, riding ahead with Mark, he pointed out.

"We have no streets as yet," Esther heard him say, "but they will come in due time. And a center green as well."

They stopped presently before the tidy Woodbridge home and Timothy and his wife came hurrying forth with friendly greetings and a ready hospitality for Prue and the twins. Esther, trying to give expression to her appreciation, was checked by the younger woman.

"La! Miz Martin! Don't say a word. It's little enough to do for a newcomer. And don't worry one mite about these three children of yours. They'll be good company for us till you get your own place."

Timothy's scholarly face appeared beside the ox cart.

"Is Prue to go to school to me tomorrow, Mrs. Martin?" he inquired in his mild way.

Esther hesitated. School for Prue amongst savages was still a repugnant idea. But it was bound to be, sooner or later, she told herself.

"If she's not needed to care for the twins or to help Mrs. Woodbridge," she answered, after a moment. Her glance went to Prue, standing slim and straight and calm in the dimming light with a twin firmly held on either side of her, and it occurred to her that Prue would never be hurt by contact with the Indians or by any other outside influence. She would only be hurt by herself. "Use your judgment, Prue," she added.

Prudence nodded, good nights were said, and they were off again, since John wanted to get up the rough narrow road onto the hill with the ox cart before dark closed in.

The first four families—the "chosen" ones—had built on the hill, Esther heard the young minister explaining. Besides Colonel Ephraim Williams and his household, there were the Josiah Joneses, the Joseph Woodbridges (brother to Timothy) and the

Samuel Browns. Ephraim was the senior white man here and the leader. He it was who had been moderator at the first town meeting held last month at which Konkapot and Umpachenee had been made selectmen in accordance with the decision to have the Indians share in the responsibility of running the settlement. At that time Mr. Jones, Ephraim's brother-in-law, had been voted constable, and Timothy Woodbridge the town clerk as well as teacher.

"This is no longer to be known as Indian Town," Sergeant added. "It is now named Stockbridge. And the Indians call themselves, not Mahicans or Housatonnucks or Skatakooks, but Stockbridge Indians."

Mark put a question. "And are they taking to Christianity?"

"Indeed, yes." John's expressive voice held a quiet pride. "I had forty converts before ever this township was established. Now I have fifty-two baptized out of about ninety. But it was my early success, I feel confident, that impressed the commissioners in Boston so that they agreed to my proposition that we gather them all together in this one place."

"Where were they before?"

"We were divided. The meeting house, which the Indians first built for me, was in Skatakook to the south of here. There also was the Great Wigwam or council place of the whole tribe of Mahicans. But they pitched their tents around the meetinghouse for only a short while since they dispersed in February for their 'sugaring-off'—an enterprise which, incidentally, the English would do well to emulate. I will tell you of it another time. The rest of the year," he went on, "they spent in their separate settlements with Mr. Woodbridge here in Wnahtukook and I down in Skatakook and the Great Mountain between us. Passage over this was difficult, therefore attendance at prayer meeting was most irregular." He paused.

Mark waited. He had felt an instant liking for this young man. He approved the courage that had led him to tackle an undertaking that could hold only difficulties at best. And he felt an ardor in him that would not readily yield to discouragements, together with a stubborn determination to achieve his goal—

qualities not lacking in himself. Moreover, he sensed that the minister reacted favorably to him. It was a reassuring beginning and the conviction that, after all, he had been right to come here, filled him once again.

Sergeant continued thoughtfully:

"I felt that the constant breaking-up because of the 'sugaring-off' was demoralizing. For best results with a people so untutored, there must be a steadiness of worship, a constancy of preaching and teaching, before a realization of the meaning of Christianity can be instilled. And the quickest way to secure these was, I thought, to establish permanent homes and then try to persuade the Indians to adopt our settled habits. In brief, it was and is my belief that they must be Anglicized before they can be Christianized. Fortunately the Colonial government agreed with me and three years ago a township was offered to the Indians and accepted by them. So, giving up Skatakook in return for this tract of six square miles, they all moved here."

"Your troubles are over, then."

The answer came with a ready cheerfulness.

"Oh, I would hardly concede that much. My plans for the school call for more money than we have at present and that is always hard to come by." His expression became concerned. "Perhaps our greatest difficulty at the moment lies in the fact that the Indians, as you no doubt know, are overfond of rum. That is our major problem."

"But how in tarnation do they get the stuff way out here in this wilderness!" Mark exclaimed.

Sergeant turned in his saddle with a quick flash in his large dark eyes. But he spoke quietly enough. "You have met Mr. Van Valkenburgh," he said. "He gets it for them and sells it to them. It is his chief means of livelihood. Mr. Van Valkenburgh is opposed to this mission, Captain Martin, because I preach sobriety and the pitfalls of drink. And if the Indians heed me, who will buy his rum? He is opposed to white settlers for the same reason. The more there are, the greater will be their influence."

"So! I see. But can't he be routed? Bought out?"

"So far he has refused to sell. However—" He hesitated; then he went on. "However, I think we have that situation in hand now—or will have at a fairly early date." He paused again and, as in Konkapot's tent, Mark noted a faint shadow of sadness pass over his features. Why, he wondered, should the minister be sad if his major difficulty was in process of being overcome? Before he could voice the question, Sergeant spoke again.

"I will leave Colonel Williams to explain that to you, I think. And now here we are at his residence."

Residence! Did it deserve so high-sounding a name? In curiosity Esther lifted herself to her elbow and peered over the cart's edge through the dusk. But indeed, yes, she thought, with surprise.

For there before her was a large, three-storied house constructed somewhat in the shape of a fort. There were glazed windows here, too, many of them, and the light shining through them lent a bright cheeriness to the scene. Before the house she saw a big yard, neatly trimmed, with a well-sweep to the side, while fences, young orchards, tended fields and a number of outbuildings were visible in the background.

Word had already come of their arrival and at the sound of their approach the big front door was flung open and Ephraim Williams, dressed in a fine wine-colored broadcloth suit with a richly embroidered waistcoat, silk stockings and buckled shoes, came out to give them welcome.

He was a heavy-set man with a pompous, blustering manner that might readily be overbearing. But Esther was so thankful to be at the end of her journey that only his expansive hospitality impressed itself upon her. At a shout from him, black stablemen in blue frocks appeared to lead away the ox, the mules and the horses, and in no time she was being helped out of the chill of the evening and into the house.

She had a confused impression of a great room where a fire blazed, where pewter gleamed and where tall white candles burned above polished glowing wood. There seemed to be many people present. She heard the colonel saying, "My wife—my daughter, Abigail—my son, Thomas—my wife's brother, Josiah Jones—and Mrs. Jones—" She saw a brown-eyed slender girl and two older women, one in a gray brocade print with a transparent fichu of sheerest gauze and silver buckles on her shoes, whom she guessed to be her hostess. She saw a lad of about fifteen, called Josiah after his uncle, a little boy younger than Andy who answered to the name of Elijah, and two little girls, Judith and Elizabeth. Quite a family, indeed! No wonder Mr. Sergeant had had to divide the newcomers. Then a slave came bringing an armload of wood. Another black man, a house servant, appeared with noggins of punch and plates of food for the visitors. But after she had partaken of nourishment, Esther sat in a daze she could no longer fight off until she finally heard Mrs. Williams speaking welcome words.

"Elijah, it is your bedtime. Put away your barlow knife and come with me. You, too, Judith and Elizabeth. Abigail, I think Mrs. Martin is sore weary. Will you help her to her room?"

Abigail's lovely young face smiling into hers and Abigail's strong young arm about her. Another room beyond this one where a second fire crackled and small rag rugs made bright spots of color against a shining waxed floor. Where there was a great tester bed with steps beside it in one corner. Where a round tub stood in another and near this a tall pewter ewer from which steam was rising. Where a pickaninny waited with white towel in hand to help Abigail help her. And a night rail still warm from the press iron lay spread out on the feather bed. Next to this, Esther's tired eyes noted a pile of tiny garments and a fresh wrapping blanket for her baby.

As she was sinking to sleep at last between smooth white sheets, with wee John lying in a cradle below her, she could not help but think drowsily that this place to which Mark had brought her might not, after all, be so uncivilized a spot as she had imagined.

Mark was observing with interest the room full of people before him. An astute judge of men himself, he sized up Ephraim Williams as a fellow to watch and experienced some wonderment that he had been selected to come here and set an example in noble living to the Indians. For there was on his broad thick features a look of greed and craftiness quite at variance with the openhanded friendliness he was displaying. Nor did his manner of joviality wholly conceal his arrogance.

Thomas, Ephraim's oldest son present by an earlier marriage, was, Mark learned, apprenticing to become a doctor, and only home for a visit. A still older son, Ephraim, Junior, likewise by the first wife, was traveling at the moment, and, though just twenty-four, was already becoming known throughout the Colonies as a man of ability. Eighteen-year-old Abigail, the daughter to whom John Sergeant was engaged to be married, was a beautiful and charming girl with a softness of manner and gracious tact that would, Mark thought, be a great asset to the young minister.

The talk at first centered on topics of general interest. On Mark's arduous journey. On Connecticut's ship-building industry. On the profitable West Indies trade being maintained by the Colonies in defiance of the repressive measures passed by the British to restrict it.

"I'm interested in the construction of your house," Mark put in presently. "It has somewhat the look of a garrison as you come on it. You don't, I hope, expect trouble in these parts?"

Williams stretched forth a thick hand and clapped a silver snuffer over a smoking candle. "Whether I expect it or not, I'm prepared for it," he said. "I've had a well built in my cellar and I keep provisions stocked up at all times in case of a siege. In addition, I plan to put a moat entirely around the house soon's ever I can get to it."

Mark looked his surprise. "But Mr. Sergeant has just been telling me that fully half of your Indians have already been converted."

Ephraim's words came out as rough and solid as stones.

"I'm not as certain of this Christian experiment as John is. I don't trust savages. Not any of 'em. Get 'em drunk and you never know what they'll take into their heads to do."

Sergeant spoke now.

"I was just telling the captain that you had found a way to lessen that danger, Mr. Williams, but I did not give the details.

Perhaps you will enlighten him, since it relates to his securing a clear title to some land here—a matter on which Mr. Van Valkenburgh has already cast some doubt."

"Van Valkenburgh has less than nothing to say about it! So rest easy on that score, Cap'n."

"I'd be pleasured to know the rights of the situation, Colonel."

"Well—" Williams cleared his throat and reached for his noggin of punch. Van Valkenburgh, he explained, in his authoritative way, had long been an undesirable resident in these parts, not only because he sold liquor to the Indians but because he was constantly trying to stir up ill feeling between them and the whites.

"He keeps telling 'em the settlers aren't to be trusted. He hammers at 'em we're really planning to rob the Injuns of their rights and that it's our intention in the end to acquire all their land hereabouts for ourselves and push them out."

"Which," John Sergeant said, as Ephraim paused for breath, "is, of course, far from the truth."

Something in his tone, gentle as it was, pricked Mark to alertness and he glanced around at the group. He caught a sharp, impatient look darted by Williams toward the minister. He heard Mrs. Williams' wheel spin to a faster tempo for a moment. He saw a small gesture of pleading stopped in midair by Abigail's little white hand as she looked at her betrothed. And he felt an imperceptible stiffening on the part of Josiah Jones and his wife. Then Williams was continuing, his voice unctuous.

"The mission can never succeed whilst Van Valkenburgh is here. It's been my contention from the beginning that he must be removed. I'd have bought him out myself had I been able. But his price was too high for me. Deliberately, I reckon, because he has no wish to leave. Lately, however, I've found a way to oust him whether he wants to go or not. Mr. Sergeant doesn't wholly approve. But Mr. Sergeant agrees that we have no alternative."

He paused.

"Tell him!" Jones urged.

"I am telling him fast as I can! The story boils down to this, Cap'n Martin. I've been able to persuade the godfathers of this project, the clergy of the Connecticut River Valley from which you come, sir, to join together and raise sufficient funds to meet the Dutchman's demands."

"And he has agreed to sell?"

"He will agree," Williams chuckled. "Gold, you know, is a great persuader."

"And we've got other persuasions," Jones added. "It was made a law at town meetin' last month that anybody caught sellin' liquor to the Injuns is goin' to be fined forty pounds. He's not goin' to like that. Not one mite."

"So he'll lose in the end. I see."

"He'll lose in the end, yes. He'll have to get out. No two ways about it." Williams fell silent and over his face Mark saw pass now an expression of cunning quickly followed by one of satisfaction.

At the same moment John Sergeant spoke again. "Let us be quite clear about all this since Captain Martin is to be one of us." He turned toward Mark. "The two hundred and ninety acres belonging to Mr. Van Valkenburgh will be bought by the clergy and a deed for these given to the Indians. Then, in exchange for this deed, the Indians will yield a good four thousand acres of their undivided land elsewhere in the township."

"Van Valkenburgh's land is already cleared and in production!" Ephraim declared sharply in repudiation of what might have been a veiled rebuke. "It's worth as much or more than the whole four thousand acres of wilderness we're getting!"

Sergeant looked at him for a moment. Then he nodded, not so much in agreement, Mark thought, as in courteous recognition of the other's speech before he continued his own.

"For his handling of the matter, Mr. Williams will receive about nine hundred acres. And it is a part of his nine hundred acres which he has kindly agreed to sell to you. So you see you will get a clear title. And you see, also," he added, rising, "that the British do not intend to rob the Indians of their property." He paused for the briefest instant, his eyes steady on those of the older man. "And now I must bid you all good night."

In the flurry of his departure with Matt and Andy, and the

departure also of Josiah Jones and his wife, there was no opportunity for more words on the subject. Doubtless John had intended it that way, Mark thought. Ephraim might be the leader
here, he told himself, and as such he might be able to trick and
deceive the Indians, but he would never trick or deceive John
Sergeant. Despite the future relationship of the two men, a challenge had been flung this night to that effect. And probably,
Mark's thoughts went on, it was John's helplessness in the present
situation which accounted for the sadness seen twice on his face.
This was not, as Williams had said, a step of which he could approve. At the same time it was not one he could stop, either. For
how could he oppose the clergy who were backing him?

Their guests gone, Mrs. Williams and Abigail made their excuses, Thomas and young Josiah had already disappeared, and
Mark and his host returned to the fire where another punch was
offered. It was then that Ephraim came back to the matter so
abruptly dropped.

"I'm right fond of John," he said, choosing his words with
care. "I'm altogether pleased that Abigail is to be his wife. But
he's a dreamer, Cap'n. And 'tisn't always possible to live in
dreams. In this day and age you have to see things the way they
are. And you have to deal with 'em according."

Mark said slowly, "When will this—eh—transaction be consum-
mated with the Dutchman, Colonel?"

"Next week. The clergy will be coming for Abigail's wedding
and the matter will be cleared up before that. Whilst you're waiting, Cap'n, we can, if you like, ride over the piece that'll be mine
and you can see what part of it suits you. It's all here on the hill,"
he added. "The way I figure it, this'll be the most valuable land
in the years ahead. There's dampness down by the river. Up here
you get good air drainage." He paused, and, with his eyes on
the noggin in his hand, he finished casually, "You sell your holdings back in Stonington for paper currency or gold?"

There was a short silence. The paper currency floated by the
Colonies in the last year or two was playing havoc with trade
and business, as Mark well knew. It had been another factor in
his decision to leave the sea. With a small fortune in English

crowns, Spanish doubloons and French gold tucked away, he had decided against continuing in a venture fraught with the uncertainty that this usage of paper money had precipitated. It was a good time to get out, he had told himself.

It had taken him six months to dispose of his property in Connecticut because he had been unwilling to accept anything but gold in exchange for it. Better less of that than a heap of the nearly worthless stuff being passed about, he had argued. So, though the full value he had set on his house and ship and share in the boatyards had not been realized, the price he had finally accepted had been paid entirely in gold. But no need to make that revelation yet, he decided.

He said shortly, "I sold in a manner that in all ways satisfied me."

For a brief moment the shrewd eyes of Ephraim Williams locked with the bright unblinking gaze of Captain Mark Martin. Then Williams rose.

"Well, now," he said affably, "I'll not keep you up any longer. After you see what I have to offer we can get down to facts and figures. Time enough! Right now I reckon a night's sleep wouldn't go amiss."

Mark got to his feet. "Aye. I won't raise any argument with you on that point, Colonel."

CHAPTER 3

The Raising

Fʀᴏᴍ ᴛʜᴇ Cᴀsᴛʟᴇ, as Ephraim Williams' place was called, the ground rose steadily but gradually until, a half mile or so above it, it leveled out onto a broad high plateau. On this elevation there were deep woods cut only by the narrow footpath that led north past a lake halfway to Yokun Town, the next settlement. It was on this plateau, sloping smoothly down to the Housatonic River in the west but stretching endlessly eastward with alternating dips and rises of wild uninhabited country, that Williams' nine hundred acres lay.

He, himself, was familiar with it, of course. Long ago he had traversed the entire Indian tract, selecting for himself those sections which he deemed most desirable and which he intended at some future time to get into his possession. The area over which he rode with Mark the following morning lay on both sides of the trail and included, at the beginning of the plateau and along its southern edge, a barren piece of about twenty acres running east and west, a marshy piece at the eastern end of this with a winding brook a half mile or so beyond it, a great stretch of heavy timber reaching northward from the barren strip and extending up the sides of a small mountain, and a slight rise, also wooded, suitable for a homestead on the western side of the trail a quarter or half mile north of the beginning of the level plateau. In several places as they rode, Mark observed natural springs.

Having covered roughly the part Williams indicated he was

willing to sell, the men came to a halt on the rise appropriate
for a homesite and there Mark recalled what he had discovered
when he had first come out on the top of the plateau. Their
horses winded, they had paused to rest them on the broad barren strip. Because of its solid rock base, few trees grew there
through the turf and an unexpected and unparalleled vista had
spread itself before the captain's eyes. With amazement and delight, but hiding both from his companion, he had slowly turned
his head to view it.

In the western distance he had seen a gracious line of green
hills lying serenely against a blue sky while still more hills extended far down both sides of the valley to the east. Now, it occurred to him that when the tract between this spot where he
presently sat and that rocky area was all cleared off, there would
be as vast and magnificent a panorama as any mariner could
ever hope to find on dry land. There would be breathing space
up here on this elevation, a limitless expanse of sky and winds
such as he was accustomed to feel blowing from the four corners
of the earth. Furthermore, judging by the quantity and quality of
the timber, the soil was good and rich. And there was plenty of
water available. Finally, stone could be dug out of that rock to
the south for a solid foundation to the house he meant some day
to build.

For he wanted this acreage. Beyond a question he wanted it.
The doubts that had beset him on his journey were gone. The
certainty that had come first with meeting John Sergeant was
bolstered anew with his findings today. Here, he felt, he could
drop anchor for the rest of his life. For up here was freedom and
solitude and the alternating peace and turbulence of nature,
things he was used to. Here, too, was a challenge—not of the sea
but of the wilderness. Yes, he could drop anchor here right happily.

At first, his thoughts went on, he would have to erect the usual
one-room log cabin. Or perhaps an English house with a great
chimney at one end and another room built the other side of it
to make a double house. Anyway, the quickest thing that could be
raised, for it was his desire to be beholden to Ephraim Williams

no longer than necessary. Later, he would duplicate the Stonington place. Already he could envision it. It would be white clapboarded, three stories high with a hall in the center and a gracious stairway winding up. There would be a chimney at each end and fireplaces both upstairs and down. Indeed, it would be better than the Stonington house, for Esther deserved better. But all this would come later.

Ephraim, beside him, was studying Mark's bearded face and making nothing of it. "Well?" he inquired, when he could no longer contain himself.

Mark, recalled to the present, put away his secret enthusiasm. "I have no desire for as much as nine hundred acres," he replied, shrugging his indifference.

Williams spoke quickly. "That suits me. I don't want to sell it all. I've a mind to hold on to most of it as an investment. A hundred and fifty acres should do you and your family, I figure. I'll let you have 'em for—"

"Hold on!" The dislike this man engendered in Mark sounded in his voice. The fellow was too ready to make up other people's minds for them. He needed putting down. And since this was a business deal, pure and simple, and they were no longer in the relationship of guest to host, the check of courtesy was lifted. Digging his heels into his horse's sides, he said, over his shoulder, "Is this all you have to show me?"

Williams stared at the other's retreating back, then kicked his own mount and went after him, an incensed surprise sounding in his voice.

"Why, man! This is the best there is to be had!"

"I'm not so certain of that." Mark flung the words behind him with a note of scornful doubt sounding in them. "What good is that marsh land? Or that stony barren tract? Waste, all of it." And, guiding Bess out to the trail, he set forth along it at a slow walk toward Williams' house.

Ephraim's jaw set. Blast it! He had put this chap down as an easy one to dupe; for what did a seaman know of land values? But last night Mark's reply to his question about gold or currency had raised a doubt. And now he recognized that here was a worthy rival to himself. The captain would not be badgered into any purchase—or bankrupt by it, either. Yet sell to him he would.

He pushed up alongside and for a moment there was only the sound of their two horses' hoofs and the creaking leather of their saddles.

"Moreover," Mark said presently, "this is a long ways off from the meetinghouse. And from neighbors. My wife's used to neighbors. I reckon she wouldn't take kindly to the lonesomeness of this way-off place. Who's to hold title to the rest of the four thousand acres you and the clergy are getting? And where is it?"

Williams smothered an exclamation. Should this man go to Bull or Hopkins or his own cousin, Stephen Williams, or his nephew, Elisha, or any of the others who were to profit like himself, and should settlers begin pushing east or west instead of north onto the hill, it would throw off all his calculations for easy and quick profit.

"It's still farther from the center, if you want to know!" he exclaimed. "Look-a-here. I'll strike a bargain with you. I'll let you have two hundred acres. I'll let you have 'em for—"

Mark urged Bess into a gentle trot and again his words came back over his shoulder. "I wouldn't be interested in only two hundred acres. If it's really as valuable a piece as you say, I'd be a fool not to take more."

This time the exclamation was not smothered. "How much do you want, then? Tarnation, man! You don't give me half a chance to meet you! Hold up a minute! How much do you want?"

Mark slowed down and Ephraim came abreast of him once more. He was blown and flustered with his anger, Mark observed with silent pleasure.

"I dunno's I want any of it," he said, his black eyes bright and inscrutable. "I'll have to think on it. But if I should decide I do —mind you, I say *if*—I'd want—well—a good half of your holdings."

"Four hundred and fifty acres? Well! I'm not willing to sell that much. Not right yet."

"Four hundred and fifty acres or nothing," Mark said.

The two men faced each other, their horses at a standstill. Ephraim was thinking swiftly. A bird in hand was worth two in the bush, and it would be many a long day before more settlers arrived who, likely, wouldn't be as well off as Cap'n Martin was reputed to be. Besides, disposing of half of this property before he had to pay any taxes on it was something to be considered, too. And getting rid of that marshy piece—

"You paying in gold or paper currency?" he demanded sharply. "Makes a difference."

"Which do you want?"

"Gold."

"Gold don't come to hand easy these days."

"Gold it is or I'll not sell."

Mark appeared to hesitate. "Well—all right. Gold—if we can agree on a price." He stared off into space, his mind going over all he had seen. "Now! How much for four hundred and fifty acres of land in a square on both sides of this trail, as far east as the brook, north to the foot of the mountain behind us, south to take in that useless rock land and west to the base of the plateau? How much?"

Ephraim pondered. Then, a trifle cautiously, he named a figure. Promptly Mark cut it by a half. Ephraim exploded. Mark waited until he had finished, then said coolly, "That's fair enough and you know it. The land's costing you nothing."

They eyed each other. Williams was furious. Mark's brilliant black gaze was unyielding. Ephraim named another figure halfway between Mark's offer and his own original price. Mark's white teeth gleamed through his beard.

"If you want gold for a thing, you get less'n you figger. I did. No reason why you should fare better'n me. Take it or leave it. C'mon, Bess."

"Wait!" There was a short silence. Then, reluctantly, Williams said, "You're a hard bargainer. I never met a harder. But you had the advantage knowing how I got title. All right! It's a deal. Now, let's get down to Timothy Woodbridge and have it in writing. Later on we'll have a lawyer fix it up all right and proper."

"We will. But between times, why bother Mr. Woodbridge?

Your title isn't clear till Van Valkenburgh sells to the clergy. Till then my word's good. Isn't yours?" And Mark put his horse to a gallop and plunged triumphantly down the trail.

Mark faced John Sergeant on the other side of the empty fireplace in Sergeant's small plain cabin.

"I wanted to tell you," Mark said, "that I hadn't the least notion a limit had been set to the number of settlers who were to come here. Mr. Williams in no wise informed me in his letters. The first I learned of it was from Van Valkenburgh after my arrival night before last."

John gestured the apology away. "I'm glad you have come. I need a God-fearing man of your caliber here, Captain Martin. So be at peace. Besides, I can assure you that if it were not you, it would be someone else. Mr. Williams is determined to offset the number of Indians here by an equal number of whites."

"Is that so? Why?"

"It is his argument that it is best for all for safety's sake in case these Indians join with those of the north who are friendlier to the French than to us. However, I believe personally—" He stopped and Mark saw the shadow that he was beginning to recognize fall upon his face again.

"Something troubles you?"

"Many things trouble me. But what troubles me most is the realization that this lovely land, dedicated to the noble purpose which is known to you, is, I fear, likely to be a battleground between the Lord and the devil."

"The devil in the shape of your future father-in-law?"

There was a twinkle in Mark's glance and John's held a faint answering one. But this quickly died and his voice came forth with sternness.

"Ephraim Williams, as you have by now discovered, is a man eager for power. He will have it, come what may. I am equally resolved that my mission and the ideal which I pursue here, shall never be betrayed. Not by or for any man's lust." He stopped, his eyes flashing.

Mark said slowly, "I have been wondering how it happened he was selected to come here in the first place."

"Alas! There are other men like him in Boston, Captain. Men who consider this whole country a plum to be picked for England. To them Ephraim Williams may have seemed the right person to protect their interests. Whatever the reason, he is here." He fell silent. Then, with a return to his customary brisk cheerfulness, he went on. "Perhaps you would like to hear something of my plans and hopes for the mission?"

Mark nodded. "Indeed, yes."

Sergeant settled into his chair. He had now in operation, he said, a boarding school for twelve boys selected as the most promising among them all. These he himself taught while Mr. Woodbridge took care of the remainder. A wealthy gentleman from London, a Mr. Isaac Hollis, was supporting the school. But already he, John, had developed more ambitious ideas for the whole project.

"I really need two masters here," he explained.

"I do not follow you."

John smiled. "My thoughts run before my words. You see, it is the Indian way to let the women do all the hard physical work. Consequently the men have many idle hours when they are not hunting or fishing in which to fall into temptation. Well, I must change all that. I want a school wherein girls are taught as well as boys. I want them to learn cooking, weaving, spinning—all the countless household duties and arts that our English women perform—while the boys learn to handle the plow and take over the planting and harvesting." He smiled again. "It is a small revolution I ponder."

"I see."

"At present," John went on, "it is only a dream. Even to handle this small boarding school is difficult, for I must not only be here but I must also travel in pursuit of my ministerial duties to other tribes west and south of here. And run my farm myself in spite of my handicap." He lifted his withered arm with a smile. "And prepare my sermons in two languages for the Sabbath, also. Of course," he added, "after Abigail and I are married she will be here to take charge on those occasions when I am away. But in time I must have a resident teacher for the boarders."

He must, indeed, Mark thought, for he could not imagine young Abigail, charming as she was, managing the dirty young savages that swarmed about this cabin. But he only said, "Mr. Williams tells me your wedding will take place right after the purchase of the Van Valkenburgh land."

"Yes."

"Which brings me to another reason for my visit here today, Mr. Sergeant."

"I answer also to the name of John."

Mark's black eyes, that could glitter as cold as ice, warmed as they rested on the countenance of the minister.

"John, then. What is on my mind is this: I want to impose no longer than is necessary on the hospitality now being extended to us. Particularly since my host is not feeling in the best of humors toward me." And he related the bargain he had made concerning the land. "For that reason," he concluded, "and also because of your impending wedding when there will be guests arriving from afar who must be accommodated, I feel our room will be more desired than our company. Do you think I can get any Indians to help me raise my cabin after I've bought my land and taken title to it?"

For answer John Sergeant rose and moved to the window. "Come here."

Mark joined him. Outside he could see twenty or more savages, bare to the waist, at work on the log meetinghouse. They moved slowly but apparently in good spirits for they were singing as they toiled.

"They will help you," John said. "I will speak to them. Every one else will help you, too."

"Good. It shouldn't take more than a day, should it?"

"By rights not that. These Indians have put up enough cabins to know how to do it in short order."

"Then we should have our own roof over our heads before the wedding." Mark's voice held satisfaction. "And now I must bid you good day, sir. But first I should like to express my thanks to you for your care and interest in my two boys while they are here."

"They are good lads."

"Andy—yes. Matt is more difficult."

"Matthew will be all right. He has found a friend in Peter, the brother of the little Marie you saw in Konkapot's tent." He hesitated for a moment, then added, "Matthew is one of those to be guided, not driven, Captain. You, perhaps, are accustomed to issuing orders." He flashed his brilliant smile on his guest as if in apology for this unasked advice and went on quickly, "How is your wife today?"

"She is recovering her strength. Abigail has been untiringly thoughtful. And Mrs. Williams, too. We are both most grateful."

"And Prudence and the twins are in good hands at the Wood-bridges, are they not?"

"Excellent. They are a fine couple and Prue is happy learning how to make an Indian cradle for the new baby." He extended his hand. "Good day, Mr.— Good day, John."

"Good day, Captain. Come again."

Mark had told Esther she had better wait at The Castle and he would come back for her when the cabin was up. But she would not wait. She had insisted on riding along in the ox cart when the men left early in the morning because she wanted to watch from the beginning the building of her home in the wilderness. And Mark had given in, since well he knew that on those rare occasions when she took a stand there was no changing her.

It was not her first trip. Mark had taken her on a pillion a few days previously to get her approval of the site he had selected before he bought it. At first she had been dismayed. The woods looked so grim and dark and forbidding. The distance seemed so far from the settlement. And not a sight or sound of a neighbor. But when Mark had ridden out onto the highest rock and told her they would, in time, have the same open view from their house, and when she had seen how happy he was over his choice, she had smothered her own feelings.

This morning she was sitting huddled in quilts in the cart, for the chill of the night was not yet fully gone from the air. Behind her back was the ship chest, rescued from the mountaintop, and all around her were their household possessions. Mark's tools, his froe and augur, his ax, his pick and shovel and blacksmith's traps, his bullet mold and powder horn and musket. Her needed utensils were somehow crammed in also—the big and little iron kettles, the churn, the swift for winding wool with its reel, the fire dogs. The wooden tub was here, too, rattling once again at the end of the ox cart.

It would be strange to live in a one-room cabin, Esther told herself. But that was what the Williamses had done when they first arrived. And now look at the house they had! Mark had promised her that theirs would be as fine some day and the cabin would then be used as a storeroom. Oh, he had his plans well made, she could see that, and it was all clear to him how everything would look when all was finished. He'd spotted where his barns and his shed and his well-sweep would go. He'd laid out his fence lines in his mind and a drive-in from the trail. He'd settled where would be the meadow for the cow they'd have and where he'd put in his rye and flax and wheat— White potatoes, too, for he was going to try them. He was happy in this venture, for certain, and it was an amazement to her that he was. From seaman to farmer was quite a jump.

Now they had reached the top of the rise and Mark cantered briskly ahead down the trail, calling back to Matt and Andy to coax Star and the mules along as fast as they could because the Indians were already waiting there.

The Indians—and Mr. Sergeant with them. How glad she was, on arriving, to see him there, too, for she still felt strange about the savages.

Somehow the ox cart was maneuvered in amongst the trees, out of the way of where the men would work and the horses and mules were tied until such time as Daisy and Bess might be needed for hauling. And now, straggling along the path to the homesite, could be seen coming still more people. Josiah Jones, and with him Mr. Samuel Brown, whom she had not met yet, and Joseph Woodbridge, the schoolteacher's brother. Esther, seated on the ground on a pile of quilts with her baby in her arms, viewed the gathering with a rising sense of excitement. All the able-bodied men in town were here, she thought, excepting only Ephraim Williams. He had had to ride down to Sheffield today, he had said, to get some things his wife wanted for the wedding three days hence. But he had sent his son, Josiah, and half a dozen of his slaves—stablemen and horse boys—in his stead. Now as soon as Mr. Timothy Woodbridge got here with Prue and the twins, there would be no more to come.

The Indians were apparently being given instructions by the minister, for they were grouped around him listening to him. Presently they dispersed. The hill neighbors and the blacks dispersed, too, gathering up their tools as they went each to his allotted task.

The men worked in pairs, some chopping down trees blazed earlier by Mark, some cutting these the right lengths, others dragging in the logs and still others squaring and notching them. The boys in the crowd were kept busy slashing down the underbrush, trimming saplings for the rafters or cutting cedar shakes for the roof.

It was amazing how fast progress was made that way. In less than two hours there was a clearing big enough for the house and the first heavy logs had been laid. And then a couple of Indians began to dig down for the clay in the ground that would be needed for building the fireplace.

Johnny whimpered in her arms and she drew him closer, turned herself half about and put his mouth to her bare breast. Every one was too busy to notice and he must be fed, for he was not thriving as he should and she could not fathom why. Perhaps when she was settled in her own house again and life had calmed down, her milk would be better. That was all she could cipher out that might be wrong. His fussy whimper ceased as he was given nourishment, and she let her attention go out once more to the group before her.

Ah! There came Prue at last, the twins stumbling at her heels. She carried the cradle she had made for the baby and, coming up to Esther, she dropped down beside her and began with sparkling eyes to explain its making to her mother.

"You get strips of wood, quite slim ones, and peel them. Then you wave those through a fire to dry and harden them. After you've done that you weave them. Then you have to bend the ends and fasten them tight with these leather thongs. It is good, isn't it? If we put a blanket inside, we can use it, can't we?"

"Indeed we can. We'll use it right now. Here's a blanket. You fix it and I'll lay Johnny in as soon as he's done nursing."

"Marie showed me how to make it," Prue went on happily, and Esther saw that her oldest child rued nothing of the past. "Ma, the Indians really know some mighty interesting things."

Matt came up now with Andy and stood inspecting the basket while Prue folded the blanket in it. "They know heaps," he said, out of the silence. "They know three ways to kill beaver and none of 'em is with a gun."

Esther looked at him. In the week that they had been apart he seemed to her dirtier and more unkempt than she had ever seen him, as if he had picked up slothful Indian ways in his association with Mr. Sergeant's boys. But he also seemed less sullen. His eyes now were lighted as they had not been since Stonington days.

"What are the three ways?" she asked.

Andy stopped his ears and moved away. Matt threw him a look of disgust and began talking:

"You can set a trap and when he goes in to get the food, the log falls on him and breaks his back. That's one. Or you can cut a hole in the ice and hide it with layin' stalks and reeds and things over it and wait by the hole. Because that's where he comes up to breathe. You can tell he's there by the water blowing. So when you see that you can reach in and grab a paw and pull him out onto the ice and then you can beat him to death with a club. That's the second way. The third—"

"Don't tell me any more," Esther said quickly. And she saw the light die in the boy's eyes at her words. She hurried on. "I'd rather you used a gun on your beaver, Matt. It's more merciful."

Matt just stared at her, the old sullenness returning to his face.

She went on. "If you must kill, kill as quickly and kindly as possible."

Still Matt said nothing. And when his father shouted for him, he turned and left her without speaking again.

Esther watched him go and sighed. But she had had to say that, she thought. An Indian lad might be callous to cruelty but not her Matt. Was it just the difference between a girl and a boy that the one had learned something constructive and the other something destructive, she wondered? Or was there a deeper difference? Not liking her thoughts, she turned to Prudence.

"Take the baby, Prue, and lay him in your basket now. Then we'll go see if all is safe in the ship chest."

It had been lifted out of the ox cart and now stood under a tree. The key to it hung around Esther's neck and she could hardly wait to unlock it and look once again at the things so dear to her.

On top were hers and Prue's best dresses. La! How wrinkled! But somewhere far down underneath was a sad iron and they would press out all right for the wedding. Good fortune she had brought their fine clothes with them, though at the time of packing it had seemed foolishness.

"Oh, I'm so glad we're to go! I've never been to a wedding, Ma. But where's the meetinghouse to marry her in?"

"The meetinghouse isn't finished yet. She'll be married at her home. Now help me, Prue. See if my pewter— Yes, thankful heart, here it all is. And here's my copper kettle and the brass candlesticks and the six silver spoons." Esther looked up, her lovely worn face kindled. "It won't be a Castle, this cabin of ours," she said, looking off through the trees, "but it'll have a sight of pretties in it just the same. And when your Pa sends back for some of the furniture we stored in the Palmers' attic, it'll be a place we in no ways need be ashamed on." She stopped suddenly on a gasp of fright. "Prue! Quick! Get Mary!"

Prue sprang to her feet and started running, for Mary, who had wandered off, stood directly in the path of a tree that was ready to topple. The Indian who had been chopping it, had spied the danger, too, and was racing forward in great leaping bounds.

Her heart frozen by fear, Esther watched the tree lean, heard its rending crack as it left its stump, saw it crash downward toward the diminutive figure of the child who, despite frantic shouts from all sides, was too petrified and confused to stir. As in a nightmare, she glimpsed the Indian give a mighty spring and fling himself upon the little girl; then he, with her, went down under a smother of green leaves.

It seemed an era before the branches had been hacked away, a lifetime before the Indian, upright and unharmed, walked toward her with Mary in his arms. She was crying a little but, by a miracle, was not hurt. The branches and the Indian had held the heavy limbs from her. All she had felt was terror.

Esther, her hand to her heart to still the pain there, dropped it now and gathered Mary to her and looked at the half-naked man before her. His face was pock-marked and scarred and ugly. And his eyes were bottomless black wells. Her instinct was to shrink but she would not permit herself this. Never again, she thought, would she think hardly of any savage, for one of them had saved her baby girl for her this day by sheltering her small body with his own.

"Thank you," she said, very low. "Thank you from my heart." And then she put out her hand. "From now I am your friend," she added.

Into the bottomless wells sprang a sudden gleam. He shook her hand once and dropped it.

"All like papoose," he said. "White man and redskin. All take fine care papoose. It is good."

And he went quickly back to work.

Every one was crowding around. Mark came swinging over, his face ashen above his beard. Prue, running back, said, "Ma, that was Aaron! That was Marie's father! Marie's and Peter's father!" John Sergeant joined them, his expressive eyes warm with thankfulness for the tragedy averted and gratification that one of his tribe had effected it. "Let us speak to the Lord who lives in the heart of Aaron," he said, and one by one all the settlers and Indians gathered close to stand with bowed heads as he prayed.

When he had finished, Mark exclaimed, "We'll tie both children to a tree for the rest of the day."

"I'll watch them, Mark."

"We'll tie them. Matt! Fetch me some rope. There's a piece by the tools yonder."

He might be rebuking her. Or he might be only making assurance against further accidents doubly sure. She did not know. She would not blame him for a rebuke. Certainly it was a woman's business to watch the little ones. It had just been the excitement of unpacking the chest and seeing all her treasures again that had made her careless for a moment. But the Lord had given her warning of the speed with which His wrath could strike if she again forgot her duty in prideful contemplation of her worldly possessions. Humbly, silently, she offered up a prayer herself begging forgiveness.

Presently her trembling ceased and she settled herself beneath the tree. Every one had gone back to work. Axes were ringing once more. Branches were flying. There was the scrape of a dry boat laden with stones as Daisy dragged it to the pile that later was to make the chimney. There was the soft thump of the pickax striking down into the earth. The twins had accepted the tying-up with docility. Prue and Andy were watching two Indians mix clay with hay for mortar, and Matt, near his father, was working like a man. The baby still slept.

The sun climbed higher and higher. Wider and wider grew the little clearing. There was a path now out to the trail. The house itself was half up. The spring was cleaned and lined with stones, and a little trough made out of a hollow log had been fixed so a pail could get under it. And now it was noon and calls were heard along the footpath and the women—squaws and whites—were arriving with food.

It was simple but ample for all. There were long loaves of crusty bread whose slices were spread with quince, blackberry and huckleberry jam or wild honey. There were wild hares done to a crispy turn, grouse plucked and rolled in clay and baked—Indian style—with Indian corn and apples. There were sides of ham with the juices running down. And there were great pails of milk for the children and jugs of elderberry wine for the adults, and tipsy cake and gingerbread for everyone. In that hour the raising became a party.

Later, the men, rested and refreshed, went back to their labors while the women, Mrs. Brown, Mrs. Jones, the two Mrs. Woodbridges and Esther, joined shyly and silently by the squaws, gathered in the shade with watchful eyes on all the children and exchanged the latest news. The foot post had arrived in Albany from New York and a letter brought over to the Williamses said that Ephraim, Junior, would be here, after all, for Abigail's wedding and would bring a friend. The Reverend Stephen Williams and his wife had fetched a silver salver for the bride and she hadn't a mind whether it would be safe to take it down into that houseful of little Indians or not. And it was true she was going to have her portrait painted in her wedding gown and the lace veil brought over from England by her grandmother. It was, in fact, being done today, which was why she and Mrs. Williams were not here.

The tongues wagged. The shadows lengthened. The children grew tired and crept back to their mothers' laps. Higher and higher went the house. The walls were all up now, the peeled logs ragged at the corners and the chinking left for a later day. The chimney was started and near done. And now the rafters and sheeting were laid and it was time to start on the roof.

Just then—suddenly—a song burst forth. It was led by John Sergeant, with the Indians all joining in to make a great chorus that echoed out through the trees and off to the distant hills.

> *"Here's a mighty fine frame*
> *Which desarves a good name.*
> *Say! What shall we call it?*
> *The timbers all straight*
> *And was hewed first rate,*
> *The frame is well put together.*
> *It IS a good frame*
> *That desarves a good name,*
> *Say! What shall we name it?"*

Mark came over to Esther and pulled her to her feet. His eyes were shining above his matted black beard. His voice was husky with his shouting and his emotion. "Give it a name, Esther."

"Oh, Mark! What shall I?" She looked around at the expectant group. "I don't know."

"Hilltop House!"

"No! Call it Broad Acres!"

"How about Home Acres?"

"Those are all good." She hesitated, looking up at Mark. "I'd like to use our own name somehow," she said. "But I don't like Martin House. Does—does Martin Manor sound too elegant?"

His great voice boomed out. "Not for the way we'll have it here some day! Martin Manor it is, folks!"

"Martin Manor! Hooray!"

"Martin Manor! May your days here be blessed!"

Martin Manor. It was settled.

CHAPTER 4

The Wedding

I T WAS NOON of a Thursday. Mark had come in for his lunch of roast corn and pumpkin pottage washed down with sassafras tea and had gone out again to ring some more trees with fire the way the Indians did as the easiest way of felling them. He was bound to clear a view to the western hills so that these would be visible from the cabin this winter, Esther thought.

She sent the twins up to the loft for a nap (they were too young to go to school yet) and then she moved about the cabin, her mind chasing hither and yon and back again the way it did when she was alone with the baby. How much better he seemed just in these three days they had been here. She stretched out a finger to touch him gently in passing. Then she moved to the fireplace where she bent down to put the iron on the trivet for heating so she could press their clothes for the wedding this afternoon. Mark didn't want to bother to dress up but he must. And she did hope Matt could get into his coat though it had been tight last spring.

She put more wood on the fire and straightened up again. It was a good fireplace. She had done as she was told and made the first blaze a small one to bake the brick out slow so it would harden well. Now with the smoke going up the chimney the way it should and the heat coming forth to meet her in the room and the swinging crane fixed in its place, she could want for none better.

She stood gazing about for a moment. Already the place had

lost its primitive look, she thought. There was a solid plank where before there had been but a flapping blanket for a door. And the wall apertures held fine glazed windows as Mark had promised her they would. The logs had been solidly chinked now and the earth underfoot packed hard and smooth. This winter Mark would lay a wood floor over the dirt. Then she would braid some rag rugs for color and warmth.

They even had some furniture, her mind went on. She had hardly thought they would so soon, any more than the ship chest they had brought with them. But the day after the raising, the neighbors had come traipsing up the hill again with a wagonload. A long bench from Timothy Woodbridge that he had made himself. A kitchen table from Mrs. Williams she said she no longer needed. A couple of stools that John Sergeant's Indian boys had built. And a hickory rocking chair from Josiah Jones and his wife. How good they had all been!

Mark, of course, had built legs and a plank bottom for their bed in the corner. The baby had his little cradle that Prue had made and the other children all climbed to the loft above to where blankets were spread over cornhusks on the floor, the boys at one end, Prue and the twins at the other.

Yes, they were fixed fine and comfortable. And with her brass candlesticks shining on top of the chest, with her best coverlet spread neatly over the feather bed and with her pewter twinkling on the table, the house had quite a civilized air.

Contentment filled her as she moved to shake out the clothes from the chest. She might dream of polished floors and white curtains and rooms enough for each of them such as she had known in Stonington, but her dreaming never interfered with the calm of her living. Today was what had to be dealt with. Tomorrow would take care of itself.

The iron was hot now and she lifted the board she had covered with a blanket and a sheet and went to work. Prue's dress first. If Esther was skimped for time on the other things it wouldn't matter so much. But Prue must look her best this afternoon. The Williamses were well-known throughout the whole Massachusetts Colony and it was likely a number of fine folk would be there.

One thing certain—Ephraim, Junior, was coming and bringing a friend. That being so, who could tell what might happen? It was a hope, at least, although not one she'd expected to entertain for her daughter so soon.

Her mind turned next to Matt. He was the only one who troubled her at all. But surely he was happier than he had been. True, he was still the silent member of the family and the distance between him and his father had not lessened a smidgen. Indeed, she sometimes felt he had gone from her, too, and strange it was to stand face to face with this lad who was bone of her bone and flesh of her flesh, knowing that the words she spoke were not those of mother to son but of stranger to stranger and that because of this what she said was often lost in space before it ever reached him. She sighed faintly. Since the time he had told her how the Indians killed beavers, it had been like that. Well, such might be the way it went with a boy child. Could be he had to put off by himself. Anyway, since Mr. Sergeant had let him remain there at his school instead of sending him to Mr. Woodbridge with Andy, his quiet seemed to her to hold less surliness than before. Mayhap, if she were patient, time would loose his tongue again.

Still she could not conceal from herself the fact that Matt was different from what he used to be. He lived a life of his own these days, secret and apart. Sometimes she had the notion he had arrived at some decision momentous to himself. But what could it be? She did not think he held to the idea of running off to sea any more, for now there was something that bound him here.

It was the Indian way of life. He seemed to admire it. And he was forever trying to copy the things that Indians did. The silent way they walked. Their skill with bow and arrow. Even their language, which he could already jabber a bit. He was down on the meadow amongst them all as much as it was possible for him to be and Peter was his boon companion. She supposed it was natural that their strange customs, their dances and weird chanting and rituals, to which they still clung, held a fascination for him, although she did not like it. But doubtless this interest would do him no harm and would pass, for as fast as Mr. Sergeant taught them to be civilized they would drop their heathenish ways and become more like Matt. **Then they** would imitate him instead of he them.

Anyway, so things were. And with her lips set firm against complaint or worry, she bent to her task.

Matt scuffed on bare feet along the trail that led home. He was alone. And with his aloneness came that strange burdensome ache in his heart that he could not understand and could not get rid of. Only when he was with Peter could he forget it. Peter told him so many things that there was no time to think about the ache. And down on the meadow with Peter's people everything was so passing different that the ache was forgot there, too.

"Some day I'll be an Indian. I'll live with them and be one myself," he muttered fiercely. "See if I don't."

He didn't belong with his family any more. That was the trouble. Sometimes he thought he never had belonged to them, that he wasn't really his ma's and pa's boy. If he were, wouldn't they treat him better? Wouldn't Pa have let him go off to sea? And wouldn't Ma have heard out his story about the beavers the way she had heard out Prue's about making a cradle? She'd listened to Prue but not to him.

They didn't care about him. That was plain. They didn't care about him except for work. The way Pa hollered at him all the time. Do this. Do that. Come here. Get a move on. And the way Ma kept pickin' on him. Where you been? What you been doin'? Have you washed your hands? It made you sick and tired. Why couldn't they let him alone?

Well, some day he'd be free of them. He'd decided that much. Some day when he knew how to take care of himself he'd disappear. He'd either go far off and join another tribe of Indians, or he'd make his way to the sea. He wasn't sure yet which. Anyway, he'd go. Soon's ever he knew he wouldn't near starve to death before he got where he set out to, like that man Peter'd told him about an' took him to see coupla days ago. Sakes! What a skeleton! He hadn't knowed how to use a bow and arrow was his trouble. Livin' on Indian land up New Marlborough way, he was, but the Injuns had tooken away his gun and give him a bow an' arrow instead. No guns allowed on their land, they'd told him. And he couldn't kill a thing with a bow and arrow. Not even a squirrel. Missed every time. Couldn't catch any fish, neither, with only his hands. Didn't know how to trap. So he'd about starved till he staggered over the mountain and some Stockbridge Indians had found him stretched out too weak to move any more and brought him to the meadow and nursed life back into him.

Well, he—Matt—wouldn't go off till he could manage better'n that. But he was learning. Peter was teaching him a heap o' stuff. An' he was learnin' fast.

He came to the top of the hill and onto the barren strip where only rocks grew. Here there was blue sky above him and against its high arch he saw now a hawk wheeling and circling.

Some day he'd be as free as that hawk. And when he came back —if ever he did come back—they'd know he was his own man.

Andy and Prue were not far behind Matt. Like him, they had been dismissed early from school today because of the wedding.

Andy walked slowly, his thoughts on the classroom. He liked school. He liked Mr. Woodbridge. And he meant to be the best pupil Mr. Woodbridge had. He reckoned it wouldn't be hard. He wa'nt the oldest boy there but he was the oldest white boy. Keziah Jones was only six. So was Elijah Williams. There were older girls—Prue and Keziah's sister, Anna—but girls didn't count. Yes, he'd beat 'em all.

He trudged along ploddingly, unaware of the bright beauty of the day, of the warm scent of the pines overhead, of the dappled sunshine at his feet, of the bird sounds all around him. Unaware of his body, even, and that he had arms and legs and was a moving, breathing, living being.

Only his thoughts stirred Andy.

Prue, on the other hand, was aware of everything as she stepped lightly over the deeply carpeted ground. She was so aware that she became what she felt and saw. She was one with the flying, fleecy clouds high in the blue vault of the sky. She was a hidden bird, now singing its heart out, now flashing into sight with a swift rush of wings. She was the brook running murmurously over smooth rounded stones. She was the cool shadow and the hot sunlight and the scampering squirrel and the immobile birch tree. And today, above all things, she was the bride. Not Abigail. By some curious mental process, she had become the promised bride herself who would this afternoon be wedded, although the bridegroom was a stranger whose face she did not know.

It was an exciting thought and it brought other thoughts still more exciting that caught her breath away as they came to her.

And now, walking up the hill ahead of Andy, she discovered a new pleasure. It lay in the controlled motions of her lissome body. In the sureness of her springing step, in the smoothly working muscles of her bare brown legs, in the feeling of power latent in her firm, flat flanks. Why, she could start and stop herself like a humming bird if she chose! As quickly, as easily. She might even fly. So thinking, she flung out her arms and felt a sudden odd delight mingled with a small terror before a mystery. Yet the terror did not lessen the delight. For what came—came. You could not stop it. You did not really want to. What you wanted was never to let life fash you. To meet it with a glad readiness, however unknown, even the scare of it.

She looked back at Andy and knew a little pity for him for what he missed by living only in his mind. But she could not think on him long because of the need for planning. Presently it was clear to her what she would do.

"I'll race you to the top of the hill, Andy!" she cried, and was off before he could reply.

Her moccasined feet seemed scarcely to touch the earth. And when she reached the summit they carried her, as if they were winged, off the trail to the right and clear across the open field up to the highest rock. Below this rock, secret and lovely, was a place she had made her own from the first moment of discovering it.

Pausing on the rim, she looked back. But Andy, who had not

responded to her challenge as she had known he would not, was nowhere in sight. And when he came he would think she had gone straight on home as he would go. Certain of this, she glanced around, her heart quickening its beat. North of her, across this arid space, the forest began. It was deep and dense and reached to the top of Rattlesnake Mountain. Pa's forest it was. Pa, himself, was in the part of it across the trail near the cabin, a good quarter mile away. She could hear the ring of his ax and his shout for Matt.

She scarcely needed to look to the south the way she had come, for she knew there were woods there, too, belonging to Ephraim Williams. And as he was not clearing his land these made as black and impenetrable a curtain for her as those on the other side.

To the north, the woods, then. To the south, the woods. To the east, down a broadening valley, a wild, uncharted wilderness, hiding in its near distance bogs and swamps dangerous to man and beast. To the west, behind her, the foot trail from Indian Town to Yokun Town. And who would think to leave it for this spot save herself? Oh, she was safe enough! Even so, she could not check a momentary inward shiver.

For a brief space she hesitated, poised against the sky. Directly beneath her the cliff fell sheerly away thirty or forty feet. But on either side of her it curved around like protecting arms and sloped down gradually to enclose in its embrace a circular sunlit glade. Nothing grew down there, as the soil was shallow, save a spreading mat of wild thyme whose amethyst flowers profusely spangled their tiny emerald leaves and filled the air with a wondrous pungent sweetness. At the farther end of this enchanted place lay a clear and gleaming pool.

The golden sunshine, the stillness, the fragrance and the glinting water laid a spell on Prue as it always did. Impossible, she knew, to descend on the right where the cliff ended in an extended mass of prickly bushes tangled with the ropy vines of wild grapes and a cluster of scraggly trees overgrown with bittersweet. But on her left it was different. For here the rock flattened to a broad ledge which swept down in a graceful crescent to form a low wall half way around the pool's edge where it met the clambering hedging bushes. And all the way there were easy natural steps cut by nature.

Across and down this ledge she moved, past diminutive wild asters and hardy ferns that clutched for life in the cracks and crevices, until she could spring the short space to the jeweled carpet below. Now she was in an outdoor room enclosed on all sides and open only to the sky. Now she was in her bridal chamber.

For an instant, flushed, uncertain, fearful, she stood quite still. Then, with a little gasp of determination, she lifted her arms, twisted her braids into a coronet about her head, stepped out of her moccasins, and, seating herself on the wall, swung her bare feet over and let them down into the water. When the ripples died away she peered in. She could clearly see bottom. She could see how the rocks shelved down in big slabs all around to make a kind of cup with a flat space in the center just big enough for her to stand in. It was here the spring bubbled up. She thought the water might come to her waist but when, after another desperately anxious moment during which all her religious training and maidenly scruples struggled in vain against this mad desire that had seized her, she pulled her linsey-woolsey dress off over her head and slid in, she found it reached to her shoulders.

Now that it was done, a kind of calm descended upon her, and, with her dark-lashed blue eyes lifted to the fast traveling clouds above her, she stood, kissed by the sun, caressed by the breeze, laved by the limpid water, held in rapture by a strange excitement that seemed to hold no possible wickedness. In her beating blood there was a tumult that was neither hunger nor satisfaction. In her heart there was a waiting that was not contentment, a poignancy that was not happiness, a knowledge that was not knowledge. Yet they combined to give a promise of all of these.

So immovable she stood that she seemed more nymph than mortal to the astonished unbelieving man on the horse high above her. But of his presence she knew nothing. She was lost to him and to the world. She had become a part of the pool, a part of the sylvan glade, a part of the sky and the wind and the water, a part of creation. Indeed, she was creation.

The numbing chill of the pool brought her back to herself. And she looked down and saw all her slender whiteness in full daylight for the first time in her life. At home in the foottub she had washed herself by inches, quickly, because some one else was waiting a turn and it had seemed somehow sinful to be curious. But here it was right and beautiful to gaze as long as she wished.

She lifted her hands in a dreamlike way, hugging herself and shivering a little at the thoughts that stirred in her. At last, with a grave wonder upon her face, she stepped out of the water and turned in the sun for it to dry her. One braid slipped loose and she unbound her hair and let it fall in bright glittering waves down her back, for it seemed to give her the cover that her returning doubts needed. Presently, forcing these into the background of her mind once more, she lay down on the scented ground with a lovely grace that revealed a nature compounded of both reverence and ardor. But then the confusion within her, with its ache and unfulfillment, became something not to be borne, and a well of tears rose up in her because, after all, she was alone.

It was at this moment that she thought she heard a horse's hoof clink against a rock. For a breath life stopped and she held her eyes closed in a terror like nothing she had ever known before. Yet if there was danger she must know it. With her body aflame, she made herself look up. There was no one in sight.

Shaking from shock, still mortally afraid, and overwhelmed at last by a consciousness of sin, she sprang to her feet, seized her dress and pulled it on, caught up her moccasins in one hand and ran on bare feet up over the ledge to the rim of the cliffs. Not that she hoped to meet any one. Not that she would not die of shame if she did meet any one. But she had to know.

She gazed in every direction and saw the world empty. She called Andy by name, knowing it would not be he, and had no answer. An Indian? Possibly. They moved on silent feet, though, and if it had been one, she would never know.

Perhaps she had only imagined the sound. Oh, she must have! It was all she could think. All she dared think.

She stepped into her moccasins and began braiding her hair with a purposeful slowness that helped calm her. Gradually her heart quieted. Gradually her hope became a certainty that no one, after all, had been near. 'Twas some small animal, she told herself, had given her that startle. A woodchuck, no doubt. They were big clumsy creatures who, scampering from hole to hole, could easily have rattled a stone loose to make a noise such as she had heard. There were dozens of woodchucks living amongst these rocks. Indeed, at her feet now was the opening to a tunnel. With this thought went her fear.

But the fear had left its mark. It had told her she had, indeed, been wicked. Oh! Would God ever forgive her? She must pray hard asking Him to. Certainly what she had done today she would never do again. For in this hour, when life had threatened as well as beckoned, something had departed from her. The delight of sweet pretense, the purity of innocent imaginings, the joy of adolescent dreaming. Reality had broken in and spoiled it all.

It was a woman who walked soberly home to the little cabin in the woods.

Most of the guests had gathered in the front yard of Ephraim Williams' Castle when Lieutenant David Reynolds finally made his way among them toward the knot of men talking beneath the largest elm. His walk was swift and graceful. His scarlet British uniform, with its white waistcoat and white breeches, fitted well his tall, straight figure; his red felt hat, decorated by a high rosette of white and gold, swung from one hand. For the rest, the ruffles falling at his wrists were of the finest net and spotless, his gold buttons and epaulets danced in the sun, his spurred black boots were shining and his dangling sword a-gleam. It was no wonder that feminine eyes followed his progress with approving interest.

He moved without self-consciousness, his easy carriage and pleasant open countenance bespeaking one who had known only the good things of life. His chestnut brown hair was drawn back into a queue and tied with a black ribbon. His brown eyes that seemed to hold tiny sparks of fire went searching over the crowd and there was an eagerness in his glance that set more than one heart a-flutter and caused more than one maiden to mistake it for interest in her alone. But the next moment he had passed on as if he had not seen her.

He came finally to his host. Ephraim, Junior, stood, big and handsome, in a green velvet coat richly laced with gold, a flowered waistcoat and buff breeches to his knees. Buckles of silver shone on his low-cut shoes and his stockings were of the finest silk. He was discoursing with some vehemence to those surrounding him as the Britisher approached, but broke off to clap a heavy hand on his friend's arm.

"Gad, David! I thought you'd got lost."

"I rode farther than I intended."

"And was I not right? Does not this land remind you of your England?"

"It does, indeed. I should like to be able to stay awhile and explore it farther." He hesitated, then added, "What I saw this afternoon was but a tantalizing glimpse." His words held a double meaning but for himself alone and would do the girl no harm. Indeed, so dazzled had he been by his vision of her, so thunderstruck by the beauty of the fancy she had enacted, that he still could not wholly believe it had not been a figment of his imagination.

"And why not?" Ephraim was saying heartily. "We would be delighted. Dave, I want you to meet these folk." And he introduced him to the others—Josiah Jones, fine today in a plum-colored suit that hung like a bag on his match-stick figure; Samuel Woodbridge, a silver snuff box in his hand; his brother Timothy, bewigged for the occasion, and a group from down Sheffield way clad in their homely buckskin breeches, leather jerkins and high-worn boots. The introductions ended, Ephraim, by reason of a natural leadership, carried on the conversation.

"I was just speaking of the recent call issued for volunteers to the West Indies. Think you we might find some willing souls in this community, Mr. Woodbridge?"

He addressed Timothy, the schoolteacher, but it was his brother who answered with a shake of his head.

"There are too few able-bodied men here as it is. And what there are should, I think, remain. Your father would agree with me, I feel sure."

"I have no doubt." The young man nodded and then turned to address his visitor with affable imperiousness.

"But come! We are not here merely to drum up volunteers for the West Indies. After all—" A touch on his arm made him break off, and, looking down, he saw Matt standing there, the unruly thatch of his hair licked down to an unaccustomed smoothness, his stocky shoulders near bursting out of the seams of his black velvet coat, his usually dark and scowling face alight with a sudden wild hope.

"I was passing, sir, and I couldn't help but hear you. And I wondered—I thought— Well, I mean! How old must a volunteer be? I know all about ships," he rushed on. "My Pa is—was—a sea captain. Belike I could—" He stopped at the shout of laughter from the big man above him and his expression changed. Seeing the hard anger come in it, Ephraim checked his mirth and spoke quickly, employing the tact and friendliness that made him so popular wherever he went.

"In sober truth, I like your spirit. And were it possible I'd enroll you for that alone. But you have surmised the difficulty correctly. Add a few more years to your stature and you'll have a better chance." His glance became curious. "You are the son of a sea captain, you say. Then you are but lately come among us. Do you not like it here that you are so ready to leave?"

Matt hesitated. His resentment at the ridicule his offer had met melted before the realization that Captain Williams was not a man to quarrel with. Some time, as he himself had just suggested, he might truly be able to help Matt escape.

He said, "I—I like the sea, sir. And I'm not afraid to fight."

"Good. I'll remember that. What is your name?"

"Matt. Matthew Martin, sir."

Ephraim nodded again and the two men strolled away. Ephraim, knowing everyone and so recently returned from travels abroad, was kept busy giving greetings. Thus absorbed, he did not notice any abstraction on the part of his companion or the way his glance continued to seek through the crowd. David was not at all sure he would remember the face he sought to recognize. After all, he had been some distance away. But surely he would know her by her hair. He could hardly conceal his impatience when, introduced by Ephraim, he must pause to converse for politeness' sake with the Colonial ladies from Sheffield and Albany and Springfield in their low-cut gowns of taffeta or kincob, whose skirts just cleared the ground to show their high-heeled slippers, whose stomachers were laced with bright ribbons and whose frills of fine lace cascaded from pretty elbows. For it was not with such as these he would find the lass he had seen this afternoon, he kept thinking. She would be, he was sure, amongst the country folk.

"A uniform helps," Ephraim observed with a sideways grin at David. "I mind when I wear mine— But wait! You must meet Chief Konkapot and his warrior."

They paused before a large group of Indians standing quietly close together in the shade. The braves, resplendent in eagle plumes and wampum, were wrapped in vivid blankets. The squaws, no less gay in full-fringed deerskin skirts topped by blouses of all colors, had woven flowers plucked from the fields into their straight dark locks. But most striking of all among them were the two leaders, Captain Konkapot and Lieutenant Umpachenee, who were garbed today in the scarlet uniforms given them by Governor Belcher, the insignia of their rank proudly visible, their long black braids entwined with feathers and hanging, most incongruously, down their backs from beneath their officers' hats.

"Some day, perhaps, more of your men will wear British uniforms, eh, Chief?" Ephraim said, in his easy way. "If the need arises?"

"If need arise, Chief Konkapot consider," he replied with slow care.

"Good. We can't ask for more than that, can we, Dave?"

David nodded agreement. He was thinking— Who would expect to find such a gathering in what must be the last outpost of civilization? And yet where else but at such an outpost in this wild, new land would the like ever be found? Indians wearing necklaces of claws and little horns mingling with Colonial ladies in silks and satins, farmers with calloused hands and woodsmen bearing rifles hobnobbing with Colonial gentlemen elegant in gold-braided coats of all the jewel colors, country women in simple cottons and clergy in sober black and white. Here they all were, rubbing elbows like equals. Amazing!

"The Indians had to be invited, of necessity," Ephraim was saying, "since my sister is marrying their minister who heads this mission. But Pa would not have them in the house. He doesn't trust them farther than his nose. And he'd like to keep them away from that!" His laugh rang out. "So the wedding will take place here beneath the trees. And the food will be served here, too. But if you want to see the gifts you will have to go inside."

David spoke suddenly. "There!" Then, recollecting himself, he went on more casually, "There must be the sea captain. Yonder by the roses. He has the look of one, think you not?"

"Where? Oh!" Ephraim's eyes found the little group, found the sunburned Mark, the only man present with a beard, at a broad stance, his brilliant black gaze surveying the scene impassively, found Esther in her lavender crinoline, babe in arms and twins clinging to her skirts, looking at everything with the flush of excitement in her cheeks, found Prue in her yellow sprigged cotton and flat black slippers, with her bright hair demurely bound about her small shapely head (save for a curl over each shoulder) and her sapphire blue eyes in her heart-shaped face wide upon him and David. Gad, what a little beauty! No one had warned him of this.

"I think," he said, with elaborate carelessness, "it is my duty as host to give a welcome to the strangers so recently arrived. Do you not agree?"

David could only nod assent. Women he had met a-plenty in his short career but never had he seen one before who affected him as this one did. He hoped he would have wit enough to speak sense when he reached her side.

"The captain," Eph was saying, in a low voice out of the corner of his mouth, "has recently bested my father in a land deal. I should hold it against him but in view of—eh—all I see, I cannot find it in my heart to do so."

They reached the little family and Ephraim bowed before Mark.

"Captain Martin, I believe. And the newest settler in Indian Town. You are happily come, sir. I have heard about you—"

"From your father?" Mark interrupted dryly.

Eph smiled. "To be sure. You made an indelible impression upon my father." He smiled again with a look that said he did not share the anger of his parent but rather admired the captain for outmatching him. "But I have also heard of you from your son."

"Matt. Where is he? I hope he has not been plaguing you."

"On the contrary, I fear I plagued him. I was unable to accept his services as a volunteer to the West Indies. Captain Martin, may I present my friend, Lieutenant Reynolds?"

David bowed. Mark's big hand came out in a crushing grip. Then Mark introduced Esther.

"And this is my daughter Prudence."

Prue's glance lifted for a fleeting instant before her long black lashes swept her cheeks again. In that instant, however, she had seen—not the big, handsome, assured Ephraim in his fine clothes, but the slender, scarlet-clad Britisher with the wavy chestnut hair, the fire-flecked brown eyes, the sensitive mouth and the firm, cleft chin.

Esther watched Prudence walk away between the two young men, her head scarce higher than their elbows. From her heritage of instinctive knowledge, the girl had put on a manner of gay yet delicate charm as surprising to herself as to her mother. It fell on her like a cloak made to her measure and both men were taken, it was easy to see.

Mark growled her thought for her. "I could wish it were some other than the son of my enemy."

"Or a stranger from afar," she added; for she had seen what

Mark had not, that though Prudence addressed herself to Mr. Williams for the most part, it had been the Englishman who had brought the color to her cheeks and the flutter to her lashes. But la! A parent was difficult to please! Had she not hoped for just this? And if not a Williams or a stranger, pray, who else?

Prue, meanwhile, her guilty worry of the afternoon temporarily forgotten, floated on a cloud. Never had she guessed to be a women would feel like this, so full of power one moment, all confidence and ease, and the next trembling and drained of both thought and speech. If only he did not surmise her uncertainties! If only these did not destroy in a blundering moment his present interest! But most of all: if only they did not tell him of her racing inexplicable joy to be with him. A thing that made no sense, but there it was all the same.

To Ephraim, her little rushing advances and instant swift retreats were but the consummate skill of a born flirt and he was ready to meet her accordingly. David, however, with his afternoon's memory of her, was less sure. Here, he told himself, was no boldness. Here, rather, was untouched innocence, something which his more experienced friend might have difficulty in recognizing. One thing was certain: she was the girl out of all the world for him. And he must not lose her. But time was short, his orders for the future unknown. How could he press his suit without startling her to flight? Or—his breath stopped—was it possible she, too, shared his same feeling? He dared not hope it, yet at the same time he must.

Again, as before, their progress was often checked. Mammas with marriageable daughters could not bear to see so young a girl swained by two. There was no fairness in that. So blocks were made and traps were laid and in one of these Ephraim was fast caught. Not David, however. Prue never knew quite how he extricated himself. She only knew that—miraculously—she was alone with him, his hand was firmly on her arm and they were moving away together toward the house.

"Shall we go in and see the bride's gifts?" he was asking.

The gifts were spread on two long boards covered with a white cloth. But the spoons and silver pieces, the brass warming pan, the fire set, the candlesticks were all only a twingling blur in her eyes. And only vaguely she saw the curtains and valence of flowered chintz for a fourposter bed, the embroidered counterpane, the stacks of snowy linen, the quilt. And, in a corner, the more practical articles—copper kettle, pewter porringers, churn, piggin, pail and loom.

There were few in the room. Only a trusted colored man left on guard against the possible sneaking thievery of an Indian, and a few other guests already moving toward the door. Adroitly the young officer placed himself between them and Prudence and then softly spoke her name. The urgency of his whisper set her blood to pounding and though she knew his daring—and her own —were unseemly, she slowly raised her weighted lids until he could see in her darkened eyes what filled her trembling heart.

He said, very low, "It has happened to me, too."

She shook her head and he had to bend his to catch her murmur. "It cannot be—right."

"Why not?"

"It—it is all too sudden." She reached for firmness but could find only helplessness. "What is it, anyway?"

His scarcely breathed reply held in its tone the gentlest of caresses. "I think we could call it love and not be far amiss."

"But—I do not know you." Dignity came to her rescue and she drew away. "Nor you me. It is folly to—"

"To give our feeling credence?"

She nodded.

"Feelings such as these are dictated by the heart, not the head."

There was a stir on the stairs outside and Colonel Ephraim Williams' booming voice broke the quiet. "Jake! We're coming! Get to the door and give the signal! Be sure the Reverend Stephen sees it! And Mr. Sergeant!"

"We should be out there," Prue said, and made a move to pass him.

But he blocked her way as Jake hurried forward, following the surge of the others into the hall. Alone with her, he reached out and took her hands and swiftly drew her to him. Thus held, with his breath warm on her cheek, he pressed his lips to hers in a long, thrilling kiss she would remember all her days.

At length she pushed against him and stood free, both hands to her fiery cheeks. "Please! This is— Oh! It is wicked!"

"No. Sudden—yes. Unexpected—" He broke off. "Prue! Little Prue! Tell me—not that you love me, I do not ask that yet—but that you will let yourself discover if you do! As I surely love you," he added.

She hesitated, her color still high, her breath uncertain. This would be not to let him go nor yet to yield too much, either. Surely that was permissible! Slowly she nodded. "But you must wait," she told him firmly. "You must not be—precipitate again."

"I will wait," he promised.

They went out, then, and joined the others. Could what she felt be read by all who saw her, she wondered? However, no one —thankful heart!—was looking her way. So, fighting the chaos within her, Prue, too, fixed her gaze on Abigail's slender white-clad form, and then, in turn, on the gravely happy face of the waiting bridegroom. By now a hush had fallen over the assembled audience and movement had ceased and the talking died away. Then as the colonel reached his place, his daughter on his arm, the Reverend Williams stepped forward in his black robe and raised his hand and said, "Let us pray."

There was no music. There was only the summer sun pouring down its golden light, the green canopy of leaves overhead and the murmur of the birds. How solemn a thing it was to be married, Prue thought, as the ceremony went on. And oh, how sure one must be! Would she some day be repeating those same promises to the stranger by her side? It did not seem possible. And in the next instant, as his arm touched hers, a warmth spread through her and she knew it was.

And now the last prayer was made, the last amen said, and the bride was turning in her place to receive the congratulations and well wishes of all who were gathered there. There was a stir of movement, a rising hum of voices, the swift appearance of black servants who began to weave through the company with trays of drinks and plates of food.

What food! And what drinks! The table at the edge of the lawn nearest the kitchen groaned under it all. Great hams and roast ducks, partridges browned and juicy, tender legs of lamb with wild honey and jellies of a dozen kinds for side dishes. For sweets there were prawns and trifles and tarts, custards and pound cake, floating islands and cream puffs. And to wash it all down one could choose Madeira wine or eggnog, fruit punch or whipped sillabub, cider or a posset. Never had there been such a feast. But the guests had done them the honor to come from afar, bringing presents, and many would be starting home that night, so they must, of course, be well fed. Besides, close-fisted and grasping as he was, Ephraim Williams, Senior, liked to do the handsome thing if it gave him importance. And he meant this wedding in the wilderness to be one long talked about.

But at last it ended. Horses were led up, took on their riders and clattered off. Those from a distance retired to change their clothes. Those from nearby drifted away on foot. The Indians melted into the landscape and soon only the house guests and the nearest neighbors were left.

Esther looked around for her family. Her baby was asleep in her aching arms. The twins, their faces smeared with traces of the goodies they had consumed, had sunk to the ground beneath a tree and were half asleep. Andy was hovering around an adult group, his ears ready to pick up stray bits of knowledge. Matt had long ago disappeared. She had seen him slipping off down the road with Peter and his sister, Marie. Mark's big figure in his blue broadcloth suit could be discerned not far off. But where was Prue?

And then Esther saw her coming forward with a light on her face that was surely not of this earth. The mother's heart jumped and her hand went to press back the stabbing pain that came in moments of stress. But it was a composed countenance that she turned on the lieutenant as the two of them reached her side. And when he bent above her hand, saying, "With your kind permission, madam, I will give myself the pleasure of calling upon you before I leave," she replied quite calmly, "Do so. We shall be happy to make you welcome. Perhaps you will join us for supper tomorrow evening?"

Her daughter had been swept off her feet into love, she was thinking. Nor could the child be wholly blamed. David Reynolds was comely, he had a warm, sweet, thoughtful manner and he seemed as struck as Prue. Yet even if that were so, Esther meant to find out much more about this young man before she let him take her first-born off with him. And to talk quietly at home with him was the best way.

CHAPTER 5

The Winter

AUGUST BRIGHTENED into September with its soft, silky days, pale-tinted and blue-hazed, then September flamed into October and the world was ablaze. Never had it been more beautiful. Down in the swamps the maples burned scarlet. Against the rocks the alder bushes threw out a warm yellow glow. All the fields crisped to russet under a brilliant sun while beyond them in the distance the hills wrapped themselves in a coat of many colors, their patches of bronze and amethyst, emerald and gold stitched together with threads of white that were the birch trees. Even around the cabin there was a steadily growing light as the woods that hemmed it in were crowned with amber.

The year was dying and Prue felt as if she were dying, too. The acorns dropping on dry leaves were the sad sound of the tears she could not shed. The blackened ferns were all her tender hopes and dreams. At night the glittering stars were chips of ice no colder than her frozen heart, while the meandering river, bound now in the shallow places by a thin sheet of glass, was her stopped life.

It had come to an end at its very beginning. The riotous pulse, the soaring joy, the bewildering happy tumult of love uncertainly discovered and tremblingly admitted—all these were over and she would never know them again.

How had it happened? She tried not to remember. She tried to blot from her mind the memory of that evening. But it kept coming back. It followed her by day and haunted her by night.

She had kept busy, she recalled, redding up the cabin for the night David was to come for supper. She had swept the floor and shined the brasses and got out the garnish of pewter for the table setting. She had plumped up the feather bed and smoothed over the Nine Snowballs coverlet. She had even fastened pine branches above the windows so that they fell down on both sides and took the place of curtains. Then, as a finishing touch, she had draped over one end of the log that was the mantel shelf the gay Indian shawl Marie had given her. It had made a wonderful spot of color in the room but for a moment she had thought Ma might not let it stay because she had eyed it critically and had said, "We want no airs tonight, Prue." "But—is it airs more than the pewter?" Oh! That had been boldness, for sure, but Ma had not taken it as other than considered reason such as one woman might give to another, for, hesitating only briefly, she had replied, "Mayhap 'tis not. Well, let be."

He had come promptly. And if the room had seemed gay before because of the blanket, how much gayer it was when he entered in his scarlet uniform! From then on it was all a lovely blur: his gentleness with the baby, his playfulness with the twins, his politeness toward Matt and Andy whom he treated like grownups. As for her ma and pa, it had been easy to see his respect, forthrightness and good manners pleased them mightily. Pa was the one had asked the questions to discover where he stood on worldly affairs, but it was Ma who had found out the things Prue most wanted to know.

His mother was dead, he said. She had died when he was in his teens. His father, who had never remarried, was in the prime of life. He, himself, was the younger of two sons. Roger would inherit the title and property, according to English law. David might have gone into politics—indeed, he still might—but he had wanted to see the world first and so had bought himself a commission in the British Army.

"And glad I am now that I did," he had said. And his brown eyes with the dancing flecks of warm light in them had gone to meet Prue's as she sat on her little stool before the fire. Then, hastily, lest her parents think him forward too soon, he had added, "Because it has given me an opportunity to see something of your great country."

"You like it? Why do you not plan to stay amongst us, then, and become one of us? An American?"

His face had sobered and Prue wondered if every one could hear the loud beating of her heart.

"It has come to my mind," he had answered slowly, "but my heart is still in England." He gave his quick smile and Prue could not guess it meant he did not want to offend any of them by saying how raw and wild this land seemed to him, for all its beauty; how fiercely frowning its forests; how wearyingly endless its vast reaches, after the cozy limits and gentler aspect of his own little island. "Besides, how could I earn a living?" He tossed off the question with a gesture and went on. "At least I shall be here whilst the French and Indians threaten."

Of all that was said that evening Prue remembered those words the clearest. He would remain here for some time, probably in the Massachusetts Colony in this section of it where danger was greatest.

"That gives me comfort," her mother had murmured, and then, lest he in his turn, misunderstand, she had added, "I mean because there will be British troops to support our militia."

He had laughed out suddenly. "I had always heard it put the other way, madam: that your militia helped support our troops."

Prue spoke softly. "Either way, it is good."

Oh, it had been a magical evening! The firelight and the friendliness and the good, simple food. The flickering candles and the easy talk. And under and over and through it all the knowledge she and he both had of the meaning of this visit. Her parents had it, too, and their unspoken approval drove away the early fears she had felt at thought of his coming, and happiness had grown in her with all the glory of an expanding sunrise. In her blue dress that matched her eyes she was, for the most part, quiet, trying not to let her glance go his way too much. But his face was a magnet. And the warm caressing quality of his voice—strange to her ears after Pa's booming tones—both gave her strength and took it from her, seeming, as it did, to enfold her like gentle arms. In a daze, she never heard when the twins clambered up the ladder to the loft. Nor was she aware of the boys following soon after. It was a small shock to discover suddenly only herself and her parents and the sleeping babe left in the room.

It was then that Mark, hearing the whinnying of the horses, had snatched up his musket and gone out to see what was disturbing them. With a murmured word of excuse, Esther had followed after and for a breathless space of time Prue had been left alone with David.

Not wasting a moment, he spoke in a low tone. "I did not think to have this good fortune."

Prue raised shy questioning eyes.

"To be able to tell you again what fills my mind and heart."

She had waited, scarce breathing. He leaned toward her so that she could feel the warmth emanating from his body. "I love you, Prue. I know I promised not to be precipitate. But that was a promise for deeds, not words."

From somewhere far away came her hushed and hesitant reply. "I still—don't understand—how you can know."

"I cannot explain. Unless it is that I feel with certain knowledge what you are. When that happens, the time of being acquainted has no importance. Can you believe that?"

"I—can try."

"Do so. Try very hard." He had smiled upon her. "Prue, listen. I am here as the guest of the Williams family for another day or two. Can we not meet again?"

"It would not be proper for us to meet alone."

"But if I am riding up the trail and you are walking down it and it should chance—"

Her small uncertain laugh held a tremor. "Well, then—" She looked up at him suddenly, her blue eyes burning stars. "I know a place! It is beautiful. I will take you there. I will show it to you." (I will share it with you, she was thinking.)

She had no idea how, in that moment, her look transported him to the same spot or how stirred he was again at his memory of a child possessed of innocence who was also a woman possessed of passion, a passion she would offer in grace and generosity and devotion to the man she loved. No wonder he forgot himself and murmured, "Yes, I know it, too."

Shocked realization came to her. He *knew*. He said he knew! He had been there, then. It had not been her imagination or any small wild creature. It had been he. And he had seen her in all her nakedness, with her thoughts visible, too, perhaps.

She recoiled as if he had struck her. So that was why he had been so swift and daring in his approach! Beyond a doubt what he had witnessed that day had given him the belief that she was a—a— She did not know the word but she knew its meaning. And she knew, too, she could not blame him. Oh, the shame of it! The searing, scorching shame of it! Yet she must endure it for her wickedness. Through the thundering in her head she heard his words.

"Prue, listen! You must listen. It was not— I can explain! Don't look at me like that. *Don't*. I beg of you. I beg—"

But she had risen, ice in her veins where before there had been fire, ice in her cold blue eyes, ice in her voice and only one thought clear. If she could not have respect, she would not have love.

"Leave me," she had commanded with dignity. "Leave me! And never come near me again."

Her mother's return had found them so. Prue, paper-white and proud in an inexorable anger; he, distraught and confused and contrite.

He turned at once. "Madam, there has been— We have had a —a misunderstanding. But I can right myself if you—she—will only give me the opportunity."

Prue had not waited for Esther to speak. "There has been no misunderstanding," she had said, with frigid calm. "On the contrary. For the first time since our meeting, we understand each other perfectly."

He did not look at her. His glance, hot and desperate, sought Esther's face.

"Madam, as you have influence with your daughter, I beseech—"

But Esther, who was aware of the lightning speed with which the distance between youth and maturity is sometimes bridged, met Prue's eyes and interrupted.

"My daughter is a woman and speaks for herself. Good night, Lieutenant Reynolds."

He hesitated, then, bowing low, he said, "This is not the end. I vow it. Kindly make my adieus to your husband, ma'am." And he went out.

He was gone. Esther, moving forward quickly, had exclaimed, "Prue! Whatever happened?"

But Prue had shaken her head and moved as quickly away. At the foot of the ladder she turned and spoke, still in that terrible calm.

"Don't ask me. Not now. Not ever."

Up in her loft beside the sleeping twins, she lay rigid for hours, suffering as she had never suffered before. Humiliation, shame, anger, a corroding sense of guilt and the anguish of a lost love —for what chance was there now that this love might ever be righted?—swept her in alternating waves, engulfing her, drowning her, casting her up finally on a desolate, lonely shore. For that night's agony there was no respite and there was no help.

Because, in order to make David know what she was not, she had had to reject him. It was God's punishment upon her for the awful sin of immodesty and play-acting that day by the sunlit pool.

It was a bitter cold Thanksgiving morning when the new log meetinghouse in Indian Town was at last dedicated. Esther and Mark, in the cart with the twins and the baby, drove down beneath a leaden sky over a foot of rutted, crusted snow, while Prue and the boys followed on foot. On their way they could plainly hear the raucous screech of the conch shell—gift of Governor Belcher to the mission—blown by the Indian, Metoxin, as a summons to all to gather for the solemn day-long services.

The crude sound repelled Esther. She said, "That's not fitting. It's almost enough to keep people away. We ought to have a bell."

Mark threw her a surprised look. It was not like Esther to be critical. Doubtless she was still bothering over Prue. He said, his voice low so the twins would not hear, "You hadn't ought to pester yourself. She has a hankering no common sense can purge out of her right now. But leave be. Life is like a voyage. If 'twas all fair sailing you'd not know how good the clear days are when they come. It takes a bit of fog to make the sun seem bright when it breaks through." He paused. "She'll make out. She's young, remember."

"That's when things hurt the most," Esther answered.

If only she knew what had happened! she thought for the hundredth time. But Prue had never told her and she had never pressed for the reason. There were only two possible conclusions, though. Either Prue, innocent and ignorant of much, had misunderstood the lieutenant's words and so his intentions. Or he, well-born and coming into their humble cabin, had felt himself a cut above her and her family and Prue no one he wanted to marry. If that were so she was well rid of him. Yet Esther could not reconcile such a thought with the kind of man he had shown himself to be. More likely Prue had misconstrued him. Only, why would she not say how to her own mother? It was surely a puzzle with but one thing plain. Prue had been deeply hurt and time was not healing the wound. Near four months now and she remained the small frozen image she had become that night.

She sighed faintly, "I suppose nothing that God wills is useless. Yet sometimes 'tis hard to accept without understanding."

He nodded. Then, hoping to lift her spirits, he said, "Come spring and there'll be three more white families here, John tells me."

The knowledge did brighten her. It could be that amongst those arriving would appear one to make Prue forget this David Reynolds.

They came presently to the settlement and passed groups walking toward the meetinghouse from plain and meadow. Most did walk. Only those up on the hill needed to ride or drive. But when the heavy snows came, which would be any day now, Esther doubted if they themselves, the farthest distant, would be able to get down at all. It was a good thing the baby was to be baptized today. She had put it off longer than was proper already. But she had had a wish to promise him to the Lord in a regular church, not the schoolhouse or even John Sergeant's home, and so she had waited.

She looked down at him lying asleep in her arms. He was still some frail and peaked-looking and she did not relish having to keep him all day in so icy a place as the meetinghouse. Why hadn't they built a fireplace in it whilst they were building? For her part, she did not believe you would be any less a Chrisitian for not freezing when at worship. In her mind it was only the danger of fire that was a solid argument against having heat in a church. But no one agreed with her. To coddle the body was to encourage the devil, most thought. Anyway, she had three hot baked potatoes in her muff and as long as these held their warmth, Johnny would not suffer too greatly in her arms.

They reached the new building and all climbed down from the cart. Prue and the boys came up and joined them. Mark tied Daisy to a tree, threw a blanket across her back and led his family inside to their pew. It was the fifth one. The Williamses, as was fitting, occupied the first; the Woodbridges the second; the large Jones family and the Browns the third and fourth. Across the aisle were the stolid-faced Indians huddled in their faded blankets, unkempt, unclean.

Esther found herself considering this separation of whites from Indians as she waited in silence for the service to begin. Why, if equality was the watchword of the mission, must they be seated apart? But of course they were not equal and never would be, for all that they held town offices and helped conduct its government. And a flashing insight into the status of the Indian, half tame, yet still half wild, and without, any longer, a world of his own, filled her with a surge of pity.

John Sergeant was a rare fine man, her thoughts went on, whose own desires were not his first concern. The Indians were close to his heart, and he was giving a life of service to them. Yet could he compass his objective with this sense of white superiority so deep-rooted a thing?

Her eyes strayed now to the slender figure of the bride, seated with her father and mother and their younger children, in her new bride's suit and bonnet of brown. It was known for a fact that the Indians were not *her* first concern. Her first concern was to get her husband to build another house up on the hill on her father's land. The cabin John had offered her suited her but little, folks said.

At this moment the minister rose, his ecclesiastical black cloak flowing over his overcoat, and, with his eyes bright with fervor, he raised his mittened hands.

"Let us all bow our heads in a prayer of Thanksgiving for this day and this hour, for the privilege of free worship in this great and beautiful land and for the privilege of being gathered here —all of us—in this new church consecrated to the Lord's good works."

His melodious voice continued. It was a long prayer and twice Esther had to reach out a hand to still the twins. At its end there came a stir in the rear, and in the waiting silence a man strode down the aisle to the Williamses' pew and sat down with them —a man made welcome amongst them by grave nods; a man in a scarlet British uniform.

Esther glanced at Prue. Her face, as always lately, was closed and pale, her eyes downcast. Only her little gloved hands, tight-clasped in her lap, admitted her disturbance. *"This is not the end,"* Esther remembered David had said. So he had come back. And what now?

The service went on. A psalm was read and a solemn dedication of the new building was made. Then Timothy Woodbridge rose and set the tune, and all joined in singing one of Charles Wesley's hymns.

> *"Jesus, lover of my soul,*
> *Let me to the bosom fly,*
> *While the billows near me roll,*
> *While the tempest still is high.*
> *Hide me, oh! my Savior! Hide!*
> *Till the storm of life is past—"*

It was a hymn for Prue, Esther thought.

The sermon now. First one for the Indians in their queer-sounding language that John had mastered. Then one in English for the settlers. It took four hours. The twins and the baby all fell asleep. Andy read the hymnbook through twice. Matt and Prue held themselves like graven images bound in their own thoughts. When at last the preaching was over, there was another prayer and a blessing before they could file out, the twins stumbling on half-frozen feet, Prue keeping in her mother's shadow, the boys lagging behind to speak to Peter.

It was the custom in New England in those days for the worshipers to bring their lunch with them and eat it at an ordinary nearby, thus re-enforcing themselves for the afternoon service and, at the same time, thawing out their limbs before a great fire. But there was no ordinary in Indian Town so the congregation repaired in groups to the nearest homes. The Williamses, as was natural, started across the road to Abigail's cabin and she, waiting for Esther at the entrance, urged her and her family to come, too.

"There is room for all," she said. "And it will be best for the baby not to have to go far." And such tenderness was in her look as she bent it on his tiny features that Esther knew at once Abigail was carrying a child herself.

Esther thanked her and accepted. Ahead was the scarlet uniform. Prue could hardly ignore the lieutenant if he ventured to address her. But where was she? Glancing around, her mother saw that she had slipped away with the Timothy Woodbridges.

"Mary—Luke—" she called to the twins. "Andy! Matt! We're going to Mr. Sergeant's house. Tell your father to bring the lunch there."

If Prue heard her, she did not turn her head. La! How set she could be!

The cold clawing at their bones as they all crossed the bumpy stretch of frozen ground. The plain little cabin with its welcome fire within. The greetings. Colonel Williams' aggressive voice, Mark's boom, Abigail and her mother in a friendly fluttering, John entering late, a glow on his face, the children fading into corners. Then the pulling close of settles and stools. The loosening of wraps. The bringing out of lunch boxes and the subdued talk as befitted the day. Esther took the potatoes from her muff and Mark tucked them down in the embers to warm them again, after which she retired to nurse her baby. When she reappeared, Lieutenant David Reynolds disengaged himself from the group about the fire and approached her swiftly. Standing between her and the others, he spoke at once urgently. "A word, please, Mistress Martin."

She looked up. His brown eyes met hers steadily without guilt or confusion. Very low, he said, "Now that you know what has come 'twixt your daughter and me—"

"But I do not know."

"She has not told you?"

Esther shook her head. "Nor is she like to now."

He stood surprised and nonplused. After a moment he said, "I had thought—I had hoped—to present my side to you. But it is her confidence to make first." Distress filled him and helplessness swept across his face. Presently he spoke again. "I am deeply sorry. Will you, since she refuses to see me, convey my remembrances to her? And tell her, if you please, I do not give up hope that all may yet come right between us."

Esther looked at him a long moment. Finally she said slowly, "You will find her at the Woodbridges'."

His face lighted. "Thank you, ma'am!"

She ate her lunch with numbed fingers. Because of Prue, who did not reappear for the afternoon service, it seemed endless. Where was she? Was David with her? Or had she sent him off again? The Woodbridges were here, all of them. Had Prue and David remained together at their house to talk? Such a thing was not seemly, but— Oh, hurry, time!

However, the afternoon prayer was as long as the morning one and the sermon longer. After that came the reception of an Indian convert to the Christian faith. It was Marie's and Peter's father, Aaron, who had saved Mary that day of the raising. How much did he understand of what John Sergeant was asking him to repeat?

"Through the goodness of God toward me in bringing me into the way of the knowledge of the Gospel, I am convinced of the truth of the Christian religion and that it is the only way to salvation and happiness. I therefore freely and heartily forsake heathenish darkness and embrace the light and the Gospel and the way of Holiness, and so now, in the presence of Almighty God, the searcher of hearts, and before many witnesses, seriously and solemnly take the Lord Jehovah to be my God and Portion, Jesus Christ to be my Lord Redeemer, and the Holy Ghost to be my Sanctifier and teacher."

Finally came the baptism of her baby, who cried out at the touch of the cold water and would not be comforted. All the time the congregation—or its representative men folk—walked up to the wooden box held by Mr. Woodbridge and dropped into it their offerings, his thin wailing filled the frosty air. Esther was thankful when, at last, she could go out with him.

A wind had risen. Mark said, "It's coming in from the northeast. We'll have more snow before night." And he went off to unhitch Daisy.

He was right. Already a few vagrant flakes floated lazily down as he spoke and Esther said, "We will all ride home. Yes, you, too, Matt and Andy. We'll pick up Prue at the Woodbridges'. Likely she didn't feel well and so stayed there this afternoon."

But Prue was not at the Woodbridges'. No one was in the house, and, disturbed and anxious now, the Martins went on up the hill.

The cabin in the clearing looked as lonely and lost as a small dark ark on a white-capped sea when they reached it, and Esther thought suddenly how meager and feeble were man's inventions against nature. But the place, filled with a dancing red light from the fire as they entered, became suddenly a bulwark against anything. For lo! Prue and David were both standing awaiting them, their hands tight clasped, their faces transfigured with their joy.

David said at once, "Sir—Madam— I have asked your daughter to be my wedded wife. And she has consented if you two will but give your approval and permission."

How had he managed to persuade her? Esther would never know. But Prue would never forget.

She had been helping the last of the Woodbridge children put on his coat and cap and mittens for the afternoon service when there sounded a knock at the front door. Thinking it was a neighbor stopping by, Prue called out, "Mr. and Mrs. Woodbridge have already gone!"

There was no answer and, with a little push of the child before her, she went to let him out before donning her own wraps. What a shock to see David standing there! For a moment, at sight of him, all the blood seemed to drain from her body and she stood weak and helpless and unable to say a word. In that brief interval he stepped inside.

"Your mother told me where I might find you," he said quietly.

The blood surged back through her veins again but now it was racing with such speed and violence she could not think.

David thought for her. To the child he said, "Run join your parents or you will be late. They are not far ahead." Then he closed the door, reached out and took Prue's two hands in his.

"I—you—we—" she began, in utter confusion at the realization that they were alone together in the house.

"We," he repeated, in his caressing voice. "Yes. That is the way it must be. *We*. I came back to tell you that. We two, Prue. You and I. Loving and living together as man and wife forever. Are you willing? You must be. For I will not give you up."

To his astonishment great tears welled up and rolled slowly down her cheeks. She pulled her hands free from his and covered her face with them while at the same time her whisper reached him brokenly.

"No. I am not—worthy—"

"Not worthy? My darling—" He tried to draw her to him but with a little gasp she retreated and sank down on the settle before the fire.

"No. Listen. Please! Please let me speak."

Again she covered her face with her hands. How small and

young and defenseless she looked, he thought, and checked his
impatience in tender pity. Presently her low words came.

"I—I've been wicked, David. So terribly wicked! That—that day
I was thinking things I should never have thought. What was in
my head was brazen and bold." She dropped her hands now and
looked up at him, and he saw her face tragic with her grievous
self-condemnation. "Oh! I wish I could forget it! I've tried! I've
prayed! But it's no use. The memory stays. And with it all my
shame. I don't—I don't deserve you, though at first I tried to
make out that it was you— Oh! Why did I ever do it? Why?
Why?"

"I think I know. And 'tis for no reason that should cause you
to blame yourself."

She caught her breath in startled surprise at the certainty of his
tone, and he saw her blue eyes widen with questioning above
her quivering mouth.

"How can you say that? How do you know?"

"Perhaps because I am older than you."

He drew a stool forward and dropped on it, facing her so that
their glances were level with each other. Then, reaching out, he
took her hands once more in his own.

"I am older than you," he repeated, "but not much. For you
became a woman that day, Prue."

"I don't know what I became," she murmured miserably.

"You became a woman with the instincts and desires of a
woman. There is no shame in that, my darling."

"Why, then, do I feel shamed?"

He was silent a moment. How could he make her understand?
Then, carefully—delicately—with a sensitive perception of her
need, he sought for and found words that would not startle, but
that (he hoped) were clear and simple and right.

"First, let me say this to you. I was not covertly spying on you
when I saw you there in the pool. I came upon that rock by
chance and, glancing down, was held by enchantment. You were
beautiful, Prue."

Her hands fluttered in his but he did not let them go.

"I do not mean just your body because I saw more than that.

I saw your spirit. For a brief and wonderful moment you let me see it." He paused. "There was poetry for me in that moment, Prue. There was a faint chiming of heavenly bells in my ears as I gazed, so that I hardly knew if I was glimpsing a vision or dreaming a dream—or what."

"You make it sound—lovely."

"It *was* lovely. That is what I want you to know . . . I had not realized until then how exquisitely balanced a woman's spiritual and physical needs can be. How earthly love and divine love can be so mingled that one hardly knows where the one begins and the other ends."

"Yes!" —breathlessly. "Yes!"

"You felt it. But you thought I hadn't. Ah, darling! But I did. That is why I told you I had a certain knowledge of you." He paused a moment. "Sometimes it happens that the person most briefly seen is the person most truly known. Well, that is how it was. I saw you. I saw desire and fearlessness and generosity and consecration harmonized in you in a beauty I shall never forget." He stopped again, then went on, his voice deepening with his emotion. "You promise a man a very treasure of love, Prue. And though I knew I was hasty and ran the risk of losing what I sought to gain—and guard—I could not pass that treasure by without reaching for it." He lifted her hands now to his lips and kissed them both before he finished. "My sweet, it is I who am not worthy. Yet I shall try to be—if you will but let me."

As he had talked, Prue's face had slowly changed. The despair on it faded, giving way gradually to wonder, then to hope, then to a dawning, incredulous joy, for, like magic, his words had changed everything, melting the ice in her heart, turning a remembered guilt into pride, disaster into triumph.

"Will you?" he was saying. "Will you marry me, little Prue?"

For answer, Prue leaned over and laid her forehead against the hands holding hers. Even without her parents' consent, she thought in that moment, she would, so wild, so jubilant, so humble yet so exalted, was the rising tide of her returning love. . . .

But of course Esther and Mark gave it, Esther saying only, "I

hope you will not carry her off to England with you to live. I
hope you will settle here instead."

"Carry me off to England!" Prue exclaimed, startled. "Oh, no!
David would never expect that, would you, David?"

David, startled himself at Prue's instant rejection of what
seemed to him the one and only course their lives could eventually take, held back his instinctive reply. Prue was a young, shy
wildling, he reminded himself. He must not rush her: not in
this first moment of their reconciliation.

"I imagine my father and brother will want to meet you," he
said smilingly. "And I should hope you would want to meet
them."

"Oh, of course!" Prue agreed swiftly. "Of course—*that*."

"Talk to me about England and your home there," Prue said.

David gave a small jump. She might have been reading his
thoughts, he told himself, for he was one who liked things clear
and the implication in his words to her two days ago that
Windemere was to be a place she and he would merely visit, had
disturbed him ever since he had spoken them. Moreover, if
transplanting was going to be difficult for her, might it not be
well for her to begin now to accustom herself to the idea?

It was the last hour of his brief Thanksgiving leave. Every moment that he had been able with decency to withdraw from his
hosts, the Williamses, he had spent with Prue. But now, soon—
too soon—he must make his farewell. And who knew when they
would meet again? Because of that uncertainty, there must be,
before he left, full understanding between them as to his plans
and expectations for their future life together.

He began telling her first of the great estate where they would
live. And as he talked, pride added itself to the deep affection he
felt for his birthplace. For Windemere had been in his family
for many centuries and history was built into its battlemented
stone walls. It had been first a monastery, then a fortresslike castle before it had come into Reynolds hands. There were high
buttressed towers from which an enemy could readily be seen approaching. There were secret passageways and doors hidden in

dark paneling and unexpected winding stairs. There was a room that held a marvelous collection of old weapons and armor plate, a gallery filled with ancestral portraits, a moat and a drawbridge, and a dungeon.

"There's even a haunted room," he finished, smiling. And then, at Prue's slight shiver, he hurried on. "At least, it's supposed to be haunted. But I've never seen anything myself."

"It sounds fearsome."

"Let me tell you some more," he said quickly.

He went on, then, to speak of matters that would be less alien to her. Of the immense sweep of emerald lawns that surrounded the house. Of the great trees ("older than any I've seen in this country") that made a park about it. Of the long sloping terrace and the quiet pool at its base that mirrored the serenity of floating white swans. Of the gardens in which old Deming, the head gardener, took as much pride as any one in the family. ("You wait till you see the roses he grows.") Of the stables and the thoroughbred horses there. Of the kennels and the dogs. Of the dovecotes and the pigeons. Of the baby lambs and the strutting peacocks—

"You're strutting some'at yourself," Prue said suddenly.

The words were as much of an astonishment to her as to him. But his account had shocked her. It had sounded so vast, so impressive, so—so affluent. It was a background completely different from her own, and, of a sudden, as he talked with such ease of it all, he had become a stranger to her. It was frightening, and in self-defense she had struck out at him.

"Why, Prue!"

"Oh, I'm sorry! Forgive me, David. I truly didn't mean that. It's just—just—"

He said, a trifle stiffly, "I only want you to know what it will be like before we reach there."

"Yes. Go on, then. Please!"

He tried to. But there was a constraint on him now and Prue, contrite, tried to help him with questions.

"There must be a vast amount of work to be done with all those horses and sheep and lambs and gardens. Who does it?"

"We have villagers who work for us. They live in cottages scattered all about. Of course, the house servants have their own quarters under our roof. And the stablemen—" He stopped a moment. "We're a community just in ourselves. You will find it not so different, really, from living in Stockbridge village. Here, you have your farmers—your slaves, too—and your landed gentry. The Williamses are an example."

"No. It's different from here," Prue answered slowly. "Everything you've said makes me know it's different." She hesitated. "But—but it's—interesting. Tell me more about the house where we'll live. Is it big?"

"Yes. It's big. I imagine it has near a hundred rooms."

"Near a *hundred!*"

They were alone in the cabin. Esther, leaving Prue in charge of the baby and the twins, had gone down the hill to see Mrs. Jones who was ailing. The twins were outside playing in a light fall of fresh snow. Andy and Matt were helping their father fell a tree. The baby was asleep. The hour—their last together—thus gave them a privacy they had not had since their first one in Mrs. Woodbridge's home.

After Prue spoke a little silence fell. David saw that she was aghast and wondered what he could say to lessen her awe and the shrinking he felt in her. Prue was thinking—a hundred rooms! And how casually he had mentioned them! Then she thought of her own humble two-room cabin and a feeling of uneasiness came over her. To dispel it she spoke with a forced little laugh.

"Well, I suppose I can get along with only a hundred rooms for the little time I'll be there."

"Prue."

At the unexpected gravity of his tone she looked at him quickly.

"When we go there," he told her, his voice gentle but firm, "it will not be for a short time. It will be for our lifetime."

Unbelieving, she stared at him. Then she shook her head. "Oh, *no,* David!"

"Yes. It is my home, darling. And I love it. My heart is there —and my future. Try to understand."

There was another silence. In it Prue felt her own heart sink to some unplumbed bottomless depth within her. She had never thought of this! But she knew there was no argument on the matter. David's tone as well as his words told her so. Besides, was it not ever the woman's duty to go where her husband went? Only —only—

"But—" Her voice sounded thin and small and uncertain as she tried to discover some valid reason that could oppose his will. "If there are house servants, as you say, what will I do with myself all day? I wouldn't want—I couldn't stand to do nothing!"

"You will be busy enough. Though you will certainly never have to work as you do here. You will live as a lady, not as a farmer's daughter, Prue. You will direct your servants. We won't live in the castle permanently of course. That will be Roger's. But there are other houses, though none quite so large or so old. Oh, you will be busy enough, directing and ordering and supervising!"

"I—I wouldn't know how to do that."

He said gently, "Darling, you will have to learn how. You will be— As my wife, Prue, you will have an established social position that will put certain responsibilities on you. You will preside at various functions. You will entertain. When I get into politics there will be important people—"

Prue's wide blue stare holding, he was not sure what, stopped him abruptly.

"What is it?"

She shook her head. "I can never do all that."

"You can learn, my sweet."

Her eyes flashed. "Well, then, I don't *want* to!"

Why didn't she want to? She could hardly say herself. Possibly timidity was at the bottom of it. The fear of not being able to play properly the role David had picked for her. It sounded too elegant to one of her simple upbringing. It alarmed her. Possibly homesickness was another contributing factor. The knowledge that she would be in a strange environment far from her own beloved family, far from the dear familiarity of this hill, this cozy cabin. But there was more to it than that, for it seemed to her that David was looking down upon her present circumstances with something of condescension. *"You will certainly never have to work as you do here." "You will live as a lady, not as a farmer's daughter."* She had not been wrong in detecting pride in his tone a while back! And this pride—this condescension—made him a different person.

I've known him such a short time, she thought, in a rising panic of confusion and doubt. Mayhap I don't know him at all.

Indeed, his next words to her convinced her of it, for he rose to his full height, and, out of his own hurt pride, said, "You don't *want* to? Do you know what you are saying? I don't believe you do. You are a child and don't know—why! I could name a round half dozen women who would give all they have to be offered what I have offered you today!"

"Offer it to them, then!"

They stared at each other in a hard-eyed anger that held for both a bitter astonishment. Where was the beauty they had known so recently? Where was the humility and confidence and joy? Then David spoke again, picking each word with a slow, stiff care.

"I must leave you now, Prue. I have to get back to Boston. I think—I'm sure—that when you think over all I have said you will change your mind."

"I fear 'tis already changed."

"What do you mean?"

She said childishly, "I mean, if marrying you means going to live in England away from everything and everybody I know and love, I won't marry you. That's all!"

"But England is everything *I* know and love, Prue."

The deep-rooted human need to be understood, to feel an assuaging sympathy that would lead to a generous yielding, held them both. But it held them apart. Yet between them, too, and almost visible, stretched a cord of love that suddenly pulled her to him. In an instant his arms were around her and, half sobbing, she clung to him.

"Oh, David! David! We mustn't quarrel!"

"No. We mustn't."

"You're—my life."

"You're mine, darling."

"It's just—just that I don't see how I—"

"Shall we leave it to time?"

She looked at him in sudden hope. That seemed safe. It was at least a temporary respite. Who could tell what time might bring?

"Oh, yes! Yes! Leave it to time. And now, David, please kiss me."

He kissed her forehead, her eyelids, her mouth. His arms hurt her but she did not cry out for she was hardly aware.

"Good-by, little Prue," he said at last huskily.

"You aren't angry? You do still love me?"

"I'll never stop."

She gave him a quick small smile. "Then—don't be strange again, will you?"

He took her chin and tilted up her face so that she saw how sober he was.

"Don't *you* be mutinous."

Her smile wavered—faded. "You mean—you mean you're still determined on our living in England? But I thought we were going to leave it to time?"

"We are. We're leaving it to time to get you used to the idea."

The stuff of his uniform was familiar. His flame-flecked brown eyes, the cleft in his chin, his hands, brown and slender and strong, the caressing quality of his voice—these things were all familiar. But there was a quality in him, a stubbornness, a resolution, and that hint of superiority that were all wholly new.

"It's terrible," she murmured, half to herself, half to him.

"What is?"

"Seeing you so seldom."

He nodded. "But listen, my sweet. There's a rumor that my company may be sent elsewhere. Perhaps to the West Indies. If it is, will you follow me and marry me there?"

"How—? How could I?"

"You could. If you cared enough."

"I do care. But—" She drew back, suddenly wrapped in a mature, cool composure. "But I will do nothing hastily."

"If I send you word from Boston—"

"Don't send me word."

"Prue, what are you saying *now?*"

"I'm saying I want to think about things a little longer before I marry you. I—I don't know you, David. It makes me not sure about you."

"Not sure? Because of England?"

"Only partly. Because of you, too. You're—different than I expected."

"I'm what I've always been."

"Perhaps. Anyway, I want to think about you more."

Time pressed him, and his desire for her, and his fear of a long separation in which her reservations would grow and her resolve strengthen against him so that he might never win her, after all, made him exclaim with desperate impatience, "Oh! For Heaven's sake!"

With these words, he put her from him, picked up his hat and went to the door. There he turned and looked back at her, knowing he was wrong to speak this way but unable to check himself. "Think, then. Think! But don't think too long, for I'm not overstocked with patience."

And he went out, leaving Prue staring mutely after him.

And now winter lay on the land and winter lay in Prue's heart. For David was gone.

Word of his departure came to Abigail through her brother, Ephraim, who was much in Boston, and she, all unknowing of the despair it brought to Prue, passed on the news. He had gone and had never written her a line. But she herself had told him not to send her word from Boston. She had said that plainly. Was it, then, for her to write him? "Don't think too long," he had warned her. Indeed, she certainly should make the first move! But how could she reach him with no known address?

Esther said, "You will just have to wait, child."

Wait! Wait with love and longing and remorse breaking her heart, for she knew now, too late, that she cared more for David than she did for herself. Why had she ever thought she didn't?

The strangeness she had felt in him was nothing to make her shrink. It was a natural pride, a natural love of his homeland and his home. She could not fault him for it when the same existed in her. And there was his future there, too. Besides, what did the Bible say? *I will forsake my mother and my father and cleave only unto my husband.* Something like that. And all her foolish thinking that David set himself above her— Why! If he truly had, he would never have come back to her at all! Oh, she had been wrong again. Young and foolish and wrong. No wonder he had lost patience.

But perhaps he would write when he reached the place to which he had been sent. It was a hope, anyway. And on it she must lean, for there was nothing else to do.

Wait—and hope. Wait—and pray. Wait—and love. For she could never stop.

December—and the log wood piled high outside the cabin door, for by now Mark had cut a swath through to the west and had his vista of the hills. December—and a barn built for the stock, the ox, the two horses and the cow he had bought for Johnny's sake. December—and the other half of the house nearly completed.

All through the fall and early winter Mark had driven himself without stint to get these chores done, especially the last, for he knew that Esther's heart craved it. Then there would be a room for her and him and the baby, with Prue and the twins left in the first cabin and the boys still in the loft. This would give the separateness and dignity to life to which she was accustomed.

So he had chopped and cut and split and hauled and hammered and chinked week after week. When he could not work outside because of the weather he worked inside. He adzed logs and laid a wooden floor. He built shelves. He made a settle with a high back to ward off the drafts. Come spring, he told himself, and he would surely start on the big house that stood so plain in his mind. The cabin then would be an ell to it. It would be the kitchen wing, with the second room a woodshed.

December—and Christmas which passed like any other day

save that there was a church service. But there were no festivities
of any kind lest these foster roistering and drinking. No special
gifts, no decorated trees, no neighborhood calling. Just a sober
parade to a solemn service and home again.

This was the last time the Martins got down to Indian Town.
After that came the days of whistling winds and shouting nights,
with the whole world lost to their sight in endless roaring bliz-
zards. Higher and higher crept the snow up the windowpanes.
Deeper and deeper grew the path to the barn till it was a tunnel well over Mark's head. The arms of the spruces and pines
sagged beneath their heavy loads. The birches swooned. The
drifts at the open rocky space where the Martin land began were
hills that no one could plow through or flounder over. The boys
could not get down to school and no neighbors could get up to
visit. They were a family marooned on a moaning lonely hilltop.

Never had there been such a winter. The running spring was
buried and Esther melted snow for water. The birds disappeared.
The wild turkeys vanished. Even the squirrels abandoned their
skittering up and down the trees and, like the bears, took refuge
in their holes. For days the sun never came out at all but was
only a pale white eye staring remotely down through a whirling
fog.

Mark did not mind. He was accustomed to outwitting tempests
and calms, cannibals and pirates, thirst and starvation. He was
ever busy making his cabin snugger from cold, his animals safer
from the menace of marauding wild beasts. He knew no fear. He
felt no weariness. And when need arose he could be doctor or
dentist, judge or diplomat. He ordered his family as he had ordered his crew, with brusque, impartial, impersonal commands
which none dared defy. Only to Esther did his tone sound gentle.
Only to Matt did it ever grow angry, for Matt bore always the
sullen air of one who would like to argue if not rebel.

Yet at night when darkness wrapped them about, when Esther
sat at her loom, when Prue busied herself making a rug of rags
she had dipped in the juices of indigo and pokeberry, madder
and hickory bark, when Matt worked at fashioning a pair of
snowshoes after the manner of the Indians, then Mark became a

different man. It was then the little ones gathered at his knee to hear such tales of the sea as held them lost in a listening wonder. Or he might get out a piece of rope and show them the various ways to twist it into knots. Or he knew a guessing game they could play with dried kernels of corn. Sometimes he would sing rollicking songs that had an endless number of verses and his rich voice would roll out until the rafters trembled. Or, if wee Johnny was fretful with his teething, he would take him into his arms and lull him to sleep with soft rumblings when naught else would quiet him. And always before bedtime he would read from the Bible in such a grave, confident way that every one knew God stood close, no matter how far off human beings might be.

Esther brought her usual philosophy to bear on the long loneliness. What mattered it that they were separate from the rest of the world? She had her man beside her night and day as she had always wanted him. She had her whole family close and safe. And there was bound to be an end to winter.

So the weeks went by and at last there came a time when Esther asked anxiously if they would have wood enough to last them?

"We must have a care with it though there's plenty more to be had if need be. What I worry about is the fodder," Mark told her.

The fodder. The fodder for the animals. The food for themselves. Yes, these grew to be worries. Esther thought she had laid in a plentiful supply but she had not reckoned on such a lengthy isolation. She must measure it out from now on—the corn and the flour, the nuts they had gathered in the fall, the berries she had dried. She must even be saving of meat, for spring was still a long way off and game growing scarcer and scarcer. It was misfortune she had not had the produce of a garden this year for preserving, but so it was. They must just make out.

By February the wolves were coming close and could be heard howling at night not far from their door. And one evening Esther lifted her face in alarm before the sound of stealthy padded footsteps on the cabin roof.

"It's a wildcat," Matt told her quickly.

Mark rose and threw another great log on the fire.

"So long as we have that roaring, he'll not venture down the chimney. We'll keep it going all night," he added, looking toward the pile of wood in the corner. Yes, there would be enough. He and Esther would each take a watch. Not until then did he address Matt.

"What makes you think it's a wildcat?"

"I saw his tracks this morning."

"Why didn't you tell me!"

Matt did not answer. What he had hoped was to kill the cat himself. If he did, then mebbe Pa would take him along with him when he went hunting, for Matt had grown keen-eyed by reason of his association with the Indians and could spot a track or spy out game quicker than his father, and he was as good a shot, too.

But Mark would never let him go. Nor did he the next morning when they saw the footprints of the animal, which had left the cabin roof some time in the night, going off into the woods to the north. Despite Esther's anxiety at his venturing forth alone, and despite Matt's dark enraged eyes, Mark said, "No. You stay here. If aught happens to me, you're the man of the family."

Mark got the wildcat that day but Matt did not rejoice with the rest. Instead he nursed his grievance. Were he really the head of the family, he was bold enough to say, he'd need to go hunting. And then the boiling pots his mother kept handy on the fire would have to deal with whatever prowled too close. Why couldn't they now just as well?

But Mark roared impatiently, " 'Tis for you to protect the house and all in it whilst I'm gone! Now clap a stopper on your tongue! I want no more bilging!"

The confinement, not hard at first because of its exciting strangeness, grew harder as dangers increased and food dwindled. Of all the children, Prue, who had found that the best way to ease her heavy, anxious heart, was to be useful, and who feared the world lost to her anyway by reason of David's unbroken silence, minded least. But to Matt winter was a cage and the hours of the long dark days bars against which he flung himself in an ever-growing resentment. He heard the wind wailing and shrieking in bursts of fury no greater than those he held pent up within himself. He watched the snow flying every which way as if it had gone crazy, and he thought he, too, would go crazy.

By early March the nuts and berries were long since gone and Esther had come near to the last of the flour and cornmeal. The meat was nigh gone, too, save for a few dried strips of venison hanging from the rafter. There was always dittany tea, though, she told herself. And she could boil the corncobs with the meat and, by adding melted snow every day, keep a stew going for a week, at least.

It was then that Mark told her he had but grain enough for two days' feed and he had decided to move the animals into the other half of the house where it was warmer for them in their weakened condition. When Esther saw in full daylight their trembling limbs and the way their bones stuck up under their hides she did not grudge them the shelter that robbed her of comfort. She could even stand the pangs of hunger that were now hers daily (for she shortened her portions in order to feed the children and Mark), because she knew that if worst came to worst they could kill the cow which had long ago stopped giving milk. The one thing she could not thole was Matt whose mixed-up churning was making him more difficult than ever. It was that night that the outburst came which she had feared and dreaded.

The twins had whimpered for more food at supper and to make them forget about their want, Mark took them up and began singing to them.

*"Come all ye, young sailor men, listen to me!
I'll sing you a song of the fish of the sea."*

He glanced around, his eyes bright holes in his gaunt, bearded face. "All of you, now! Join in the chorus!" And he led it, with Prue and Andy and Esther lifting their voices and the twins trailing behind.

*"Then blow ye winds westerly! Westerly blow!
We're bound to the south'ard so steady she goes!"*

Mark went on to the next verse alone, bouncing Mary and

Luke on his knees to keep time, bringing small smiles to their tear-stained faces.

> *"Oh, first come the shad, the biggest of all,*
> *He clumb up aloft and let every sail fall."*

He stopped. "Sing, Matt! What the devil's the matter with you!"

Esther saw Matt's mouth close like a trap. Mark, with his glance hard and angry on his son, continued the song.

> *"And next come the mack'rel with his striped back,*
> *He hauled aft the sheets—"*

The song came to an abrupt halt. "You goin' to sing or ain't you?"

"I don't have to."

Mark glared at him. Then he exploded. "By the tarnal! You just keep yourself dense a-purpose! It means small shakes to you if you swap talk with ary one of us or join in family doin's or not! Well! I don't hold with such ornery ways! Sing! Or I'll knock your noggin off!"

His anger scalded Esther's heart. She knew Matt was the unhappy prisoner of his own deep groping desires. She said quickly, hoping to appease the answering wild fury in her son's eyes. "Leave be, Mark. We can make out if he doesn't care to be one with us."

But to Matt she was saying that they could get along without him.

Two days later, when the last grain had been meted out, Mark shot the deer. A slight thaw that gave a hope of spring, and a freeze that took it away again, had laid a hard crust on the snow and Mark went off early in the day on his snowshoes. Esther watched him vanish amongst the trees with her usual worry. What would he find, anyway? There was nothing—nothing—roaming the wilderness these days save wolves and foxes. Not a marten. Not a mink. Not even a woodchuck.

But Mark caught sight of the antlered head not far from the

cabin. The buck's weight had taken it through the crust and he was floundering in deep soft snow with a broken leg. Mark shot him quickly, and, thinking him dead, went close to cut him up before the wolves appeared. But in his dying spasm the deer reared up, plunging, and the great spread of his horns ripped through Mark's coat sleeve, tore a deep gash in his arm and punctured his shoulder. Mark shot again and then, ignoring his pain, went swiftly to the butchering.

Esther heard both shots. She heard the responsive howling of the wolves coming nearer and nearer, almost at once, and, watching from a window with fear in her heart, she presently saw Mark staggering through the forest, a bloody burden on his shoulders, one arm—his crippled arm—hanging useless and dripping by his side.

"Matt! Run help your pa! Prue, take the baby. Andy, if you're bound to be sick at the blood when he gets here, step outside. Mary, you and Luke tear up these rags for me—"

A few moments later Mark came in, followed shortly by Andy. Esther was ready. Deftly she cut away the ripped sleeve of her husband's coat. Then, with the water she always kept hot by the fire, she washed out the deep cut and the hole in his shoulder and applied a styptic of ashes and cobwebs. When the bleeding had stopped she cleaned the wounds gently and laid hot coon grease on them. Finally she bound him up. While she was working she saw how thin his frame had grown with all the work he had done and the scanty rations he had had, but she said nothing. Please God this winter was near gone. And with what he'd brought in today, they'd last it out now.

"I had to leave the most of it for the wolves," Mark was saying regretfully, "but here's steaks and stews enough, I reckon. And here's venison broth for my stock," he added. "That'll keep life in 'em till I can get down off the hill."

It was not until that moment that Esther missed Matt.

"Where is he?" she asked, looking around. "Didn't he go meet you, Mark?"

"Yes. He helped me to the door."

"Where is he? Call him, Andy."

Andy's near-sighted eyes looked from his mother to his father in distress at what he had to tell.

"He's takened his snowshoes and gone down to Indian Town. He said he figured he was light enough not to fall through and he could get down afore dark."

"But—where's he gone?"

Even before she heard it, Esther knew the answer.

"He's gone to stay with Peter. He says you don't need him any more. You've got food and spring's comin' soon. He says—" Andy swallowed. "He says he's not comin' back."

CHAPTER 6

The Terror

It was August and summer hovered over all the land. Level lakes of bright yellow covered Mark Martin's hay fields. Along the trail's edge to Indian Town the tall grasses were heavy with seed. Birds could be heard in an increasing variety of songs. Robins sounded from early dawn to dusk. Blue jays screamed. Song sparrows trilled. Warblers filled the soft air with their music. Now and then, high amongst the foliage there was visible, like a flash of sunlight, an oriole's wing, or the flaming dart of a scarlet tanager. While from the forest which still stretched wild and dark behind Martin Manor came the steady drill of woodpeckers testing out ancient trees. It was hard to believe that danger lurked anywhere, that Indian raids, directed by the French government—by-product of the war on the continent between that nation and the English—were terrorizing the countryside to the north. But so it was, and beneath the beauty lay a tense and uneasy waiting.

By now the house that Mark had imagined stood in serene and simple dignity on its wide expanse of emerald lawn facing the western hills. A few magnificent oaks and elms shaded it but all the rest of the woods down to his line by the rocky strip had been cleared away for the view he had envisioned when he bought the property. The view was there, ever the same, yet ever-changing as the seasons rotated, and a source of endless pleasure to the seafaring man whose eyes were accustomed to gaze on far horizons.

Across the trail connecting Yokun Town with Indian Town, a transformation had taken place, too. Heavy timber had given way to a small open area and down this young apple whips marched in straight columns, bravely defiant of wind and weather. Farther along, Prue's secret place of beauty had been quarried and great stones hauled by sled from it to form the foundations for the new house and for the barn that stood four-square and solid as a windbreak to the north and west.

Mark had realized his dream.

For Esther, too, grown accustomed to the solitude, content-ment had deepened with each passing year. The big house with its fanlight over the front door, its wide hospitable center hall opening both at the front and at the rear, its beautiful carved balustrade, its heavy seven-paneled doors leading into spacious rooms—four downstairs and four up with an attic above—its wide-throated fireplaces and lovely mantels, was far finer than the Stonington house had been. It was furnished finer, too, with well-made pieces of pine, butternut and maple, and all the lovely things Mark had brought home from his voyages to distant places. More important, there was space here for each member of the family. Esther and Mark had their bedroom behind the keeping room, with Johnny, now nearly seven, in the small room across the hall in the rear of the best parlor. Upstairs, Prue and Mary, Andy and Luke each had their own sleeping place while Matt had chosen to remain in the loft of the ell, the original cabin. He had cut in windows and built steep narrow stairs to it and could thus go and come without observation or question.

Matt was as big as his father these days, with all of his brawn and bulk and all of a man's desires pounding fiercely in his blood. He was taciturn still and had remained unforgiving toward Mark and unresponsive to Esther, doing what he had to do about the farm in a silence that spoke neither of submissiveness nor rebellion but only of endurance. And when, two years ago, Ephraim Williams, true to his promise, had come for him to go with his re-enforcements that had been ordered to relieve the troops besieging Louisburg on the island of Cape Breton, he had left like a shot arrow. It had been a bitter disappointment to him that they had arrived too late to see action, for Louisburg had already surrendered. But he was likely to be called to the militia again any time that the Indians and French threatened too close to home territory. And it was for that he lived.

The need to escape, to prove himself, to stand alone and assert his independence was stronger in Matt than ever. But now he wanted more. He wanted a say in affairs, a say that would be listened to. He had been shocked when his ma and pa had decided to give away the money that had come to them after Ma's father —the Grandfather Richardson whom Matt had never seen—had died in Boston. Never in the world would *he* do such a thing. Oh, he liked John Sergeant all right! And he liked the Indians as much as ever. Peter was still his best friend, and Marie— His thoughts went off on a tangent as Marie came to mind.

He was alone down by the river gathering up the last of the hay there while he was thinking these things.

Marie was Marie, he told himself, pausing in his work. There was no one like Marie. No white girl he knew had her slim grace, her dark beauty or her intuitive knowledge of him. Marie could walk like a shadow by his side and bring him peace when he knew only chaos. Even so, even caring about her and Peter as he did, he would have kept that money rather than donate it toward an Indian school.

He recalled the time this spring when the letter came from the lawyers. They had all been at the table finishing the noon meal when John Sergeant rode up with it. It had been in the pouch with the mail for the Williamses brought that morning by a traveler, and Abigail, thinking it might be important, had sent him up with it.

He had looked tired, Matt remembered, his natural joyousness dimmed a trifle, his usual zeal and energy lacking from his manner. Esther and Mark had spoken of it after he had left.

"He is worrying," Esther had said.

He had cause to worry, Matt thought. His wife, insisting on his building her another house on the hill near her father, had driven him into debt. He humored her too much, his thoughts went on. She had beguiling ways and she worked them on him. When she had said she was afeard of the Indians coming and wanted to be near her pa's fort-house, John gave in. But neither he nor Matt's father really thought there would ever be an attack here. The settlement still had many more Indians than whites. If there was trouble it would be north of here the way it had been on and off for the past four-five years.

He picked up his pitchfork and began tossing loads of the dried hay onto the wagon, rejoicing as he did so in his own great strength, in the feel of taut muscles obeying his command. If danger should come, he was thinking, the major would summon him and he'd be off with a whoop and a holler. Mebbe this time he'd see a little excitement.

He finished the area around him, clucked to Daisy and moved to another spot. His pa wasn't able to do things like this any more. His shoulder and arm had got stiffer and stiffer and he could no longer swing a pitchfork or a shovel or a maul with any ease or power, since the time the buck deer had gouged him.

Matt went back in his mind now to that day and its unexpected aftermath.

With what violence of emotion he had sped over the hard crust of snow to Indian Town and Peter's home! With what mingled defiance and certainty and trepidation he had knocked at their door!

Peter had opened to him and he had said gaspingly, "Peter— I've come—I told you I would some day! And—well—here I am."

Peter had glanced over his shoulder toward the dark interior and from the shadows Aaron had moved forward, his face a mask. Marie had followed him, her wide shining eyes fixed happily on Matt.

"You will live here?" she had asked. "Like you always tell me?"

Matt had nodded, looking not at her but at Aaron's ugly, pock-marked countenance.

"Peter told me there would be room," he said to the old Indian.

The waiting silence had been awful. Matt could remember even now the sinking sensation at the pit of his stomach. Because if he could not stay here—then what? He had not thought any further. He stared for an interminable moment at Aaron, who stood with his arms crossed over his chest, his bright opaque glance revealing nothing. At last he had spoken. "You have home."

"Yes, but—"

Matt had hesitated over all the words he wanted to say and could not bring himself to utter, and Peter had intervened for him. "He likes us. He likes our ways better than white ways. He would take ours for his own."

But Aaron had shaken his head. "Not good. Make trouble. Go back." And he turned away decisively.

Matt, desperate, had cried out, "I can't! I hate it there! I'll never go back! Never!"

It was then that John Sergeant had stepped forward from a dim corner and had laid a kind hand on Matt's rough head.

"There is sickness in this house, Matthew. Grave sickness. I am here now to pray for Aaron's wife. You cannot add to his burden at this time. Come home with me."

It had been several days before Mark's wounds and the weather had permitted him to follow Matt down off the hill and Aaron had promptly sent him to the minister. Matt, who had seen him approaching, had hidden behind a door and had heard the interview between the two men.

"I'd a good mind not to come after him at all!" his father had exclaimed. "But Esther is heartsick. And I, myself, want no son of mine living with savages." He had pounded his great fist on his knee as his anger rose. "What ails the lad! I can't fathom him!"

"He wants to do things. Hard things. He wants to fight them and beat them and you are preventing him. You had best face it, Mark. 'Tis his thwarted desires that twist his heart."

"Thwarted— Gad, John! The boy's got a *duty!* Besides—"

John's quiet voice had interrupted. "I have told him that there is one hard thing for him to do right now and that is to return home and bide there till he is older. I have told him he must conquer himself before he can conquer life."

In the short silence Matt had heard his father's heavy breathing.

"Aaron's wife died," John had continued. "And soon Aaron and Peter will be going to their sugaring-off. I have suggested to Aaron that he invite Matthew to accompany him. And I suggest to you that you allow him to go. Let him go from here in the next few days. Living in the woods in the winter the way the Indians do will be an adventure to satisfy him for the time. After he has experienced it he will, I believe, come back to you. When he does, listen to his tale, for I gather from what he has told me that he feels you are not interested in what he has to say. So welcome him back and listen to him."

This was how it had worked out. Matt, knowing ahead that he was not to be lambasted for running away, had returned home after the sugaring-off and no rebuke was ever administered to him.

But it was that incident, of course, and John Sergeant's wise part in it that had prompted his parents to share with John the money that had been left to them, last spring. It was a way of showing their appreciation, of repaying an obligation.

Indeed, it was more than that. It was much-needed tangible support to John's dream school which was getting financial help from nowhere else in the Colony,—a fact that plagued him as much as his indebtedness. The trouble was that the French and Indians occupied every one's thoughts these days, Pa had said. In vain, John had written to governors, to college presidents and to wealthy friends asking for gifts of money so that he might begin building. The letters went unanswered or brought forth only refusals.

Just from England, Pa had continued, was Mr. Sergeant receiving any help. From there Mr. Hollis, who had always been a benefactor, continued to forward money with explicit directions for its use. He wanted it to educate twelve chosen Indian boys. But Mr. Sergeant, busy going from hill to plain where he read Scripture to the savages (which he had translated into their language), busy with study groups at night, busy calling on the sick and traveling far afield to preach to other tribes, could no longer maintain a school in his home. He had no time. And his hope that Abigail might take over its running in his absence had proved impractical. She had her own tasks—weaving, spinning, baking and looking after her two small children, Electa and Erastus.

Finally it had been arranged that the chosen twelve, Peter among them, should be sent away to Newington, Connecticut, until the schoolhouse could be built here. They were now receiving instruction from a Mr. Kellogg, who knew the Indian language. It was as good a fix as could be managed but it was not good enough to suit the minister who chafed against the obstruction of his purpose, worried not to have the boys under his direct control and was anxious lest they be not receiving all the teaching that should be given them.

"That's why he's low in spirit," Pa had finished. "He's had a mess of troubles. Sickness—debt—disappointment. He's beat out by them." And Ma, looking at the letter from the lawyer she still held in her hand, had been struck by a sudden thought.

"Captain Martin," she had said softly, a flare of color coming to her cheeks. "We have prospered here and are still prospering. I say we should pass on what has come to us to further this most worth-while work. We should help Mr. Sergeant build his school. What do you think?" And she had waited for his answer. Indeed, all of them had held their breath while he considered. At last he had nodded slowly. "I will write the lawyer this very day and ask if we may do this," Ma had finished, with satisfaction on her face and in her voice.

Matt had been stunned. Stunned—and angered. That money, or part of it, was his! Least it would be some day. What right had they to give away what belonged to him? He had spluttered out a protest but they had shamed him into silence. However, out of his stifled rebellion a determination had been born. He would

get money himself. Some day—some way—he would get his own
and it would be his that no one could touch.

The horn that was blown only when there was trouble or danger of some kind now sounded on the still August air. Startled,
Matt dropped his pitchfork. Then, looking up over the sloping
land, he saw Prue standing in the sunlight with the horn at her
lips and beside her on his horse, Major Ephraim Williams,
Junior, in his scarlet uniform.

Indians! By the tarnal! Indians!

He tossed his pitchfork onto the load he had gathered, leaped
to the wagon, snatched up the reins and shouted at the mare. The
next moment she was straining toward the house while he, his
black eyes bright, his face alive and eager, was thinking, Cracky!
This time he'd see things happen or he'd be a gone Josie.

Prue had been working in her flower garden before the house
when the beat of a horse's hoofs made her rise from her knees
and look down the trail toward Indian Town. At once she recognized Ephraim.

Her heart gave a quick jump at sight of him, not because his
was a disturbing presence but because she could never see him
without thinking of David Reynolds. Where was he now? What
was he doing? Had he put her out of his mind forever by this
time? Alas! She feared so.

The last she had seen him had been the day he had left her in
anger. Shortly after that she had heard he had been sent away.
For three long, endless years she had waited in the hope of hearing where he had gone so that she might write him. Finally, he
had written her from Barbados just before he had been ordered
back to England. It was a letter that had brought her immeasur-
able joy, for in it he had reasserted his love and opened a path-
way back to him. Quickly she had replied. But since then it was
three more long years and she had heard nothing further. Perhaps Ephraim would have news of him, though she thought it
unlikely he would waste time in talking as there seemed to be an
air of urgency upon him.

But if he was pressed he did not spare her his customary appraising look when he drew rein before her—a look that invariably put her on guard. How little he changed through the years, she thought. Save for some added weight, he appeared the same as when she had first met him, affable, assured and attractive. His increasing responsibilities in the Colony had only increased these characteristics.

Before he could speak, Esther appeared, her instinct already warning her of his errand, her hand, as always in moments of stress and anxiety, pressed against her heart where the pain that had lived with her so many years was growing more insistent. Seeing her, he swept off his hat and addressed her and Prue together.

"Good day to you, Mrs. Martin—and Prue. I've come recruiting. Where's Matt?"

"Down by the river."

"Please call him. Where's the captain?"

"He's at Mr. Sergeant's."

"I've just come from there. Somehow I missed him. And Andy?"

"Andy—" Not Andy, Esther thought. He was never meant for fighting. He was always separated from violent action by the need first to weigh and measure its cause and probable result. He would be shot dead a dozen times before ever thought came clear to him and he could draw a bead. Indeed, a musket was not familiar to him, so much did he dwell in his mind. Even his own hands weren't familiar to him. Besides, he was but a scrawny, near-sighted fourteen.

"Andy couldn't tell an Indian from a tree at ten paces. You know that, Ephraim. Anyway, someone should be left here."

Prue looked up at him, her voice quiet. "What is the news?"

"There's a rumor the Indians are gathering and mean to attack Fort Massachusetts. I need more men there. At the moment it's but weakly guarded, so many have returned home to get in their hay."

She nodded and moved toward the horn that hung fastened to one of the pillars of the porch. Eph's eyes followed her, noting for not the first time the fluid grace of her figure, the shining beauty of her hair bound in braids about her head, the lovely shape of her scarlet mouth as she raised the horn to her lips. She was a woman made to be kissed, he thought, but he doubted that she ever had been. She was too cool, too remote. Still he had known women like that who, once wakened, were more rewarding than the easy ones. He remembered, too, that a while ago—at the time of Abigail's wedding—Prue had had sparkle enough. Were the fires merely banked? It would be interesting to discover. Despite the pressure of his errand, Ephraim Williams could think these thoughts.

Esther was saying, "Matt will go. But—do you need the captain?"

Eph turned his glance on her. Esther's sandy hair was quite gray now and the delicate tracery of fine lines in her skin had deepened, but the shape of her face and her expression still held beauty. She had been brave to continue to live up here on this lonely hilltop as she had done, with the wilderness at her back, not a neighboring house in sight and her children small and helpless save for the two oldest. That little tyke coming out the door now with the fair hair and great gray eyes must be her youngest. Ephraim frowned thoughtfully, remembering that the favorite pastime of these treacherous savages was to seek out an isolated home such as this. And with Andy the nearest to being a man—should he, Eph, take both Matt and his father—she would have scant protection.

"How is your husband's arm?" he asked.

"It grows stiffer. He won't say so but it does. It is his right arm," she added.

He nodded. "He'd best stay here," —slowly. "The doctor is going with me. My brother, Doctor Thomas. And some of the Indians from the meadow and a few men from Yokun Town and down Sheffield way. But I'll want and need Matt."

"Matt's tearing his heart out to get to you right this minute."

They stood silent as Daisy, once over the brow of the slope and urged on by the boy, labored toward them at a gallop. Esther moved to the mare's head when Matt stopped by the corner of the house and sprang to the ground.

"What is it?" he demanded breathlessly.

Ephraim told him and added, "Make ready fast as you can."

"I'm ready now. Just got to get my gun."

He rushed into the house and was out again in a moment, gun in hand, jacket on his arm, an old cap jerked slantwise over his thicket of black hair, powder horn slung about his waist. Ephraim nodded at him approvingly. He was a stalwart lad with a stout heart—and a fine shot, to boot. It was good to have him in the company.

"Go down to The Castle where the others are gathering. I'll see you there."

"Wait, Matt. I'll fix a bite of food for you."

"Let him go, Mrs. Martin. He's a-foot. I'm riding. I'll carry the packet to him."

Esther nodded, turned Daisy about and, with a slap on her flank, started her toward the barn. Then she moved to the front steps. Behind her Ephraim's words came clear to her ears.

"Would you consent to walk a little way with me along the trail, Prue? It's been a long time since we have visited together and may be a longer ere we meet again."

"I had best not delay you," Prue began, when Esther turned at the door.

"Please go with him, Prudence. The twins are likely on their way up from the Joneses'. They've been playing with Keziah and Abigail. You can meet them by the rocks and see they don't dawdle along the path." Her eyes turned toward the forest behind the house while she was speaking, as if, already, she saw shadowy shapes there. But mingled with her anxiety over the savages was concern for Prue, now nigh twenty and still unwed. Ephraim Williams was no more her first choice for a son-in-law than earlier, but there'd been no one in the three new families suitable for Prue and—oh, dear heart! What a mess of unrelated worries a body could stew up at one time!

She reappeared presently with johnnycake, dried venison and a bit of salt pork tied up in a small parcel. "And here's a change of socks," she added. "Matt can tuck them in his pocket. Thank you, Ephraim. He's that frenzied, he'd go off without his head if 'twas loose. Shall you be starting north today?"

He nodded. "I, myself, must go to Albany first. But I'll get to the fort before trouble breaks, I hope."

He had dismounted and he and Prue now set forth side by side. Watching them as they turned down the trail, Esther noted that Ephraim was studying Prue as though nothing else were on his mind. It was strange what power a pretty woman had to scatter a man's brains, she thought, and calling Johnny to her, she went toward the barn to unhitch Daisy.

Prue walked in silence, her calm face never showing her inner turmoil, for she meant to break her silence today and speak of David, to ascertain his whereabouts if possible. The restlessness that was on her was something she could ill bear longer.

Her mind went back to his letter. Long before that came she had sternly schooled herself to forget her adolescent love, but each spring the ache of her memories of it and of him had returned with increasing poignancy. She had tried to put her mind on her garden. Diligently she had toiled amongst her herbs— pennyroyal and horehound, mignonette and clove, lovage and lavender, sage and saffron, summer savory and winter savory. For bloom she had planted Canterbury bell, sweet William and stock. She had set out lupine and laburnum, fragrant pink and ragged robin, with heartsease for a border.

Yet for all her efforts she—then a passionate, lonely seventeen —had known no heart's ease herself. Only restlessness, only hunger, only regret. For if she had it to live over, she would go with him without question to the ends of the world.

And then had come his letter.

Dear Prudence,

This may surprise you—this letter. I do not doubt it will. But I must write it in hopes of bringing to a fresh beginning the love for you that lives in me and will not die. I have kept thinking you might feel inclined to write to me. Perhaps you have done so and it has never reached me. Or perhaps my last words to you (and I could cut my tongue out for them) has made you feel 'twas for me to write first. At any rate, in humility, in tenderness, in devotion now, I do.

I have let some time elapse since first resolving to pen this letter to you, partly because the arrogant pride, to which I plead guilty, held me firmly to silence, partly because I felt that you needed a space before you would be able to see our future together in another light. I pray that the time you have had has been enough. But even more fervently I pray it has not been too much and that, during it, you have not put me irrevocably from your mind and heart.

For, Prue, one thing has come clear to me above all others in the absence enforced upon us by my military duty, and that is that you are and always have been and always will be the woman I desire above all others. I do not want to live the rest of my life without you, and to that end I have thought upon the difference that divides us—the only difference, dear heart—and have come upon a compromise that should be fair to both and equally satisfying. Why can we not plan to spend a part of each year in America? Surely in that way neither of us will be either too selfish or too sacrificial. Will you not write me at once before I leave here, telling me you agree and approve this suggestion? I shall wait in hopes of your letter until the day of my departure. After that, if no word has come, I shall dwell in darkness, having seen the light by which I want to live and blunderingly put it out.

My love is yours, Prue, as it has ever been. And my constant hope is that soon—*soon*—you will consent to be my wedded wife.

Yours
David

How joyously she had sped her reply to him, accepting his compromise! Since then—nothing. Had he never received it? Had he tired of waiting? ("*I am not overstocked with patience.*") If only she could know!

Ephraim's voice broke in upon her thoughts.

"I feel it would be advisable were you and your family to move down to the settlement until the present threat is ended."

Startled, she looked up at him. "But—we are some twenty miles and more from Fort Massachusetts!"

"True. Still you are very isolated. I would feel better were you nearer neighbors. Abigail could take some of you. The Castle could take you all but—"

She interrupted quickly. "Pa will never go there save under duress."

Ephraim's hand came out and caught her arm and she saw his face suddenly transformed by an ancient hunger. Shocked, she could only stare at him.

"Perhaps we two can heal the breach that exists between our parents," he heard himself saying, much to his own surprise.

Prue recovered herself and shook her head. "That is not possible," she replied, speaking with composure as she tried to draw free. But her indifference to his words stung him like a gadfly. With a hasty glance behind to assure himself they were well hidden by trees from Martin Manor, he dropped the reins of his horse and took her in his arms. She held quite still beneath the fiery tempest of his kisses until at last he angrily let her go.

"What manner of woman are you!" he exclaimed.

She drew away, unruffled, cool.

"Were you not an old friend—and ignorant—I would be vastly incensed."

"Ignorant?"

"That my heart is already given elsewhere."

It was his turn to stare as he tried to guess who it could be. There were so few possibilities in Indian Town. Then he felt her hand on his arm as light as a leaf.

"Let us go on being friends because as such I have need of you."

"By gad! What—"

"Ephraim, tell me, please, if you know. Where is David Reynolds?"

A memory came to him. A memory of David and Prudence going off together to look at Abigail's wedding gifts, of David's acceptance of his—Eph's—invitation to remain over for a day or so; of his going to supper at the captain's and his abrupt departure after that. So they had loved—and quarreled. And this was why Prue had remained single all these years. David, too, for all the pursuit of him by willing females, had never succumbed to any of them so far as Eph knew.

But if David did not turn up again? If he failed to reappear? This girl was comely. Her father, the captain, was well-to-do. She came of good stock. She would fit into any scheme of living which he, Ephraim, might settle upon, once these skirmishes with the French and Indians were ended. Finally, love did not flourish in poor soil. She could be made to forget.

He said, "I know nothing whatever about him."

"Nor how he can be reached?"

He shook his head.

She took her hand from his arm and stood silent, a shadow on her face. "I am sorry. But if, perchance, you do come upon him, will you tell him for me that I—I was very glad to receive his letter and that I answered it?"

"If I do," he conceded.

He considered for a moment the advisability of taking her in his arms again but decided against it. She was not one to be handled thus. Not yet. He said only, "And if I don't? Will you try to forget him—for me?"

Her clear blue eyes met his in quiet consideration. He had a goodly measure of charm, she was thinking. He was able, kind, respected and liked. And lives were meant to touch and merge. Yet hers touched no one's. She was only half a woman and so only half living. Caught between emotions deep as life itself, she answered slowly, "I will—try." And even as she spoke, the echo of those same words to David sounded in her ears.

She had not been flattered as he expected her to be, he found himself realizing in piqued astonishment. It was she conferring a favor, not he. The thought pricked him to a doubt. But before he could say anything further, three figures appeared over the brow of the hill down by the rocks. They were Mark, hurrying back from the minister's upon receipt of the news from Abigail, with a twin on either side of him.

Ephraim swung quickly up into his saddle. Prue looked into his face.

"God be with you," she said gravely.

Ephraim nodded. "And you," he replied.

And he galloped away.

It was early in August that day when Matt went off to Fort Massachusetts. For the next two or three weeks time went by on the slow and heavy feet of fear. And then, one day shortly after the twentieth, Prue was working in her flower garden when she heard the sound of swiftly running steps. Straightening up, she looked toward the road and saw an Indian racing by on his way from Yokun Town to the village, his black hair streaming in the wind. For a moment her heart stopped, until she recognized him as a Stockbridge Indian who lived on the meadow.

"What is it?" she called.

The runner hardly slackened his pace but over his shoulder came hoarsely shouted, frightening words.

"Fort Massachusetts burned! All men captured or killed!"

Prue stood paralyzed. Esther, who had heard their voices, came quickly from the house followed by John and the twins. Mary's brown eyes were alert and fearless through the fallen tangle of her chestnut hair. Luke, munching an apple, was calmly curious. John's face, just losing its babyish curves, held an expression of alarm.

"What is it?" Esther asked, in her turn.

Prue turned slowly. "Fort Massachusetts. Ma—it's gone! And all the men—" She could not go on.

"Killed?"

Prue whispered, "Or captured."

Esther let out a gasp and her face turned dead-white while her hand crept up to hold her side. "Matt!" she murmured. Then— "Blow the horn for your father and Andy. They're in the potato field. We must get to The Castle at once! Even now they—" She cast a furtive glance over her shoulder at the forest. "Did he say they were coming this way?"

"He didn't say."

"Blow the horn! Then saddle Bess. I'll gather up a few things."

In response to the raucous summons, Mark and Andy came hurrying with Daisy at a gallop and potatoes rattling loose in the wagon. Mark heard the news and issued quick orders. In no time the family cavalcade was making its way down the hill, Prue riding Bess, her mother driving Daisy, with young John and Mary and Luke beside her and the wagon loaded with hastily snatched blankets, food, grain, the garnish of pewter, the family Bible and whatever else had seemed most valuable or most needed in the few moments there had been. Behind her came Mark afoot, his rifle cradled in one arm as he urged Star along, while Andy led the cow. The chickens, save for the pet Luke clutched in a close embrace, must be left to fortune, as well as the pigs and cats.

Strange, Prue thought, as she rode, the day was just the same. The saw-toothed spruces still stood clear against a sapphire sky. The cut hayfields still dreamed tranquilly beneath the summer sun. The blackberries still hung alongside the trail, polished and glistening as if they had been freshly enameled. And down by the white rocks bees still bumbled lazily above the spreading purple thyme. The day was not changed. Only their hearts were, as the anxiety that had filled them turned to agonized grief and terror. Prue tried to think of Matt lying bloody and dead somewhere and a sob clutched her throat for all his youth and courage and defiant strength destroyed. How terrible it was to die before you had begun to live! Dear God, did the same awful fate await them all? The Indian had said the fort was burned and every last defender gone. What, then, stood between the mission and a shrieking horrible butchery? Nothing save a few miles of primeval forest in which the savages were at home.

They were not the first to reach the acknowledged stronghold. Abigail Sergeant was already there with her six-year-old Electa and little Erastus of four. Mr. and Mrs. Jones and their four children—Anna, Keziah, Abigail and Elijah—streamed ahead of the Martins across the lawn, their arms filled with their most treasured possessions. Prue could see Anna bearing her best dress and baby Elijah trotting along on fat uncertain legs with a stranglehold on a kitten he held upside down in his small pudgy hands. The Browns were visible in the distance topping Brown's Hill—as the western slope had come to be called from their house located part way down it—while up from Indian Town straggled a line of figures, the Woodbridges and the three new white families.

Within The Castle all was noise and confusion. Mrs. Williams stood in the hall issuing directions to the black house servants who hurried about, their eyes rolling in their heads, shuttering windows, pushing heavy furniture around as added barricades, and gathering up silver pieces, rugs and other valuables to bear to the cellar for safe keeping. Josiah Williams, Matt's age, was shouting orders from a rear door to the stable boys. Elijah was trying to smuggle his dog, unseen by his mother, across the floor to the safety below. Judith and Elizabeth, both a year or so younger than Prue, met the villagers as they poured in and led them to the Great Room where small children huddled in awed silence in corners and Colonel Williams, red-faced and imperious, could be heard clearly above the hubbub.

"Nobody has call to fret! There's room for all and a margin of safety in the matter of time, I reckon! Just let my wife first get to the cellar the things she wants down there! Then we'll follow. Now about what happened—I don't know much more than you do. All I can say is what I got from the runner. The doctor—my son, Thomas—left Fort Massachusetts the day before the attack with fourteen men to seek re-enforcements from Deerfield. Seems half the defenders were down sick and had to have help. He and his company got through safe. But the next morning, Monsieur Rigaud and some seven or eight hundred Frenchmen and Indians surprised the place and all that weren't killed were captured."

He paused for breath and looked around at the taut faces and harried eyes before him.

"I thank the Lord for Thomas," he went on. "But—" and his voice broke for a moment—"I've no news of my eldest. I know not if Ephraim got there before the slaughter or not. I've no news of the men who went to Deerfield with Thomas, either. Who they were, I mean. But I'll say this!"—and his voice strengthened and became hard again—"Fort Massachusetts will be rebuilt! And if those devils come down this way now they'll meet more'n they expect to!"

The devils did not come down that way. And Dr. Thomas, riding in, disheveled, gaunt and weary to the point of exhaustion a day or two later, brought them the reassuring news that they would not this time. He also brought more details of the tragedy.

He and his men, he told his attentive listeners, must have walked right through the enemy which had already encircled the fort. They were no doubt allowed to pass because to have attacked them would have been to warn the others. Major Ephraim Williams, his brother, who had been in command, was not there when he left. It was likely he was safe. But for the twenty-two men, three women and five children left behind, he feared the worst.

Out of the heavy silence Prue asked the question that neither Esther nor Mark could find voice for.

"And our Matt— Was he one of those?"

Thomas nodded an unwilling assent.

There was a stir and a murmur of commiseration on the part of the villagers that was interrupted by the doctor. A lad from Yokun Town was safe, he went on. Two mission Indians were safe. A couple of men from down Sheffield way and a boy from Sheffield North Parish—these had all been with the doctor and were safe. But Matt— Whether he was only marched into captivity or whether he was killed by now, he could not say.

John Sergeant came over to Mark and Esther who seemed stricken into immobility. "Let us not grieve yet. All may still be well with your son. Captives are often ransomed. Let us hope. Let us pray."

A woman's shrill voice was heard. It was that of one of the newcomers amongst them, a woman who had not borne well her imprisonment for two days 'mongst crying children and nervous women with rations scarce and a constant threat in the air.

"Pray! We got to do more'n pray! We got to prepare ourselves for anything. Anything!" she finished hysterically.

Her husband—Nathaniel Piggott—joined her. "Yayuh. Makes me feel mighty uneasy livin' here in this place, I kin tell you. How do we know we won't all wake up some night murdered in our beds by these Injuns we're tryin' so mighty hard to help? We'd ought to run 'em out of town afore that happens, 'pears to me!"

John turned on him, his great eloquent eyes glowing with indignation. "The Stockbridge Indians are different! They are truly our brothers! Some of them faced death along with our own people at the fort. Never forget that! No! They are our best protection. I am sure of it. And the work of regeneration must go on." He looked from Esther to Mark and back again to Esther. "What say you, Mistress Martin?" he asked gently. "The savages have caused you to suffer. Has your feeling toward our charges changed?"

Esther wet dry lips and summoned speech from a numbed mind in support of the minister and his work. "Regeneration is our best solution," she agreed quietly. "If I had fear of the Indians at this mission—which I have not—I would still say that."

John Sergeant nodded. Mark boomed angrily, "I echo my wife's words! Now have done with roiling up a hurrah's nest in folks' minds! There's real enough trouble without that!" He looked at the doctor who had sunk onto a bench and was eating like a starved man from a plate Abigail had brought him. "When do you reckon it'll be safe enough for us all to go back home? If they had been going to attack, wouldn't they have done so afore this?"

Thomas Williams looked up. "They'll not attack. Not this time. They've retreated to Canada. God knows why! The way here was open. But they've retreated, burning and pillaging as they went. It's my opinion it's safe for all to return home."

The Martins were the first to depart. "I can't thole pity," Esther told Mark in a low voice. "It undoes me. And all tears do is weep away a woman's strength. Let us get back to where we can keep busy with work."

Work. Work and wait—and hope. For how long? Days? Weeks? Months? Matt had been difficult to live with. He had been wrong-headed most of the time. But he had a deep-hid kindness that life might have brought out. And he was the oldest son. It was a bitter burden on the heart to think of him as gone.

It was a week later that Peter appeared at Martin Manor one night when the family was at supper in the big keeping room. No one heard his footsteps. He did not knock. The door stood open to the September night and there he was.

"Peter!" Prue exclaimed, seeing him first. "You gave me a startle. I thought you were at school in Newington."

"I have left. It is not a good school. Mr. Kellogg does not teach us. He makes us work on his farm instead. All the time we work. There are no lessons. None."

"Tarnation!" Mark exclaimed.

Peter nodded. Esther said, "Will you have something to eat, Peter? You are welcome to join us."

He shook his head. "I come to ask a question. But already it is answered. Marie is not here."

"Marie? Why, no. Why should she be?"

"She is not at home." He hesitated, then he went on, his voice dropping a little. "I have heard about Matt. My heart is sick with yours. But I think he will survive and in time return to you."

"Why do you say that, Peter?"

Again he hesitated. "Matt has—understanding of Indians and Indian ways," he answered, after a moment.

This was something Esther had not thought of and it gave her encouragement. Her voice took on a note of added warmth as she said again, "Come in, Peter. Please do. Let me give you a bite of supper."

But he shook his head. "I go to find Marie." And he vanished into the night as silently as he had come.

The days passed. Ephraim returned to Indian Town but he did not come to see Prue. She heard of his brief visit through Mark who had met him in the village.

"He never got to the fort," Mark said. "But he is held blame-
less for its destruction, nevertheless. And he assures us it will be
rebuilt. He has gone now as our representative to the General
Assembly."

He had come and gone, leaving no message for Prue. He had
not, then, seen David Reynolds.

Would she ever know aught of him or of her brother again?

CHAPTER 7

The Redemption

THE TRAIL WENT THROUGH endless woods, up shaggy mountains and over rivers. It led almost due north to Canada. Matt's eyes watched it sharply, noting marks on the trees, remembering campsites, counting the streams they crossed, for he meant to escape and make his way back home. He was so set on this that he paid no attention to the other prisoners. He did not care what happened to them, if they dropped out or died. He cared only about himself.

Now that his hands were no longer bound he could walk more easily. And though he was always hungry and had to drag a heavy sledge behind him by means of a leather strap across his chest that cut into his flesh, he was better off than most. Youth was on his side. And he had not fallen ill with dysentery as had so many others. And he bore no wounds.

He had been lucky there. When the morning stillness had been broken by that sudden hideous screeching outside of the fort and shots had begun to pour into it, he had known a moment of stiff terror. His mouth had gone dry and his heart had nearly burst within him. But he had sprung for his gun just the same and had picked off several of the leaping devils with exultation and rage mounting in him. Then he had heard some one exclaim, "Cracky! There's hundreds of 'em!"

That had cleared his brain. And he had seen it was true. Yelling, howling, waving their tomahawks aloft, they had swarmed forward in countless numbers with as many more Frenchmen visible behind them. What good was it going to do for twenty-two men to try to stand off nearly a thousand? They would only all be killed. He had known they must surrender.

He had retreated then to a corner and leaned his rifle against the wall and stood with his arms hanging loosely—waiting. The air rang with musket fire and the sounds of blows and shouts. Curses and groans filled his ears. He had heard children crying, women sobbing, the bubbling gasp of dying men. He had seen bounding bronzed bodies topped by ferocious painted faces all mixed up with little yellow flashes of fire and sprawling figures and red blood spurting. Then, in less time than it takes to tell it, his waiting ended, for the white flag had gone up. They were still killing in a frenzy, however, and he had picked up his rifle again and held it ready to swing if necessary, his eyes hot and hard.

But when they came to him, he thrust his weapon out suddenly across the bodies of two of the savages, holding them off for a moment while he said, in the Mahican language, "Take it. It is yours. I am yours."

His first battle—and it was a defeat. Yet it was not his fault.

He had become the prisoner of the larger of the two Hurons to whom he had surrendered. He was an ugly-looking fellow, with one eye gone and a wide scar down the side of his face, who had been pleased with his good fortune at first, for he thought he saw in Matt a rich prize. His clothes were good. He was well-fed. He would bring a big ransom.

Then as the days had passed, a doubt had entered the Huron's mind, for Matt knew Indian ways too well. He walked like one, soundlessly, with a free and arrogant swing. His face was as impassive, his black eyes as unafraid. When they camped he was skilled in selecting birch poles, stripping them and setting up a shelter of bark and skins with a layer of hemlock and spruce boughs inside for a bed. He scooped up cornmeal mush, hot or cold, out of a pot with his hands and ate it in an accustomed fashion as did the other Indians. He knew how to load the sledge with its pack of kettles, dirty blankets, stolen shirts and provisions. He had the trick of saving a coal of fire which he carried in his powder horn from camp to camp. And, finally, he could read the Indian signs on the trees and speak the Indian language. He even knew how to make a bow and arrows for it.

Did all this mean he was not the son of a wealthy white man, after all? That he was an orphan, perhaps of mixed blood, whatever he wore given him, and with no one to redeem him who could pay a good price? The Huron watched him closely and decided at last that was it.

Matt sensed the change of attitude in his captor from interest to puzzlement, to resentment, and then to indifference. It was at that point that his hands were freed as he walked and the Huron's watchfulness grew less vigilant. And that was the moment that Matt began to make definite plans for his escape.

For the most part they traveled in single file, the strongest leading the way and the stragglers, the sick and the wounded, sometimes being left more than a day's journey behind. Monsieur Rigaud, who was in command, had a tent which was pitched every night for his cot-bed but he was the only one with such a luxury.

He was seated one day on his bed, a small, neat figure, playing solitaire. They had camped in an open place on the shores of a great lake where the whole party was forced to wait until a storm, which had created mountainous waves, would permit them to embark in their small craft for the last leg of the journey to Quebec. At the moment the rain had ceased but the wind still raged outside his frail shelter.

His mood was one of disgust. This expedition had hardly been worth the effort: only thirty captives. Indeed, not that many, for some had been killed in the attack and others had died along the way. Unfortunately they had had to let a dozen or more men escape the day before, fearing to warn the fort if they fired on them. *Bien!* And how much money would twenty or less captives bring? What he—Rigaud—had hoped was that they might take at least a hundred prisoners. That would have been rewarding.

He smoked morosely, staring at the cards before him. He disliked this warring on the British in America, anyway. It seemed to him a wholly futile endeavor. The country was too vast. You took a place here and lost one there and what good was that? If the French could ever seize and hold the Ohio Valley country, it might be another story. But that was a matter for the future.

Right now the governor in Quebec—more or less of an imbecile, in Rigaud's opinion—could do no more than order frequent attacks on the exposed English outposts, hoping thereby to bring discouragement to the hearts of the colonists and, at the same time, to swell the size of the French purse by demanding high ransom money for the prisoners that were taken. *Le bon Dieu* knew the money was needed badly enough!

Money! There it was. The root of all evil, all anxiety, all despair. He, himself, needed some to pay his men who did not like the paper script issued by the intendent whenever gold arrived late from France—which it always did. They suspected it, and with good reason. As a matter of fact, he could well use some money himself. He had pressing debts to be settled and when he got back to Quebec there was a certain lovely lady. . . .

The squeaky voice of a pallid young lieutenant with a feeble growth of down on his upper lip was heard at his tent flap. "Monsieur Rigaud, there is a woman here desiring to speak with you."

"One of the prisoners?"

"No, sir. She has just arrived."

"A woman? Just arrived? Come in, Lieutenant. Your news intrigues me. What does this woman look like?"

"She is young, sir. A young woman."

"Ah!"

"She is an Indian, sir."

"Oh." The Frenchman's voice held disappointment. He fingered his small mouth a moment meditatively. "What tribe, do you know?"

"I am not sure, sir."

"Well"—indifferently—"send her in. With an interpreter."

"She speaks excellent English, sir."

Rigaud raised an eyebrow. An Indian girl who spoke excellent English had a complicated sound and for a moment he considered refusal of her request to see him. But curiosity got the better of him. Besides, it would be a diversion. He slapped at a mosquito and said again, "Send her in."

He resumed his card playing. At a small rustle by his tent door a moment later he looked up to see before him a slender girl standing beside the lieutenant. Her black blown hair, kept in order by a ribbon, was silky with cleanliness. Her hands were clean as was her fringed deerskin dress. But it was her eyes, dark and beautiful against her golden skin, that held his gaze the longest. Set in the delicate oval of her face, they were large and liquid, shadowed by long curved lashes, and holding in their depths alternating fire and fear—a fascinating combination.

"Well?" he demanded brusquely, sharpening his voice against her appealing loveliness.

A pulse throbbed in the column of her throat before she ventured to reply. But once having started, her words, falling on his ears melodiously, came with a rush.

"Monsieur, first I thank you for your kindness to allow me to come before you. I ask it for this reason. It is among your prisoners a young one by the name of Matthew. Matthew Martin. I beg permission to—"

"Martin," he broke in. "A young lad, you say. Is he of great strength? With black hair and eyes? And a proud solitary manner?"

"Yes! That is he! Is he—is he well, Monsieur?"

"He is well."

He stared at her unblinkingly and she could not tell if he was friendly or unfriendly. He was neither at the moment. He was only sad at the weight of his years which seemed heaped upon him all of a sudden as the picture of Matt rose before his eyes. At last he said, "What do you want of him?"

Her lashes drooped, then swept upward again bravely.

"Monsieur, I love him."

"Well! By *le bon Dieu!* So you love him. And you have come, I suppose, to be with him. To stay in his tent and go with him to Quebec. Another mouth for us to feed. And who will redeem you when he is redeemed?"

She shook her head. "You do not understand. I have not come to stay with him. I have come to pay ransom for him so that he may go back with me to Indian Town where we live."

He leaned against a blanket which he had stuffed behind him and was silent a moment. This was, indeed, diverting: love always was—or almost always.

He said, "And how much are you prepared to pay?"

"How much do you ask, Monsieur?"

A shrewd one, he thought, and replied gruffly, "I never knew before of any Indian having money."

She merely smiled. There was a silence broken by him as he addressed the lieutenant.

"Find the prisoner and bring him here. No! Wait! Find the Huron who holds him. I will speak with him first."

He went on with his card playing. Marie stood, a silent, patient figure in the shadows. How they could wait, these savages, he thought. He wondered when she had eaten last. But they could travel for days on only berries and water. He would not give himself concern about her. Yet this was strange, her having money.

He looked up suddenly. "You must have stolen it."

Her glance did not waver. "One does what one has to do," she told him gravely.

"You love him very much, eh?"

She bent her head in acquiescence.

"Will you not be caught for your theft when you go back?"

Before she could reply the lieutenant returned, followed by the Huron. He was bare save for a breechclout. He did not look at the girl but stood with folded arms saying nothing.

Monsieur Rigaud signaled for the officer and the girl to leave him. "Go out of earshot," he added. Then he turned to the Indian.

"She has come for him. For your prisoner."

The Huron made a growling sound in his throat and shrugged.

"You are willing to let him go?"

"It is good if he goes."

"Why do you say that?"

"There is Indian blood in him."

"You are sure?"

The Huron gestured. "Does not her coming here prove it? He has lived with Indians. And he has lived with whites. No one will pay a fat ransom for one like that." He gestured again. "He is nobody. Nothing."

Monsieur Rigaud was thoughtful. "Perhaps you are right," he agreed. "She said they lived together. Well, then, since you do not care and there is nothing to be gained by holding him—for she has nothing—we will let him go. *Oui?*" He looked up as the other grunted approval. "It is settled, then. At least we will save the food he eats." He laughed. "Will you be kind enough to send the young man in question here to me? And as you go out, if you will tell the lieutenant to come back with the girl I will be obliged."

Confronted again by Marie, with the officer outside the tent this time awaiting Matt's arrival, Rigaud's voice took on a stern note.

"This proceeding is somewhat irregular. However, I am allowed considerable freedom of judgment. Acquaint me now with the amount you have to offer for your Matt'ew."

This was the moment. With a trembling hand Marie reached down into the neck of her gown and drew forth a tiny deerskin parcel that she had concealed in a pocket sewed inside.

"It—it is not exactly money, Monsieur," she murmured. "But it—they—are worth money."

"Ah! Ha! I suspected as much. Well, let us see."

She approached him and laid the packet in his outstretched hand. Unfolding it, he saw glittering before him two exquisite silver buckles mounted with blazing diamonds set in the form of the letter A. Turning them over, he saw a date engraved in the silver, *August 16, 1749.* Some well-born maiden would miss these from her wedding slippers, he thought.

Steps outside caused him to flip the deerskin over the treasure and tuck it beneath the blanket behind him.

"It is enough?" Marie breathed.

"It will suffice," he replied, as softly.

And then the lieutenant and Matt entered. Matt did not at first see Marie who had retreated to the shadows but stood, bold and at ease before the Frenchman.

"You sent for me?"

Rigaud looked up, a small smile playing about his mouth.

"I sent for you—yes. I sent for you to tell you that we no longer desire your company. Is not that very amiable of me? Yes, I think it is." He paused to toss a hand into the air. "Pouf! What I am saying is that there is some one who desires it more."

"What do you mean! What trick is this!"

Behind him Marie spoke. "It is no trick."

He whirled and stared. Then, with a hoarse, incredulous cry, he reached her in a great stride and laid his hands heavily on her shoulders.

"Marie! *You*—here! How—why—?"

"It is a long story, M'sieu Matt'ew, but you have a long time in which to hear it on your journey home."

"Home?" Matt turned to the Frenchman. "You mean I'm—I'm free?"

Rigaud nodded, his eyes bright with amusement, with envy, with satisfaction. "Love is a miracle, is it not?"

Matt's head was swimming. He did not understand. He could not believe. Had his father sent ransom money? Had he secured a letter through Major Ephraim from the Boston government? That must be the way of it for the major had not been at the fort. He had been safe elsewhere. However, this was not the time for asking questions. Rigaud was waving an impatient hand of dismissal and Marie was tugging at his arm and murmuring, "Come. It is arranged."

He said only, "I shall need a gun, Monsieur Rigaud."

Rigaud looked at the lieutenant. "Give him one." He nodded toward a few heaped in a corner. "And powder enough for their journey."

They went out. The lieutenant came to attention again and looked at Monsieur Rigaud, who looked back at him with a cool, level glance.

"She had no money, after all. Only a bauble or two. Trinkets of little value. But you know how the Indians are. Anything that gleams is precious. Besides, there is no one else to redeem him. He is not pure English." He patted a yawn. "Ho! Hum! Love is wonderful, indeed. One could not destroy its beauty with a refusal, could one? As Frenchman to Frenchman, I ask you. I ask you, also, is it not a pleasant role to play for a change—that of cupid, instead of that of murderer? I greatly prefer it myself."

The rascal, the lieutenant thought, he's got something. But what, I'll never know. Saluting, he replied squeakily, "You are correct, M'sieu. You are correct—*absolument.*"

The nearer he came to Indian Town the less Matt wanted to reach it. For the first time in his life he was free—and himself. For the first time he had come to his full stature. He had conquered a hard thing—fear—there at the fort. After that he had endured physical discomforts, fatigue, hunger, humid days and bitter nights, the torment of mosquitoes and the pain of running sores from the strap over his chest. Moreover, throughout the past week he had proved he could sustain himself in the open. But most of all he had discovered the pleasure of being the recipient of a woman's loving care and thought. How could he go back now and dwindle to the size and shape his ma and pa expected of him? It was impossible.

He looked at Marie sitting wrapped in a blanket beside the campfire. She had hid the blanket in the bushes just this side of the lake before she came for him. Hidden there, too, had been a knife and a trap for small animals, a pouch of dried corn and a little pot for cooking. She had thought of everything. She had been courageous and clever. And as she led the way home she had been tender and gay, laughing when he laughed, quiet when he was quiet, deferential to his manhood as no one had ever been, never arguing, never speaking her mind, proud of his prowess and content in his companionship.

Feeling his glance upon her she raised her eyes and answered his thought as if she had been inside his mind and heart. "There is a cave on Rattlesnake Mountain. It is but a half-day's journey from here. It is deep and warm. And there is a spring nearby."

He remembered it well. Peter and she had taken him there years ago. Then he came to sit down beside her, cross-legged, Indian fashion. For awhile they said nothing. She watched him tossing acorns into the flames, his hair thick as a bush around his face, his eyes brooding.

Presently she spoke again, her voice soft. "There are your people. And there are my people."

"Yes."

"They are two different worlds."

"Yes."

"You could live in my world. But I could never live in yours."

He was glad she knew it, too. Their two worlds were irreconcilable. Try to bring them together and there would be only pain.

Suddenly his mind was made up. Long ago he had wanted to dwell in the Indian world but he could not bring it to pass. Now he could. He was free.

"The cave will be a good place," he said.

They sat awhile longer while the darkness grew about them. When the trees had all melted together and become a single blackness, he rose and dragged a great log to the fire that would burn all night and keep the animals away. Then he said, "It is time to sleep. Keep the blanket. I will stay by the fire."

She rose obediently. Nearby was a pile of dried leaves. On this she lay down.

"Good night," he said gently.

"Good night."

He had chosen her way of life and her people rather than his own, she was thinking. It was good.

The days slipped by. Matt hunted and trapped while Marie cooked their simple meals and fashioned warmer clothes for them both out of the skins of animals he had shot or trapped. At night he whittled little wooden dishes and cups by the light of the fire as she sat watching. He made a low table for them to eat from seated on the ground. He drove four stakes into the earth in a corner of the cave and fastened saplings up and down and across it and then laid a thick mattress of sweet-smelling pine and cedar branches on it for a bed for her.

"I will kill a bear," he told her, "and we will have its skin for a rug when it grows really cold."

She nodded. She was happy. And so was he. Nothing drove him. He could sit and watch a woodchuck or a bird or a beaver all day long. He could just listen. Or smell. Or lie in the sun and feel it on him. No one was there to tell him to do anything. All Marie wanted was to serve him. And he knew that he loved her.

But as the woods took on their brilliant autumn coloring and the leaves began to drift down, she sensed a difference in him. He was possessed by a restlessness. He would leave her and be absent for long hours, and when he came back he went into his own thoughts so that she must take refuge in hers. And his was a strange land to her while hers was a wild country to him. She got the notion of trouble in her head. Once she followed him and saw him standing at a place halfway down the mountain where, through the woods, he could glimpse a bit of Martin Manor. He could see down there the pumpkin-colored barn and a corner of his father's hayfield. She watched him staring at it for a long while and at last she crept back without his knowing she had been there. That night she said, "You want your people."

"No," he replied.

"Yes, I can feel it."

It was that night that Matt knew they would never be sadder —or more happy—again.

And then one day, early in November, Peter came.

It was a cold day of bright, fitful sunshine with a high wind chasing great gray and white clouds across a sapphire sky. When the clouds were lowest they opened and spilled tiny particles of snow into the air that danced in the sunlight like sparks of fire.

"It is magic!" Marie cried, laughing and clapping her hands like a child.

But Matt did not laugh. He was staring at Peter striding toward them over the rustling leaves.

Peter looked at his sister. Then he looked at Matt. "There is news," he said.

He sat down with them before the cave opening and held his hands to the little blaze to warm them. For awhile he did not speak. Matt's eyes were hot and eager on his friend's face. What news had he? Was it of his family? Or of more Indian attacks? Or—his heart jumped—had some one other than Peter made the discovery of their life here?

"Konkapot has gone to the happy hunting grounds," Peter said at last.

"Oh!" The exclamation came from Marie. Matt said, "That is sad."

Peter nodded. "Without him, Umpachenee stumbles. There is no leader for us any longer. We have seventeen fine English houses in the settlement. We have cows. We have plowed fields. We have many baptized into the Christian faith. But we no longer have a strong leader."

"You still have Mr. Sergeant."

"Mr. Sergeant is good and does all that he can. But Mr. Williams is powerful. He can twist matters so that Mr. Sergeant is often helpless. Mr. Sergeant is not able to keep white families from coming and settling on our land."

Matt and Marie both knew this was not what Peter had come to tell them, but they did not say so. They waited.

Presently Peter continued. "There is to be a grist mill at the eastern end of the town by the running brook there. Mr. Williams is having it put up. There is to be a store some time soon as well. Mr. Williams will have this built also."

Neither was this explaining the purpose of his visit, Matt thought, and waited again.

"Mr. Sergeant has begun to erect his new school. It will have three fireplaces and a cellar and many Indian boys from outside will come to it. It will be finished next year."

"That is fine." Then Matt leaned forward, unable to contain his impatience longer. "We know nothing. We left the prisoners on the shores of the great lake."

Peter nodded. "I followed Marie's trail to there. Then I found you had returned together here."

"Does any one else know?" Matt asked quickly.

"It was not my concern to tell," Peter replied. "However, our father, who is growing old and feeble, was anxious about his daughter. Him I told." He looked at Marie. "He is glad you are safe and well. He wishes you would return to his house."

Marie's glance sought Matt's but he did not meet it. There was another silence before Peter went on.

"A letter has gone from the government in Boston to the government in Quebec asking the price of redemption for the prisoners from Fort Massachusetts. A list of the names of the prisoners was sent in the letter. Major Williams saw to this." He paused a moment and now he looked at Matt. "The reply that has come back states that one Matthew Martin is not to be found among the prisoners who have arrived. Monsieur Rigaud has reported that he escaped."

So now they are waiting and watching for me to appear, Matt thought.

"A decision must be made," Peter finished.

Matt got up and walked away among the trees. There was a great heaviness in his heart and a great turmoil in his mind. He remembered the day it had started. He had been watching the squirrels as they busily gathered nuts for the winter and, recalling that bitter year when he had been small and their scant provisions in the cabin had so nearly run out, he had said to Marie that she must store up a supply, too. She must gather nuts and berries, he had told her. And she must hang up meat to dry so that they might not starve when the snows came.

She had laughed. "Starve? But you can always shoot."

"My powder is nearly gone," he had told her sharply.

She had looked startled, more at his tone than at his words. "Then you can shoot with your bow and arrow, or set a trap. I do not fear! But I will be a squirrel and gather nuts if you wish."

He had known then quite suddenly that the Indian way of life would not satisfy him, after all. It was too planless, too casual, with too much left to chance. The Indians never knew or cared where the next meal was to come from. They simply trusted that a lucky shot would bring something to the pot when needed. They wanted nothing. They hoped for nothing. If their future was like their present it was good enough.

He had walked halfway down the mountain that day until he could glimpse Martin Manor. He had seen the bare brown fields from which he knew his father and Andy had dug up the summer crops—potatoes, carrots, turnips. He could imagine the barrels in the cellar where these had been providently sanded down for good keeping. He remembered his mother's pantry that would now be stored with various kinds of glowing jars of fruits and vegetables. He thought of all the neat, careful ordering of their lives down there, all the thrift, all the looking ahead, and abruptly he had asked himself what he was doing up here on the mountain? What of his old desire to make his way in the world? To get money for himself and become some one whose word would be heeded? The white man's heritage of ambition was in his blood and there was no escaping it. He still loved Marie, of course. But to live as her people lived was not, when he faced it honestly, to be free. It was to be shackled to purposelessness.

He walked blindly now, all the hate of his family that had sustained him hitherto in his self-imposed exile, melting within him. He walked kicking at the leaves, his great hands clenching and unclenching. He thought of Marie's devotion and watchful care and he told himself he could not leave her. She must come home with him, after all. She must conform to her man's ways as woman always had. Surely his mother would help her. They would be married. Mr. Sergeant could not refuse them even though it was not customary.

He turned and went swiftly back to where the two were waiting for him. "A decision is made," he told them.

Peter nodded. Then, speaking slowly and with care, he said, "Before you tell it, there is still another matter. A slave boy has run away from Mrs. Williams' house. They think it must be he who cut the diamond buckles from the wedding slippers belonging to Mrs. Sergeant. She did not notice these were gone for some time. She had wrapped the slippers in a cloth with some silver she was taking to The Castle for safe-keeping at the time of the terror. First she took the children, leaving the silver in her empty house. Then she came back for that. But in all the haste and confusion she did not unwrap the bundle until weeks later, long after the danger was past."

He stopped. Matt looked at him, wondering what this had to do with him. Peter went on then, his eyes downcast. "At first suspicion centered on some one else. On some one who disappeared before the slave boy did. On some one who was seen entering and leaving Mrs. Sergeant's house that day: on—my sister, Marie."

Matt whirled toward her incredulously. "You? No! You didn't!"

But she lifted her great eyes to his face and in them he saw an admission of guilt without shame.

"You took the buckles?"

She nodded. "For you. There was nothing else to do. Mr. Sergeant was not there. I had meant to ask him for money. But he was not there. And there was no time to be lost. The other silver was too heavy," she finished simply.

Matt was staring at her as if she were a stranger and her hand went suddenly to her throat while a little sound came from it like that of a small animal hurt.

"It makes a difference?" she asked. Then she rose and moved toward him and stood looking up at him, speaking with quiet dignity. "Listen. You were gone. No one knew where or if you were alive or dead. I had to find out. There was no one else. Peter was not there. He was at the school in Newington. Mr. Sergeant was not there. My father was too old for such a journey. And—this I ask! Could your father have followed you as I did into enemy country through the wilderness? You know he could not! He would have been shot. But I—an Indian girl—was safe." She threw back her head and her eyes blazed suddenly. "Strike me! Kill me! But never try to make me say I am sorry I did this thing! Or that I was wrong! For I cannot!"

"You gave them to Monsieur Rigaud?"

"Yes."

"Why didn't you tell me!"

"You did not ask."

It was true. He had assumed that his first bewildered thought had been correct, that she had come bearing letters from people of influence and that there had been a promise to pay if she had not actually had the money. In the happiness of his sudden release and the days after that, he had never inquired.

"And now," Peter was saying, "if you return—together—much must be explained."

Suddenly Matt saw it in the right perspective. "But it will be forgiven! My father will repay! It is nothing, after all. It was not for herself that she took them. It was for a good purpose. For me. No one will ever—"

Peter was shaking his head. "It was a bad deed even if it was for a good purpose. Always that will be remembered. Whatever the reason, Marie stole Mrs. Sergeant's diamond buckles. Our father, who is old and wise, can understand and forgive. So will others because you, Matt, are safe. But every one will not do so. For one thing, how can any one be sure she has not kept them and has them still—these buckles? It is said that you escaped, not that you were ransomed."

Matt frowned. Now why had Rigaud said that? Oh, to be sure! So that he might keep the buckles himself. His head began to whirl. He did not know what to do or think.

Peter went on: "At first, perhaps, people will believe it if you say you were ransomed. But not forever. A finger will point. A voice will say, 'We do not know that for a fact. The report has it that Matt escaped. He, himself, did not see her give the buckles to the Frenchman.' And if ever aught else is lost from the settlement it will be that way. Therefore, our father thinks it will be better for my sister to come back with me now. He will tell that she has been away on a visit to another tribe and I have fetched her back. Matthew can then return by himself as it is expected he will."

He stopped. Matt stood silent. Marie waited for him to speak. Nothing was said and at last Peter spoke again. "It is the only path of true happiness, our father says. He says this is so not only because of the buckles but because you have been together and there is no remedy for that."

Matt turned slowly to Marie and saw a little pulse hammering in her throat. "Peter! Leave us!" he exclaimed harshly.

Peter went away. When he was out of sight, Matt stretched out his hand and laid it against the little leaping pulse to quiet it. But it still jumped. Marie did not stir. Matt's hand dropped.

"It is—to protect you," he said at length, heavily. "And not only you. Do you not see? After all Mr. Sergeant's work with your people—with your father a Christian now and a member of the church— Don't you see how it would hurt—too many?"

There was more to it than this lame talking. He knew it and she knew it. It was as Peter had told them. They had been together and there was no remedy for that. Yet she said nothing. She simply stood there and went quickly away from him inside herself. She was lost from him forever this time and they both knew it. After an interminable moment, she nodded.

"This way only you and I are hurt."

"Yes. Only you and I."

"That is your wish."

"Marie! You said yourself we are two people! Two worlds!"

"It is true." She stepped back, reached for her blanket and wrapped it about her with a dignified gesture of finality. "I will follow Peter. I will go home to my father as he wishes and as you wish."

He put out a hand, but she would not see it and he let it slowly fall. He wanted her to wait. He wanted to try and tell her how happy he had been with her, to thank her and reassure her—if that were possible. But it was not possible. There were no words for such feelings. Anyway, she was gone, without ever looking back, and in sadness and loneliness he watched her go.

He could live in either of their worlds, he was thinking. But because he could and because he had, he could live in neither. In both he was there, yet not there. What was the answer for him? He had not found it yet.

He glanced about. Then he kicked at the fire and put it out. After that he went into the cave and ripped up the table he had made, threw away the cups and dishes he had whittled, destroyed every vestige of their life together.

At last he started slowly down the mountain toward Martin Manor, his heart both sick with misery and buoyant with relief.

CHAPTER 8

The Lord's Will

WINTER CAME BRINGING SNOW that dimmed the horizon, blotted out the hills and darkened a persistent sun. Then the winds roared out of the north. They swooped across Mark Martin's exposed hilltop, shrieked down his chimneys and went wailing off high in the tall tree tops. Daily the cold pinched the nostrils and cut like a knife blade into the lungs. Daily the snow mounted higher on either side of the tunnel dug to the barn and the woodshed. And daily Prue's heart sank lower in her breast.

For though Matt was home, David Reynolds had not appeared. And where could Prue look now? Not even the thought of Ephraim Williams was any comfort to her, for he was never there.

"I will forget everything," she resolved. Yet she could not forget. It was only the pressure of untoward events with the coming of spring that pushed her own sadness into the back recesses of her mind.

It had been a hard winter for all. The French and Indians had continued their depredations against isolated outposts. News reached the settlement that an American corps had received a decisive defeat at Fort Clinton. De Lery captured Fort Bridgman. Saratoga fell and its people were massacred. As a result of all this the inhabitants from Albany to Boston began to flee to the interior for safety.

What was to be the end? The little mission with its scattering of English homes encircled by a thin fringe of wigwams waited and wondered. But it remained untouched. John Sergeant moved steadfastly about his work, unhurried and unalarmed. Dark figures, huddled in their winter clothes, safely trod the cleared trail from east to west to the meetinghouse. In the north the woods loomed silent and menacing—but empty. And finally the winter passed.

With the coming of spring the minister's dream school was completed. The Mohawks appeared to look it over and grunted their approval. Yes, they would send their sons here to be educated. Some Delawares would come, too. And a few of the Oneidas. To this end, John invited Mr. Kellogg from Newington to settle amongst them and assume charge of the visiting boys. He had never learned—or never believed—that the man had not treated the boys as he should have when they had been with him in Connecticut. Besides, Colonel Williams approved the choice and was backing him. It did not occur to the minister that this very backing might be suspect. He was simply relieved that, for once, he and Abigail's father were agreed. Timothy Woodbridge, of course, was still to teach the local Stockbridge lads and Abigail was to take care of the girls.

It had a fine progressive sound. But it was not all either fine or progressive. For the Indians had lost some of their first enthusiasm for tidiness and morality. With Konkapot dead and Umpachenee falling into slothful habits, there were many cases of transgressions on the part of others of the tribe. John, never losing faith, slaved and prayed over the sinners, exhorting them to better behavior, but Ephraim Williams, remote in his Castle, watched with a secret triumph the gradual deterioration and continued making his own private plans. It was as John had said to Mark long ago: the Lord and the devil, in the shape of the minister and the leading citizen, were fighting for control here.

Prue was thinking of these things one day on her way home from calling on Mrs. Woodbridge. It was late of an afternoon in early May. The willows were out down by the brook, their long pale yellow streamers waving gently in the light breeze. Wild columbine happily swung their tiny garnet bells above the crevices in the rocks to which they clung. There was a buzz of bees in the air all day long while with the creeping dusk thousands of tiny unseen frogs sent out their wild discordant song that seemed to come from everywhere at once—earth, air and water. It was a harsh and strident sound, and the din of it made Prue's ears ring. But it was the poignant loneliness it evoked that caused her to hurry her footsteps toward the surrounding warmth of home and family, since for her it held no paean promise of nature's fulfillment.

She came into a strangely silent house. Her father and Matt and Andy were, of course, still out in the fields making the most of the last bit of daylight. No doubt Luke, reliable at thirteen, was doing the milking, with Mary and Johnny as helpful assistants. But why was Esther not heard moving about in the keeping room, singing as she prepared their supper?

"Ma!"

There was no answer. More sharply Prue called again. This time a weak voice whispered a reply. Frightened, Prue pushed through the half-closed door from the hall and saw her mother prostrate on the day bed near the fireplace, one hand feebly clutching her heart, her blue calico work frock and mob cap awry as if she had fallen suddenly.

Prue flew to her side.

"Ma! What's happened? What's wrong?"

"The Lord—giveth—and the Lord—taketh away—"

"No, Ma! *No!*"

"Blow—the horn—"

Once again the raucous summons. Once again the men of the family pelting up from the fields. Once again terror. Once again a race to The Castle. But for a different reason this time. For Dr. Thomas and the minister.

They were too late. Before they arrived Esther's eyes had closed and her hands lay folded quietly on her breast. How old she looked, Prue thought. How old—and tired. You never noticed that when she'd been alive. You never noticed, either, how firm a hold she had on everything because she'd been so gentle. No one could take her place. No one. Yet some one had to try.

Prue. It was for Prue now to manage the big family. It was
for Prue to run the busy household.

Matt took their loss hard . . . as hard as anyone, Prue told
herself, even Pa. Pa seemed to lock his grief away where 'twould
hurt no one but him. But Matt—

Or was something else troubling him, too? She could not be
sure. Anyway, he was difficult again, his dark face brooding and
fierce, his temper short. It was as if his body caged a wild beast.
He'd been so, in fits and starts, ever since his return, but lately
there was no peace in him at all.

One day, a week or two after Esther's death, when he came
in from the barn where he'd been preparing with hackles and
swingling knives the flax that had been stored there, she faced
him with quiet determination. Best let the wild beast out, she
had decided, and grapple with it in the open.

"Matt, is something plaguing you?"

He stood before her, his face begrimed, his clothes covered with
the fibers and dirt of the flax. He had swingled nigh onto forty
pounds that day and he was weary. But a bond of unspoken
sympathy existed between him and his sister and he found it
hard to be curt with her. For a moment he seemed about to
speak. Then he shrugged and turned away.

Prue followed him and laid a gentle hand on his arm. "Tell
me."

"Oh, all this talk!" he burst out.

"Talk?"

"Ephraim was back for a night. He told of disputes in Boston."

"What disputes?"

"Now that we have two legislative houses, the one for the
Crown and the other for the Colonists, there's ever quarreling."

She was puzzled. "You mean over New Hampshire? But it's
no concern of yours if Massachusetts has lost jurisdiction over
that territory. What matters it to you?"

" 'Tis not that so much."

"What then?"

His eyes narrowed to a black glimmer. "You've heard of our triangular trade?"

"I've heard of it but I haven't foxed out its meaning yet."

"Why! England has ruled we shall sell to none but her! And what have we to offer save agricultural products and fish, neither of which she wants? We *live* by our commerce! Such a ruling strangles us!"

"So—?"

He tossed back his head, all his fiery rebellious spirit flaming clear on his face. "So we trade, in spite of the law, with the Indies and Africa! To them we send what we have and what they need, and from them we get what we want and can use! Sugar! Rum! Slaves!"

"But—it's all illegal."

He nodded.

"You would join them," she said slowly. "You would still go to sea. That's it, isn't it?"

"It was always my wish," he said sullenly.

"I know."

"Andy's grown now. And Luke is getting big. Pa has not so much need of me."

"But he'll not like the thought of you joining smugglers, Matt! Going against the law!"

"Is England to rule us forever?" he exclaimed sharply.

She stared at him in horror. "Matt!" she whispered. "Why, that's—that's treasonous!"

"Then there's more than one traitor in America."

He stood there, stubborn and defiant. She shook her head.

"Let me think on this."

"Think all you want. But I've about settled my mind."

She looked at him and saw it was so, then said, "Pa's broke up enough. I want no words."

"There'll be none."

He swung from her and went out.

Two nights later Peter appeared. Seeing him, Prue thought suddenly how long a time it had been since he had come there. Not once all winter. Nor Marie, either. In the absorption of their own affairs, they had neglected these good friends. She spoke cordially. "Peter! You are a stranger. Come in."

"I seek Matthew."

"Matt is out in the barn. But don't be in a hurry. Tell me, how is your father? How is Marie?"

"My father grows feeble."

"Yes. I know. I have heard he is troubled by an unknown ailment. Remember me kindly to him. He is a good man, Peter. We've never forgotten what he did for us the day of the raising."

Peter's black inscrutable glance met hers in silence for a moment. Then he said, "My father loves all children." He paused. "I will find Matthew now."

"Tell Marie to come up and see me," Prue called after him. "I have some clothes for her."

A few moments later she saw Matt and Peter emerge from the barn together. They stood talking in the May sunlight. She could see Peter's face, grave and urgent. But Matt was turned from her. Presently he gave a start, turned sharply to Peter and said something. Then they went off down the road—running.

It was late when Matt returned. Every one had gone to bed and only Prue, wakeful and worried because he was not in, heard him open the ell door and go up the narrow creaking stairway to his old room there. For awhile longer she lay thinking of him, recalling her mother's last words about him.

"Be patient—with Matt. He's all—awry. I know not what—"

Prue had reassured her. She loved Matt, too. And she knew, from her own hunger, that what he needed was a woman. Had he found one on his journey home from his capture? It seemed unlikely. It was wilderness he had traversed. Yet what had kept him so long? Two months and more had he been gone. He had said he had sores and waited in the cave on Rattlesnake Mountain for them to heal, and he had showed the marks on his chest to prove it. But it was more than that. Doubtless, though, Esther had been right. He'd enjoyed his solitary living, for during it he'd proved himself as good as an Indian and all of a man.

Well, she could be patient as Ma had asked, Prue decided, and, turning on her side, she fell asleep. So soundly she slept that she never heard the creak of the stairs again a little later. She never knew till morning that Matt was gone.

"Where?" Mark demanded furiously when Prue told him. "Where away this time?"

"To sea," Prue answered as gently as she could. "Where he's always hankered to go."

"You sure?"

"He spoke of doing so just a while back."

Mark went to the door and stood gazing out at the hills. Long ago he had put the sea from him and had found contentment here on this wind-swept plateau. He had found a companionship with earth and growing things that had fully satisfied him. The sea had meant battle and destruction: destruction of the life of men as well as of sea monsters; destruction, sometimes, of fine ships, too. The fields meant battle with the same ungovernable elements that challenged a man's skill and knowledge, but in the end there was creation.

He said at last, "Let him go. He'll learn a few things."

He went out, moving heavily as he had done since Esther's death. Prue looked at the circle of faces left around the table. Andy was peering with near-sighted anxiety at his older sister, his thin frame hunched above his plate. Luke's fair open countenance was calm as he leaned stolidly against the back of his chair and finished his bread and butter. Mary's round brown eyes held a bright interest and a lively anticipation of what might happen next, while little John, the baby of the family, who was tempered so fine that every least disturbance was a desperate crisis to him, sat in a tense and quiet waiting. The close safe walls around his life had already fallen once with his mother's going. Were they falling again today because of Matt?

Andy said, "More work for me now, I suppose."

Prue nodded. "But you shall go to college just the same, Andy, come fall."

"You sure?" he asked worriedly.

"I promised Ma."

Mary spoke eagerly. "I can do everything he can do. Just as good! Mebbe better."

"You can help me in the house, Mary. It isn't fitting you should work in the fields."

"I'd sooner!" Mary's tone held impatience.

"I know. You'd sooner be a boy than a girl. But the Lord made you a girl and so a girl you'll have to be." Prue smiled down at the pixy face of her little sister. What the child had said was true enough, though. Her small wiry frame, only half the size of her twin brother's, was tough, her motions quick and sure. She'd be better than the awkward, slow-moving Andy when you came right down to it. And she loved the out-of-doors. It was so much more adventuresome.

Luke spoke, his words holding some scorn for Mary. "*I* can help Pa. Nobody else needs to! I'm near as good as a man right now. He said so."

Prue nodded. "Yes, he did. You're big, Luke. And strong. And willing. You're a great comfort to him."

Johnny's high voice broke in. "Don't quarrel! Oh, don't *quarrel!*"

Prue went to him quickly and laid a hand on his head. "Why, Johnny, we're not. This isn't a quarrel. We're just settling things. A Portuguese parliament, Pa calls it."

"You *sounded* like quarreling."

She laughed and ruffled his hair. He must grow out of his tender sensitiveness, she was thinking. Doubtless life would take care of that. But when it had, what would he be like? She loved him as he was. His responsiveness to beauty touched an answering chord in her and his companionship, as he followed her about her tasks, was a joy.

"We are sorry to have Matt go," she told him. "We'll miss him. But some day he'll come back. Until he does, though, we'll all have to do what we can to take his place. That's what we were saying, Johnny."

He sighed with relief. "All right, then. Can we play the word game now?"

"Yes. We'll play the word game whilst I wash the dishes."

The word game with Johnny took the place of the musical

rhyming Prue had never had time to get right. But some day *he* might, she thought to herself.

The whir of the spinning wheel and the snapping of the clock reel prevented Prue's hearing the knock on the door. This was work for evening hours but the baking was done, enough soap was made for the next month, there were candles a-plenty and the linen was already spread to bleach on the grass in the sun. She could weed in her garden—that ever needed doing—but the flax was ready now and she'd best get it out of the way before she had to go to work carding wool for a new suit for Andy to take to college with him in the fall.

It was Johnny who looked up at the second rap and saw the slave boy in the open doorway to the kitchen.

"Here's some one from the Williamses' place, Prue."

Prue stopped her work and rose.

The little black boy touched a finger to his kinky hair, rolled his eyes and stuttered out his message. "Marse Sergeant say p-please c-come."

"Come where? Is some one sick? Mistress Sergeant?"

"No'm. Mist'ess Sergean' not sick. Injun sick. Please c-come."

"Oh." An Indian sick was bad, because it might mean a plague of some kind. "What Indian, Tobias?"

The black eyes rolled wildly. "He s-say you k-know. He s-say you good f-frien' dis Injun. He say name b-but ah disremembah."

Marie? Peter? Aaron? Prue knew them best. It must be Aaron. Peter had said only last week he was getting weaker all the time.

"Aaron? Was the name Aaron?" she asked.

A wide grin of relief spread over the slave boy's face. "Dass it."

"I'll come right away."

"Mist'ess Sergean' say Johnny kin stop wiv 'Rastus."

"Yes."

She turned back into the room. Johnny was already standing waiting. They would have to walk because Mark had the two horses. He was letting Luke harrow his first field today while he himself plowed another. Andy was picking up brush and loading the ox cart in the apple orchard. She would speak to one of them as she passed and tell where she was going.

The three of them set off down the road. It was a lovely summer day in early June and Prue's heart lifted as she walked. Now was the time when the wild roses bloomed, when strawberries lay like tiny rubies in the grass, when the combined warmth of the sun and moisture of the earth drew forth the peculiar fragrance of fertility hidden through the winter in the brown earth. Prue lifted her head and sniffed the air joyfully, her eyes on the clear hills. From somewhere came the ringing sound of an ax and the swish of a crosscut saw.

It was good to be alive, she thought. Was Matt alive? He had been gone ten days now. Had he got aboard a ship all right? Or had he been caught in that rioting against the British in Boston —a runner had brought the news—and been impressed into service on one of their ships? The question took the edge off her pleasure and she drew a faint sigh. It would be months before she could be certain of his whereabouts.

They passed Mark and she called out her errand. They passed the rocky strip and, as always, Prue's glance went to the high place that overlooked the little pool. It was despoiled now, half filled with great hunks of stone that had fallen in when Pa had quarried out blocks for the foundation of their house and barn. Despoiled like the fragrant turf surrounding it that was dug up and overlaid with chips and fragments. Despoiled like her own romance.

But she would not think of that.

They came to The Castle. Just beyond it was Abigail's beautifully proportioned little house, a tribute within and without to her good taste and intelligence. It had lost its stark newness by this time and the weather had given it a soft silky look. The carven door stood open and there was Abigail with her baby, John, in her arms and five-year-old Erastus clinging to her skirts. She waved and Prue waved back.

"Tobias will take you the rest of the way," she said to Johnny. "I'll get you when I come back."

Alone she went on down the hill at a faster rate. She passed

the Joneses' place and reached the little village. It looked peaceful and quiet beneath its great spreading trees. The English
homes—several more now than when she had first arrived—were
exceedingly neat, their fences trim and tidy. There were two or
three cows wandering back and forth across the trail that cut the
settlement from east to west. A pig was loose and a little Indian
boy was chasing it. Laughter came through one open doorway,
singing through another. John Sergeant must be proud of what
he had wrought here, she thought.

But which was Aaron's house? She was not sure. She paused
to inquire of an Indian who was sitting beneath an elm and discovered he was in a drunken stupor so she went on and asked
the little boy who was chasing the pig. He spoke perfect English
and gave her clear directions. She thanked him and continued
on her way.

A few moments later she stood before the closed door of a one-
room cabin. And now a vague uneasiness seized her. The house
was surrounded by Indians seated on the ground. They were
wailing together in a soft minor key, bending their bodies and
beating their breasts as they wailed. They paid no attention to
her and her knock could not be heard above their mournful
chant, so she opened the door and went in.

Fetid air with the smell of death in it struck her forcibly as
she entered. For a moment she recoiled. Then she heard the
minister's voice and she moved toward the shadowy corner where
he was. Peter stood aside as she drew near and gave her room.
But the flow of John Sergeant's reading from the Bible continued
without interruption.

Prue looked down. A figure wasted to skin and bones lay on
a thin pallet of straw on the floor below her. Save for the scars
on his face she would never have known it was Aaron, but these
stood out white against the brown parchment of his skin that
was drawn taut over his high cheekbones. Elsewhere it fell in
deep wrinkles and folds. His eyes were closed, his toothless
sunken mouth half open and through this, coming in short fluttering gasps that blew his puckered lips in and out, she could
hear his labored breathing.

The rich deep music of John's voice broke through her shock and pity:

"I am the door. . . . I am the good shepherd and know my sheep and am known of mine . . . And other sheep I have which are not of this fold. Them also I must bring and they shall hear my voice. And there shall be one fold and one Shepherd."

There was a silence. The leaves of the Bible in John Sergeant's hand turned with a slight rustle. Prue looked around for Marie but did not see her. Before she could wonder, John was reading again.

"Who shall separate us from the love of Christ? Shall tribulation or distress or persecution or famine or nakedness or peril or sword? . . . . For I am persuaded that neither death nor life nor angels nor principals nor powers nor things present nor things to come nor height nor depth nor any other creature shall be able to separate us from the love of God which is Christ Jesus our Lord."

For a moment the labored breathing seemed to stop. Then it went on again and with its coming came also faint whispered words.

"She—is come."

John put down his Bible. "Yes, Aaron, she is come. Shall I speak?"

"Speak."

The minister rose from his knees beside the pallet. Accustomed to the dimness now, Prue could see his face. How serious it was. How tired and how inexpressibly sad. She looked into his dark eyes, ordinarily filled with the flash of a brave and bright spirit, and saw them, instead, suffused with tears.

"Prudence, I have grievous news. Your friend, Marie, was called to her Heavenly Father a number of days ago." At her low, surprised exclamation of sorrow, he raised his hand. "Wait. There is much to tell and little time in which to tell it." His glance went to the dying man and then came back to Prue. "Marie died in childbirth. She has left a son. There is now in this house no woman to rear this son. It was Marie's wish that he

be raised to Christian ways in a Christian household. Therefore—"

There was a stir on the pallet. Prue looked down and saw
Aaron's eyes wide open. They stared up at her, holding her transfixed by their fierce, burning, silent demand. Suddenly, with a
superhuman effort, he lifted himself to one elbow and began to
speak. He spoke in his own tongue, pausing every moment or so
for John to translate for him.

"He says for you to recall the day of the raising of your first
cabin roof. . . . He says it is his desire to remind you, without
pride on his part, of how the tree fell that day and he ran forward and threw himself upon your sister and shielded her body
with his own lest she be hurt."

"I remember."

"He says it is a happy memory to him the way your mother
spoke to him when he bore her child back to her . . . 'From now
I am your friend.' Those were her words, he says. And she put
her hand in his to seal the promise."

"I remember that, too."

"He says he told her that Indians and whites all love papoose
the same. That is why he did what he did. And she smiled upon
him and thought, with him, that it was so and it was good."

"Yes."

"He says that these words he speaks now he could more properly address to your mother. But she has been called to the Great
Father and you have taken her place. Therefore he speaks to
you."

Aaron fell back in sudden exhaustion and for a moment there
was silence save for his panting breath. Then, lying still with his
eyes closed, he began again to push the words out slowly and with
great difficulty.

Carefully John translated. "He says an Indian never forgets a
kindness. He says it is his belief that your mother, likewise,
would not now forget her gratitude to him if she were here.
What he asks, he says, is that you take Marie's son into your home
and bring him up as your own. It is his dying request, as it was
Marie's."

Prue looked at the face on the bed below her. Even in its terrible emaciation it held a look of pride. He murmured something more and John bent to catch what it was.

"He says only in this way can matters be evened between your two families."

Prue did not have to think. Aaron was right. Her mother would do this. She turned to Peter. "Where is the baby?" she asked quietly.

"A neighbor has him. I will bring him."

Peter slipped away. Aaron's face slowly took on the color of wet ashes and John opened his Bible again.

"I am reading from the fifteenth chapter of Corinthians, Aaron. 'For since by man came death, by man came also the resurrection of the dead . . . That which thou sowest is not quickened except it die. And that which thou sowest, thou sowest not that body which shall be, but bare grain, it may chance of wheat or of some other grain. But God giveth it a body as it hath pleased Him and to every seed his own body . . . So also is the resurrection of the dead . . . It is sown a natural body but it is raised a spiritual body . . . The first man is of the earth, earthy. The second man is of the Lord from Heaven . . . For this . . . mortal must put on immortality. So when this . . . mortal shall have put on immortality, then shall be brought to pass the saying that is written—Death is swallowed up in victory.' "

The door opened and closed and Peter was by her side. Prue turned and held out her arms. Then, looking down into that tiny white face in which enormous black eyes stared angrily up at her, she thought she saw a faint resemblance to some one she knew. For a moment she could not think who it was, until—suddenly—she remembered Matt's long delay in returning home the previous fall—his story of living alone in a cave. And Marie? Where had Marie been? She looked into John Sergeant's face and saw there her confirmation. This was Matt's baby. There was no mistaking it. The truth lay in those small features as well as on the faces of the other three around her.

Ice and fire flooded her heart. Matt's baby! Marie's baby, too. Oh, what did it matter? It was a baby that was inexorably bound to her by blood ties. It was a baby that was helpless and alone in the world since its mother had died and its father had run off without acknowledging it. It was a baby that would be raised in filth and poverty and ignorance unless she saved it. It was a baby sent to her by the Lord's will.

Only in this way can matters be evened between our two families.

She raised her head. Shame and pity and sorrow sounded in her low voice but it was her own thwarted mother instinct that spoke above them all.

"I will take the baby. I will love him as my own. And I will name him—Aaron."

CHAPTER 9

The Captain's Daughter

IT WAS DARK THAT SAME NIGHT when there came a knock on the front door of Martin Manor. The twins and Johnny were long since in bed and asleep as Prudence had planned they should be. She and Andy and her father were all in the keeping room. Andy was reading by the light of a candle. Mark had taken off his heavy boots and was sitting in his socks smoking his pipe and staring silently at the flames leaping in the fireplace, for though it was June the night was chilly. Prue was mending. At the sound of the knock Mark reared up his head.

"Who in tarnation's that this hour of the night?"

"I think it's Peter. He always makes the sound of an owl before he comes near so as not to fright us. I marked it just now. It must be he."

Prudence rose and went swiftly into the hall. Mark heard her shoot back the heavy iron bar and open the door, heard her say, "Thank you, Peter," heard the door close and the bar fall into place again. Whatever had Peter brought that could not wait till morning, Mark wondered? And why hadn't he come in for a visit as he usually did? And, finally, why had he knocked at the front this time when always before he had gone to the kitchen? Not that Mark minded. It was a little thing and he had never held with Abigail's fussiness on such matters. It was simply strange. Thinking these things, he looked up curiously as Prue re-entered and saw her with a small blanketed bundle in her arms. There

160

was no mistaking what it was by the way she held it. Yet he stared, puzzled and incredulous.

"What on earth you got there?"

"Matt's baby boy, Pa."

"Matt's—!" Mark leaped to his feet as if the words had been electric. His pipe clattered to the floor, and he faced Prue, amazement and outrage struggling together on his countenance. Andy sat staring owlishly at them both, held to quiet by his own astonishment as well as by his realization that whatever this meant lay chiefly between the two people before him.

"Matt's—and Marie's," Prue was saying.

For an instant there was a dead silence. Then Mark let out a great oath, the first Prue had ever heard pass his lips, and strode toward her. A chair stood in his way and he threw it aside sending it crashing against the wall. But for all his violent approach, Prue never stirred save for a slight protective tightening of her arms about the baby.

"How do you know that!" he demanded, in his most terrifying captain's voice, as he towered over her, his eyes afire. Matt's son, he was thinking. *That's* why Peter came to the front door.

"Peter told me. They lived together in the cave atop Rattlesnake Mountain. He found them there. 'Twas the reason Matt was so long in coming home."

Andy could see the chords of Mark's neck swell with his fury. He watched his good hand clench and unclench by his side. He heard his deep hard breathing and thought Prue must be shaking in her shoes. But she stood calm and cool as you please.

When Mark finally spoke his voice was choked and rasping. "What in tarnal's the brat doing *here?*"

"He's here because Marie died giving birth to him, because Aaron died this afternoon, because Peter is going away from here with one or two other Indians where there are not any whites who will take away their land and hurt their people. There's no one else to care for Matt's boy but us, Pa."

Astonishment at her daring overtopped Mark's anger for a moment.

"Why, you—you—! What the devil are you sayin'! You mean—"

Prue's blue eyes met her father's steadily. "I mean he's to live here with his own kin. That's what I mean."

He thrust his face close to hers. "Are you in your right senses? Whose house is this, anyway?"

"It's your house. But if you don't want your grandson in it, then you don't want me, either. And I'm right to say this, Pa."

Her words brought Mark up short. He saw with sudden clarity that this slip of a girl standing before him was her mother all over again, yielding in small ways but unchanging in her final beliefs.

He felt suddenly helpless and his thoughts churned wildly in his head. He told himself that his family was already broke up enough with Esther's passing and Matt's going off. He couldn't stand it to lose Prue, too. It was she who steadied the helm now and held the rest of them together. Indeed, in more ways than that he needed her, for a man could not manage without a woman to do for him and Mary was far too young.

Slowly he straightened and stepped back a pace. Prue, seeing she had won the first advantage, moved past him and sat down in the rocker before the fire, cuddling the baby against her as it began to whimper.

"Don't you want to see him, Pa?"

"No! I don't!" Mark pulled himself together and came to the attack once more. "The child's a half-breed! That's what he is. That's all he is! Well, I tell you again I'll have no stinkin'—"

"Stop!"

Prue's blue eyes held an unexpected flash of steel and there was a ringing command in her voice that checked him a second time. With surprise he discovered that she was his daughter, too. He waited, and she went on in an even tone. "If he goes, I go. I mean that. So think well before you speak further." She looked from him to Andy. "Get the cradle for me, please, Andy. I brought it from the attic and it's waiting in the parlor all clean. His name's Aaron," she finished.

Andy stumbled to do her bidding like one dazed. Never had he thought to see his father silenced thus. Prue was brave, all right. But already Mark had recovered.

"Aaron. Even named after an Injun, by—! Where would you go?" he added, with a sudden shrewd hope.

"Mr. Sergeant would take us in. Or Mr. Woodbridge. I made sure."

Prue put the small bundle in the empty cradle that Andy had fetched and rose to her feet once more. Confronting her father, there was such a look on her face of pleading, of sadness, of wisdom and of dedication that he held his tongue till she had finished what she had to say.

"This baby was born of love, Pa. Matt loved Marie. And Marie loved him. 'Twas wrong, mayhap. But one is not always able to see clear when—when love is steering the course. So it was with them, I'm fair certain."

She paused a moment to let her own past sink back out of its hurting.

"You'll say they should not have done this thing. But 'tis done. There's naught for us now but to make the best of it. Besides— have you forgot the debt we owe to Aaron? Ma would remind you. Ma would say we must keep this child and give him all we can in return for Aaron's gift to us of Mary. That's what she would say, Pa."

Mark faced her motionless and answered never a word.

Prue continued. "We owe a debt to Marie, too. She ransomed Matt. It was she took Abigail's diamond buckles and with them bought Matt's freedom."

Mark sat slowly into a chair. Prue came and knelt before him and never had her voice been more tender, Andy thought.

"I know what you're thinking. You're thinking of the disgrace of it. You're thinking of what you can say to the townsfolk and still hold up your head. Well, nothing at all need be said about the buckles. No one knows of that but Peter and Matt and us three here in this room. Not even John Sergeant knows. If it's brought out now, all 'twill do is mar the repute of a dead Indian girl whom every one loved that knew her."

Mark put his head in his hands and made a sound like a groan.

"As for—for the mixed blood in our little Aaron—" Prue

paused a moment. "Pa, it's good blood on both sides. We can be proud of that."

He raised his head and his voice came ragged. "I can never be proud that Matt did this thing."

Prue seemed not to hear him. "All we need tell the world is that we are repaying the debt we owed to Aaron. There's not a soul here but knows of that and not a soul but will admire you for your high honor in thus settling it."

There was a silence. Andy hardly dared breathe. Mark said suddenly, "Let me see him."

Prue drew the cradle close and turned back the blanket. The baby lay asleep. In his eyes there was a startling resemblance to Matt. There in miniature was the same uncompromising chin, the same mutinous mouth, the same wild black hair growing every which way above a broad white forehead.

"It will be but a matter of time afore the world sees the father in the son," Mark said, in a heavy tone.

Prue rose. "Then so it must be."

She stood straight before him and her next words fell like those of a Solomon come to life, Andy thought. Never had he dreamed his sister was like this, so resolute, so clear-sighted, so righteous.

"Pa, this community is trying to do something new. The white people were asked into it to set an example to the Indians. If one fails in setting that example, must not all the rest of us do our utmost to rectify that failure?"

Mark made no answer. Prue's steady voice continued.

"Long ago Mr. Sergeant said to you this would be a meeting place for the Lord and the devil. I heard you tell Ma so and that he counted on you to be on the Lord's side. Can you leave it now for the matter of your pride? A puny reason, He would think."

Still Mark said nothing and Prue's voice grew softer.

"When I left Aaron's house this afternoon, Mr. Sergeant came with me. There is grief in his heart for this thing that has happened, as there is in yours. But he found comfort in his certain belief that you would not suffer harm to come to one of his charges without doing what you could to remedy that harm." She paused. "He said for me to remind you that in the Lord's sight we are all brethren."

Mark spoke at last.

"How can you know this would be Matt's wish? Why! He himself scud off from his child! He had no hankering to acknowledge it! Why should we?"

"It is my belief that Matt ran not so much from his child as from his shock and grief. He did not know Marie was to be a mother, for she would not see him all winter. It wasn't until she lay on her deathbed that she let Peter come for him. No. He ran from his guilt and his sorrow. But he will return. And then— then he will be grateful, I feel sure. If not—" Her eyes held the strange look of a desire that has been both lost and found. "If he has no wish to claim Aaron for his own, I shall keep him myself."

She stopped. The logs fell apart with a soft sighing. Then a small fretful sound came from the cradle.

"I must go warm some milk," Prue said.

She went out to the ell. Mark sat staring into space. He looked, Andy thought, as if something had broken in him. The baby's wail grew louder. Mark reached down for his forgotten pipe and slowly cleaned it with a farrier's nail. Then he got up, took his shoes and left the room. Prue came back with a small pitcher of milk, poured some into a shallow pan and warmed it over the embers. Presently she poured this into a cup, put in it an eagle's feather she had clipped to make a hollow tube, and let the baby suck the nourishment that way.

Andy spoke softly. "I never thought I'd live to see the day Pa'd give up the ship."

Prue's eyes brimmed with tears. "I had to do it, Andy. And— and in my heart I'm afeard of what Matt may say." The tears rolled down and she finished in a whisper. "Sometimes the ways of the Lord are hard to understand."

CHAPTER 10

The Glory and the Promise

A BIGAIL SERGEANT was having a small quilting party. To it she
had invited to come the women who were nearest her age
—her two younger sisters, Judith and Elizabeth, Anna Jones, two
newcomers, Mary and Amy Stiles, and Prudence.

Prue always liked to go to Abigail's house. There was usually
some new wonder to be seen there. Last time it had been her
watch, a possession coveted by all feminine hearts but owned by
no other in the settlement. This time she had little goldfish
brought from China that swam endlessly about in a small round
clear glass bowl open at the top. All Prue had to do was prop
Aaron up in young John Sergeant's chair, which he had out-
grown, and the child would sit for hours watching the fish while
Prue sewed.

Today the tongues of the visitors moved as fast as their needles.
Gossip, rumor, fiction and fact must all be sorted out and Abigail was the best one to do this since she had, through her large,
sprawling family, the most contacts with the outside world. Right
off, Anna Jones asked if it was true that the people in Northampton where Jonathan Edwards had for so long had his parish, were
turning against him and wanted him put out?

Abigail said it was. "He frighted his congregation so with his
talk of hell fire and damnation that many have been saying harsh
things about him. He has really lost his influence, 'tis rumored."

"La! What's to happen now?"

"John says there'll be a vote to see if he's to remain in his pulpit. But I had rather speak of another minister than Mr. Edwards." Her glance touched with loving mischief on the face of her sister, Elizabeth. "I mean a certain Reverend Stephen West. He's seen a good deal in Indian Town lately. What can be the reason?"

There was a sly smiling at the blushing Elizabeth. Some one asked if she was planning to have the bans read soon? Some one else lightly said she had better before there was a scandal.

At this there fell a sudden silence broken almost at once by Anna Jones. If Prue wanted a cutting of Mrs. Jones's Seven Sisters roses, Anna would be pleased to fetch a couple up to her some day soon, she said. Ma had told Anna she was to give that message, she added. Though, in truth, Ma had said nothing of the kind. It was only Anna's tenderness of heart making her speak out like that and change the subject to save Prue embarrassment. For every one knew by now that Prue, at twenty-two and the oldest among them save for Abigail, was destined to be an old maid. Besides which, there sat Aaron next to her, the illegitimate son and living image of Matthew, her brother, who'd been gone near a year now and not heard from once. And while Prue must be well aware of what folks thought about her being still single, and also of what they knew about Aaron, still and all it could hurt mightily to hear too much talk of bans and proper marriages and scandals.

"How's Andy making out at the college down in New Jersey?" Abigail asked, as ready as Anna to protect Prue, whom she loved as a sister.

"Very well," Prue answered evenly. "He's working hard, but he enjoys it. He loves the world of his books."

"Speaking of books, I have a copy of *Pamela* here if any one would like to have it. John thinks 'tis not the kind of story should be in a minister's house so it will be a favor if one of you will carry it home with you."

There was a chorus of cries demanding the book, but Prudence spoke first. Since she had no time for putting together words out of her own thinking, she was hungry for the printed words of others.

"Is Mr. Sergeant feeling better this week?" Anna inquired now. "He appeared to us to look quite poorly Sunday last."

"He is poorly!" Abigail's tone held a sharp anger. "He's working himself to death over his savages! I feel that he is hardly rewarded for his faithful service. I lose patience often. But he never does." She sighed. "He is too good a man."

The talk turned now to lighter matters while Abigail prepared her tea table. Amy Stiles asked if any one had heard of the newest sight Boston had to offer? It was a curious musical machine and along with it went a posture boy who could make his muscles do the most extraordinary things. They rode together—the machine and the boy—in a cart through the streets but he would not perform without payment . . . Then Elizabeth wanted to know who present had a good receipt she might copy for a sack posset and also for potpourri . . . And Mary Stiles told of a new kind of plaster that was being sold down in Connecticut. It would crawl after any pain or disease wherever it went on the body. Would wonders never cease! First the Franklin stove that would burn both coal and wood and now plasters that could follow an ache till it was routed!

Abigail had begun to cut her pound cake into thin slices when there came a clatter of hoofs outside and a man's voice was heard calling to a slave boy to come hold his horse. Quickly she went to the window and saw her brother arriving.

"It's Eph," she said, and moved to open the front door to him. But it flew wide before she got there and the Major came in.

"Greetings, sister." Then, following her into the big kitchen, his glance went swiftly around. "Ho! A posy of women! I'm just in time to take my pick."

"What brings you this time?" Judith inquired. "We had no word you were coming. Have you news?"

"Yes. Good news." He stood before them all and imparted it with delight of the importance given him in so doing. "The British and French have signed a peace treaty at Aix-la-Chapelle."

"Peace! Oh, Eph, really?"

"Does that mean no more Indian raids?"

"It should. But—"

John Sergeant, who had heard Ephraim's arrival, appeared from his study behind the dining room across the hall. He did, indeed, look ill, Prue thought, seeing him close. Poor man! Even with his school built now things were not running too smoothly.

"But what, Major?" John asked. "I heard your news and 'tis good. But what qualifies it in your mind?"

"Well, the British have agreed to give back Louisburg in Cape Breton to the French and that hardly sets well with those of us from New England who wrested it away against terrible odds in a cruel battle that lost us many good men. It was a great victory for us and now—so it seems—all for naught. It's—well, to speak truth—it's put a strain on the relations between the Americans and the British which are already strained enough, what with the trade rulings and . . . ."

A knock on the rear door interrupted him. Abigail went to open it and then turned to her husband. "John, there's an Indian here wishes to speak to you."

John went out to the back entry only to come back the next moment and make his excuses. Umpachenee was in trouble again and he must go to him.

"Drunk?" Eph asked carelessly.

"I fear so."

"Wherever is he getting the stuff?" Anna exclaimed.

John made a helpless gesture and then went away.

Abigail now poured tea for all. Ephraim served the ladies first and, after taking his own cup and a piece of cake, ate and drank with his eyes seeking out Prue, suddenly realizing he had not seen her in a long time. Indeed, just before the burning of Fort Massachusetts was the last, and that was over two years ago.

He was glad, now, that he had heeded his pricking doubt on that occasion and had kept away from her since, for she had turned out to be a strange kind of woman, strong-minded and high-handed. None other he knew would have the boldness to foist a child born out of wedlock—and a half-breed at that—onto her family. Oh, to be sure, her motives had been noble enough! But the fact remained that a man married to her might find it mighty uncomfortable at times. Yes, he'd done well to keep clear of her.

Now, seeing her serene and lovely face bent above the quilting to which she had returned, he found she still excited his curiosity, if nothing more and, moved by it, he decided to give out, then and there, a further piece of news. He addressed his sister but his words were meant for Prue.

"Do you recall a certain Lieutenant David Reynolds who was attendant at your wedding, Abigail?"

"Oh, very well! But la! So much time has passed since then I'd forgot all about him. What of him?"

"I recently learned he's been at Louisburg ever since its capture. No doubt he'll be leaving there soon, though, since it's to go back to the French." He was watching Prue's hands which had begun to tremble over her work.

"Will he come here, think you? I'd like to see him again."

"I have heard he will."

Suddenly Prue's needle plunged into her finger drawing blood. She put it in her mouth to suck and began folding up her quilt with the other hand.

"I fear I'll stain the goods," she murmured. "This bleeding does not stop. But I should go, anyway, for Aaron is getting sleepy."

"So this is Aaron." Ephraim put down his empty cup and strolled across the room to cast his bold and knowing look down at the child. "I've heard about him."

Prue rose. "I am not surprised," she said quietly. "You seem to hear everything. Abigail, this has been a most pleasant afternoon. Good-by, Judith and Elizabeth. Good-by, Amy and Mary. Anna, please thank your mother for me and tell her I should dearly love to have a cutting of her roses."

She lifted Aaron from his high chair and stood him on the floor.

Ephraim said, "It will be quite a walk for the little fellow up the hill. Let me put him on my horse."

"Thank you. He's too small for a horse."

"I'll hold him. Come! Up you go!"

He bent and swung the boy to his shoulder. Aaron made no sound before the swooping attack of this total stranger but only looked at him out of dark enigmatic eyes.

They went out, the three of them together. The slave boy yielded the reins and Aaron was lifted into the saddle. Held there by Ephraim's strong arm, he evinced no fear but rode soberly, his small straight back very erect, his glance fixed on the horse's bobbing head before him.

They were well out on the road before Prue interrupted Ephraim's casual talk. She spoke in a level voice, her eyes straight ahead. "Ephraim, you puzzle me. I do not know if you are friend or foe. You've acted strangely these last few years, avoiding me as if I were the plague. No! Wait! 'Tis so and you know it! But it does not matter. Only one thing you must tell me at once, whether friend or foe. Did you deliver my message to David?"

He parried with amused enjoyment of her. "It does not matter? Truly? You are hard on a man, Prue. Did you not know my visits home were brief? And do you not recall you gave me little encouragement to lengthen them?"

"Nor do I now. You kept your distance, I think, because you had not delivered my message. Is not that so? You must tell me!"

It was a better reason to admit than the real one, he thought. "I will tell you, then. I did not deliver your message in person because I did not see David. But when I finally learned of his whereabouts I managed to send word through another who was traveling to Canada on official business there with the governor. Naturally I could not repeat it quite as you had given it to me. It seemed better to leave your name out so I merely asked my friend to report that Martin Manor had received his letter and had replied to it immediately with great joy."

She turned toward him, her face alight. "Oh, Eph! You're good! And I thought so hardly—I am ashamed. Think you he understood?"

"I'm sure of it."

"Why do you say that?" she asked breathlessly.

"Because of what I reported to you in Abigail's house."

"But how can I know that meant what I want it to mean? How can I be sure? There was nothing in it just for—for me."

He looked at her flushed, eager face with an admiration not wholly untinged with regret. "You do still love him. After all this time! It's an amazement to me. Surely such faithfulness deserves a rich reward."

"How can I know?" she repeated impatiently. "All you said was he was returning here. Oh, Eph! I beg of you—" Her voice broke and tears came to her eyes. "It's been too *long*," she murmured.

It was past understanding, Eph thought. David, too. When there were so many charming and willing women in the world! Yes, it was past understanding. But it commanded a certain respect.

He said, with more than his usual kindness, "There was another part to the message that I have not given you yet. I had to see you alone for that. The rest that was transmitted to me said, 'Kindly give my regards to those at Martin Manor and say to them that I will be seeing them shortly.' Now! Can you not rest assured from that? And am I friend? Or foe?"

Prue looked up and through her tears now shone a lovely radiance. "Friend, Eph. Now and always. From my heart I thank you. You can never know, for I cannot tell you, how much this means to me."

"I am not blind," he replied. "Though I think till now I may have been."

She did not hear him. Of a sudden the glory faded from her face and it became taut and miserable with a fresh uncertainty. For how, with Ma gone, could she spend half her time in England when she was so needed here? Moreover, when David appeared, he would find her with a child, a half-breed, whom she was pledged to raise as her own until Matt came back—and forever, if he did not want him. And what would David, born of

English gentry, say to that? Oh, truly! Hope and despair seemed forever mingled!

It was June and the fields were filled with red and white clover, daisies and yellow buttercups. In the morning sunshine cobwebs made a sparkling coverlet over the timothy. At night what seemed like a fall of snow was the paleness of Queen Anne's lace in the moonlight.

Through the days and the dusk of days and the starlit evenings Prue watched and waited for David, for hope would dominate all other feelings. Was he not returning to see her? Surely there was hope in that! At those moments it seemed to her that time had never gone so slowly, then, thinking of Aaron and dreading the telling about him, never had it gone so fast.

She was alone when he came. She had left the supper table early to go out into her garden and plant the rose cutting of the Seven Sisters given her that day. She heard footsteps but there was nothing familiar about the tall figure in tan buckskin and leather jacket she saw swinging up the road. It was not until he turned in at their lane and smiled upon her and she glimpsed the remembered warm lights in his brown eyes that she rose from amidst her flowers and looked upon him with a wide gaze in which love came and went like a frightened bird.

He said only her name but somehow in the saying of it all was asked and answered. She looked at him, hope transfigured into certainty, and the next moment she was in his arms.

"This—this is a dream," she murmured, drawing away finally.

"A dream no longer. And thank Heaven for that! I never had your letter, you know. It must have reached the Indies after I left there."

"But Eph's message found you!"

She ran her hand slowly down his brown sleeve and then, seeing what it was for the first time, she looked up at him in question. "This is not your British uniform."

"No. I have laid that aside."

Her face reflected her uncertainty. "You mean—?"

"I have left His Majesty's service for the time being, my sweet. But now tell me. Where is your little Aaron?"

She caught her breath. "You—know?"

"Yes. I know. I met Mr. Sergeant on the plain."

"And you—don't mind?"

"Why should I mind? It is a brave and beautiful thing you have done. Yet you were always brave and beautiful. From your wild-bird girlhood when I first saw you, you have always been brave and beautiful in my eyes."

The dear caress of his voice! How it moved her. But not to the joy he had expected. Instead, he saw her face anxious with a new worry.

"What is it, Prue?"

"Ma. She's gone, David."

"Yes. I know."

"But—don't you see? I—it complicates all our plans. How can I—now—go to England? My place is here."

He lifted a hand and laid it on her forehead, then drew it slowly down her cheek until he cupped it beneath her chin.

"Yes. It is. I do not dispute you. That, little Prue, is why I have secured permission to lay aside my British uniform. You bear a heavy burden, darling. I have come to help you with the carrying of it."

The grave sweetness of his reply plucked at her heartstrings. He had done this of his own volition. Oh, truly! He did love her to let his England go! But she could only say, "Come!" and, taking his hand, she led him into the house.

Prudence and David were quietly married in the parlor at Martin Manor. John Sergeant conducted the simple ceremony at which only the family was present—and Abigail. Prue came down the stairs in the blue David loved on her the best, joined him there, and together they walked into the flower-decked room. There was no uncertainty regarding their love in either of them. If tears trembled beneath the surface, they were tears of joy, for this was their moment of glory.

John stood before them gravely sharing their happiness, his measured tones rich and meaningful in their ears.

"We are met here together to witness the joining of this man and this woman in the holy bonds of matrimony."

Prue heard every word. They sounded to her like silver bells chiming. Yet even as she heard, her mind took her back to that day long ago when she had wondered if she would ever stand by David's side and repeat the solemn vows she was repeating now.

"Do you, David—?"

"I do."

His voice sang through her as it always had. His warm brown eyes met hers in a look that clearly said, *The years we have missed will be forgotten in the bliss of the years that lie ahead.*

"And do you, Prudence—?"

"I do."

She did not hear Pa suddenly clearing his throat. She was not aware of Luke's attentive face or Mary's wide gaze or Johnny's rapt, mystified attention or little Aaron's sober mien. There was only herself and David in the fragrant, June-filled room. And John Sergeant pronouncing them man and wife.

"Whom God hath joined, let no man put asunder."

No man and no thing could ever do that, Prue thought. Not again! They had been through their Gethsemane and now ahead lay a life rich with the promise of everything shared in a trusting and untroubled peace. Not a tremor of fear marred the perfection of that moment for her.

As for David, there was no question in his mind of the depth and sincerity of his love for Prue. But of his decision to forsake his homeland and take up his abode here in this rough, tumultuous country amongst these sturdy pioneers, he was less sure. His loyalties ran deep. His obligations to his King were ever-present in his mind. Should he have left his service in the British Army to form a personal allegiance here? The doubt had pricked him more than once. Moreover, he felt a trifle strange and ill at ease before the blunt, outspoken Mark, the domineering bluster of Colonel Williams, the crudity of some of the new settlers and the tart dryness and elbowing quality he sensed in all these independent colonists. Could he have done so, he would have carried Prue back to his beloved England, but there had been no possibility of that. Perhaps later. . . .

But the future must take care of itself.

CHAPTER 11

The New Minister

IT WAS SUMMER AGAIN and Prue had been married for more than three years. It had been a period of happiness beyond anything she had ever imagined. David's sweet gentleness, his quiet reasonableness, his calm imperturbability were so different from anything her own men folks had shown her. He never raised his voice as Pa did. He never lost his temper or succumbed to moods as Matt had. He never was preoccupied with his own thoughts as Andy used to be. Day after day and night after night slipped away and the hours brought her only peace and an ever-deepening contentment.

By now Mark was a rollicking youngster running around everywhere and baby Esther was a newcomer to Martin Manor. In her care for them, and for little Aaron, Prue found herself completely absorbed so that outside affairs became remote and of less and less importance.

"I shouldn't be this way, I suppose," she said to David one time. "I should care more that things are at sixes and sevens here in the mission. But even if I cared, what could I do about it?"

They were in their upstairs bedroom where sunlight flooded in and fresh white curtains billowed gently in the soft breeze from the open windows. It was early in the morning and David was about to go out into the fields with Pa to start on the haying. But he paused now to reply to her question. There was nothing she could do, he said. It would take a strong man to put a stop to Ephraim Williams' rascality and now that John Sergeant was dead there was no strong man.

John had preached his last sermon shortly after little Mark was born. A week later, with his family mourning upstairs and his friends grieving downstairs and the Indians gathered in a sad silent waiting on the lawn outside his house, he had passed from this world to the next. It had been more than the passing of a man. It had been the passing of an era. For with the minister's death there went one of the last of those courageous souls who pioneered in Christianity, who moved with his flock fearlessly into a wilderness, there to suffer with them whatever hardships and dangers beset them.

Every one had wondered who—and what—was to follow.

What had followed was two years of devilish machinations on the part of Colonel Williams. It was his privilege, as leader of the community and as a member of the wealthy and influential Williams clan, to name a successor to Mr. Sergeant. But he said it was difficult to find just the right man. What he meant was that he wanted time in which to perpetrate certain dealings before anyone came who would supersede his powers. The things that had gone on during this interval were known to Prue because they were known to Mark but the reverberations of his wrath about it reached her as from a distance.

"I feel—apart," she went on now. "I can't help it. My life is up here on the hill and not much that happens off it seems to matter."

He nodded. "Unless it affects some one of us," he suggested.

"Yes." She smiled, not really believing it ever could or would, and then, in one of those sudden uprushes of love that so often overtook her, she tried to explain to him, not her lack of concern for the mission, but her great joy in life with him.

"I'm so wonderfully happy, David. Do you know at all how happy I am?"

"Tell me."

Her glance went out through the window for a moment. "I feel—rooted," she said at last, softly. "Like one of those trees out there. I feel fixed forever. And I love the feeling! Every day I want to be able to do what I'm doing now—sit here and see those same hills and fields and fences. The same orchards, the same barns. I don't want anything ever to change. Least of all you," she finished.

He was moved. "Do I really suit you so well?"

"Perfectly. That's why I say, don't ever change." She paused, her face sobering. "I didn't dream happiness could be so—so complete a thing. It makes me tremble sometimes."

"Why should you tremble, dear one?"

"For fear something will happen and it won't last."

"It will last as long as I do, Prue."

She was silent a moment, reveling in the certainty his words gave her. Oh, she was foolish to fear! She was, indeed. Yet how could anything so perfect endure in this imperfect world?

"There's only one thing I'd have different," she said presently.

"What is that?"

"I'd have more children. I don't believe I could ever have too many."

His eyes smiled into hers. "Well, you've made a good start." And he bent over the cradle where little Esther lay, her exquisite beauty and dainty perfection of body catching at his heart the way it always did. It was a different feeling from his pride in his son, yet his love for both was equal. And then his hand came out and lightly touched Prue's face with the worshipful love she invariably stirred in him.

She was born to her role, he thought. Her wisdom and her heart were great enough to encompass not only their two children but also the adopted Aaron and Pa's children as well. His was not made to stretch over quite so many people. Luke was all right, although quite unimaginative. Mary, however, he found trying. She was so ever-present, so full of curiosity, and so irresponsible. There were times when he wanted to be sharp with her, yet he never was. For Aaron he had no feeling whatsoever, though he was kindness itself with him. Only Johnny touched a responsive chord in his own nature. But that was easily explained. Johnny was like Prue. . . . Prue! Prue! How deeply he loved her! But her words had disturbed him somewhat, for if she rooted any deeper, how could he ever uproot her?

He stood a moment while she leaned her cheek against his warm palm. Presently he went away, leaving her rocking the baby in her arms. Alone, her thoughts wandered from one to another of her family.

Aaron, by this time, was as much hers as if he had been born to her, she mused. There was nothing strange any longer about the sturdy straight-backed boy now more than four years old. She had ceased to be disturbed that he talked little and was unusually self-contained and sober. So might Matt have been at his age. So, indeed, might be all little Indians. And, belike, 'twas Pa turned him silent, she told herself, hardly ever speaking to him and looking at him most of the time as if he wasn't there. It distressed Prue that Pa was that unforgiving toward him, though she knew it was not so much that the boy was half Indian as that he represented a fall from a place of honor on the part of Matt, the oldest son Mark had. That stuck in his craw. That made the youngster a constant thorn in Pa's side. But she never lost the hope that some day he would change.

As for the twins, Luke was nothing but comfort to her with his steady ways and even temper, but Mary was a bit of a worry, to be sure, by reason of her restless hankering for excitement. It was ever people she must have. New faces and new places were what she liked the most. How she loved going down to Sheffield on Pa's rare trips there! And how eagerly she hung on the words of anyone who had been farther afield!

But doubtless that was the age she was, Prue's thoughts went on. Once she found herself a husband she would drop her will-o'-the-wisp ways and settle down like any other matron. The only thing that really bothered Prue was her trick of talking all the time, yet never saying what was in her mind. She hid behind a constant fall of words so you couldn't ever rightly get a hold of her. But oh! Pretty as a picture she was, with curly chestnut hair and big brown eyes and tiny scarlet purse of a mouth.

Then there was Johnny. Ever since she had ushered him into the world on the mountaintop he had been especially close in her heart. Johnny would do something or be something notable some day, she was sure of it, if he could just be protected till that day came. Sometimes it troubled her that he was so thin-skinned, that he bore the hurts of everybody as if they were his hurts. At twelve the tears would start, or he would shiver and shake in a way that made little Aaron stare in silent, bright-eyed scorn. But give him time and she was confident he would grow up to a sufficient strength. It would be different from that of the others. It would never vaunt itself and it would never be unmindful of weakness. Yet it would take him through whatever dangers and hardships might beset him in life. Yes, she loved Johnny in a very special way, understanding him and knowing his need and seeing him solitary amongst the other children as she did.

Andy was out of her charge now. He had finished at the College of New Jersey and gone to New York to study law for awhile after graduating. Then—such an astonishment!—he had declared he was going to the Ohio River country to start his practice. No one of them had ever thought Andy had that much adventure in his soul. Matt had it all, they had believed. (Matt! Where are you now? What are you doing? 'Tis over four years and not a word from you.) Yes, Andy had taken them all by surprise. Mark had said he was crazy. There was no law in that wild land yet. Indeed, since France had announced it was her territory and England had refused to accept the statement, there'd more likely be war more than law, Mark had said.

However, Andy had gone, anyway. If there was no law, then that was the better for him. He would take it there.

So he had sold to David his sixth of the farm that Mark had given him when he reached twenty-one. (By this time Mark owned five hundred and forty acres, having bought a strip from Mr. Jones so as to be able to offer each of his children a subsistence of ninety acres.) He would never be a farmer, Andy had declared, and David would need for his growing family more than Prue's share which, together with the house, Mark had presented to her at the time of her wedding.

It had all come out nicely, Prue thought, for not the first time. Pa had needed David, with Matt and Andy both gone, and David had wanted to stay. The love of land was in his blood as it was in that of all Englishmen. And now, with title to one hundred and eighty acres, he was independent. To be sure, they worked the land together—he and Luke and Pa—and all lived together as one family at Martin Manor, still Prue felt it gave David a good feeling to realize that, if he wished, he could establish himself separate and apart with his little ones. That he might still dream of establishing them separate and apart in faraway England simply never occurred to her.

Yes, Prue was happy. Almost perfectly happy. All she needed was for Pa to notice Aaron more—and to hear from Matt that he was alive and well.

A few days later Pa came stamping into the house, roaring out Prue's name so commandingly that she hurried to him to find out what was on his mind.

"That committee's been heard from!" he told her, wrath in his black eyes, wrath in his voice. "Leastways, Boston's been heard from now that the committee's reported back to them!"

"Committee?"

"Yes! The investigating committee. You remember! I told you! I told you I'd finally got Timothy Woodbridge to write to the commissioners telling all that was going on here."

"Oh, yes!"

Poor Timothy, she thought. It was on his thin, bent, scholarly shoulders that the cloak of Mr. Sergeant's authority had fallen. But the cloak did not fit. He was too mild-mannered and peace-loving, forever hoping Mr. Williams wasn't as bad as he was proving to be, forever praying things would work out better if they were left alone.

Pa was storming up and down the keeping room.

"He wrote, all right! I saw the letter. He registered plain and clear the complaints of the Indians. He told how Eph had taken for himself a good four hundred acres of their land in the village. And he told how white families—Eph's friends—are swarming in here at his invitation when he's got not a smidgen of right to bid them." He stopped in his pacing and faced Prue, his glance an icy glitter. "And he told, too, how the visiting Indians—the Oneidas and Delawares and Mohawks—ain't been satisfied with Mr. Kellogg's being in charge of teaching their sons and how they wanted a committee to come and look into things here. Well, they came. But much good it's done!"

"Why? What's the matter?"

"Here's the matter. I just found out. Took a deal of piecing together of different bits of news, but here 'tis. Did the committee talk with the Indians when it came here? No! Did those men talk with Mr. Woodbridge? No! They talked with Eph Williams. That's who they talked with! 'Twas he met them when they arrived. 'Twas he entertained them at his house, filling them up with his stories about everything. How he'd needed this bit of land to protect his stream. And that bit because it fetched up next his crops. And how another Indian was in his debt and couldn't repay any other way than in property. Then when he was asked about the new settlers he gave out they were related to folks already here and he hadn't had the heart to tell sons and daughters they couldn't follow their own parents." He stopped. "Lies!" he roared. "All lies!"

Prue nodded slowly, her mind was going over the names of the latest comers—the Pixleys, the Curtises, the Nashes, the Willards, the Barnards, the Taylors. Certainly they weren't all sons and daughters of the original families! Brigadier General Joseph Dwight wasn't. He had come a stranger among them, with his bodyguard, Lawrence Lynch. How wicked Mr. Williams was to pretend a thing like that!

"And then," Pa went on, "having filled 'em up with his fancy tales, he filled 'em up with good food and drink so's they didn't want to stir anywheres to find out anything different than what he told them. And now the word is that all his claims to that

Indian land are to be allowed! All that's to happen is that the Indians will get a small sum of money to 'soothe' them."

"The new settlers are to stay?"

He nodded.

"And what about Mr. Kellogg?"

Pa sank into a chair, his anger suddenly gone, replaced by a deep gloom. It was strange and yet rather wonderful, Prue thought, how deeply he felt about the mission. She knew he had cared greatly for John Sergeant when he had been alive. She knew that to have him go was, for Pa, like the going of another member of his family. The minister's counsel had not always been heeded but his comfort had never failed. John had known, as no one else ever had, the anguish Matt had given Pa, the deep loneliness he had felt when Esther had been so suddenly taken, the turmoil and rebellion that had filled him—and still did—at little Aaron's presence in his house. And while the preacher had not been able to change any of these matters, he had helped Pa to bear them.

She waited now for his answer to her question.

"Nothing's been done about Mr. Kellogg," Pa told her at last. "He's still here. He's still in charge of the visiting Indian boys. I'll never rightly understand why he was invited here in the first place when—Peter told us afore he went away!—he never treated the lads right down in Newington. John was too trusting, I guess." His brows came together and the force of his anger returned to him in some measure. "But you mark my words! We've not heard the last of this."

"You think—"

"I think Timothy's goin' to have to write to Boston again. That's what I think. The Indians don't like it that their complaint about Mr. Kellogg wasn't paid any attention to. It's got their dander up so they're gettin' ready to leave. They're a-goin' to fold up their tepees and go away—all eighty families of 'em. And the commissioners won't like *that*."

How little they would like that, indeed! For they knew full well that the tiny mission at Stockbridge held a relationship to the Colonies out of all proportion to its size. It was the mission that was keeping the powerful Mohawks friendly to the British and it was because of this that the Boston authorities kept pouring money into the place. With the French getting so bold in the Ohio Valley, it was absolutely essential for the English to keep on good terms with Chief Kendrick, the most important leader of all the Six Nations, in case of an outbreak of hostilities.

"We need a minister here," Pa concluded. "Tain't right we should be without one so long. We need some one will stand up for the Indians the way John did. But who it will be I don't know."

It was Jonathan Edwards.

When the second letter from Mr. Woodbridge reached Boston (as Pa had prophesied), bringing consternation with the news of the departure of the disgruntled Indians, it was to the deposed preacher from Northampton that the authorities turned.

For Jonathan Edwards was a strong man, and his integrity, his religious fervor and his moral leadership were unquestionable. Moreover, he was known to the Stockbridge Indians, having visited there often, and was liked and trusted by them. If he would accept the charge there and if Mr. Kellogg were replaced by a teacher of Mr. Edwards' choosing, the anxious council was certain that the Mohawks and the Oneidas and the Delawares would return to the mission. Only so could the delicate balance between savage and settler be maintained. Only so could the council feel at ease again in these dangerous times.

When Pa heard of the appointment he was immeasurably pleased and he was one of the first to call on the new minister after his arrival.

"I reckon from things Mr. Edwards let slip, he didn't want to come here at first," he reported to Prue. "Seems he didn't really hanker to preach again. He'd druther do nothin' but write. But he was persuaded this was his duty."

"Who will he get to take Mr. Kellogg's place?"

"A Mr. Gideon Hawley. He—Mr. Edwards—has made out a plan for him to follow that he thinks will be suitable and please the Indians. So now I reckon with General Joseph Dwight, who's Mr. Edwards' friend, handling the finances and Mr. Hawley doin' the teachin' and Mr. Edwards at the helm steerin' the course, the mission will sail along on smooth waters." A deep rumble of laughter rolled up in him. "Old Eph's met his match this time! I'll stake money on it!"

And there was in his voice a note of personal triumph as if it had been he, himself, who had secured Jonathan Edwards for the Indians.

As Mark had expected, Ephraim Williams was not pleased.

In his Great Room in his Castle on the hill, he sat stiff and erect and enormous in a straight, high-backed chair with a pitcher of cider and a glass on a silver tray beside him. He had been there upward of an hour silently smoldering and fuming at the changes that had been wrought under his nose and without his permission. He had not wanted that strait-laced, iron-willed, fearless, fighting old man here breathing out his hell-fire-and-damnation sermons. He had wanted someone younger and more pliable. Ezra Stiles would have been just the one. Samuel Hopkins would have been next best. But neither of these men was here. Jonathan Edwards was here.

At first, knowing the minister's passionate interest in writing and knowing also his reputation for absent-mindedness, Ephraim had hoped he would prove to be the kind of person who would immure himself in his study and let things go along as they always had without interest or inquiry. Instead—this whirlwind.

Ephraim did not like it. He could not endure high-handedness on the part of anyone other than himself. But more than that, he could not endure the feeling of helplessness that had fallen upon him with Edwards' arrival. He did not like to feel helpless. And by the eternal! he would not remain helpless! Yet what could he do?

He poured himself another glass of cider and gulped it down. Then he plopped the glass back on the salver with a vehemence that brought the sound of a sharp crack. He stared at it furiously and bellowed for the house servant. Jake came hurrying, his black face fearful. Marse in a powerful bad mood dis day. Not nothin' pleasured him. Not nothin' a-tall.

"Get me another glass! And fill that pitcher up with ice! Don't take all night about it, either!"

Jake sped away. While Eph was waiting for him to return, he got up and walked about, flapping the coattails of his fine broadcloth with his big, thick hands. He could hardly contain himself. If he couldn't think of a way to get hold of the reins in this town again—

Suddenly he stopped short. For a long moment he stood in silence, staring at nothing out of the window. When Jake came back he was still staring and Jake put the tray down with its tinkling pitcher and fresh glass and tiptoed quietly out of the room again.

Ephraim returned to his chair and sat down without even seeing the refreshment waiting for him. A light had been lighted in his brain and by it he was spinning a web of planned action.

He was not helpless. Not yet. Not by a long sight. What had ever made him think he was? Take Mr. Kellogg. Just because he had been ordered from the school did not mean he had to leave town. In fact, he wasn't going to leave town, for by remaining here he could be of great use, indeed, of even more use than before.

The colonel chuckled. But it was a sound that had no mirth in it.

And take General Joseph Dwight. A fine man, Dwight—a man of the world like himself. That being so, it was not unlikely that their opinions might be identical on more than one future occasion; that their views on—say—the best good for the community might exactly coincide. The colonel had talked to Dwight more than once and had found him a most practical fellow. Practical —and agreeable. Most agreeable. He had, indeed, seemed to lay himself out to be agreeable. Now why was that?

His eyes screwed up to tiny pinpoints of brightness. The answer was simple. Dwight wanted to be agreeable to Abigail's father because her soft and lovely beauty, enhanced by her late bereavement, had greatly attracted him. Ephraim had no doubt at all that she was the woman the young colonel would like to marry. Well, his own influence on his daughter was not negligible.

He chuckled again. Then he poured himself a glass of the ice-cold cider and drank it with slow appreciation, smacking his lips as he finished, his early anger forgotten in the plans he now clearly envisioned for the future.

It was a May Sunday in the year 1752, nearly a year later when Jonathan Edwards leaned one arm on the big Bible before him, bent his tall thin body forward slightly, fixed his eyes on the congregation and began to speak. His tone was quiet but beneath its calm were the hot fires of a hidden volcano.

"The title of my sermon this morning is—Sinners in the Hands of an Angry God."

Prue's mouth settled into a firm line of unspoken protest. Jonathan Edwards was a good man, there was no doubt about that. It was fine that he was here because of the Indians who had sorely needed him. But he was certainly very different from John Sergeant. John had believed in a God of love while Jonathan's God was an avenging God and he preached dire warnings of the awful end that awaited unrepentant souls. It made him a fearsome leader.

He was saying now with a grave and impressive fervor, "If you continue in your enmity a little longer, there will be a mutual enmity between you and God to all eternity. It may not have reached this point yet but at any moment death may intervene and then reconciliation is impossible forever. As you hate God, He will hate you forever. He will become a perfect enemy with a perfect hatred, without any love or pity or mercy. He will be moved by no cries, by no entreaties of a mediator—"

Ahead of her, Prue could see the impatient jerk given to one of the old colonel's big shoulders. It was plain what he felt about the minister's words! He was opposed to them as he was opposed to the man. But where did General Joseph Dwight stand now that he had married the widow Abigail? He had first been a friend of Mr. Edwards, yet could he remain so and at the same

time be a member of the Williams family? Every one was wondering.

The low voice with its well-banked fires continued while Edwards' glance roved searchingly over the lifted faces below him.

"But this enmity will be mutual; for after death your own
enmity will have no restraints but it will break out and rage
without control. *When you come to be a firebrand in hell—*"

A movement at her side made Prue look down. Johnny had
shrunk against her. She could feel his tenseness and she could
see his young white countenance in which his eyes were downcast
as if he were afraid to look up.

And that was the truth. To the young lad the preacher's pene-
trating, forceful tones sounded hynotically above him, a vague
threatening menace. He could endure it as long as those dark eyes
passed over him unseeingly, but if he chanced to lift his gaze
and their glances locked, then the voice, saying all those dreadful
things, was directed straight at him. Then, try as he would, he
could not make his look let go, and the voice beat upon him—
on him alone—thundering in his ears, roaring in his head, till
something inside him broke in a silent screaming, and he was
left, helpless, quivering and terrified, unable to speak, unable to
move.

Prue reached down and took hold of his hand and held it
tight in hers. It was cold and sweaty. Her eyes moved onto the
twins. But she need never worry about them. Luke, who lived by
the rhythm of the seasons, had a sturdy common sense that was
his own protective shell, while Mary's seventeen-year-old mind
danced lightly away from all that did not interest her. Nothing
seemed to bother Aaron. Prue pulled herself back to the sermon.

"—when you come to be a firebrand in hell, you will be all on
a blaze with spite and malice toward God. Then you will appear
as you are . . . spitting poison at God and venting your rage and
malice in fearful blasphemies. . . . You are ten thousand times
more abominable in His eyes than the most hateful venomous
serpent is in ours—"

I won't listen, Prue thought. I will think of trees instead. I
will think of the tall elms beside our porch and the way the

crocuses I planted make mats of gold under them every spring. I will think of purple lilacs against our white house. And the hills pasted black against a sunset sky. How can as kind and gentle a man as he is talk the way he does?

On her other side there was a slight movement also and she turned her head and met David's eyes. He felt as she did about these sermons. It was one more instance of their perfect accord. How marvelous it was that there was no separateness between them on any matter. Oh! Life with him was good and beautiful! Why did Mr. Edwards always speak as if it were a terrible thing? Indignation stirred in her for not the first time. But the voice was going on, rising and falling inexorably. There was no escape from it, not even in your thoughts.

"Seeing we are such infinitely sinful and abominable creatures in His sight . . . is it not immensely more worthy of the infinite majesty and glory of God to deliver and make happy such poor, filthy worms, such wretched vagabonds and captives—"

Again Prue's vital spirit protested. We are not worms! We are not vagabonds and captives! He—he degraded people. It was unbearable. And now listen! He was saying that we were born wicked. Even babies.

"As innocent as young children seem to be to us, if they are out of Christ, they are not so in God's sight, but are young vipers, and infinitely more hateful than vipers . . . Indeed, they are naturally very senseless and stupid, being born as the ass' wild colt—"

Thus, certainly, had Johnny been born. But he was neither senseless nor stupid. And to call him a viper was ridiculous. Prue, who had a store of simple, wholesome beliefs, felt her indignation turn to a rare anger. It was a good thing, she told herself, that the minister was reaching an end or she might shock every one and disgrace herself by walking out. Yes, she might! And then her thought trailed away to the wonder as to how this man could hold a congregation as he did when he was not a popular person at all? Perhaps it was the confidence and authority with which he spoke that lent power to his words. Well, whatever it was,

they were all—Indians and whites—in the palm of his hand right
this moment. Almost you could hear a pin drop.

Edwards moved a little in the pulpit. He slowed his voice and
spaced his words and said impressively, "The bigger part of men
who have died have heretofore gone to hell. You"—he paused to
point an accusing finger—"you who now hear of hell and the
wrath of the great God and sit here in these seats so easy and
quiet and go away so careless—"

The hand within hers moved spasmodically and Prue saw that
Johnny's gaze was lifted and held by the man above him, that
those dark compelling eyes were looking straight down into the
wide gray ones of the boy and that though he wanted to, he could
not tear himself away. One by one the awful words fell into the
waiting silence—for him, for *him*—while the finger pointed.

"—by and by you will shake and tremble and cry out and shriek
and gnash your teeth . . . Indeed, it would be a wonder to me if
some that are now present should not be in hell in a very short
time before this year is out. It would be a wonder if some persons
that now sit here . . . in health and quiet and secure, should not
be there *before tomorrow morning*."

There was a gasp from Johnny. Quickly Prue gave his icy hand
a small squeeze but felt no response. She could see a shudder pass
over his body and suddenly her rebellion against this kind of
preaching was no longer to be borne. From last August when Mr.
Edwards had arrived to now was enough. She lifted her head and
looked at the minister and her blue eyes blazed with the resolution that had come to her. Through the last hymn and the last
prayer she held to it with steadfastness. Then they were outside
in the warmth of the summer sunshine. They were moving, as a
family, across the common, going toward their wagon and their
cold lunch packets. With quiet decorum they greeted their neighbors and sat down on the grass to eat.

But Prue, watching Johnny, saw that he left his food untouched. He did not even take a sandwich into his hand and she
guessed it was because it trembled so that he was ashamed. Then
she saw how his eyes were darkly circled and she remembered
that often lately he had cried out in his sleep. Once or twice he

had walked, awake yet not awake, down the hall from his room. And she knew that the time to act on her resolution was now.

She looked at David. "I will be back in a moment," she told him.

Rising, she adjusted her high-crowned bonnet, tightened its strings beneath her chin, smoothed down her stiffened petticoats under her fulled overskirt, and made her way with a faint rustling of her fawn-colored moire gown across the road to John Sergeant's first little house opposite the church where—somehow —Mr. Edwards had packed himself in with his wife and all his children. Here she knocked at the closed door. From within she heard the sound of soft, happy voices and she thought how strange it was that a man could be two such different people. At home he was gentle and his children were playful with him and he with them, yet in the pulpit—

Mr. Edwards, himself, opened to her. Behind him Prue glimpsed Sarah, his good and beautiful wife, clustered about by her brood. Mrs. Edwards looked toward the guest and smiled a welcome, while Esther, the oldest daughter, soon to marry Aaron Burr, president of the College of New Jersey, called out a friendly greeting. But Prue shook her head.

"Please do not disturb yourselves. I seek a word with Mr. Edwards, if I may interrupt him for a moment?"

"Certainly."

The minister came out and the two moved off together to a little distance but in full view of the interested spectators across the road on the common. Prue lifted her head and though the border of her bonnet was shaking at her own temerity, her blue eyes held his unwaveringly.

"Mr. Edwards, I came to tell you that I am not staying for the afternoon service."

His face, which could be sweet, and had been in the relaxation he had found in his family group, turned swiftly severe. Towering above her, he bent his head and fixed her with his quick, dark look.

"And why not? Are you ill?"

"No, sir."

"Is some one ill in your family, then?"

"Yes, sir. I mean—well, not yet. But he may be. Indeed, he *will* be unless I take him home now at once." She paused a moment and the ribbons that laced her bodice fluttered with her quickened breathing but she forced herself to calmness and finished. "I am speaking of Johnny. Your sermons frighten him, Mr. Edwards."

"They are meant to."

"But they frighten him so he will not eat! And he sleeps poorly!" She controlled herself again. "Mr. Edwards, if I may be so bold as to say so, you assert God at the expense of humanity. I—I do not find it good. Indeed, I find it dangerous."

He stared at her. She did not give ground. Presently he spoke. "You astound me. What you say makes me tremble for your soul. I—"

But Prue's soul was not her present concern. She interrupted. "Please! Mr. Sergeant said something once that I have never forgot. The words are to be found, I believe, in Ecclesiastes. They are: 'Man should remember that God approves of joy.' Oh, Mr. Edwards! There *is* joy in the world! And we need more of it! We—"

"Child! Be still! Joy, you say. What joy can there be when we are all sinners? You do not seem—"

"But I do not believe we are all sinners. Not as you believe it. Oh, I cannot listen to you! Forgive me but—I am taking Johnny home. I am taking him because your God, your cruel, avenging God, is hurting him. I wanted you to understand."

There she stood, slim, defiant, fearless. Jonathan was shaken. No one had ever spoken to him like this. No one. Suddenly he was very tired. This place that he had thought would be a haven of peace was turning out to be a stormy petrel. Only yesterday Mr. Woodbridge had come to warn him against General Dwight. He, Jonathan, had not heeded. He was sure his old friend was dependable. There was Mr. Kellogg, too. And now this girl— He fixed her with his dark glance but he did not want to answer her or punish her. He did not know how at the moment. How could you reach a person who refused to be terrified?

He looked down at her and even from the distance where they waited, Mark and David could see his dis-ease of spirit. He said, "We will discuss this again when I have more leisure."

Prue bent her head. "If you wish. But I have nothing to add. Nor will I take anything away." She put her hand on his arm in a brief, silent plea and then moved quickly back to her family.

Mark said, "What in tunket were you sayin' to the minister? He looked as though you'd choked his luff for fair."

Prue hesitated. She had been bold and reckless past all conscience, she knew. And what the consequences would be she could not rightly guess. Rebuke and punishment had been dealt out for far lesser offenses—for running into church out of the rain, for instance: or for wearing too much finery. But while matrimony and motherhood had added to her tenderness, they had also added to her strength. With David by her side she was afraid of nothing. She looked at him, then at Johnny's taut face, then at Mark.

"I simply told him, Pa, that Johnny and I are not staying for the afternoon service."

Simply! Mark could only stare at his daughter, for this was out and out heresy. Or near to it. The twins stared, too, open-mouthed. David was startled, yet met her eyes with comprehension, for he shared with her the concern she felt over young Johnny.

"Then none of us will stay," he began decisively, but Prue broke in.

"On the contrary, David. You and Pa and Mary and Luke and Aaron will remain. Only Johnny and I are leaving."

"I will stand by you, Prue."

She laid a hand on his arm. "Please," she said quietly. "Thank you. But please remain. It is best so. We will take the wagon. The rest of you can walk home. It is a beautiful day."

Johnny asked a bewildered, frightened question. "But—but won't we fry in hell?"

Her answer came out round and clear and positive. "If I am not afraid, you need not be."

David thought, My fearless Prue. He knew it would be useless to try and swerve her from her purpose. Whatever she thought was right to do, she did. It was an amazement to him to discover every so often that through all her sweetness there ran this streak of iron; but when it appeared, he acknowledged it, as did Mark who said now,

"Let her jump ship if she's so minded. Like as not she knows what she's about."

"Come," Prue said to Johnny. "We'll go home and help Mam Beck take care of the babies."

Ah, David told himself. There was more to it than Johnny, then. She was uneasy leaving the two little ones at the house with only the colored woman and the redemptioner there. Mam Beck was devoted and fairly intelligent but the redemptioner—a stupid boy who would soon work himself out of service—could be panicked were there another Indian scare as there had been last year at Yokun Town, the peace treaty at Aix-la-Chapelle notwithstanding. At that time one woman had been shot and several homes burned. Yes, 'twas this was in Prue's mind now as much as Johnny, for sure, though what put it there of such a sudden he could not fathom.

As she had spoken Prue began picking up chicken bones and pear cores and putting them in a paper. Johnny's untouched sandwiches she wrapped again in a neat parcel and tied with string, then, holding these in one hand, she mounted into the wagon with David's help while Johnny scrambled up beside her.

"You may drive," she told him.

Through the knots of people they slowly made their way, Prudence nodding pleasantly to all as she passed and taking no note of their surprised and curious faces, Johnny intent on his driving as she meant him to be. Once out on the road and going up the hill toward home, she began talking easily.

"This is the time of year I like best. Hear all the birds, Johnny! There's a warbler chattering. When we get home we must see if the baby robins have left their nest in the apple tree yet. It's time."

Johnny, flapping the reins on old Daisy's fat back, slowly relaxed. Prue could feel the tension leaving him in each of his long, deep sighs. Presently she began to sing.

> *"Love divine, all love excelling,*
> *Joy of heaven to earth come down."*

She finished the first verse and said, "I like that hymn, Johnny, don't you?"

"Prue, are you sartin we won't burn in hell?"

"Perfectly certain. Sing with me, Johnny. 'Jesus, Thou art all compassion, Pure unbounded love Thou art.' That's why I'm sure, Johnny. Because if we are loved by our Savior with a pure unbounded love, which means a love that never stops—Well, such a love as that wouldn't dream of letting us burn in hell."

"But Mr. Edwards said—"

"Mr. Edwards tells only part of the story. When he gets around to telling us the other part—the part Mr. Sergeant always told us about how much God loves us—why, then, we'll go back and listen to him again. But not before."

She heard his quick, incredulous gasp. "Cross your heart?"

"Cross my heart."

He straightened on the seat. He threw back his shoulders and his head went up and his eyes shone.

"And now," Prue said, "I'm hungry. There was little chance for me to eat there. I was too busy talking." She reached down and opened the parcel she had tucked between them. "I'm having a sandwich. Do you think you can eat and drive, too?"

Johnny nodded. "Sure I can."

She could never prove it, Prue thought, but however wrong she might seem to be for this morning's wicked behavior, she was certain, in her heart, she was right.

CHAPTER 12

The Dilemma

JONATHAN EDWARDS rode silently through the September sunshine down the blazed trail to the west and so off toward uninhabited country. He needed solitude to straighten out the turmoil in his mind and these lonely rides offered him the only means of securing it. Behind him his little house was a Babel of feminine voices with all of his daughters aiding his good wife cut out and make the fans and caps that helped to eke out his slender resources.

His pockets now were filled with the scraps they did not need, for paper was short and thoughts for his writings often came to him when he went off like this. Then, before they were lost to his memory, he would halt his horse, pull forth a small piece and write down the words he wanted to remember, pinning them onto his long black coat when he had finished. Sometimes his mind was so active that he would return home fluttering like a veritable scarecrow, to the great amusement of the villagers. Of this, however, he was scarcely aware. The point was that the ride had yielded rich results.

This morning, he told himself, he must not think only of his next book. He must come to a decision, without further postponement, as to what he was going to do regarding the lovely young errant in his present parish—Prudence Martin Reynolds. God give him guidance!

He reached a gate and was about to dismount to take down the bars when a small bare-footed slave boy in ragged clothes appeared from nowhere and did it for him.

"Thank you." And then, as the youngster pulled his kinky hair respectfully, he added perfunctorily, "Who are you?"

"I'se Jake's boy. I'se Marse Williams' boy."

"Oh, yes. Well, thank you."

The minister rode on. *Williams*. Now how had he secured for himself land down here? And when? He drew a sigh from the long cavernous depths of his body and shook his head despairingly.

Thinking of Williams brought his mind to Joseph Dwight who had married Abigail Sergeant, John's widow. It had never occurred to him that so fine-seeming a match might bring disaster in its wake. He did not fully believe it even now despite Timothy's warnings and all the rumors that were afoot. He could not believe it. If there were wrong doing, and his old friend was mixed up in it, then he was being used as a dupe, he was sure. Anyway, he could not concern himself with Joseph now. The stories about him were still only guess work. But Prudence Reynolds was a bitter fact.

What a clamor there had been over her withdrawal from the church! Some had said she ought to be excommunicated and others had replied that if she was, they, too, would leave the church.

It was surely a dilemma for him through which he could see no clear-cut path. To do nothing was to risk a complaint against him made by the powerful Williams clan and led, of course, by Ephraim, for dereliction of duty. Yet to punish was to risk a serious split in his congregation. Either way he might lose his parish—and he had no wish to go through that experience again.

Furthermore, Captain Mark Martin was a man he respected and liked. He was a Christian in the best sense of the word. He was, moreover, a friend of the Indians and an enemy of Colonel Ephraim Williams—a strong ally for Edwards to keep on his side. Would he remain so if his daughter were banned from the church?

He jogged along now deep in despair. He had already talked

with Prudence more than once only to find her continuing in
her gentle obduracy. She must be guided, she had said, by her
own conscience. And she could not feel that she was wicked to
desire him to preach of a God of love since Mr. Sergeant had
always done so. She was sorry, but a young boy's health of mind
and body hung on the issue between them. And he, Mr. Edwards,
could not fright her.

So was he to alter the whole content of his sermons for this
unyielding young rebel? When all of his thinking and writing
and preaching had been based during his entire life on the beliefs
he was expressing in the pulpit now? It was unthinkable! Yet
what was the answer to the problem?

He turned his horse about and rode homeward without finding any answer. He came to the gate again and started to dismount to open it when a bare-footed little slave-boy clad in
ragged garments appeared from nowhere and did it for him.

"Thank you." And then, as the youngster pulled a kinky forelock respectfully, he added, "Who are you?"

The little fellow rolled his eyes. "Why, suh! I'se de same boy
I was when you went t'roo heah befo'!"

"Oh, yes, of course." He started on and then drew rein on a
sudden thought. "You belong to Mr. Williams, I think you said."

"Yessuh."

"Is this his land now?"

"Yessuh."

"I thought it was Indian land."

"Y-yessuh. B-but he done tole 'em to lay off clearin' it cose it
was next to his'n. An—an' so it was mo' propuh fo' him to have
it."

"I see."

He rode on, reached his little cabin, gave his horse to an Indian, and was met at the front door by his wife.

"Mr. Hawley and Mr. Woodbridge are here waiting to see
you."

"Thank you, Sarah."

He went in. The room was emptied now of feminine figures
and the clutter of sewing material. Two men rose from the settle

as he entered—the slender, worn Timothy Woodbridge and the stockier, younger figure of Gideon Hawley.

Timothy spoke. "I have distressing news to report, Mr. Edwards."

To neither of the teachers was the news they brought surprising. They had tried to warn the minister of a complication of events if Mr. Kellogg was not made to leave town and if General Dwight, as resident agent, was not checked on. But Edwards had refused to listen. What harm could Kellogg do without authority, he had inquired? And who could question the integrity of General Dwight? So he had steadily turned a deaf ear. But anyone else would have known it was impossible to live within old Ephraim Williams' orbit, as the general had been since marrying his daughter, without being contaminated by his wickedness. And anyone else would have known Mr. Kellogg had been deliberately detained here by Williams to make trouble.

Well, the trouble was here. Woodbridge came to it bluntly. "The Indians are leaving again."

"Leaving? Why?"

"They say you have not kept your part of the bargain. Mr. Kellogg is still in the school."

"But he has no rights there! He cannot teach or—"

"No, 'tis true he cannot teach"—Hawley's tone was bitter—"but he can interfere with my teaching. And he has no authority. But he usurps it."

Into Jonathan Edwards' eyes came now a flash of fire. "How?"

"He contradicts my orders. He's in the school every day as if he belonged there. Indeed, he says he does. And how can I keep him out? Then, while there, he contradicts all I say and criticizes constantly, creating the utmost confusion. The Mohawks say their boys do not know who to listen to, Kellogg or me, and they are so disgusted they are going away."

There was a silence.

"That isn't all," Woodbridge said, after a moment.

"Sit down, then, my good gentlemen," Edwards said wearily. "And let me hear the rest."

They took seats. Mr. Woodbridge, who had spent his life work-

ing for the Indians with the same devotion that John Sergeant
had shown, was pale and shaking with his indignation.

"There's to be a new school," he said. "A boarding school for
Indian girls."

"By whose order?"

Timothy gestured. "Whose but Colonel Williams?"

"What right has he?"

"Have you forgot? The colonel had himself made resident
trustee of the mission quite some time ago. And his son, Ephraim,
Jr., who is much in Boston, is on confidential terms with the
governor there. Moreover, Elisha Williams, his nephew, was appointed to the board of the Society for the Propagation of the
Gospel when he was in London last. And now, with Mr. Dwight,
his son-in-law, in control of the school funds, who's to stop him?"

"Well"—Jonathan spoke slowly—"perhaps a boarding school
for the Indian girls is needed. I know 'twas in Mr. Sergeant's
mind."

Timothy leaned forward. "But it's to be built on Sergeant
property, Mr. Edwards. On Abigail's land up on the hill. And
after it's built she will sell it to the government at a handsome
profit."

Jonathan's brows came together. "How do you know this?"

"We know the colonel,"—dryly. "Besides, 'tis common talk
amongst themselves, so the servants hear and they talk. Oh, it's
true, all right! What's more, Abigail plans to be made mistress
of the school. She will thus be able to educate her children free
as well as draw down a nice salary for herself."

There was another silence while this sank in.

"That, however," Hawley went on presently, "is not what con-
cerns us personally so much as the rest of the news."

"There is more?"

"Aye. Hark to it. General Dwight expects to take over both of
the boys' schools himself in due time. Then he will dismiss us
and, when he is ready, put his own son in charge. He will dismiss
Kellogg, too, I have no doubt. But he will surely be paid off
handsomely as he departs. For Mr. Kellogg is to make such

trouble for us that complaints about us will warrant our dismissal."

Edwards sat back and, folding his long hands, fixed his eyes upon them as he revolved his thumbs thoughtfully.

"This may all be just rumor," he suggested at last. "I— Somehow I cannot believe that the general would—"

" 'Tis more than rumor, Mr. Edwards," Gideon Hawley said sadly. "These are clear-cut plans. Mr. Kellogg, as we have said, is already putting them into effect."

"Moreover," Timothy added, "I faced Mr. Dwight with the accusation myself today and he did not deny it." He leaned forward to add a final word.

"And did you know, Mr. Edwards, that in that store Colonel Williams had built in the village at government expense, the Indians can buy liquor? You were wondering—we have all been wondering for a long time—where they got it. Well, that's where. They can buy it—and no questions asked."

Jonathan Edwards softly struck one closed fist into the palm of the other hand. When he spoke his voice was rough with his emotion.

"My friends, please leave me. I must think upon these matters. I would not wish to take hasty action but"—he rose to his full towering height—"rest assured that action I will take!"

Left alone, Jonathan resumed his seat and pondered in silence a long while. Confusion in the school situation, disgrace in the settlement, discontent everywhere. In addition, furtive schemes afoot to defraud the Indians of their best friends and teachers, a means already well established to destroy their character by taking advantage of their greatest weakness—drink—and at the same time a fraudulent cheating of the government. For what? Why! For the benefit of the Williams clan only! To increase their finances!

The wrath of a righteous man was aroused. Laying aside all his own writing, laying aside the unresolved problem presented by Prudence Reynolds' withdrawal from the church (transcended now in importance by this new business), Jonathan Edwards turned his attention to the distressing matters brought to him by

Mr. Hawley and Mr. Woodbridge. He sat down and wrote to the commissioners in Boston. It was a letter written with his usual directness and force, mincing no words and giving the commissioners permission to publish what he had told them.

The authorities were impressed and deeply disturbed, for there was no possible doubting Edwards' honesty. It was certainly an ugly situation and it left them but one choice. The government wanted order kept in the school and it wanted the Indians satisfied. Well, plainly, from this account, order was not being kept and the Indians were not satisfied. Therefore, the power of the Williams family must be curtailed.

Up on the hill Mark Martin shook his head over all these happenings. It was now winter and more than six months since Prue's withdrawal from the church. And though he understood and sympathized with her reason, he had always been bothered by it. Did she not feel, he asked her one night, that she could return soon?

"I'm feared your action may redound to Mr. Edwards' harm," he said. "He is a very strong man and he is needed here. But Williams will oust him if he possibly can just because he is so strong. And now you have given him a good reason. We've not heard the end of this matter yet, mark my words. That, together with all this upset over the Indians—" He paused. " 'Twould be a sorry day, child, if you were to contribute to Mr. Edwards' dismissal. Why couldn't you leave Johnny home here with Mam Beck and the little ones and you go with the rest of us once more to service?"

"We sang 'Throw out the life line' again last Sunday," Mary said, her eyes dancing. "And every one knew you were meant. Then, after that, we sang 'You are drifting far from shore, Leaning on an idle oar, You are drifting, slowly drifting, drifting down.' " She was greatly enjoying all the turmoil and excitement of life these days.

There was a faint expression of anger on David's face as Mary spoke, while Prue's eyes flashed.

"No one need worry about me!" she exclaimed. Then she answered her father.

"Johnny is too grown up to leave at home. He is rightly of an age to go with me. If I go without him, he will think he has to burn alone in hell and his fears will return. But if I risk punishment with him, he has no fears at all." She shook her head and finished slowly, "No, Pa. My family—Johnny—means more to me than the mission. This may be wrong but so it is. Therefore we will both remain at home through the rest of the winter, anyway."

Mark said nothing more. But he was thinking to himself that there must be some way through this Sargasso Sea and, if he could, he'd find it.

"He came too late," David said. "Jonathan, I mean. He came too late to save the Indians. The power to run things was already in Ephraim's hands. In the school and in the village. No one could stop him. No one can stop him now. You'll see."

Mark lifted his great shaggy head and his hard black eyes glimmered on his son-in-law. "I'm surprised at you," he reproved. "We *will* see. By the Great Horned Spoon, we will! I'll stop him myself if no one else does."

Luke spoke for the first time. "Trouble thick as dogberries everywhere you look," he remarked cheerfully. And he rose to go out to the barn to check over things there before going to bed. But at the window he stopped short.

"Dang! See that!" he cried, an unusual note of excitement in his voice.

"See what?"

"There's a fire in the village! A big one! The sky's all red with it! Looks like the whole settlement is burnin' up. C'mon, Dave! Let's go!"

The fire was in the schoolhouse where Mr. Hawley taught. It was beyond control before Luke and David got there. The building, the furniture, the books were all gone in a red ruin. How it had caught no one knew though many conjectured without mentioning names. Who had it in for Mr. Hawley? No need to ask. And those that were agin him had the means to pay a fat bribe to somebody to do the dirty deed if they were so minded. Oh, o' course it might ha' been carelessness. Some young Injun might ha' been smokin' in his room. Mr. Hawley and the boys were lucky to escape with their lives.

When news of this disaster reached the commissioners on the heels of Mr. Edwards' letter they were more than ever alarmed. Things were definitely getting out of hand at the mission. As a consequence, Mr. Edwards received a notice to the effect that the situation about which he had written would receive prompt attention and, at the same time, Colonel Ephraim Williams was sent a severe and well-deserved rebuke.

Ephraim Williams was not a man to take a reprimand lying down. The letter delivered to him from the Boston government put him in a rage. So they did not approve of his daughter for head mistress after hearing from Mr. Edwards regarding her! And he was to do nothing about discharging Mr. Hawley or Mr. Woodbridge yet, since a committee wished to confer with the minister before General Dwight took over the two schools! The more he thought about it the more apoplectic he grew. Never before had he been crossed in this manner. Never! Then he quieted down and began once again to scheme and plot. First he called on his nephew Elisha, telling him that he must at once try to persuade Jonathan to back down on his stand regarding Abigail. Or, if he could not be persuaded, then Elisha, in his position as a board member of the Society for the Propagation of the Gospel, must do some bullying.

But Mr. Edwards was not one to be either persuaded or bullied.

So old Ephraim called on his son-in-law, Joseph Dwight, and ordered him to draw up a long argument setting forth all the reasons why Mr. Edwards was not qualified to continue to hold the pulpit in Indian Town.

"Write that he has never preached to the Indians in their own language," he prompted. "He understands it but he has never once preached in it. Pay no mind if they do all talk English!" he interrupted the younger man's objection. " 'Tis a point against him! But the best one," he went on, "is the matter of Prudence Martin. Recite how she has defied the power of the church and he has done nothing about it except sing hymns and pray. No punishment has been administered at all." He rubbed his hands together gloatingly. "That'll make a mark, I warrant!"

To his surprise it did not. The report, presented by Ephraim, Jr., was turned down in Boston and no action was taken against the minister. As the Boston authorities saw it, the final contest for the prize of the North American continent was about to begin. The Six Nations were needed to adhere to England's cause. If the Indians wanted Edwards in control of their affairs and did not want Dwight or the Williams clan, there was nothing more to be said.

Ephraim, finding himself balked at every turn, was beside himself. There was but one thing to do, he finally decided, to regain the power which he felt was slipping away from him. That was to buy out every one of the white farmers who belonged to Mr. Edwards' faction. Once he became economic master, he would have the full say of things. He had money enough to manage this, he told himself. Now let's see. Who were the families he'd best go to first?

He made a list, taking no one into his confidence, not even Joseph Dwight and Abigail. Then late one dark spring night he set forth on his planned rounds.

He came to Martin Manor first. If he could break up Mark's holdings he would at least weaken his strongest opponent, he had figured, and a full rout could come later. Sitting on his horse under the trees, he bellowed for David Reynolds to come forth. Mystified by the summons and the possible reason for it, David complied.

"Dave, I want to buy your land," the colonel said to him bluntly. "The strip you got from Andy."

The old man had always rather appalled David. Now he was astounded by him and his crude demand. But he replied courteously enough after a moment, "I've no wish to sell, Mr. Williams."

"I'll pay you twice what it's worth."

"I've still no wish to sell." David peered up through the darkness, trying to ferret out this strangeness. Was the fellow drunk? "What's back of your offer, sir, anyway?"

"Want it. That's all. Never did aim to sell such a chunk to the cap'n. Figured to get it back some time and now's the time. See here! I'll even go more than twice what it's worth."

This made David suspicious but of what he did not know. He simply shook his head, stifling his resentment of the old man's insensate, insistent demand. Ephraim lost his temper.

"You fool! Don't you know money's power?"

"Land is power, too," David replied quietly. "Surely you must agree or you wouldn't—"

But the colonel, with a muttered curse, dug his heels into his horse's side, wheeled and galloped off. No use wastin' more time here.

Dave went slowly back into the keeping room. Mark was sitting in his socks. Prue was darning. Mary was carding wool. Luke was mending harness. They all stopped their work and looked up curiously as they waited for David to speak.

He said, his tone angered at the memory, "He wanted to buy my share of the farm. Tried to *make* me sell it to him."

"What for?" Mark asked sharply.

"He wouldn't say. Except he'd always meant to get it back."

"But to come at this hour—" Mark's bright glance met David's, and grew brighter. "He's up to something. We'd best follow him."

David nodded, albeit unwillingly. He did not like being drawn into neighborhood quarrels. He would prefer to stand on the side lines. But a sense of loyalty to Prue's father impelled him to take a part in this one, and to go along with him now.

"I'll come, too!" Luke exclaimed. But Mark shook his head. "You stay here. Can't all the men folks be away at one time."

In a moment he and David were hurrying down the hill behind the sound of galloping hoofs. They found the colonel's horse tethered to a post before the house of one of Jonathan's stanchest supporters. They waited outside, hidden behind some bushes until Eph finally came out. In the blackness they could not see his face but they heard his triumphant chuckle and saw him slip a piece of white paper into his pocket.

They followed him to the next farm where, apparently, he met with less success for he emerged shaking his fist above his head.

"You'll be sorry!" he was heard to shout back at the slammed door.

Mark and Dave knocked at the same door when Williams had gone on his way. It was opened only a crack. "I tol' ye once—no! Now git!"

"Nat," Mark interrupted, in a low voice. "Let me in. It's Cap'n Martin and Dave."

The door opened wide and Nat Piggott, who had been afraid of the local Indians when he and his wife had taken refuge in Colonel Williams' cellar at the time of the terror, stared at them angrily above the flickering light of a candle he held. "All I want's to git to bed. What in tunket's goin' on 'round here that folks come callin' this hour o'night?"

"What did he want, Nat?"

"Wanted to buy my farm. Must be crazy."

Mark said only, "Get on your shoes and come with us."

"What for? Don't aim to 'tall." But Nat was putting on his shoes as he spoke. "What for?" he repeated, rising and reaching for his gun.

"You won't need that."

"Mebbe not. Mebbe so. Figger to take it, anyways. Gorry! What's that skunk up to?"

"I figure he's trying to buy everybody out that's a friend of Mr. Edwards. Then, likely, he'll get in some more of his friends and have things all his own way."

Nat blew out the candle, laid it down on a table, stepped out into the darkness and spat. "He *is* crazy."

They went on to the next farm where, again, the colonel's horse was tethered and where, again, he came out in a fuming anger. This farmer, too—David Pixley—was persuaded to join Mark's ranks and for the next couple of hours they followed Ephraim, who, except for his first call, was rebuffed everywhere. Defeated, and puzzled by his defeat (Had money lost its value?)

the colonel finally started back to his Castle as dawn broke. But he left behind him a sizable crowd of disgruntled, disgusted, angry men, Indians as well as whites, gathered together in the village who had heard the story and who had had more than enough of Ephraim Williams' high-handed ways and selfish furtive schemes. Elnathan Curtis was there. And Stephen Nash. And John Willard and Joseph Barnard—all those latest settlers whom Colonel Williams had brought in as his friends before Mr. Edwards' arrival. But they were less on his side now than he had expected them to be. Lawrence Lynch was there, too, only he was not taking sides against his master, General Dwight, having it in his mind to work out his redemption and set himself up here as a free man some day.

"Well, folks! What about this?" Mark called out to them all. And a chorus of voices answered.

"He'd orter be punished!"

"Yayuh! Can't let him get away with what he tried to do!"

"The durn skinflint!"

"The skunk! Thinks he's God A'Mighty hisself!"

"Hangin's too good f'r him, I say."

"Well, now, *is* it!"

"Yes!" Mark spoke up quickly. He was the leader and as the sense of the mob came to him he asserted his leadership. "It's too good. Listen, men! Let's just run him out of town. Scare him to death and run him out of town. 'Twould be more fun than a hanging. Come on! Follow me! But leave your guns behind. We want no bloodshed."

"How about tar and feathers?" some one called.

They began chanting.

"Pitch, tar and turpentine make an awful plaster,
The more you try to pull it off, the more it sticks the faster!"

Up the hill they swarmed, their singing growing louder as they neared their goal. Not all had complied with the order to drop their guns. Others had picked up heavy sticks. Still others had caught up coils of rope that they carried slung over their arms or shoulders, while the Indians brandished tomahawks. And as they saw the house with its surrounding moat and solid barricading doors before them, they began to shout and throw stones and shoot off their guns into the air. Suddenly above all the tumult there rose the blood-curdling yells of the savages. David took no part in all this. He was there with them—yet not with them. For the wild, exuberant lawlessness that had grown out of the whole night's work repelled him. These people were as untamed as their country, he thought. They were a rough, unruly crowd, seeming to love disorder and violence for its own sake. Never had he felt so alien and alone as in that moment, for it illumined for him a stark, unhappy but undeniable fact. America was not—and never could be—the home of his heart.

Ephraim Williams, meanwhile, who had first thought he was safe enough in his fortlike Castle, changed his mind when he heard the Indians yell, and, peering out from an upper window at the surging throng, he was sure they had come bent on killing him. In a voice cracked with terror, he ordered his wife to gather some clothes together into a bundle. Then, seizing it, he ran down the stairs as fast as his weight and his age and his trembling legs permitted, and out to the stables where his horse stood still saddled and bridled. Mounting while a slave boy clumsily fumbled with the roll of clothing, trying to strap it on behind, he clapped heels to the flanks of his mare and dashed out amongst the trees that stood between his place and Martin Manor. Thus hidden, he came in due time to where the trees ended and the barren land began, and there he emerged onto the road to Yokun Town.

But Yokun Town was not far enough away. Nor was Pontoosuc. Ephraim Williams, scared as he had never been in his whole life, did not feel safe until he reached the outpost of Deerfield a day or so later.

Mark, hearing of his final destination, said with satisfaction, "Well! The devil's been routed. And the school's been saved for the Lord and the Lord's works. I only hope John Sergeant can look down from heaven and see it for himself."

David said nothing. And Prue thought that the happenings of the mission had, indeed, reached into her life and family.

And what of the dilemma she had posed for Mr. Edwards? It was Johnny himself who resolved it. He came to his sister one day not long after the colonel's flight and said, "I'll go back to church meeting with you now if you want me to."

"Will you, Johnny?"

"Yes. I'll just sit there and think about Mr. Sergeant's God. That's all. I won't let Mr. Edwards' God get into my mind at all."

She looked deep into the wide gray eyes of the boy and saw them clear and unafraid.

"Pa says for me to fill my noggin with dreams and plans of my own making. Then there'll be no room for the fears and doubts others may try to put into it. He's right, isn't he?"

"Yes. He's right, Johnny."

"It's—" His brow creased with his effort at lucid thought. "It's what's in your own head that's important, not what's in other people's. It's your own private ship chest."

Prue gave him a quick hug. "Yes. That's what it is."

Johnny had found his strength at last, she thought happily.

Johnny went away and Prue lifted her eyes to the hills, to the view that was as dear to her as it was to Mark. Now she was free to return to the fold of the church from which she had never relished feeling an outcast. Now she could ease Pa's troubled conscience, but better than that, now she could take her rightful place by David's side once more. How loyal he had been! Never a word of protest had he given her though she was well aware of his unspoken disquiet.

"My cup runneth over," she murmured softly. "Surely goodness and mercy shall follow me all the days of my life and I shall dwell in the House of the Lord forever."

CHAPTER 13

The Return

THE MARCH SUN shone down with the warming beneficence
of spring on the little settlement at Indian Town. The village was recuperating from the reverberations of its own thunder.

Ephraim Williams, Senior, was gone for good. That was for
sure. His wife had followed him to Deerfield where he had moved
in with another Williams of the family, and from there he wrote
back orders to his young son, Elijah, left in charge of The Castle
until Ephraim, Jr., could appear on the scene and take command.
The villagers knew all that through the Indians who had been
approached by Elijah to sell him some wheat straw so that he
could lay a cock around each tree in his orchard for winter protection as his father had told him to do. Oh, he was gone all
right!

Well, good riddance to the old man. And good riddance to
Mr. Kellogg, who had faded from the scene with the colonel's departure. Yes, the turmoil had subsided. Jonathan Edwards was
in supreme command of affairs here, Abigail had retired into
domesticity—which, perhaps, was what she had always wanted—
and her husband, General Dwight, (who, it turned out, had disliked his involvement) now had his head full of other business,
for war with the French was only a matter of time now and he
had been called to Boston to help deal with it when it came.

The little group huddled in the sunshine on the porch of the
store was discussing all these matters when two strangers rode
into sight. No one knew who they were and they all watched in

silence as they made their way across the roadway and came up to the stoop.

One of them was a tremendous man, nigh the biggest they'd ever seen, and he was dressed most outlandishly in a heavy pea-jacket with his trousers tucked down into enormous boots. He had some kind of a visored cap on his dark, clubbed hair, too, and a canvas duffle bag bulging with things lay across the horse's back behind him. He wore a thick black beard covering most of his face and above this there was something faintly familiar about the bold black eyes. But no one could place him exactly. The other fellow was younger: a pindling youth with a pimply face that had on it now a scared look.

It was Elnathan Curtis who spoke first. "Howdy, strangers."

The big man answered for the two of them, the boy being able only to open his mouth like a gaping fish from which nothing came but air.

"Howdy."

He looked at them all coolly and there was something in his glance that sent a tingle down their spines and held them from further speech. It was John Willard who finally came out with the thing they'd been thinking. Letting his eyes run over the frayed and knotted rope bridles, he said, " 'Pears like Indian horses you got there."

"They are."

There was a slight stir among the men. At the rear of the porch an Indian detached himself from the shadows and came forward. Deliberately he stepped down to the ground and laid his hand on the neck of the young lad's mount. After a moment of silence he made a brief announcement.

"Schagiticoke."

There was another stir. Only a few from this tribe lived in the settlement. The rest made their home in the surrounding mountains. They were known to be quarrelsome and great care was always taken never to provoke them.

John Willard spoke again, a trifle grimly. "How'd you git 'em? An' lest you think I'm pokin' my nose in whar it's no bizness t'be, I'm the constable here."

The big man looked at his companion. "Tell your story," he ordered.

The youngster wet his lips and tried to speak but his voice cracked and his wits were addled by his growing fright, and presently the big man interrupted him impatiently.

"I met up with this—this stripling at the inn in Springfield. When he found I was coming this way he asked to join me. I had a hoss but he was afoot. Part way over the mountain my hoss stepped into a hole and broke her leg. So then we were both afoot. Little further on he gave his ankle a bad turn. Hurt him all right, I reckon. Anyway, it slowed him up considerable." He paused.

"We came to a place where these two hosses were tied to a tree with some buckets of sap setting on the ground nearby. I was ahead. I didn't know what he was doing till I heard a shot. Then I looked back. He was on one hoss and was leading the other up to me and two Indians were running down out of the woods yelling at him. He—" He stopped and swung his head around toward the boy. "You tell now."

The lad rolled his eyes wildly. "I—I shot one," he croaked. "I d-didn't think. I was s-scared. I was s-sartin' they'd scalp me if I didn't kill 'em fust. So I s-shot one."

There was a complete and utter silence.

"He's dead," the other went on. "I'm fair sure he's dead. He never moved after he fell. The second Indian bent over him and when he straightened up agin his hand went to his tomahawk at his belt and that's when we lit out. Seemed best to keep his hosses to help us on our way,"—dryly. "Harm was done then."

Willard said slowly, "Harm's done, all right." He turned to the Indian. "Will you see these critters git takened to the rightful Schagiticokes?" He turned back to the newcomers. "Git down."

The big man was already on the ground and slinging his duffle bag over his shoulders. The boy scrambled down quickly, his pink pimples standing out like pox on his white terrified face.

"Now, then, I got to git your names and where I kin lay a-holt of you does any trouble come out o' this." Willard looked at the young lad inquiringly.

"I'm— M-my name's Jim Davis. I—I ain't goin' anywheres special. Reckon I could stay here effen they was any w-work I c'd do. Leastways till this blows over. Oh, Lordy! You b'lieve I'll be hung?"

"Injuns don't hang folks," Willard said with deliberate cruelty. "They jest burn 'em alive. Or else kill 'em inch by inch."

"Oh, L-Lord have mercy!"

The big man spoke. "You'll find me on the hill if you want me. At Martin Manor. I'm Matt Martin."

John Willard looked at him in surprise. "Well, I'll be dogged! Didn't know the cap'n had airy other son than the one went west."

"Reckon you haven't been here long."

"Two—three years."

"I've been gone five or six."

"That accounts." But the constable's glance remained curious. How come no one ever mentioned this fellow? Must be sump'n about him not good. He said tentatively, "This Andy son—a lawyer out'n Ohio er some'ers—he writes home onct in a while."

Matt's eyes became black ice. Some one nudged Willard in the ribs and there was a slight general movement of retreat. Matt said, "You want I should leave any money with you for this mess?"

Willard shook his head. "Do we want money I'll come ast fer it. First off I'll tell Mr. Edwards. He'll likely hev to report to Boston." He looked at the shaking lad who stood clinging to the railing. "You'd best go with me to see him, too."

"Who's Mr. Edwards?" Matt asked.

"He's the new minister here."

"Where's Mr. Sergeant?"

"He died. Canker of the throat took him off back in 'fortynine."

Matt nodded and turned away.

Indian Town had changed and yet it was the same, he thought, as he swung up the hill road. There were many more whites here than when he had left, more neat fences and houses and barns, and fewer wigwams and foot-loose pigs and trees. Indeed, quite a sizable clearing had been made. The road through the village had been widened, too. The store was new and he glimpsed a green down by the church near the Indian burial ground where Konkapot lay. He wondered if Marie had been buried anywhere near the old leader.

He had long since ceased to think of Marie with any emotion, although she would probably always remain a tender memory because she had been the first and there had been a healing for him in her love that he had never encountered later. Probably the reason was that he no longer had need of healing. He was whole and complete within himself. He had no requirement of a woman save to satisfy his physical desire.

Immersed in his thoughts, he swung along at a steady pace over the ground where traces of snow still remained. Seemed a dozen lifetimes since he'd run away from here that long-ago night. In spite of all he'd seen and done since then, that hour in Marie's cabin stood out clear in his mind and he could even now recall all that had overpowered him then: the shock and horror, the sense of guilt, the pity, the helplessness, the hate and rebellious confusion. Well, he'd got over it right enough, and death, new then, had become an old story long since.

His memories became a flood at this point, tumbling over one another like the waves of the ocean in their haste to reach the shore.

Boston—and the smell of the sea in his nostrils. The great dark mysterious hulk of ships lying still and silent in the harbor. The night's blackness. The chill damp. The slippery wharves and the hurrying figures of men all around. Then—suddenly—an uproar back in the city a ways and a shouting milling crowd coming toward him and himself caught up in the midst of it, fighting for his very life. Oh, it had been wild! But his blood had sung and his fists had flailed and when 'twas over he was running fleetly alongside another man till they could drop off the wharf and hide in the underpinnings beneath.

"What—was it?" he had gasped.

"Britishers." The voice had a Scottish burr, the tall frame

folded up in the dimness was powerful beside him. "Hae ye nae
kennt? They try everywhaur t'impress our lads into service on
their ships. But ye're a brawny mon an' so be I. An' they've not
got the twa av us th' noo." A growl meant for a chuckle had issued softly from his throat.

"I want to go on a ship, all right," Matt had said. "But not on
a British ship."

"Whut ship, then? Ye dinna ken? Ye could come abaird th'
schooner whaur I be. She's a guid enough vessel, though her
maister's an auld rapscallion. Ontemperate he is. Wi' a rage in
him like to a seethin' cauldron. 'Twill boil over th' nicht, I'll
warrant! But syne we've lost some lads I doot not ye'll be gi'en
a welcome f'r all his bloody anger." Again that growl in his
throat meant for a laugh. "Oh, he'll gi' ye a welcome! For 'tis
na in him t' see a guid mon wasted."

So Matt right away had got a berth on a sailing vessel. His
Scottish friend, Alec MacDonald, a sandy-haired man about ten
years older than he, had turned out to be the ship's carpenter,
but Matt ranked no more than a "boy," for all his size, because
of his inexperience. Days, then, of sweeping and clearing decks,
of coiling up rigging, of loosing and furling the light sails, of
standing watch and going aloft and learning to draw and knot
yarns.

It was during this apprenticeship that he'd come to understand the reason Pa had not wanted him to go to sea at the
tender age of eleven, for life aboard, even for one as big as he,
had been hellish. He'd not been able, at first, to "pare his opinions and hold his tongue," as Alec had advised, and injustices,
jealousies, thievery, maliciousness and sadistic abuse had brought
him to a quick fury that had only served to fetch the cat onto
his bare back more than once or to feel the hard fists of some of
the crew. But he'd survived.

That had been the first trip and it had taken him to Africa. He
had been amazed to discover the world was so immense a place.
Week after week of solitary sailing over leagues and leagues of
ocean. Seemed they'd never get anywhere. But eventually they'd
reached the coast and a "factory" where blacks were held in

waiting for shipment to the Indies. They'd sailed back with the hold packed full, the men laid, like spoons, front to back, manacled, and dying by the dozen. At Barbados, those that had survived had been sold in the market there at a price that had made Matt's eyes pop out. Five to seven hundred dollars apiece! A man could get rich quick in that business, he'd said thoughtfully to himself.

He came to a halt here in his thoughts as well as in his climb, for he had reached the barren strip and the sight of what lay before him brought a sharp and sudden understanding to him.

He'd been all over the world. He'd seen everything. He'd seen palm-fringed beaches where the sand was soft as a white velvet carpet beneath your bare feet. He'd seen rocky headlands and swampy plains, gray deserts and dark jungles. He'd seen islands where emerald-green mountains turned to purple in the twilight and the air was filled with the perfume of jasmine and the melody of falling water. He'd seen primitive hamlets of mud huts and the white turrets and towers of ancient cities, and pagodas and palaces and simple, charming pastel-colored homes. He'd been in places where the sun shone hot all year round and you wanted nothing but to lie in the shade and make love to the girl by your side. And he'd been in places where it was forever cold and the glitter of ice and snow near blinded you and the breath on your beard turned it brittle, and a freezing mist crawled through your skin into your very bones to turn you bloodless so all you wanted was just to survive. Oh, he'd seen aplenty! For from first mate to captain to prisoner to pirate and back to captain again compassed everything. But never till he returned here with fresh-opened eyes had he seen a place that held so much of the best of what he'd seen and known.

Here was stretch enough for the eye and space enough for limb. Here were friendly mountains in a lovely line against the sky that did more than change from green to purple, for these took fire every fall and blazed all colors as the Caribbean peaks never could. Here was summer, too, lying under the dead brown ground—he remembered it well—fragrant and soft as a zephyr. And winter, also, if you wished, that glistened and gleamed with its own beauty but would never last too long. Here were winds strong enough to unhair a dog should you hanker for them. And a trackless wilderness at your back door if you hankered for that. And even a strip of bare rock and a swamp to keep it all in proper balance. Water? Well, there was a bit of a lake not far off, but could be you'd tire of water as Pa must have.

There lay the sudden understanding. Some one thing—if not more—you had to yield up in your old age and Pa had yielded the sea once he'd taken from it what he wanted. But where, besides here, could he have got so much else he'd needed and remembered and loved? His own black eyes, hard and cold and bright, like Pa's, glimmered softer with his new-found knowledge.

Slowly his glance took in the scene before him, seeing it, too, changed considerable since he'd beheld it last. More trees were chopped down now and more neat orchards set out across the road to the east. There was a new barn over there, too, a sizable one, directly opposite the house. There were more hayfields, more fences, more stock in the pastures. He could see sheep in an enclosure behind the new barn that hadn't been there when he'd left. He could see a pair of oxen working 'stead of only Star. And two colts were frisking in the field as if today was the first time this season they'd been let out.

It all looked prosperous.

His look swung to the house. There it stood, beneath its great trees, lovely as any pastel island place, more inviting than any palace, spacious, dignified, serene. You couldn't compare it with anything else you knew. It had its own air, its own charm and appeal. What changes had taken place in it, he wondered? Almost, he was afraid to go forward and find out: for changes there must be since nothing stood still.

Somewhat amazed at the stir of feeling within him, he picked up his duffle bag that he had let slide to the ground. As he did so he heard from a distance, the low rhythmic beating of drums— Indian drums. They were telling about the killing that day. They were calling the neighboring tribes to the funeral. They were saying—what?

It worried him. He hadn't done it. It wasn't his fault. Yet he was mixed up in it and so it did not make for the most auspicious homecoming.

He set out again. He could see far off two men with the oxen, one plowing, the other harrowing. He could see the rich brown earth rolling up and lying gleaming in the sunlight. There were more men amongst the apple trees pruning them, and in the distance two others erecting fence posts. But none observed him and in their bulky winter outfits he could not tell one from another. Pa must be there somewhere. And Luke, mebbe, growed up to a good size now. And some Negroes, most likely, since no two men alone could do all there was to be done.

He moved along. And now he asked himself the question he had not faced before. Why had he come back?

He was not sure himself of the reason except that he'd reached a turning point in his life and had not decided what way to take from here. He'd made his pile: some in triangular trading, more in piracy. He had part of his fortune banked in Boston, the rest —the gold and silver that had been his share of loot captured— lay buried deep in a spot on the southern coast. Nobody knew where except the raw-boned, dour-faced Alec who had stayed by him through everything and who was now waiting in Boston Harbor in charge of his ship there. Oh, he was sailing on his own bottom these days, all right! And mayhap that was part of coming home, too—to show Pa he was. But mostly it was to sort out his thinking, find out if this was the place he wanted to settle down—when he got ready to settle down—or if he wanted a bigger place, a city, where life was gayer, where there were more women, where he could, if he chose, build up for himself a fleet of ships instead of having only one. He didn't know. He was torn in two already, both liking it better than he remembered or had ever thought he would, and not liking it. Lord! Whatever would a man *do* here? That is, if he didn't want to rip up the earth and make things grow? And he was never a one for that.

Well, time would tell. He'd see 'em all—the family. Especially Prue. To Prue he felt the closest. Yes, he'd let 'em all know about him and what he'd done. He'd stay for a spell. But if he wanted to light out again he would and nobody could stop him. He was his own boss, just like he'd planned to be.

Prue was alone in the house when Matt appeared. She was sitting at the maple butterfly table in the big keeping room polishing the brass candlesticks when the doorway was darkened, and, looking up, there stood the biggest man she had ever seen. For a moment she did not know him in his strange seafaring clothes and with his heavy beard half covering his face. Then she saw he was a younger edition of Pa and her hands flew to her cheeks. "Matt!"

"Yes. Matt." He came in to tower above her, exuding confidence and power. It was more than physical. Matt had found himself while he was gone, she told herself. He was all of a piece now. "Well, am I welcome?"

She let out a gasp and got to her feet, and, reaching up, laid her hands on his great shoulders in quick contrition.

"Yes, of course! Oh, *yes,* Matt! You're *so* welcome! You gave me such a startle I—I couldn't think. Oh, but 'tis wondrous good to see you! We've thought about you so many times. We kept waiting for a letter—waiting and hoping—and when none came—" She gave a shaky little laugh. "Well, we just didn't know if you were dead or alive. Why didn't you write, Matt? Just once?"

"I didn't rightly know what to say at first. Then—" Then time had seemed to make an unbridgeable gap between him and home, seemed like. But Prue was speaking.

"You could have said where you were! You could have said you were well! You could—" She broke off. "Oh, dear, never did I mean to be a scold the very first minute you set foot in the house. Forgive me. I—" Suddenly a sob in her throat choked off all her words so she could not go on. She could only stand there looking at him with her blue eyes swimming.

"Well! Now!" Awkwardly he patted her arm. "What's all this for? I thought you were so glad to see me."

"I was—I am—"

Aaron. She must tell him about Aaron right away. But she was afraid. She searched his glance for kindness—Ma always said there was kindness deep hid in him—and met only a bright inscrutability. Pulling herself together she stepped away and as she did so he noticed her figure for the first time. It changed him somehow. Gentled him. She heard it in his voice.

"You're married."

She nodded.

Slowly he lowered to the floor the heavy duffle bag. Then he took off his cap and dropped it on the table.

"Who's the man?"

"David." Her voice rang with her happiness. "David Reynolds. You remember him, don't you? We have two lovely children, Matt, and this summer a third will come. Oh, there's so much to tell you! I don't know where to begin."

"At the beginning. But sit down whilst you do it." He pulled forward a rocking chair for her and then took a straight one himself. He straddled it, sitting backward on it with his arms over its top. She heard it crack and thought anxiously it would break under him, and then wondering why she wasted a caring thought on a thing like that when so much else was of greater importance between them. *Aaron,* her mind kept saying. But she could only speak of trivialities.

"I ought to ring the bell and call everybody. We have a big bell on a post outside now instead of that awful horn." She started to rise but he threw out a huge hand in an imperative delaying gesture.

"Wait. Let me get caught up first." He stared away through the window a moment. Then, abruptly, he said, "I miss Ma."

"Yes."

He turned his bright black eyes on her. "I'm sorry she's gone. That's a fact. I always liked her. It always galled me she didn't like me."

Prue's glance widened with surprise. "Why, Matt! She loved you! I think most of all she loved you because you were her first-born son and— Why, her very last words to me were of you." A sudden insight came to her. "Belike some of your trouble here when you were young was all in your own head."

He considered that. "Could be," he said. Then he gave a short hard laugh. "But not all of it."

She said quickly, "Let's not go into the past any more. 'Tis over and done. And there's a new sheet to write on now." She paused, her breath coming a little faster. "Just remember, when Pa comes in, that he's been mightly lonely without Ma all these years. Besides"—well, she'd come to it at last—"he set a store by you no matter what you think he thought, and you can't blame him if he was cut up bad when you—"

Her voice died as light running footsteps were heard across the front porch. The next moment Aaron came in. He stopped short at sight of the stranger there and stared at him in a questioning silence that seemed to Prue to stretch on and on like some terrible enchantment. There he stood, tall for his years, straight as an arrow, black-eyed, black-browed, watchful and wary as an animal. At last she spoke.

"This is Matt, Aaron. You've heard me tell of Matt many a time. He went off to sea, you know, but now he's come back." Let him take it from there, she thought. He knows! He sees! It's for him to say what he wants.

But Matt was a statue frozen into silence as well as immobility. And, with a startled look at the wildness that had leaped into the face that he turned on the boy, Prue spoke again quickly.

"Will you do something for me, please, Aaron? Will you run out to the fields and tell Gramp and David and Luke that Matt has come home? Find Mary and Johnny, too. I think they're with Mam Beck and the babies. I think they all went to the orchard to watch the pruning."

He nodded but he did not stir.

"Well—run along."

He backed away, his look fixed as firmly on Matt as Matt's was on him. At the door he turned and fled on fleet silent feet.

Matt said hoarsely, *"Who is that?"*

"That's your son, Matt."

He gripped the chair back with both of his big hands. Then he slowly rose, swung it from between his legs, set it down carefully and walked over to a window where he stood with his back to Prue. Her voice followed him in shocked amazement.

"Didn't you know?"

He swung about, his face a storm of emotions. "No! I didn't know!" He moved his head like a man coming up out of deep water. "God Almighty! I don't know why I didn't! Could be I was too frenzied over Marie. Could be I didn't rightly take in all Peter told me." He stared at Prue. "I always thought the baby died, too."

"So you didn't run away from him. Oh, Matt! I'm glad of that!"

"No. I'd never—" He stopped. "Well, I don't know as 'twould have hindered me, either." He stopped again. "Who knows? The whole town?"

"Just about."

"Does he?"

She nodded. There was a silence. Then he gave a short laugh. "Fine welcome he gave his pa."

"Matt, don't." She looked at him gravely. "He was waiting for you. I always told him to wait for you to move first." She hesitated. "Are you angered, Matt?"

"Angered?"

"At me."

He frowned. "I don't know what I am."

Matt was in a tumult. He felt a strange, queer-feeling pride that he had fathered a son. It gave a sharp point to the future that he had never thought on before. And 'twas Marie's boy. There was pleasure in that thought, too, but no shame. He'd seen too much to let that part trouble him. Yet there was some resentment, though he was uncertain at what. The boy's attitude, perhaps. The way he'd stood off. And—finally—there was the thought that if he took a woman to wife she might not—

Prue was saying, "Aaron died and Peter went west. I couldn't leave him there with the Indians. Not your boy, Matt." Her blue eyes beseeched him.

He said nothing.

"Besides—Aaron asked me to take him." She told him, then, about that. "I couldn't refuse. Don't you see I couldn't?"

"No, you couldn't," he agreed slowly at last.

She dared to draw a breath of relief while he prowled about the room seeming to fill it with his great size and restlessness. "I bet Pa hated it," he threw out presently.

"At first," she admitted reluctantly.

"And David?"

"David thought I did right."

There was a silence, then, "How is Pa now?"

"He's—well—he's never unkind, Matt. It's just—" She paused, searching for the right words as she saw his face darken. Then she hurried on, changing the subject. "If you don't want him— If you feel angered and don't want him, I'll keep him for my own. He's like that, anyway, to me."

"He calls you Ma?"

"No. I told you it's been the truth between us from the start. He'd have found out some day. And maybe in a cruel way. You know how people are."

The storm that had stood on his face cleared abruptly. "I know how you are."

She rose and went to him and laid her hands on his arms. "It's all right, then?"

He looked down at her. A son. He had a son. Yes, it gave a point to the future, and if he couldn't manage his own woman. . . .

"I'm—obliged to you, Prue."

"Oh, Matt!" Suddenly she thought of something. "Are you married?"

"No. Why?"

"I was afraid you might be. I was afraid you might want to take him away. David said you might—"

"Does he want me to?"

"I don't mean that. But he's yours. David always kept reminding me so I wouldn't feel too badly if you—" She stopped. "What I'm trying to say is that David wants me to have what I want—if it's possible."

Matt thought, She would like to keep him. Perhaps 'twould be best, though he wasn't sure.

"Well, it's possible," he said. "Most likely I'll go off and leave him to you again." He paused. "Takes thinking. Not all that's happened to me has fashed me like this has." He bent down to pick up his duffle bag and her hands fell. When he straightened up he seemed to have put the confusion and uncertainty of the past few moments from him. "My old room in the ell still empty? I'll stow my gear if 'tis."

She gave a start. "Oh! Aaron's there now. You see, when the babies came it grew a little crowded upstairs. Besides, he likes to be off by himself—he's like you, Matt, that way—but if you want, he can go in with Johnny across the hall downstairs here."

He thought a moment. "No. Let be. That fixes it hard and fast. If we don't have sand in our ears before morning we'll get acquainted."

"Sand in your ears?"

"A sailor's way of naming a shipwreck."

The keeping room that night looked like an Oriental bazaar, so filled was it with the things Matt had brought back from his travels. Yards of silk—sky blue, carnation red, April green, spring lilac, sun gold, and all richly embroidered—were flung over chair backs. Brass bowls from India, *cloisonné* boxes from China, lacquered dishes from Japan, perfume from Arabia, high-backed tortoise-shell combs from the Celebes, shell necklaces, pearl necklaces, gold necklaces, bracelets and rings were strewed over the tables. Luke stood fingering a Damascene dagger, glittering and bright. Mary pirouetted in a brilliantly flowered silk shawl with a deep fringe that reached to her knees. David smoothed with affection a leather wallet from Morocco. Prue hung entranced over some pieces of fine linen and delicately drawn laces. Johnny curiously examined ivory tusks carved into a line of marching elephants, little figures of monkeys and strange fat-bellied gods, while beside him Aaron eyed, but did not touch, a heavy knobbed stick with fierce-looking spikes that was the weapon of some primitive tribe. There was something for every one, even the babies, though Matt had not known of little Mark's or Esther's existence. He had brought along the wooden shoes and the string of bells as curiosities. But Mark, taken in charge by Mam Beck, had gone clattering up to bed in his Dutch footgear and long before this Esther had fallen asleep with the bells beneath her pink satin cheek.

It was all unbelievable, Prue thought, as she relaxed, heavy with her child, in a rocker withdrawn a little from the rest of the group.

She thought back a few hours.

Pa had come in last behind the excited young folks. She had forgotten to tell Matt that he looked older but perhaps it was as well, for the sight of him, thinner and grayer than Matt remembered and with the spring gone from his step, had caught him to a shocked surprise. Could be it had softened him a bit and made the first minutes easier. She could sense Pa was glad to see Matt again, that a hope rose in him they might yet be friends. But some constraint had held him—Thought of his own harshness? Thought of Aaron?—and he had hesitated. It had been Matt who had put out his hand first as if experience had wiped out all youthful unreason, and Pa had gripped it hard. So the first hurdle had been got over. But each remained wary of the other, seeming to agree their best meeting place was on the common ground of Matt's adventures at sea. To her surprise, she had sensed a wariness in David, too, though she could not fathom why.

"How did you come by your captaincy?" Mark had asked first thing, soon as they all were settled. Oh! It was easy to see he was ready and glad to live over his own life in Matt's!

"That was when I got back from the Orient," Matt had replied. "A trip I made after I'd given up thought of whaling. I signed on a privateer, then, sailing for the Caribbean. But we were attacked by a Spanish ship off Cuba and the captain was killed. I was the mate so the command came to me."

"Did you beat 'em? The Spaniards?" Luke had demanded, stirred from his usual calm by all this strange talk.

"We scuppered her,"—briefly. "But not till we had her treasure." He had gestured. "Some of this stuff is from the hold of that ship. "

Pa had leaned forward, impatient at the interruption, wanting only Matt's story. "And then?"

"Well, then, we went on our way."

Prue called Aaron to her now and whispered to him that it was time he went to his room. "Matt's to share it with you while he's here. It's his, you know, really. So you sleep next the wall and leave the greatest space for him."

Aaron nodded and slipped away, taking nothing with him, saying nothing, showing nothing of what he was feeling about this unexpected arrangement, and Prue stifled a small sigh. It was the only way the boy was difficult. She never knew what he was thinking. She didn't know with Mary, either, it was true. But at least Mary gave out a voluble chattering though it said nothing of her true thoughts.

Matt's words pulled her back. He was giving his father a strange-looking, long-stemmed pipe, saying, "Mebbe you'd like this, Pa."

Pa took it, nestled the bowl in the palm of his hand and lifted it to his nose. "Has a good smell. Know the wood?"

"I've heard. But I forget. Outlandish kind of name."

Pa began pouring tobacco in and tamping it down with his thumb. "So you went on your way," he said remindingly, and, looking up, his face grew stern in the old way. "I don't hold with privateering, you know."

Matt laughed easily. "Well, when our leading citizens in Boston outfit us and our governor commissions us, who can say it's wrong?"

"Just the same—"

"No use talking, Pa. It's what's going on. And why not? The backers get their cut and are pleased. The public gets its goods cheap and is pleased. The captain reaps a rich reward himself— if he's lucky—so he's pleased." He paused. "To my thinking, the fellow that risks his life has as much right to profit as the fellow that only risks his money. I had clear orders from the governor to prey on French ships in the Indies." He paused again. "But to tell truth, it wasn't till I turned captain on a pirate's ship that I really got my pile."

"Captain on a *pirate's* ship!" Mary sucked in her breath, her brown eyes round with her excited wonder. Oh, what a life her brother had led! Would anything ever happen to her? Would she ever see the world as Matt had? Or must she, like him, go out to meet it?

"Tell us," David said. He was interested in spite of himself, for he was not drawn to this brawny, hard, adventuring brother of Prue's. If he should decide to stay here, what effect might he not have on them all? Already Mary was thinking and wishing crazy things, 'twas plain. If little Mark were older— But thanks be, he was a baby still. He left off thinking and waited for Matt to speak while Mark's gaze screwed up to coal-bright pinpoints of eager light.

It made an incredible tale. Had Matt heard it himself from some one else, likely he'd find it hard to believe. Oh, it hadn't been strange (he told them) that his ship had been overpowered by two others painted black and flying the skull and crossbones bold as you please, for the weather had been heavy with a dark grayness folding sky and sea and water together so he'd not seen them till they were on him. He'd put up a fight but the odds were against him from the start. And when fireballs set his sails ablaze and the enemy's guns raked his decks, sending his men down like ninepins, there was nothing for him to do but strike his colors.

That part was understandable. But for him to have been able to fix a bargain with the pirate captain to save not only his own skin but Alec's, too, and those of the crew still left to him, was something else.

Yet so it had been. And he related how it had happened.

The handsome blond leader, elegant in damask waistcoat and breeches with a heavy chain of gold about his neck and a great ruby on his thumb, strolling up to Matt's riddled bridge where he stood, torn and bloody, had been too insolent. Thinking his end had come, anyway, Matt had decided to match him.

"Captain Nikola," the pirate had said, bowing mockingly. "At your service."

"Captain Martin," Matt had replied shortly, standing stiff and unbending and full of hate.

Lightly the other had swung his sword that hung in a jeweled scabbard by his side, both liking and not liking the proud giant before him. "I have no need of your men," he had said. "They may die. Different amusing ways that will be decided later. But I could use a better navigator than the one I've got."

"My navigator has been killed," Matt said. "Yonder he lies."

Nikola let his look stray to the fallen figure. "Aye. Well, doubtless you can do as well."

It was then (Matt said) his bold thought had come to him, born of the other's insulting tone.

"Doubtless," he had agreed. "But there's a condition."

Nikola had lifted an eyebrow. "*You* name conditions?"

"I do. 'Tis this. If I'm to live, my men live, too."

"To stir up trouble on my ships? Blast your impudence! Do you take me for a fool?"

"Rather"—Matt had told him coolly—"a wise man not to refuse me. Listen! The days of piracy are not what they were. There are fewer of you sailing the seas nowadays. When you take prizes you need crews, for you lose men in every encounter and cannot trust your captives. Yet if you dared to trust them—" Deliberately he had paused.

"Speak on! Tell what's in your mind!"

Matt had shrugged. "Who knows? Some might make good pirates. Since our lives depend on it, we ourselves might. What harm to try us? If we prove unsatisfactory you can always kill us later. Only time would be lost. Nothing else."

So that was how it had been for weeks and months till the day came when four prizes were taken and three of the masters on those vessels killed. He was trusted by then, so it was he who had, by free election of all, been made captain of one of the ships. After that it was his ship (though Nikola took good care to have the majority of Matt's crew made up of his own men) and, when booty was taken—gold, silver in coin or bullion, church plate and other riches—and a dividend was made, six portions were Matt's according to custom.

Thus another year passed making the second since his defeat at the hands of the pirates and making him a rich man.

Aye, it was a strange tale, Matt concluded, but the sea could yield others stranger than that, he would wager on it.

No one had moved during this recital. Now David said, with a smile glinting in his brown eyes, "There's a kind of wry humor in the thought of a man's being forced to make his fortune at peril of death, whether he wants to or not."

Matt nodded carelessly. David was all right for Prue, he guessed, but he himself liked a man less stand-offish. For a brief moment their glances met and in it David saw himself as Matt saw him—a stranger in their midst. Would he never feel like one of them, he asked himself? And knew, again, as he had the night Eph Williams had been driven away, that he wouldn't. One had to be born here to companion with them. There was a saying that Englishmen took England with them wherever they went. But not here. Here an Englishman lost England—if he wasn't careful. And now Mary's voice broke into his thoughts.

"But don't stop there!" she cried. "Oh, Matt! Don't stop there!"

Prue's eyes sought Johnny. He was sitting on the floor, his slender adolescent frame tense and still, his hands clasped about his knees, his gray glance wide. Never had he heard such a tale. It was terrible. But it was wonderful, too. And it was true! *True.*

"Yes. Tell us how your escaped, Matt. Johnny will never be able to sleep until you do."

"Well—" Matt was silent a moment. "It was simple," he said. "When we ran into the path of a British man-of-war, I permitted her to overtake us—accidentally on purpose—and capture us. We were all brought to trial in England for piracy, of course, but Alec and I were acquitted. The only ones," he added.

"And how did you manage that?" Mark asked gruffly. These were doings unlike any he'd ever known and, bold and dashing though they sounded, there were things left unsaid that disturbed him. Why hadn't Matt managed to fake poor seamanship before so much time had gone by and surrender much sooner to a

British vessel? The loot before him gave him his answer. It had not been the challenge of danger dared or a curiosity for far places that had lured Matt to the sea. For him it had been a quick and easy way to amass a fortune. He stared at his son, seeing him grown into an alien pattern, a stranger, after all.

"Alec had a relative living in London," Matt was saying. "A lady of quality and some importance and influence. Word was got to her of our plight and at the trial she rose and declared she had known us both well for many years and she would swear the tale we told—of impressment into piracy—was true. Not only that, but upon our release, she would vouch for our good conduct in the future. On her reputation for uprightness we escaped. Although"—again his easy laugh—"her youth and beauty helped considerable in affecting the jury, I must admit."

"Oh, Matt! You should have married her! Didn't you want to?"

Prue spoke. "Mary, you are much too curious. Johnny, off with you now. It's our turn to talk and we are going to tell Matt of Andy and his life in the west. You know all about that, so good night."

Reluctantly Johnny withdrew.

Prue went to the drop-lid desk and rummaged through it for Andy's last letter. Just as she came on it and turned with it in her hand the drums in the hills were heard again.

Mark reared up his shaggy head. "Must be something's happened. I've been hearing those drums on and off since afternoon. Don't like the sound, either."

Matt met his eyes.

"Something *has* happened. I can tell you about that, too."

CHAPTER 14

The Revenge

THE LAST SNOW of that year fell like softly blown mist. It obscured the world for a few hours, then it drew away beneath the white light of the sun, leaving the tops of the slender birches fantastically blurred with frost so that they looked like enormous plumes pinned for decoration on the alabaster shoulders of the hills. There followed, after that, unexpected days when the amazed wind paused in its final blustering as an emerald sheen appeared like magic to cover the forbidding earth. Eager ferns began to poke up their furry rounded heads, lilies thrust furled green lances through dark sod, red buds formed on the maple trees and wild violets made purple patches in the cold shade. Presently in the forest bluebirds flashed and robins called while early mornings brought the raucous sound of crows flapping hungrily over the fields.

It was spring. A time of growth and yearning. Prue, feeling the push of vigorous life within her own body, knew an increasing lethargy and peace. But to her younger sister, Mary, the unseen force that laid gentle fingers on the swelling buds of the apple trees, that made the ground quiver and crack open to the silent demands below it, brought an unbearable pressure of vague compelling desires. When would she begin to live? And where? And how?

Others in the great house were affected, too. The sap no longer rose in Mark's body as it once had and it was getting to be an effort for him to last out the day in the fields. Could be his worry added to his weariness, too, for unease stood in the air and a tense watchful waiting filled every man's mind in Indian Town.

The Schagiticokes had had their funeral—an elaborate ritual to which many neighboring tribes had gone—and then had waited for justice to be brought them. But at the trial in Springfield, whither Mark had accompanied Matt and young Jim Davis, Matt had been completely acquitted, and Jim, convicted of manslaughter, only slightly punished by a short stay in jail there. The judgment was based on the argument that it was difficult, if not impossible, for a young stranger passing through the land, to differentiate between a friendly local Indian and an unfriendly Indian from the north. But the sullen acceptance of the verdict and the ensuing silence of the savages had told all too clearly that they were not satisfied. Even the Stockbridge Indians (some of whom had already enlisted to assist the English in their war against the French) and the visiting Mohawks, Oneidas, Tuscaroras and Delawares, maintained a strange and unhealthy quiet.

Mark had gone to Mr. Edwards in his concern and had succeeded in turning the minister's attention from his books long enough to persuade him to write to the government in Boston. It was gravely important, Jonathan wrote. The Schagiticokes were unreliable and mischievous. They could stir the embers of a smoldering resentment into flames amongst the Mohawks and Mahicans living in their midst. And then what? The mission lay in a strategic position between north and south, between east and west. And with the French spreading the rumor that the English intended, sooner or later, to swallow them all, would it not be wise to send a subsidy to calm them? It was a matter on which the authorities procrastinated for weeks, but eventually the sum of twenty pounds was sent.

Yet now, as summer hovered over the land, Mark knew they were still not appeased. The money had, rightfully, been interpreted as a bid for safety rather than as belated justice. Only Matt, of all the men folk, seemed unaffected by the brooding anxiety. And this was strange because he, perhaps better than any of them, was aware of the dark workings of the Indian mind.

Was it that he did not intend to linger here long but to return to his waiting ship and his life at sea so that his own plans held a greater importance to him? Mark could not tell. He could only look at his son with puzzled eyes in alternate pride and disturbance.

He was proud when Matt strode about holding little Mark crowing ecstatically on his shoulders. Or when he bent in silence above baby Esther's cradle, held in thrall by the petal softness of her hands, her flashing dimpled smile, her long-lashed, golden-brown eyes. Or when, with Aaron mounted before him, he rode boldly, without embarrassment into the village to the grist mill or to the store or even down to the wigwams and tepees of the Indians on the river. The two of them—his small son and he—seemed somehow to have established a bond of understanding and liking, from the very first night when they had shared the same room, though no look or touch ever passed between them to indicate it.

But Mark was disturbed when he saw Matt's gaze go over the farm with a hard calculation in his bright eyes. What was he thinking? It was impossible to guess. Once he said, "You've given Prue her share of the land and David has taken title to Andy's acreage. I'd like my piece, too."

Ah! Jealousy! Was that it? Mark said, "You thinking of staying?"

"I'm thinking of Aaron."

There was a flash of the old antagonism between them, but only a flash and instantly gone. Mark debated the matter within himself and finally decided that Matt's interest in the property augured well. Once the sea had served him all he wanted of it, he'd leave it, as he himself had. And Aaron, for whom Mark had not provided, should, of course, be considered. Mark was just, even though resentment died hard in him. So he deeded to Matt ninety acres north of the Manor House toward the lake and Yokun Town, which, like the remainder of his holdings (save the one hundred and eighty now being worked and already owned by Prue and David) was undeveloped. A strip of ninety acres, partly cleared, lying south of the big house, he was saving for

Mary, so that she could be neighborly with her sister when she married, while Luke and Johnny would go east toward the brook and up the mountain.

Matt thanked him and there the matter ended. And before the tragedy that struck the household a day or so later, it was forgotten.

It was a hot summer day in July and all the Martins save only the two youngest, who had been left at home in Mam Beck's care, had gone to church. For Prue it would probably be her last appearance there until her baby came.

Mr. Edwards was in the middle of his lengthy sermon and the congregation had settled down to its various ways of giving him their attention when the church door flew open and a wild-eyed, disheveled man rushed breathlessly up the aisle.

"Injuns!" he gasped. "They're on the warpath! On the hill! Killin'! Scalpin'! Oh, Lord! Have mercy on us all!"

Instantly bedlam arose. Every one started up. Cries of fear and horror filled the air. Questions were hurled. Men and women hurriedly made for the door to race back to the protection of their homes or to race south to the greater protection of the large populace in Sheffield North Parish. In vain the minister raised his voice, exhorting his people to a faith in the Lord and calm in this crisis. They paid no heed. Jostling, pushing, moaning and calling, they crowded by the astounded Stockbridge Indians and vanished. In no time the church was half empty.

David, springing to his feet at the stranger's burst of electrifying words, reached him first and held him fast by one arm.

"Which house?" he demanded.

The man shook his head and continued his babbling, incoherent story. He had been riding from Yokun Town. As he was on his way along the hill road, he saw an Indian run out of a house dragging a child with him. He had yelled at the savage who had dropped the child and lifted his tomahawk, but had changed his mind, snatched him up again and disappeared into the woods. He had then entered the house and had seen—

"Such sights! Oh, my God! The slave woman murdered and lying in her own blood. The babe's head crushed—"

"*Which house?*"

David's expression was terrible to behold. At his elbow now stood Prue, her face drained of color, her blue eyes wide and staring. Above her Matt towered, a volcano ready to erupt, and close around her were clustered old Mark, Mary, Luke, some of the Williams clan and the Dwight family. The hill. They all lived on the hill. But Martin Manor was the most isolated of the three homes there.

The man rolled his eyes toward David and went on as if he had not heard the question.

"There—there was another Injun in the house when I got there. But he ran off when he saw me. He'd done his work—"

"Blast you! *Which house?*" Matt roared, seizing him from the rear by the shoulders and shaking him as if he had been a rat.

The stranger gulped. "I—I'm tellin' ye! I'd jest come out of the forest. I'd jest got to the first farm—"

"Ours, David." Prue heard her hoarse, strained voice as if it were another's. "It was our place. Hurry! Mary—Johnny—stay here. Go with the Woodbridges. Or the Joneses—" How could she think of any one save her own murdered children? "Luke, we may need you."

Matt's huge figure pushed by her purposefully. David said, "You'd ought to wait here, too, Prudence—"

She beat off his restraining hand. "No! No! I must go with you! I must know!" Her voice rose hysterically and she caught her breath. *Heaven help me. I must be calm. What has happened, has happened. I must be calm. There's another life—* She put her hand to her throat and moved blindly down the aisle after David.

Matt had the horse and carriage ready when they got outside. He lifted Prue up beside David as if she were no weight at all. Luke and Pa swung up behind. Then Matt, on Bess that he'd ridden down, went thundering off ahead of them.

Not a word was spoken. There was only the pounding of Daisy's hoofs as David, his face still set in that terrible look, leaned over the dashboard and unmercifully lashed her back.

Already Matt was out of sight. He had turned off the village street and was half way up the first steep rise.

Prue caught hold of the edge of the seat and tried to hold herself steady. Behind her Luke stood up and put his hands on her shoulders and, somehow balancing, drew her tight against his firm young body. She heard the click of the rifle Pa was loading which he, like all the other men, had carried to church with him. She saw little groups of people, already on their way to the North Parish, scramble hastily aside, as, lurching and careening, they tore past them.

Over the first rise now and Daisy's sides heaving. She was too old for such a race. But David gave her no respite. The whip whistled through the air and the mare tossed her head and strained every muscle. Past the Joneses' house where little Elijah, Aaron's playmate, stood on the lawn staring. Past Abigail's lovely little home. Past the Castle—and a part of Prue's mind registered a thought.

"If old Colonel Williams were here he'd be herding us into his place. He'd never let us every one run away."

The top of the hill at last and there was the house. It looked so quiet, so peaceful under the trees. The day was quiet and peaceful, too. The sky was blue and serene, the sun bright. How was it possible death stalked abroad?

Matt's horse, Bess, was where he'd dropped the reins and left her in the driveway. Daisy's labored breath came clearly to Prue's ears as David jerked to a halt at the front steps. He was the first out of the carriage with a stern "Wait here" to his wife. But before he could follow Matt inside, Matt was out again, carrying young Mark. A colored slave boy, a small playmate, trotted whimpering at Matt's heels. Prue held out her arms, a great sob breaking from her.

"Mark! My little boy! Oh, thank God!"

"Steady, Prue. Steady the helm. The lad's unharmed."

Matt handed the frightened child up to his mother. Then he stood there, unable to speak the words he must say, his huge frame crumbling as if all the strength had gone from it.

Prue, holding Mark tight against her, looked over the child's head to Matt in an agony of suspense. David, after one glance at him, went by into the house. Pa followed. Luke remained behind her, supporting her still.

"Tell me," Prue said, tight-lipped.

He shook his head.

"They've killed her, Prue. They—they threw her against the wall. Her little head's broke open." His big hands slowly balled into fists. "They killed Mam Beck, too. And they've taken Aaron."

Mark was gasping out his story between his sobs. "Mam Beck see'd 'em c-comin'. She hid Jonas an' me in de fevver bed an' tol' us to keep still as mices. But I was scairt, Ma. I cwied—"

Prue scarcely heard him. In her imagination she was seeing a savage bend over her beautiful baby girl as she lay asleep in her cradle. She was seeing his dirty brown hands reach out and pick her up and, holding her by her tiny feet, hurl her again and again against the wall. She was seeing that bright curly head dripping blood, that little face mashed—

A shudder went over her and, sickened, she swayed and nearly fainted. Then she felt Luke's fingers tighten on her shoulders, felt the leap of life within her own body and, with a superhuman effort, pulled herself together. She must not do that. She must think of her unborn child. Of little Mark. Of David.

"I'se still scairt, Ma—"

She closed her eyes and laid her trembling lips against Mark's tousled hair. "Hush. You needn't be. You're safe now. We're—" The shudder came again, pain with it this time so that she went rigid. *Oh, God, not now! I can't stand it now!*

Matt's voice came to her from far away.

" 'Twas the Schagiticokes, I'm fair sure, taking blood for blood accordin' to their law." He stopped. "I'm going there. I'm going to their mountain place and—"

Unheard by him, Pa had returned. He stepped close to the carriage, his features old and ravaged by what he had seen, but his voice was unflinching in its firmness.

"You're not goin'. Are you mad? It's you they blame."

Matt turned, and in that moment the old enmity, quiescent

until this moment, flared to new life between them. Mark continued. "You may care naught for your own skin but there's others to think on. There's Prue. And David. I'd say they've been punished enough."

There was a silence. Prue gazed silently into space, not heeding them. Little Mark still trembled against her. Luke released his hold on her shoulders, jumped to the ground and went into the house to help David. The slave boy stood sniffling. The two others, Mark and Matt, looked steadfastly at each other, bitterness in the eyes of both.

Mark finished his say.

"There's the peace of the whole valley to think on, too. 'Tisn't jest you. Nor us. It's all the white folks hereabouts. Leave be! This is a punishment. Let it stand as such. Let it be an incident ended. Not a war started." He paused. "You'd not likely find Aaron, anyway. If they haven't already killed him, they've well and good spirited him out of your reach. Depend on it."

Matt said, "You never wanted him here. You never liked him. You're glad he's gone."

The hard black glance of the son met the equally hard black glance of the father. There always had to be something come between them, Mark thought. Now it was Aaron. Even though he was gone.

A whisper above their heads broke the moment.

"Help me— Get some woman— It's my time—"

CHAPTER 15

The Scattering

PRUE'S LITTLE GIRL WAS BORN without any woman's assistance.
There was only David to help her. David's deft, knowing
hands, that had brought so many baby lambs into the world, were
strong, gentle and efficient. And young Luke, calm and steady,
was within call when needed.

Every moment of that dreadful day was indelibly imprinted on
Prue's memory. Pa's start of surprise as she broke into the talk
between him and Matt. His quick order: "Ride to the village.
Get some one!" Her own words: "Take Mark with you, Matt.
Tell Mary to care for him. Or Abigail if you can't find Mary—"
Before she finished, another spasm of pain caught her and she
gasped, "Help me—down—first."

Her wait, then, on the porch as Matt rode off with the two
children (for Mark clung to his playmate and would not go without him) and Pa went upstairs to tell David and to assist him
and Luke with their grim work of cleaning up her bedroom. Her
call for Becky, Mam Beck's young daughter, and her realization,
in the silence that followed, that the terrified slaves had all run
off long since and she must wait alone. The sounds from above
of slow footsteps carrying something heavy, of quicker footsteps
bearing something small and light. Oh, God in heaven! Was this
real? Was this frightful business true? David hurrying back to
her then, his face still wearing that terrible look, and saying
sharply, "I think we'd better try to return to the village." But
she had shaken her head. "I'd never get there."

"Darling, the slaves are all gone. There's no one—"

"There's you. And Matt will bring some one."

He had stood distraught and uncertain until she had said, "You'd best make haste." Then he had given her shoulder a quick pressure and had left her again. Presently she saw two horses go galloping by, coming from Yokun Town and ridden by a man and a woman. And she had wondered about them briefly until another paroxysm seized her and drove all thoughts from her head. And now there was the sound of water slopping upstairs, of a brush scrubbing on bare boards, of furniture being shoved about. And then David was beside her once more, the lines down the sides of his mouth and around his nostrils deep and dark. But the terrible look was gone and only compassion and love and an anxiety he tried to conceal stood in his brown eyes.

"I'll help you upstairs now, Prue. It's—all right there now."

The slow climb and her own bedroom at last. She had hesitated at the threshold, her blue eyes going over it in quick dread. *How can I go in here?* But it was sweet and airy with the snow-white curtains stirring slightly in the summer breeze and the sun gleaming on the dark mahogany of the tall fourposter and lighting up the silver pieces on her dresser. Nothing of the tragedy that had so recently been enacted there showed save for the damp bare boards on the floor and the horrid stain on the wall that David had not been able to get off—and that the chair he had pulled before the stain did not quite hide. Shrinking, her eyes riveted on that while her fingers tightened around his arm.

"Don't think!" David said quickly. "Except of the future and the new one coming."

She shook her head. "Where is God's mercy?" she had murmured. Then— "David, promise me something! If they come back —kill me! Kill us both first."

Quickly he promised.

She drew a trembling breath. "I should be willing, I know, to die any way God pleases. But I'm not, David! I'm *not!* I can never be willing to be butchered!"

"You won't be—" sternly. "Have no fear."

It was out—the dread they both had of the Indians returning.
And now she looked at the empty cradle and could not withhold
her tears. Great sobs rent her until David had to hold her up,
and though she tried to control herself, she could not, for the
pains were on her again and it was all too much anguish. Body
and soul—it was all too *much*.

When at last she had got herself, with David's help, undressed
and down onto her bed, she lay wondering, in a moment of respite, if the savage murdering of her baby had been a punishment
sent her because she had refused to go to church for so long? But
if so, it was a punishment on David, too, and that was not fair.
And a punishment, as well, on a sweet little innocent that had
never done a thing wrong. And if it was a punishment, why was
another child being sent her? Oh, surely it was for consolation!

But her torment had returned and this time it was a torment
that did not cease. It grew into a great and terrible storm in
which overwhelming darkness was suddenly riven by a blinding
light, in which a mighty sea rolled over her, tossing her, buffeting
her, pummeling her, dashing her onto the shore again for a moment's gasping breath, and then roaring upon her once more,
rushing her in its terrible turbulence almost into oblivion. But
not quite. Oh! If only she could lose full consciousness! The
thought came to her in that moment, knife-sharp and gleaming,
that dying would be so easy. It was living and taking all it
brought you that was hard. If she could just die—

And then, through that turmoil, she heard the pounding hoofbeats of a horse and, with it, her own high, despairing scream
that went wailing off into the wild wilderness of her pain.

It was days before she knew what Matt had learned in the
village.

The two Indians, fleeing from Martin Manor, had encountered
a small group of whites coming from Yokun Town. A Mr. Stevens
had been shot from ambush, but a young woman in the party
and another man had managed to escape. It had been their
horses Prue had seen and wondered about as she waited on the
porch.

These added killings had brought panic. All the rest of that day people from Yokun Town crowded into Indian Town. And when warning was sent north to Pontoosuc, most of the inhabitants in the small group of cabins in that frontier town joined the refugees fleeing south. In the mission itself the Dwights, making all haste, hurried off to Sheffield North Parish, not even stopping to put shoes and stockings on little John Sergeant, and directing a slave to follow them with their baby, Pamela. The slave, too frightened to be thus burdened, had dropped the baby under a bush and had taken to his heels alone. But Lawrence Lynch, General Dwight's indentured servant, had found her and picked her up and hastened after his master.

It was to the Irishman that Matt had entrusted young Mark and Jonas, since Mary, with Johnny, had, long before this, been swept along in the procession with all the others. Aside from the local Indians, only Mr. Edwards remained calm in the whole community. Practically all of the rest had departed, Matt reported.

It was no wonder that he had not been able to find a woman anywhere to come to Prue's aid at her birthing.

Days passed. In the north, ten miles west of Fort Massachusetts, the village of Dutch Hoosac was destroyed by a large force of Canadian Indians. Tension and fear increased with this happening and some of the refugees moved south from North Parish into Sheffield proper and even farther down into Connecticut. But when a force of soldiers, upon the order of Commander Israel Williams, arrived at Indian Town and began building a palisade for a fort around Mr. Edwards' new large home which he had erected on Main Street, the people of the mission drifted slowly back.

Matt chose this time to take action. He went down to the plain and across the meadow to the little tepees and houses that had remained peaceful and undisturbed throughout this whole tumultuous period. And there he found an Indian he had known in his boyhood who was also a friend of Peter's. Him he persuaded to go to the mountain place where the Schagiticokes lived to ask—

for him—about Aaron. He would pay a ransom, a large ransom, whatever sum they named, for the return of his son. Would Umpaunee give this message to the chief? And if Aaron was not there, would Umpaunee discover, if he could, whether the boy was dead or alive, and if alive, where they had taken him?

The trip was unsuccessful. Umpaunee returned and reported that the sachem had not been interested in a ransom, nor had he been willing to reveal whether Aaron was alive or dead. But he had permitted the Mahican to go through the wigwams and Aaron was not to be found in any one. Even when Umpaunee had called his name aloud only an echo had come back. The eyes of the sachem, Umpaunee concluded, were empty, and looking into them, Umpaunee had seen that Matt's son was gone for good.

Not long after this Matt left Martin Manor. To the question in Prue's desolate face, he said only, "I don't know."

"Matt, please write."

He looked at her strangely.

"What is it?" she asked.

"By rights you should hate me."

She shook her head. "It was not your fault," she said sadly. "So why should I hate you? Please write," she repeated.

He nodded, then he went away. She could not blame him, what with Aaron lost to him and the curtain of mistrust and dislike dropped again between him and Pa. But she would miss him. He was a great tower of strength, and in these anxious times a comfort for that reason. Though she doubted she would ever feel comforted again, or know full ease and happiness.

By early winter the villagers had returned. Zeke, Mam Beck's husband who was a house servant, reappeared with his daughter, Becky, as did most of Mark's field help and in due time, as the men of the community came back from the south, the soldiers were withdrawn.

But oh! What a winter it was! Prue would never forget it. She could not rid herself of the awful imagined horror of Esther's death, as, over and over, the picture of it rose in her mind, even in her sleep, when she would start up with a choked cry, until David's arm drew her back to wakefulness and a shuddering sadness. Aaron, too. Again and again she was pierced with the anguished fear that he had met a similar fate, or, if not, that he was suffering in the hands of his abductors and would, if he lived, soon forget all he had learned with her, reverting to uncouth savage ways. It was a thought she could hardly bear.

Yes, it was a cruel winter—with little Faith proving to be a colicky baby and difficult to feed, with young Mark troubled by nightmares from his experience, with the cold so severe it froze the river solid, together with all the running brooks, and the snow dropping endlessly day after day from the gray burdened clouds.

It was that winter, too, that David so surprised and shocked her, bringing her, for the first time in their lives together, a worrisome uncertainty.

He came up from the village one day with a letter which he handed to Prue without speaking. It was from England, one of those rare communications from his brother, Roger.

Roger was writing (he said) to inform David that their father had died. Death had been sudden, though not unexpected, as a slow deterioration had been going on for some time. Now, of course, Roger was master of Windemere and, as such, he intended to sell off a part of their vast holdings. If, however, David had any desire to own some or all of this property, would he kindly send word at once before it was put up for sale? It was that portion lying at the extreme eastern tip where the river turned, and would include both copse and open fields.

"I have no wish," the letter went on, "to deprive you of this if you would care to have it. I well remember your love for our home place. However, your marriage to an American girl and subsequent settling down in the New World may have changed your sentiments. You will recall you have written us but a few times, so, whether or not you have lost interest in England and your future here is a question in my mind. In regard to the latter —the political prospects for you are fairly bright at the moment but may not remain so should you absent yourself much longer.

I might add that there have been enquiries concerning you from people in high places, but, not knowing your intentions or plans, I could not answer for you. Under the circumstances and with so much depending on it, I suggest you return here as soon as possible if you are so inclined."

Prue put the letter down in a stunned silence. All thoughts of David's future lying in England had long ago been forgotten by her and he had become so integral a part of their way of life here on the hill that she could not imagine his ever leaving it. Nor could she bring herself to believe that he wanted to. Indeed, had he not voluntarily said good-by to the idea when he had first come back to her? She could recall his very words. *"I do not dispute your place is here now. That is why I have laid aside my British uniform. You bear a heavy burden and I have come to help you with the carrying of it."*

But she must speak.

She said, "I'm sorry to learn your father is gone, David. If you had known he was failing, you might have gone over to see him. Did—did you love him very much?"

"Love him?" David answered slowly. "I would hardly use that word. I respected him, I admired his integrity, his sound judgment, his sense of fairness. But he was a cold man. Harsh, aloof, self-contained. And after my mother died he became more so. He asked nothing of me, not even my presence. He never showed any curiosity about my hopes or plans or interests. In a way, we were strangers to each other for all the blood tie. That is why I never felt compelled to keep in close touch with him. It was my mother I loved," he concluded. "I have the tenderest memories of her gentleness and sweetness."

"You are like her," Prue said quickly.

"I don't know."

"Yes. You are. And Roger?"

David's smile was faint and oddly twisted. "He's the one should be in politics rather than me." (And I should be master of Windemere, he was thinking. For I love it more. I could never sell one inch of it to anyone. But since Roger seems determined to do so, I will take his offer. It will at least keep our holdings in one family, if not in one name.)

There was a short silence. In it Prue waited for him to answer her unspoken question. But he seemed lost in his thoughts. Finally she put it to him, certain she already knew the answer.

"What will you do, David?"

"I will go there."

She looked at him as if she had not heard aright.

"But—is there any need? Can you not simply write him and thank him, telling him you are not interested in his land? That your future is here?" She stopped abruptly before the strange look on his face.

"I'm—not so sure."

Again she could hardly believe her ears. "You—you mean—"

"I mean I want to go, Prue."

The quiet words so quietly spoken held under beautiful control his surging passionate desire, yet she could feel it and she was aghast. She murmured, in uncertain bewilderment, "You are planning, then, to—to divide your time—our time—between here and England? The way you once proposed?"

"Yes."

She could only gaze at him. All in an instant her whole world was topsy-turvy. What was the matter? Where had she been that she was so unprepared for this? But he was speaking again.

"And I would like to have you go with me on this first trip."

"Go with you? Oh, but I can't, David!"

"Are you saying you do not *want* to?" he asked her.

The question took her back over the years to an earlier time when she had so spoken, and suddenly she was cold with fright. She spoke quickly.

"It is not that. Truly! It is not that at all! It is leaving little Faith. Surely you don't believe such a thing is possible?"

"Of course not. We will take her."

"David." Prue sought to control the agitation and dismay she was feeling. "The baby is not six months old. And she is slimpsy because of her premature birth. She has digestive ailments, as you know, since I had to wean her so early. How could I ever feed her properly on such a voyage with all its dangers of sea sickness? It is a risk we dare not take."

He regarded her thoughtfully but made no reply.

"Then there's Mark," she went on, gathering encouragement from his silence. "He is subject to croup in the winter. I question how the damp and bitter cold of the ocean would affect him."

"I had not thought of those things," he admitted.

She could not be certain from his tone if he agreed with her that these were important considerations. But the need to convince him that it was not just her own unwillingness, but others, who stood in the way of her joining him, drove her on.

"If Mary were more responsible I might be persuaded to leave her in charge of both children and the house. Certainly she is old enough. But I could hardly be sure she would even see to proper meals. Much less give my baby the special care she needs right now." She drew a trembling breath. "Perhaps it is my fault. Perhaps I have not done the right thing by her that she is grown up to such flighty ways. Still I do not know how I could have done differently. I think, no matter what, she would be as she is, gay and altogether charming—but frivolous."

She fell silent at last. His gaze, as he listened, had left her face and gone out of the window. Yet she felt he saw nothing there. Just as she thought she must break if he did not speak soon, his words came to her.

"There will, I fear, always be some sound reason why you cannot go with me." He turned his head toward her and she saw his face gravely and sadly reproachful so that compunction filled her.

"No, David. No. Later—truly! I will join you. Indeed—" She hesitated only a moment. "Indeed, I will go now if—if you command me."

"Prue! Prue! You know I will never do that. How can I command your heart? And if your heart remains behind, what pleasure would I have in your company?" He rose now and, turning from her, moved to the window where he stood with his back to her for a long moment. She waited uncertainly. Did he mean he was abandoning his idea? If not— Oh, she would like to be submissive in her love for him but there were times when

she could not be! And this was one of them. For there was still
another argument—

He wheeled suddenly to face her. "There is one more reason
I am surprised you have not mentioned."

"The Indians?"

"Yes. The Indians."

"I did not forget. How could I?" She shivered slightly, and he
came instantly back to her and took her in his arms, holding her
close. The land could wait, he told himself. Politics could wait.
He was not much interested in them, anyway. But he would not
leave Prue while a French and Indian war was threatening the
Colonies. Not with such memories as she had.

"I will not go," he told her. "Rest assured, little Prue. For a
moment I thought we both might, but now I see we can't. And
I will never leave the country with you exposed to such danger."

But he had wanted to go, she thought. Indeed, did he not still
want to go? That was the worry and uncertainty that stayed with
her, until, a few days later, she brought up the subject again.

"I've been thinking, David, about your—your hope to rear-
range our living so that part of it may be spent in England. It *is*
still your hope, isn't it?"

"When things calm down—and the children are old enough—
yes. Why?"

"I've been thinking about it," she repeated. "In the beginning,
years ago, when you first proposed it, it seemed to me an excellent idea. Certainly it was fair. But—"

"But what?"

She turned an earnest anxious gaze on him. If she could just
say this so he would understand and believe her! So that this
problem might be settled once and for all and not forever hang
over her head!

"But now that I am older," she said carefully, "I view it in
quite another light. And I do not believe it is a practical or
happy solution."

"I should like to hear your reasons."

"Because—and this has come to me but lately so that I may not
voice it well—because your loyalties will ever be in England,

which is your birthplace, as mine will ever be here. Thus, even though we may be together, we will be apart." She paused, searching his face to discover if what she visioned with such clarity was realized by him at all. "It will be—dreadful, I think, for us to be so divided in our thoughts and desires and duties." She stopped.

"Go on."

"Please believe I am not trying to dissuade you, David! I understand only too well your feelings. Oh, I do! Have I not the same for here? I am only asking you to consider that the way you would have us live is no right way. We would be spending a good third of the year on the sea, straining to reach a home that would not be a home for one of us. Indeed, though we could lay claim to two, we would actually have none. How could we have when we remain nowhere long enough to take root?"

I feel rooted—like a tree. And I love the feeling. I don't want anything ever to change. That was Prue. It would always be Prue. But he, himself, had already been uprooted. Still he did not try to answer her and though his silence nearly stifled her, she would not rest until she had finished.

"There would be, too, crises that would delay our departure at times, or, perhaps, necessitate one of us traveling without the other. Right now we are confronted by such a situation because of the children and the threat of war—both matters over which we have no control." Her voice grew softer. "And, David, should you, too often, return to England without me—" She shook her head. "No love should be subjected to such a test."

She waited, as the silence stretched itself out, hearing her own hurried breathing and the wild and desperate hammering of her heart. Why did he not speak? And why—oh, why!—was it given a woman to see so much further than a man in matters like these?

"You are forgetting, aren't you," he said at last, "the test of love your own mother endured when your father went off for years at a stretch?"

"Ah! But he was not going to live in comfort in a land where half a dozen women were waiting who would be glad to take her place!"

His startled half smile held both chagrin and pleasure that she had remembered his long-ago words. "Are you jealous?"

"I could be, David," she said soberly.

There was another silence while David's fingers drummed lightly on the chair arm.

"You have not pointed out one thing," he said presently.

"What?"

"That I have already torn myself free from England."

"But I thought of it. And I—I could not help but ask myself if you had not been happy here that you could not consider remaining? Oh, David! Tell me! Why isn't this home to you? What more can I do? What more can I give you than I already have?" Her voice broke now and her blue eyes filled with tears. Instantly he was beside her, embracing her, comforting her, and in that moment he relinquished his dream. Yet his doubt remained. Would he ever feel himself an American at heart?

"Darling, it *is* home. Yes, it has become that. Because you are here. Because you have given me all you promised and all I ever dreamed of."

"Have I? Truly? I've tried. But oh! I would not want our *not* going to divide us, either!"

"Nothing will ever divide us. Nothing."

"Then, David—"

He stroked her hair a moment before he replied. "I think, if you could go with me, just once, some of your—uncertainties—would disappear. There are many things about England you would love."

"I will go—once."

"Is that a promise?"

She nodded. It was settled. He, himself, had settled it. *"Nothing will ever divide us."* She could ask for no more.

It was a year later, in the summer of 1755, and the French and Indian War had, months before, broken out, when one day Prue heard hoofbeats on the road. Looking from the window, she saw Colonel Ephraim Williams, Jr., riding in great haste toward Martin Manor and with foreboding in her heart, she moved to the porch to greet him. She was followed by Faith, no longer a slimpsy child, but vigorous and strong, with David's golden-brown eyes and Prue's golden hair and her grandfather's square resolute face.

Elegant on his black horse, in his scarlet gold-laced uniform, with white buckskins and gleaming boots, he came galloping up to the steps. As he drew near Prue saw that his usually cheerful face today wore an expression of anxious gloom. Drawing rein before her, he did not even give her the usual greetings but demanded at once, "Where are your men folks, Prue?"

"Getting in the hay from the east meadow."

"Summon them, please."

Prue's heart sank as she moved toward the bell rope hanging from the post at the foot of the steps.

"What is it, Eph?"

He shook his head. "To tell it once is enough."

While they waited for the men, who had shouted a response to the wild ringing of the bell, she said, "I was grieved to hear of your father's death."

He nodded. "That was one of the matters brought me here. The Castle is mine now. But until this fighting ends, Elijah will have to run the place for me. I'm leasing it to him. And now that I'm here, I'm recruiting for the Lake George campaign."

"I thought as much. Who's to command that?"

"Sir William Johnson. He's most influential with the Indians, you know, and has been promised three hundred Mohawks by their chief, Kendrick."

"I see."

This was the third campaign that had been planned, she had heard David tell Pa. General Braddock, with strong British forces, was even now attacking the French along the Ohio, while Governor Shirley—General Shirley, for the emergency—was to strike at Niagara. Before she could say more the wagon careened up to the barn across the road, with Mark and Luke rocking in the seat and David and Johnny and a Negro riding on the half load of hay. Tossing the reins to the slave, the four others sprang to the ground and hurried to the house.

"Well?" Mark demanded at once.

"Braddock's been defeated. Word has just come."

Eph's voice held the heavy surprise he was still feeling, for Braddock's army of British regulars had been considered invincible. He looked down from his horse onto the group before him and nodded in comprehension of their unbelief, confirming his words at the same time.

"Yes. Twelve hundred chosen men put to rout, more than half of them killed, and Braddock dead."

"Braddock? Dead? How in tarnal did it happen?"

"From all I have learnt, the British don't understand how to fight Indians. They marched in open formation without advanced guards or scouts. 'Twas stark madness."

David said, "I thought Colonel Washington was to—"

"Washington wasn't even to go. But he begged to be allowed to, so, having no rank whilst serving under a British general, he was made an aide-de-camp. As such he offered to scout ahead of the troops through the woods but his offer—indeed, all his experience with Indians so hard come by lately at Great Meadows—was rejected."

There was a silence. This was a blow of major dimensions, all knew, and what it meant to the family listening was clear to each of them. With Braddock defeated, the Lake George campaign took on a greater significance than ever. Yet no one spoke and only Prue moved as she went to draw the baby back away from the feet of Eph's horse.

"Seems young Washington's come out a hero," Eph went on. "If it hadn't been for him and his masterly handling of the remnants of the troops, they'd have been all wiped out. He kept the provincials in order and covered the retreat of the regulars when the general fell."

Luke said quietly, "If you have room for me in your regiment, I'll join you."

Eph nodded but his face did not lift.

"I have room for you—and more. We're all in this up to our necks." He reached into a pocket and drew forth a letter. "Here's what Governor Shirley has ordered. 'I desire there be none but right good men enlisted and none under five feet five inches without their shoes unless—' " His glance flicked to the fair-haired Johnny whose wide gray eyes were staring at the paper in his hand. " '—unless they are young enough to grow to that height.' "

Prue saw Johnny straighten up and she cried out a protest but Johnny was ahead of her. "I'm more'n that now," he said.

"No!" Prue's tone was sharp. "Eph, no! He's too young! Isn't there an age limit?"

"None downwards. Only the other way. 'None above forty years old.' " He folded the letter and put it away. And now his look moved to David who was not yet forty by several years.

Prue lifted blazing eyes to the man above her and her voice rang hard.

"You can't have them all. I won't permit it. Not David, too." She flung out a hand and caught her husband's arm and held it tight as he made a move toward Eph. "No, I say! No, David, *no!*"

His look upon her as he released her hold on him was as gentle and kind as ever but his answer came with an unqualifying firmness. "It's not for you to say what I shall do, Prudence. You forget yourself."

"I don't! It's you who forget! There's danger here as well as elsewhere!" She flung herself forward ahead of David and finished to Ephraim. "You can't take all my men away from me, Eph!"

"Prue. Keep silent." David turned to the colonel. "If you need me, I'm ready."

"David! How can you! You said you would not leave me! You promised scarce a year ago you would never leave me while there was this danger."

"I promised I would not leave the *country,* Prue."

Eph's eyes, gazing on Prue's agonized face, held the softness she invariably inspired in him. Unmarried still himself, it had occurred to him more than once that he had perhaps missed his best chance in Prue. Well, be that as it may, the opportunity was gone. She was David's wife and a more devoted couple he did not know. But she had suffered, even with the love he gave her, and through no fault of his. She had suffered more than any one in the mission. And if he could reassure her now it would not be amiss. Besides, she was right. There was danger here as much as farther north.

"I'll not need you, David," he said. "Not yet. Luke and Johnny will be enough. What about Matt?"

"He's gone from here long since. We don't know where he is now."

Prue sank down on the step with her knees trembling under her. She had won. But David had rebuked her before she won and was not pleased at her victory. Certainly she should never have been so bold as to speak for him. Yet greater than her contrition at that moment was her great fear for her brothers. Oh! It was going to be terrible to lose Luke and Johnny! For Luke, curiously, she had little anxiety. He was calm and resourceful and would always be able to look out for himself. But Johnny— Her glance went to him where he stood beside Eph's horse, and his slender young back, with the wavy light hair growing too long on his thin neck, had a vulnerable look, while his bony shoulders, squaring to the unaccustomed load of maturity thrust so unexpectedly upon him, smote her with pity and fear. Johnny was too sweet for war. He was much too sweet and sensitive. Oh! All this was killing her by inches! It was! It was! And if David ever left her to go to fight, too, she would be finished!

The Flat, Albany
July, 1775

Dear Prue,

There is good chance that I may now write you fully of what we have encountered since leaving our beloved home and family last week, as there is delay and confusion here and we are not like to march soon. Anyway I am taking time by the forelock since it is bald behind.

We arrived in Albany in great heat. Some of the men have fallen sick of it but Luke and I are well. There are still men to come from Connecticut and New Hampshire and there are many Mohawks to appear. Did you know our own village got up a company of one hundred Indians? Our regiment is made up of an astonishing number of men by the name of Williams. The Reverend Stephen is our chaplain, Dr. Thomas is our surgeon—and there are many others. You would think, being surrounded by such a contingent of his own kin, that Ephraim would be in good spirits. But he is much depressed, not only by Braddock's defeat but by his belief that the Mohawks will not appear as promised. Indeed, so gloomy is he over our prospects that he has made a will which he had me to witness for him. In signing, I could not help but observe some lines he had writ in which he has left the land west of Fort Massachusetts, given him by the Colonies for his services, to be kept for a free school, provided the town and the school both are named after him. I think this to be a very fine gesture, though some there are from home who say that the sins of his father have shamed him and, since his death, he would make amends by spreading a fairer perfume with his own good name.

I must end this as word has just arrived that we will dally no longer. Do not distress yourself with worry about me, dear sister. I have put myself into the Lord's hands (*our* Lord's, not Mr. Edwards') with every hope and confidence and with very earnest humble prayer. May He likewise keep you and the little ones safe in our absence. With love to every one, I subscribe myself,

Your very affectionate brother
Johnny.

The letter was like Johnny in little flashes, Prue thought, yet not like him on the whole, for she could never imagine Johnny, the dreamer, Johnny, the imaginative, Johnny, the tender-hearted, who hated hunting and could hardly bear a family argument, in the bloody thick of war.

Prue learned of the result of the Lake George campaign weeks later through a letter sent by Dr. Thomas Williams and relayed to her through Elijah. Relayed to David, rather, for Elijah would not meet Prue's eyes.

"Seems nigh the whole outfit walked into a trap," he said. "Took their time gettin' up to Lake George, diddle-daddlin' along the way. Dieskau got wind o' the campaign, anyway, through letters to Braddock the French picked up off the battlefield where he was killed. So he up and marched down to meet Johnson's men. Set an ambush both sides of the road and routed 'em good and proper, then followed that up with an attack on their camp."

"What of Luke? What of Johnny?" Prue interrupted, in a desperate impatience. What did she care about the details of the battle? It was only her brothers that mattered to her! But David, who had caught the appeal flashed to him by Elijah, admonished her.

"He's coming to them, Prue. You might ask, also, what of Eph?"

"Killed," Elijah answered briefly.

"Oh, no!" Prue's shocked voice held a swift contrition for her selfishness.

Elijah nodded. "Shot through the head and fell dead." He pulled a letter from his pocket. "Here's what Thomas says: 'It was the most awful day my eyes ever beheld. There seemed nothing but thunder and lightning and perpetual pillars of smoke. But I never saw braver men. Young Luke, especially. Though mortally hurt, he continued to load and fire till he fainted from loss of blood. I doubt he will survive the homeward journey as I had to amputate the leg. Please inform the Martins of this sad circumstance and tell them we share their grief in our own loss. I can think of no other comfort for the way ahead looks extremely dark for all of us.'"

Elijah folded the letter, still not looking at Prue. "Well, that's all," he said roughly, at last.

Prue could only nod. Luke. *"Mortally wounded,"* Dr. Thomas had said.

And she had been so sure about Luke.

Dark, indeed! 1756 was the darkest year Stockbridge was ever to know. Indian runners, bringing the news, were anything but reassuring about the war. Montcalm had taken Oswego and raised the French flag there. The soldiers at Fort Henry had fallen sick and were further demoralized by the ruling that no Colonial officers could rise above a captaincy. Closer to home, at Fort Massachusetts, two commanding officers were scalped and tomahawked while hunting one day. The little village shook and shivered.

Johnny came back for Luke's funeral and stayed long enough to help get in the winter's crops but went off again, a boy full grown into a man. David went this time, too. All Prue's tears and words had not sufficed to hold him. Indeed, in the end she sent him.

"Do you think I want it thus, Prue, my darling?" he had said. "But I cannot see it any other way. My King needs my services. This land he holds is in peril."

"Your wife and your children are in as great peril, David," she had reminded him. "With you gone we are left with but one sergeant and five privates here in the village to protect us. Oh! I beg of you to think of that!"

He came to her and took her in his arms.

"I do think of it," he said, in moved quiet. "I have gone over and over the whole matter. It is a question whether to protect you single-handed and alone here against an onsweeping enemy or join myself to troops and go to meet and defeat that enemy before ever it reaches here. This latter seems to me to be the wiser choice." He looked down at her, his face, his voice, entreating her. "You have never failed in understanding, my dearest one. Do not fail me now."

Prue's blue eyes beseeched him silently. He went on, his tone never more caressing or tender.

"In moments like this a man cannot think just of his own wishes and his own loved ones. He must consider a greater need —that of the whole country and all the people in it. Suppose each one of us decided to stay by his own hearth? We would have no army at all and there would be no safety anywhere." He paused but Prue could only shake her head.

"You know this. I see it in your face," he continued. "You know you are not the only woman whose heart is being torn. You know you must rise to an equal courage with those others." He kissed her forehead, her eyes, her mouth. "My love has not and will not fail you because I leave you now," he finished. "You know that, too. It is just that my duty has first importance and I must do my share. In your deepest self you would not have it otherwise."

She nodded at last slowly. "Go then—since you must—" she said brokenly. "And God keep you."

He was right. Oh, she knew he was right! And she could never have let him go with any resentment standing between them. But it was hard to be a woman. It was mortal hard.

Only Jonathan Edwards was undisturbed throughout that time. He took refuge from all rumors and from his large family in his small study which was just big enough to hold his chair and his hexagonal revolving desk and his books. Here, unmindful of danger, he buried himself.

Yet he found time from his work, to pen a letter in the spring to his daughter, Esther, married a few years ago to Aaron Burr, president of the College of New Jersey, and now the mother of a two-year-old daughter and a baby son named after his father. Would she not come to make him and her mother a visit? She need not be disturbed by all this talk of Indian savagery. The village was peaceful. She and the children would be safe.

Esther compromised by leaving her babies at home and coming alone, only to spend her time in dread and terror, hardly able to sleep. Visiting one day at Prue's, she said, "I don't know how you stand it alone up here. Especially after your awful experience." She looked at Prue with admiration and commiseration mingled in her glance.

Prue gazed into distance for a moment without answering.

"Sometimes I wonder myself," she said, at last. "I can never let the children out of my sight these days for an instant, because I can never forget Aaron and Esther. Oh! These are truly dreadful times!" She sighed. "And as if constant fear were not enough, our farm is being sadly neglected now that so many of our field help have gone into service, too. Sometimes I think I'm living a bad dream," she ended.

"It's horrible!" Mary declared. "We don't dare do a thing! Or go anywhere! We just sit—and wait. And *wait*. I'm like to die!"

Esther's friendly voice held sympathy as she impulsively addressed the younger girl. "Why don't you come back with me when I go? You would meet people. There would be concerts and lectures and teas. You could go to New York and see the sights there. It would be a little change for you, at least. Then, if the college does move to Prince's Town, as it seems certain of doing, you could help me. That is, if Prue can spare you."

Mary's pretty young face kindled to sudden eager light and life. What a miracle! The thing she had thought of herself and wished for but had not known how to bring to pass! Rushing to Prue, she dropped on her knees and threw her arms around her older sister. "Oh, Prue! Could you?"

With Mary's departure the exodus would be almost complete, Prue thought. Yet how could she deny this proffered pleasure to her sister? Prue knew she was restive and unhappy and it worried her that Mary's youth was slipping away and that she had, till now, had little pleasure in it. Before she could speak, Mary rushed on.

"*You* don't mind sitting in the center of a dead calm! Oh, the worry—yes! You mind that, of course. But the quiet you love. And it's always quiet here whether there's a war or not. Well! I'm not like you! I don't want life to revolve around me! I want to do the revolving! I always have. I want to be on the outside edge, whirling and spinning myself, even if the breath is scared clean out of me! Let me go with Mrs. Burr! Let me see a little of the world! Say I may!"

Prue laid her hand on the girl's head and smiled faintly. "Of course you may. Go pack up all those lovely silks and satins Matt brought home. You can have them made into beautiful gowns while you are down there."

"Oh, *Prue!*"

I shall miss her, Prue thought. But it is David I miss the most.

It was a year later and winter lay on the land. Prudence, waiting by the south window in the big silent house for Pa to come
with the sleigh and drive them all to church, gazed with lack-
luster eyes at the world outside. It was a blue world. The sky
was gray-blue. The trees rising against it were blue-black and
the snow was blue-white.

She felt like the landscape before her, growthless, with all of
her life withdrawn into a cold, ungiving ground. Would she ever
come alive again? Not until her family was gathered about her
once more—what was left of the family, she sadly corrected herself.

She had been scattered as the family had been scattered. With
each one's going had gone a piece of herself. Now she was left,
shrunken and small and no good to any one. Even her tears had
dried up. She could think without weeping of all those lost to her
never to return. Of her baby, Esther. Of Aaron. Of Luke. What
was worse, though, was to think, without hope, of those that were
left. David. Johnny. Matt. Andy. Mary.

David and Johnny were off somewhere with that great army
that the British had sent to America. Undismayed by all the
French successes of the first three years of war, the English, under Prime Minister William Pitt, were planning to wage a vic-
torious, able prosecution of the war. When David had come home
the last time he had been most enthusiastic.

"Twenty thousand regulars have been sent over here under
General Abercrombie!" he had said joyfully. "With the militia,
that makes us fifty thousand strong. It's the greatest army America has ever seen!"

She did not like David in his role as soldier, she thought now.
He seemed to have grown away from her somehow, to have become less American and more British. (As a commissioned officer
he had been welcomed back to their ranks.) And yet that was a
foolish notion of hers. Wasn't everybody British—really? All except the Dutch settlers, of course. She, as much as he, had English

roots. (She must remember that when the time came to go to England with him—if it ever *did* come.) Anyway, let him find gladness in the promising new army if he could. Let him get what pleasure he might out of all this killing.

Her mind turned to Johnny. If she imagined a change in David as a soldier, there was no imagining about the change in Johnny. Or was it only that he had grown a hard, protective shell over his secret self? That underneath he was still the same? She could not be sure. She only knew he presented to the world an alert aggressiveness in strong contrast to his early dreaminess and timidity. He had grown to full stature, too, and while not the giant Matt was, nor as square and solid as Luke had been, his tall, spare body held a steely strength implicit in every easy, graceful movement.

Matt. Matt had written—finally—from the west where, on a hunch of his own, he had gone to hunt for Aaron. He had written from Andy's cabin in which he had found his brother ensconced with a wife. Hannah kept his place neat and his clothes mended and was a fair cook, Matt wrote, but more praise than that he could not offer. "She's plain as a pike and has a sharp tongue, to boot. I'd not look twice at her. Howsomever, I suppose Andy had to have some one to do for him and there aren't many petticoats to choose from out here. Moreover, if the Injuns come she's as good as a man with a gun and you know how Andy is—all thumbs." He finished, "No trace of Aaron yet. I begin to give up hope and shall be returning soon to my ship and my life at sea."

As for Mary: she had not come back. At first she had been having too good a time to think of returning. "So many people!" she had written. "So many parties! So much to do! Oh, I love it here, Prue!"

It had been an adventure for her. Just the kind she had always hankered for. And if her letters did not give Prue all the details she would have liked to have, Esther Burr supplied a few. "Your sister is very popular," she wrote. "Indeed, perhaps too popular for her own good. She is in danger of having her head turned by all the admiration she is receiving, particularly from gentlemen.

But I am sure the good common sense that is her heritage will restore her to a proper balance in the end."

Ah, but it hadn't. When the New Jersey College moved to Prince's Town, and, shortly after, Esther's husband had become so gravely ill, Esther had sent another letter.

"Mary is no longer with me. The quiet of this country village was not to her liking, and with Aaron's sickness, I was not able to provide any entertainment for her. So she went to New York where she has been visiting around amongst her new acquaintances. And now today I have just heard that she has started on a journey south. I do not know who is accompanying her and I do not want to worry you unnecessarily. But I thought you should know this in case Mary had not had time to write you herself—and her going was a sudden decision, I was told. She means to look up her brother Matthew who, according to your letter to her, has made Charles Town his base for his trading vessels."

This brought an agony of alarm and anxiety to Prudence. It was all so vague! With whom had Mary been staying in New York? With whom had she set out to find Matt? And by what mode of travel? Oh, Mary! Mary! My wilful, wild little sister! Why do you not write and answer all these questions that weight down my heart?

But only one short missive had come. It had been written from Virginia and said only, "Dear Prue, I am well and on my way to visit Matt. Forgive this short note. I will write at length as soon as possible. My love, Mary."

Since then—silence.

The sound of sleigh bells broke into her dark, anxious thoughts and she rose from her chair, fastened her bonnet under her chin, buttoned her sealskin coat and called to Becky in the ell.

"We'll go now. I'll take Mark. Do you bring Faith. Mark! Come down! Faith, where are you?"

Mark, eight, was almost old enough to go to the long church service but of course the four-year-old Faith was not. However, never again would Prue leave her babies at home. Becky could take one or both to Mrs. Edwards' house and wait for her there.

The children came running. Becky helped them into their warm clothes and the four went out to Pa waiting in the sleigh.

Jonathan Edwards looked down with a sad and solemn countenance on his congregation. Many familiar faces were absent because of the war, but there remained a goodly showing of white people—older men and women and children—with a larger sprinkling of Indians. For though sturdy pioneers could count eighteen families amongst themselves, the savages still outnumbered them almost two to one. However, this disparagement would not stand much longer, he thought. For when Chief Kendrick had failed to deliver all the Mohawks he had promised for the Lake George campaign, which had resulted so disappointingly for the English, the Boston authorities had lost interest in its support of the mission. Funds had ceased to arrive, and this fact, together with the enlistment of most of the older boys, had necessitated closing the boarding school. Long before this he had sent the six remaining children down to his friend, Dr. Bellamy, in Connecticut, making their safety in these times his reason. He really doubted, in view of government indifference, that the boarding school would ever be opened again.

"Change," he told himself. "Change. It is the law of life. We fight it. But it comes. It has come to me more than once. It will come, also, to my charges. There is no earthly help against it."

He leaned over the pulpit and began speaking.

"My friends, I have a message for you this morning. It sorrows me to deliver it but I see no escape." He paused. "As you have been apprised, my son-in-law, Dr. Aaron Burr, recent president of the College of New Jersey, has been called unto his Heavenly Father. The governing body at the college has seen fit to do me the honor of requesting me to take the presidential chair in his place." There was a slight stir in the group of people before him and he paused again. "After careful deliberation and much against my personal inclination, I have decided that it is my duty to accept this offer. Today's sermon, consequently, will be the last I will preach here in this pulpit to you." He paused a third time. "For my text this morning, I have selected the twenty-eighth and twenty-ninth verses of the twentieth chapter of the Acts of the Apostles. 'Take heed, therefore, unto yourselves, and to all the flock, over the which the Holy Ghost hath made you overseers, to feed the Church of God, which He hath purchased with His own blood. *For I know this, that after my departing shall grievous wolves enter in among you, not sparing the flock.'*"

Prue, hearing these words, knew a little flare of her old indignation. Lugubrious, always! Why must he be so? In these terrible times a note of hope was desperately needed. Yet he never supplied it. Truly, she was not sorry to have him go.

But Mark, solid and immovable and heavy-hearted beside her, felt only that the text was prophetic. For this was the end of another era, and the future of this noble experiment, uncertain when John Sergeant died, looked gloomy, indeed, with Mr. Edwards' resignation.

Who, now, would take his place? Who, coming, would fight for the mission as he had? Or feel concern if it failed or succeeded? Only John Sergeant's son, named after him, cared for its fate: he—and the faithful Timothy Woodbridge. Yet the one was too old and timorous and the other too young, and neither was an ordained minister.

A curious thought twisted its way into his mind now. If the Lord could not work out His plans fully, was it any wonder that men failed in theirs? For Matt, riding the high seas again, carrying on his illicit traffic with Canada and the "sugar islands," piling up his ill-gotten gains, one more shipowner making it impossible for the English to starve out the French West Indian possessions into submission, hurting—not helping—the war's successful conclusion— And Mary, following her own secret, wilful course with no thought for her family, were certainly no part of his design when he came here so many years ago.

What was to be the end of it all? What was to be the end?

CHAPTER 16

The Visit

IT WAS A MAY MORNING after the ending of the French and Indian War when the letter came. David brought it to Prue—a David returned sound and well from the fighting as, thankful heart! was Johnny, also. (Andy had been killed. He and his wife, Hannah, had fallen together in a senseless attack made against their settlement.) Waving it above his head as he rode into the driveway, he called out to her where she was sitting on the porch steps holding the new baby named after her brother, Luke.

"I think it's from Mary!".

Mary. Her heart turned a somersault and then lurched into a heavy dreadful thumping so that she could not speak a word.

David dismounted and came toward her and from somewhere Pa appeared. He came with the slow, heavy tread that was customary now as if the spunk had all petered out of him. She could not blame him. Two of his sons dead—Andy and Luke—and Matt far away now he was married and settled definitely in Charles Town. (Might he have remained here had Aaron ever been found? It was something she would never know.) Mary's absence, too, had hit Pa hard, even though he had long ago given up expecting much from his children. What they did to you (he had said once) and to your hopes and dreams for them, they never knew and never would know till they had young ones of their own. Still Prue had had the feeling that though Mary had taken herself out of his home and out of his heart, closing the door to both herself, she could open them again if she so wanted. His coming at David's call now seemed to prove this.

She found her voice at last.

"Read it aloud, David. My arms are full." She fixed her eyes on the letter as if she would pull the words straight off it.

Yes, it was really from Mary at last. She was in Charles Town with Matt, having arrived there just in time for his wedding after many vicissitudes. She was well and happy and about to be married herself. *Married!* Oh, dear Lord! Now all the curious questions and sly gossip and meaningful looks from villagers could be put an end to.

" 'I am going to marry Alec MacDonald,' " David read. " 'Perhaps you recall that Matt spoke of him that time he came home to visit. He has always been Matt's friend and right-hand assistant. He is considerable older than I, and Scotch in all ways, but oh! he is good to me, as he has ever been, and I love him with my whole heart.' "

"Pa! That's fine news!"

He grunted. "Go on, David."

" 'I am not sure,' " he continued, " 'if you and Pa can ever forgive me for running off as I did without consulting you and for my subsequent long silence. But my experiences were not all of the pleasantest and I could not bring myself to trouble you with an account of them. I would like now to admit that I was reckless and foolish, showing little sound judgment and only an avid desire to go beyond the confines of Stockbridge and see the world. I can but plead my youth for such headstrong selfishness as I have shown, and, if I have erred, the Lord has punished me by a mort of anxieties that turned me ill for upwards of a year. However, He must have forgiven me also, else He would not have directed Alec to me and put it into his heart to care for me as I hope some day to deserve. Should this explanation suffice to satisfy you and Pa—for I can never make a fuller one—and should you want to see me again, Alec says we can easily come some time when one of Matt's ships sails to Boston. Please let me know if we will be welcome, for oh, Prue, I have missed you all so much! And I do so long to see you again!' "

Prue looked up at Pa whose dark face was a perfect mask for his feelings, and her voice came clear and gentle, yet with a demand in it, too.

She said, "The past, whatever it held, has been lived. I shall never question it. And I shall write her at once that I long to see her. What word shall I put down for you, Pa?"

Mark wheeled so that only his broad back was visible.

"Tell her I say she and that husband of hers better come north here soon's ever they can." He paused. "Might put a message in for Matt, also. Tell him I'd be pleased to meet his wife, can he ever see his way clear to make us a visit."

He stumped away. David sat down on the step beside Prue whose eyes, filled with happy thoughts of the future, were now on her cinnamon roses, now on an eagle suspended high in the blue vault of the sky and now on the tiny green fingers of new leaves uncurling in the trees overhead. For a moment he laid his hand over hers in a gesture of wordless understanding, then he rose to take his horse to the barn.

Prue remained where he had left her, brooding happily. Everything was turning out so much better than she had ever thought it would. David had definitely renounced England and was content here. To be sure, he did not feel as she did about the land on this broad hilltop, nor, likely, would he ever. Only she and Pa shared that feeling. It was not something she could put into clear words. It was—well—a kind of religion that defied expression. Luke had felt it when he was alive. But no one else in the family ever had. Johnny might stand spellbound before thin, black hills pasted flat against a scarlet sky or snow shadowed to a lavender light at evenfall, but he took little delight in the rich returns of the good earth. David did that, at least. As for Mark—

Mark was only twelve and so too young to know for sure what his feelings would be.

She laid Luke on a blanket beside her and then picked up Mary's letter to read it again. La! What changes she would find here when she got back! Two schools, one for the white children and a separate one for the Indians, now that the whites so out-numbered the savages. Much of the Indian land transferred to the hands of the white settlers by a law passed that made it al-lowable for debts to be settled that way. (This was thanks to Elijah Williams, town sheriff, who was a chip off the old block if ever there was one.) Dr. West, husband of Elizabeth Williams, the minister in place of Jonathan Edwards. Sheffield North Par-ish named Great Barrington now, Pontoosuc changed to Pitts-field, after the English Mr. Pitt, and Yokun Town called Lenox. Oh! But their tongues would wag! In her turn, she—Prue—must hear all the details of Matt's wedding and what manner of girl it was he had married, for she knew nothing beyond her name— Myrtle Avery—and that she was of French descent from a fine family that had been one of the early settlers in Charles Town.

But now to write and get the letter posted to Mary and on its way. The letter was sent. But it was several years before Prue saw Mary again.

At last the house was ready. The big rooms had been aired and cleaned and, flooded with sunshine, smelled sweetly of lavender and beeswax. The new spinet in the parlor, which Faith was learning to play, glowed warm and bright from the polishing she had given it. In the keeping room the nosegay rug on the floor had been taken out and beaten and scrubbed on the lawn until all the colors sparkled like new. The dining table was stretched to its uttermost length and extra chairs brought down from the attic to accommodate every one. Bayberry candles stood on man-tels and tables in their gleaming brass or silver holders. Curtains, fresh-laundered, stirred against the glittering glass of the win-dows.

Out in the pantry preparations had been made, too. Here pies of all kinds lined the shelves while jars of assorted colors filled the cupboards. In the ell, known now as the "cold room," were hung hams and venisons and sides of beef. Pans of milk stood ready for skimming. Cheeses gave off tantalizing odors. There were little mountains of white eggs and brown eggs heaped in baskets on the floor while from the cellar the fragrant aroma of early fall apples filtered up through the house.

Prue, slender as the girl she had been when David married her seventeen years ago, her braids still a shining gold coronet about her head, moved swiftly to her tasks in her full-skirted blue woolen homespun dress, directing and checking everything. Becky was in charge of the five-year-old Luke and was to help Mary with her three children. Old Cindy, successor to Mam Beck, was the cook. Zeke, tottering on thin old legs, but proud of his white coat for this momentous occasion, lugged logs to the fireplace, while his giggling young granddaughter, Pearl, helped him and was, in addition, responsible for carrying hot water and warming pans to the bedrooms, when needed.

Faith had her responsibilities, too. Thin and knobby-kneed and plain of face in her adolescence, with her straight bright hair flying and freckles standing out clear on her pale skin beneath her big brown eyes (the only claim to beauty she had), she energetically made beds and dusted. But young Mark, now sixteen and ready for Princeton, watching all this activity, was disdainful. "You'd think at least the King were coming. And it's only Aunt Mary and Uncle Matt."

"Do you remember them, Mark?"

"I remember Uncle Matt. He was huge. And he had a black beard. When he dug me out of the feather bed that day, I thought he was a giant and I was most as scared of him as I had been of the Indians." He paused. "All I remember about Aunt Mary is she was pretty."

Yes, she was pretty. Was she still? So much time had passed since Prue had seen her! Never had she thought 'twould be five years from the day Mary's letter came before she made her visit. But first she had had twin boys—Keith and Kim—and then a little girl, Phoebe, had been born to her, and well Prue understood that traveling with three such babies was impossible.

It had taken the threat of war again to unite them. When an anti-Stamp Act congress was organized to meet in New York this fall, Matt had written that he was coming north to be present at it, since his occupation—trading—was profoundly affected by all England's threatening attempts to stifle it in the Colonies, and he wanted to know, first hand, what the country was planning to do. He added that he was bringing Myrtle and that Mary and Alec and all three of their children would also come. But Myrtle preferred to leave their two girls at home. Would Prue have room for them all?

Would she! She could hardly wait. Johnny felt the same way, for Mary's letter had stirred his sympathetic imagination when he had read it, while Matt, ever since his dramatic return to Martin Manor loaded down with fabulous gifts and filled with adventurous tales, had always been something of a hero to him.

Dear Johnny! Why had he never married? He was tall and slender with thick fair hair, deep gray-green eyes under curiously pointed heavy lids, a puckish, slightly crooked smile, charming in its sudden radiance, and a body that moved with a steely grace. Just the kind of man a girl would set her cap for—and many had right here in this village. But he had proved aloof and elusive and not a one had so far caught him. Yet he was twenty-six, old enough to have a home and family of his own long before this. He seemed, to Prue's thinking, to use self-containment as a kind of armor, the way he had used weapons in war. What was it he was afeard of, she wondered? She could not imagine. But ever since he had come back he'd kept himself hid from her. Not with surliness, as Matt used to. Nor even with a flow of talk, as had Mary. His was a gay, quicksilver, teasing evasion. He would come to the brink of revelation and then, with a laugh, sidestep and go off whistling that catchy new tune made up by the British to poke fun at the American Army and adopted by them as their own. "Yankee Doodle" it was called. Yet she suspected, for all his brightness and lightness, that he was lonely and longed for love as a traveler on the desert longs for water.

And Pa, nothing could hide from Prue his wish to see both his children again. Errant they had been and he was not one to excuse them for their sins. But the ache to have an open space of friendliness between him and his oldest son had never left him. As to Mary—he must see for himself that all was at last well with this wayward girl child of his.

David, of course, was glad for Prue's present rejoicing since he was always happy when she was.

So Martin Manor, with its welcome ready, waited for the visitors.

They came by stagecoach from New York to Hartford and by stagecoach again from Hartford to Egremont. From there they journeyed on horseback with arrangements made for their trunks and boxes to be hauled by oxen later to Stockbridge. The twins, Kim and Keith, rode in panniers as Mary had when she had first arrived. Alec MacDonald bore his precious baby girl in his arms, himself, not being willing to trust her to any other way.

The clattering of hoofs was heard long before they reached the crest of the hill and Prue was out on the lawn to greet them when at last the little cavalcade turned into their drive. How splendid they looked! Matt, shaven as she had never seen him, was altogether transformed in his elegant riding suit of bottle green and his gleaming boots, with his hair clubbed in the latest fashion and a silver-handled riding crop shining in his hand. Marriage and money had wrought wonders, to be sure! Beside him rode a small, dark slip of a girl, lovely to behold with her quick black eyes and her warm red mouth and her ebony tresses loosed to a pretty cloud about the pure oval of her face beneath her scarlet hood. The tall bony man with the sandy hair who was dressed in sober brown and held the baby so carefully was Mary's Alec, of course. But it was Mary that Prue saw the clearest. Mary, in an apricot velvet riding habit with an orange plume framing her chestnut curls, who slid from her mount and ran toward her sister with a half sob and half laugh, crying out, "Prue! Prue!"

Prue held her off at arms' length for a second, unmindful of the stylishness of her clothes, only searching her face with tender, anxious gaze. Mary looked just the same save for one thing. The restless questioning of her sparkling brown eyes was gone and in its place now there glowed serenity. The headstrong girl who had wanted to see the world, had, indeed, seen it, only to discover its confines were bounded by her own heart.

"I'm all right," she murmured, breathlessly. "Oh, Prue! I'm—all right!"

"So I see, my darling."

There was no time for more, for now came Pa, calling out Mary's name and laying his good hand on Matt's shoulder at the same time in an unusual display of feeling. And Zeke was lifting one twin from a pannier as Faith lifted down the other, with little Luke yelling and screaming and prancing about in a paroxysm of excitement over having playmates his own age. His cavorting frightened Myrtle's horse which suddenly reared, and had she not been an expert rider she would surely have been thrown. As it was she kept her seat until Johnny leaped forward and caught the bridle and led horse and rider away from the commotion. A moment later, when a slave ran up to relieve him, Prue saw him reach up his arms, his hair gilded by the sun, his lifted face alight with his ingratiating smile, and pick Myrtle from her saddle as if she had been a feather. For an instant they stood there, the dark-haired girl, heart-high to him, and he with his hands still clasping her tiny waist under her fluttering scarlet cloak. In that brief span of time Prue felt, rather than saw, the blinding rush of sudden feeling that held their glances locked and their breath stopped. Then Johnny's smile slowly left his face and he stepped away.

"You must be—you are—Matt's wife," she heard him say.

Myrtle nodded. "Yes," she answered. (Was there an unconscious note of regret in her soft voice?)

Prue looked down the long board and met David's eyes. He smiled. He knew this was what she had wanted for years—her family, except for Aaron, gathered together again—and she smiled back.

It was what she had wanted, indeed. But she had never reckoned on complications with their return. Matt did not guess. Humility was not one of his virtues, and his complacency made him blind. After all, he had won Myrtle. The victory was his. What more was there? That he had not reaped and never would reap all the spoils had never occurred to him. Would he ever know? And if he did, would he realize it was not so much another person that separated him from his wife as a force he could not combat? It would not be that he had lost her but rather that he had never truly had her.

For Mary had told Prue of their marriage. It was strange, Prue had observed to her sister when they were alone together, that two weddings in the same family held such a discrepancy in ages between husband and wife.

"You and Alec I can understand, now we have talked," she had said. "But Matt and Myrtle— Does she love him, Mary?"

"Not as I love Alec," Mary had replied. "She was dazzled by him, I think. He's quite impressive, as you've seen. And he has a commanding way which a woman likes if there's kindness with it. But it was her father, whom Myrtle adores, and who was in financial difficulties, who put considerable pressure on, I believe, to have the match go through."

"I see."

It was clear, then. A girl of eighteen, her fancy untouched at the time, had been flattered by the attentions of an older man, fascinated by his assurance, his knowledge of the world, his power, perhaps swept off her feet by his passion and urged on to acceptance of him by harried parents. Now, five years later when she had come to understand life—and Matt—better, she had met a younger man—Johnny—a man her own age, as different from Matt as day from night.

David, head bent, was saying, "Bless Thou this food to our use, oh, Lord, in Thy good mercy. Amen."

Phoebe, in the high chair discarded long ago by Luke, banged on its arm with her spoon and then threw it from her, instantly crying for it as it hit the floor.

"We'll have no peace and not a chance to talk with her here," Mary said. "Can Becky take her?"

Prue nodded and Becky was summoned.

"What's the matter with her?" little Luke inquired, as she was borne screaming away. "Is a pin sticking her?"

Mary laughed. "No, she's just tired from her journey."

"Did I ever cry like that, Ma?"

"Well, you used to howl for your food, I remember. I could never keep you filled up."

"That's why I'm so big now." He looked across at his cousins. "I'm bigger'n both of you," he bragged.

Kim, slow of speech and sober, like his father, answered nothing, but Keith, with Mary's quick spirit, instantly stuck out his tongue.

Alec transfixed his two boys with a look. "Mind y'r manners 'n say y'r prayers," he told them. "Keep y'r feet on the heevenly stairs. F'r troobles will coom by threes 'n pairs, less'n ye mind y'r manners 'n say y'r prayers." He paused. "Be biddable, noo. Be verra biddable 'n verra carefu'. 'Tis fair warnin'."

The twins, both staring solemnly back at their father out of the bluest blue eyes Prue had ever seen, nodded obediently and retired into silence. Luke, impressed, did likewise.

Prue sent Alec a fleeting smile. She had liked him at once and knew from that first moment that she need never worry about Mary again.

But now Matt was speaking in the booming voice that was so like Pa's used to be. "It's as well we left Lucy and Mary-Etta home, I reckon. Lord! What a bedlam we'd have had here!"

Johnny's head jerked up and he spoke to Myrtle as if he and she were alone in the room. "It's hard to believe you're a mother," he said.

Prue broke in quickly. "Oh, we'd have managed well enough, Matt. I'm sorry you didn't bring your girls. But tell us about the anti-Stamp Act congress and what happened at it."

Politics. They were off and she could listen. But she gave them only half her attention. The rest was focussed on David, carving expertly, on the white-coated Zeke lest he forget to pass something, on the loaded table to be sure glasses were kept filled and the small dishes circulated. Between times her mind kept going to Myrtle.

What was it about her that had captivated Johnny? She was built with the softness and fragility of a bird. Everything about her was soft. Her small hand folding up boneless in yours, her great, shining black eyes, her voice— Ah! Her voice! It was the kind would drag over a man's heart, plucking each string of it with every uttered syllable and leaving an echo in its still places long after she was silent. She was just a soft, helpless-seeming creature. Yet something in her had leaped to a recognition of something in Johnny. Their spirits, winging together on instinct alone, had mated in the fraction of a second before either had said a word. And now what?

But perhaps they didn't know what had happened to them any more than she had known when she had met David. Or perhaps she—Prue—was just imagining.

She was recalled to the men whose voices had grown heated. Matt, leading the argument, was having his say in this house as, long ago, he had dreamed of doing. And all were listening. He was addressing David who leaned back against his chair, his face grave, the little flecks of flame in his eyes hot with worry.

"I tell you there's trouble brewing and the fire under the pot grows fiercer all the time. Who decided we should have to pay for quartering a permanent force of British here? Not us! *We* never asked for them!"

"You were glad enough they were here two years ago, time of the Pontiac outbreak," David reminded him. "And who can say when this land will not be attacked by other enemies of England?"

Matt thrust himself forward, his eyes hard. "And who can say that troops stationed here won't take away what liberty we have?"

David's glance dropped to his hand that began shoving his knife about on his plate. All this strain of dissension sickened him. England might have made mistakes but America was too brash and impulsive. Surely time would work things out—if these reckless Colonists would only show patience. "The question, of course," he answered slowly, "is how much liberty you want."

Johnny turned to him in surprise. "You?" he repeated.

Pa's heavy voice cut through the moment. "If any more enemies attack us, I reckon we can take care of 'em. Our troops are no longer green. And we've a good leader in George Washington. To my thinkin', it's not the matter of whether England should have a bigger army and more garrisons here that's raising ructions. It's the way she's imposing taxes on us. Like James Otis said, the Navigation Acts and all such else were tax laws passed by a foreign legislature that never had our consent."

"You're right, Pa. That's the crux. And we don't propose to stand for it." Matt turned to David again. "You'd know that if you'd ever heard Patrick Henry in Virginia last May as I did."

"He's a fiery hothead, isn't he?"

"He may be. But what he said made sense!"

Young Mark, his face scintillant with the excitement born of all this unusual talk, turned toward his uncle. "Is New York the only place that's to have a Sons of Liberty organization? Why can't we have one here, too?"

"You can. You should. They should be formed everywhere— and will, I warrant, if the press takes up the matter."

Faith asked, "What is the Sons of Liberty group for, Uncle Matt?"

"It's to strengthen—you might almost say legalize—our decision to buy no more British imports whilst these taxes are put on us." His eyes flashed around the table and came back to David once more. "I wish you could have been with us down there in the city, David! It gave me heart. All nine colonies sent representatives. James Otis was there. And Livingston of New York. And John Dickinson from Pennsylvania. Our state sent Mr. Rutledge who took me in with him. There was determination as well as seriousness in all that was discussed there."

"Determination? What did you determine?" David asked. "Aside from organizing the Sons of Liberty?"

"I'll tell you! We determined to send petitions to the English government. And with a declaration of our rights and grievances. Mind you! We claim only those rights that all other Englishmen have, so Britain must give heed. What we say is if we're to be taxed we want to be represented. That's the gist. We complain also of the Stamp Act, of course, which is the greatest folly England has ever committed. Why, agents risk their very lives trying to collect it!"

"I know." David sighed faintly and shook his head. "It's all a sorry business." He was silent a moment. "Benjamin Franklin is in London. He's fearless. And able. Perhaps he can present the American viewpoint so it will be better understood."

"He will try. And I prophesy the Stamp Act will be repealed."

"If it is," said Johnny, "let's hope England doesn't think of something else to take its place."

Matt spoke grimly. "If she does, 'twill be most—*unsafe.*"

"Why don't we get free of England? We don't need her running us, do we? Why can't we run our own country?"

Young Mark's impulsive question electrified every one. It was David who spoke first, his face white as death, his voice stern as it rarely was, but trembling, too, with his emotion.

"That, son, is treason. Let me never hear such words pass your lips again. Prudence, I think we are ready for our dessert."

Was the shadow his words seemed to cast also the figment of her imagination, Prue wondered? Or was it, in truth, thrown upon them by the passing of dark, invisible wings?

CHAPTER 17

The Party

PRUE HAD DECIDED, before Mary arrived, to open her house for a party. People would want to meet Matt's wife and of course they were curious about Mary—about whom there had been so much conjecture. This would be a chance to end once and for all any unkind gossip that might remain concerning her. Mary was here with her husband and her three children. Let folks come meet them all and see for themselves how happy she was. So the house was polished and shined up once more, the best china brought out, the finest cakes made, almonds glazed, possets of eggnog prepared—and the townspeople arrived.

Abigail Dwight came with Pamela and Dr. Erastus, with whom Abigail was living since the recent death of her husband, the general. Young John Sergeant, who had inherited his father's missionary spirit and was studying theology under Dr. West, put in an appearance with the minister and his wife. The two Woodbridge families had been invited, also, of course. And the Stiles girls (now married), the Joneses, the Browns, the Pixleys, the Curtises, the Willards—indeed, all those earliest settlers—as well as the Ashleys from Sheffield, and the Sedgwicks from Great Barrington, who were taking a lead in affairs during the present unrest.

The affair started off well. The twins were on their best behavior, as was Luke. Faith's plainness, as she whisked about, was transformed into something resembling prettiness by her pleasurable excitement. Alec, tall and somber-looking, impressed every one with his solid worth and charmed them with his Scottish accent. In him they saw a sturdy, if foreign, replica of themselves. But it was really Matt and Myrtle who commanded the most interest. Mary, the guests soon discovered, was, after all the talk about her, merely another matron like the rest. Matt, however, whom they remembered as a sullen obstreperous lad sowing his wild oats early, was become a man of the world, wearing fine clothes with ease and speaking with authority, while his tiny exquisite wife, seeming soft and helpless as a kitten, effortlessly extracting gallantry from blunt, outspoken men, and with a low drawl that sounded odd in contrast to their own clipped terse speech, was an alien among them.

Prue was glad this was so. Mary had slipped, without awkwardness, into the place where she belonged. Let them stare at Matt. Let them go home and talk about Myrtle. But let Mary alone. This was the way Prue wanted it. Her satisfaction was not to last, however. Oh, Mary survived! But Myrtle gave them more subject for gossip than Prue had anticipated. Was it a demon of mischief prompted her? Or the desire—thwarted till now by Johnny's avoidance of her—to be near him and to speak a whispered word into his ear?

For after that first day he had seemed to forget her presence. Shorthanded when young Mark had departed for Prince's Town, he was up and out in the morning before Myrtle appeared, and at noon he ate hurriedly. Then, at night, when she might have expected something different, he was off to a meeting somewhere. Matt went to these meetings, too, as did Alec and Pa. David stayed at home. Plainly, he, like the Williamses and the Dwights and a few others, wanted to keep clear of embroilment and believed, as they did, that matters would simmer down best if let alone.

But Myrtle, accustomed to more attention from men folks, had grown restive under this regime, as had Mary. For Mary, however, there had been no challenge lying hidden beneath such desertion, while today was Myrtle's first opportunity to seize this challenge and reply to it.

She was seated on a low stool before the blazing fire, surrounded by an eager group and looking, so tiny she was, more like a girl Faith's age than the mother of two. Her black hair was curled and fell prettily over her white shoulders. A beauty patch high on one cheek called attention to a dimple there. Her gown, the finest in the room, was a silver brocade cut low in the neck, the skirt shaped with padded panniers and edged, as was the square neckline, with scarlet lace, and all the time she talked, one small silver-shod slipper kept tap-tapping the floor while her eyes roved from those around her to the tall, aloof figure of Johnny across the room.

"Indeed," she was saying, in reply to a question, "Ah am enjoyin' mahself greatly. Ah love it heah. How could Ah help it? Yo' hills in October— Ah nevah saw anythin' so breathtakin' in mah whole life. Of course theah's some things is a lot different to me," she admitted, her glance going to Johnny again. "Fo' instance, Ah can't rightly accustom mahself to the way you men folks go out and work in the fields alongside of yo' slaves all day. Home our men folks jes' ride aroun' inspectin'." She shook her head in admiration as she spoke, lest her words seem unkindly critical. "And then, too—" She hesitated.

But a chorus of voices urged her on. After all, it was diverting to learn how you appeared to strangers.

"Well—" Myrtle looked from one to the other with those great, shining, black eyes of hers. "Prudence tells me you all nevah have any plays up heah, or any readin's, not even Shakespeare. And that you frown most severely on dancin' pahties. Now that's a mighty big shame, seems to me, 'cause—" She shrugged. "Well! Wheah's the harm? Were we all down in South Ca'lina right this minute, han'some men and lovely ladies like I see 'roun' me, we'd— Wait! Ah'll show you!"

She sprang up and went with a little rush to Johnny and slipped her hand into his, turning him with her to face the roomful of people.

"Faith! Do you go to the spinet in the parlor and play that little air Ah taught you!" she cried, her face sparkling with her daring. "Then Ah'll teach you-all the steps of the minuet! Matt,

take Prudence! Alec, show Pamela! Mary, choose a pahtnuh, too,
and we eight will form a set an'—"

She stopped abruptly, seeing, in startled unbelief, all the faces
before her grow rigid and forbidding, mouths closed grimly and
eyes that had been friendly a moment ago, staring at her now
with the anger of outrage and horror. It was Mr. Theodore
Sedgwick, the rising young lawyer in that area, who came swiftly
to the rescue with his usual grace and tact.

"You must forgive us. We've lived so long alone here behind
our hills that our viewpoint on some matters has become fixed.
Possibly time will change it. Who can say? Meanwhile, please
accept our thanks for your generous impulse—and our regrets."
He bowed deeply.

The moment passed and the tension relaxed. But Prue, a
frozen onlooker, had seen something she had never seen before.
Here in this room were gathered, in their best bombazines and
broadcloths, the lean and the plump, the tall and the short, the
old and the not so old and the young, each as different and
separate and strongly individual as nature could make them. Yet
in them all was a likeness, too, that stood out clear and unmistakable. For there was in each some of the shrewdness of old
Colonel Ephraim Williams, now long since dead, the idealism
of John Sergeant, the integrity of Jonathan Edwards, the goodness of Timothy Woodbridge. And with all this, the likeness,
also, born of a group loyalty that refuses permission for any person to act on moral matters except as the group decrees, a likeness brought on by years of hell-fire sermons and the steady
denial of all joy.

Only Matt and Myrtle in that assemblage seemed not to belong, Prue thought: Matt, by reason of having broken away from
this pattern in his youth, and Myrtle because of a different and
far more lenient upbringing. Or was there yet another? she asked
herself, her glance passing to Johnny who stood with Myrtle's
hand still in his.

Yes, there was. Something about him—the set of his mouth,
the veiled glimmer of light between his narrowed eyes—told her
that Johnny was a rebel, a nonconformist, too. This, then, was

the reason he had kept himself so well hid. No wonder! It was the only way he could possibly live here. But if it were true (her mind went on), she was probably the cause of it, setting him the example she had by withdrawing from the church for his sake during Mr. Edwards' ministry and teaching him not to be afraid of the consequences.

These thoughts all went through Prue's head while Mr. Sedgwick was speaking and, as he finished, she saw Myrtle flash a glance upward into Johnny's face, asking him silently, if he, too, condemned her. His reply was clear enough. Sakes! Couldn't the whole room see? Prue felt her spine tingle before his answering look, for it was a second recognition, a second flaming which, this time, demanded acknowledgment. "Nothing"—it seemed to say—"that you may do is wrong in my sight for I love you." Then Myrtle's hand fluttered away from Johnny's clasp and they moved quickly and soberly apart.

It was at this moment that Faith came to Prudence and plucked her sleeve, her young face puzzled and disturbed.

"Ma, there's some one on the porch. I don't know if he's come to the party or not. He looks—he looks summat like an Indian. Did you invite any Indians?"

What now? Yet Prue was glad for the interruption as she turned and went forward swiftly to the front door that Faith, in her uncertainty, had closed. Opening it, she saw standing before her in buckskins, a tall stranger whose long black hair fell in disorder about his bronzed face but in whose black eyes there was an eager light of recognition and hope, and whose features were Matt's own.

For a moment she stared without speaking. Then—"Aaron!" she said breathlessly. "Oh, Aaron! Is it you? It *is!* Oh, come *in!*"

"What else could I do, Matt?" Prudence asked.

"Nothing, I reckon."

"He lived here as one of us when he was small. He was part of the family."

"I know."

"It never occurred to me not to ask him in. I—I had to."

"I know," he said again.

They were alone together in her bedroom the day after the party. Faith was in school. Myrtle had gone riding with Johnny for the first time since her arrival. David and Pa were in the fields and Alec had taken the three small boys for a walk. Aaron was not here. Last night he had gone down to stay in the home of some Indian when he had learned how full Martin Manor was. But he had promised to return today to talk with Matt. He had come back (he had said to their eager questioning) because he had never forgotten their goodness to him. It had lived with him through the years, warring with the goodness of the Indians until —finally—he had decided he wished to return and take up again a white man's ways. The white girl he had married, who had been captured by the tribe that had held him, and who had no family left to her, had helped him make up his mind. She was in the village now.

"That's it, I suppose," Matt said.

Prue looked at him inquiringly. He was frowning as he paced about the room, completely at a loss for the first time in many a year. Pausing before her, he threw out a great arm impatiently.

"I mean that he's always been accepted by us as an equal. But these things are different in the South. Oh, they happen, all right. Myrtle knows that. The plantations are overrun with mulattoes and half-breeds, but they don't ever come to the front door. They're kept in the background—in their place, and their place is never under the same roof as the wife of the master. That was the insult."

"She wasn't shocked, then."

"Just at that. She knew I— She knew I'd seen the world and was no innocent when I married her. Southern women sense these things and ignore them." He paused for a moment, amazed at the freedom with which he was speaking to this sister of his. But so he had always done, hadn't he? He went on. "Only, as she puts it, she never expected to have the proof of my early indiscretions thrust in her face. Oh, she's angry! I've never seen her so. And I don't know what to do. I can't deny him now. It was never in my heart, anyway. I'm proud he's come back." He paused, then finished, "What's more, he's the only son I have."

There was a little silence. In it Prue shivered slightly in the cold of the room and asked Matt to put a light to the logs Zeke had laid in the fireplace. The frown was still on his face as he bent to do her bidding but when he straightened up she saw it had cleared.

"There's just one thing," he said. "Pa gave me ninety acres before Aaron was carried off. I'll give them to him. He can build a house on them and live there." He looked at Prue. "He'll be your nearest neighbor. Will you mind?"

"But of course not!"

He flung himself into the wing chair and stared at his boots. "Myrtle will never understand it. Never. Much of what she has seen here has been strange to her. Our tightlaced notions— Well, you know from yesterday." The darkness left his brow and a faint smile appeared. "It was good as a show to see all their faces, wasn't it?" Then the smile faded. "It's all right for *her* to choose a convention to oppose," he finished dryly.

"It's—whatever we're born and bred to that forms us, isn't it, Matt?"

"Is it? Could be." He stared at the flames. Then he rose to his feet. "Well, this ends our visit," he said. "As soon as I get this property transferred to Aaron, we'll take our departure. She won't stay with him around."

Prue nodded, her look going out of the window to where, in the distance, she saw Johnny and Myrtle riding. It was best so, she told herself reluctantly. Then her glance moved nearer.

"Here comes Aaron now, Matt," she said. "He's had his hair cut. He's—quite fine-looking." She raised her glance to her brother. "I'm glad you're doing this," she finished quietly. "I'm very glad."

"That's something. I'm not sure about Pa."

"Pa won't object."

He left her and for a few moments she remained alone with her thoughts, going over the excitement created yesterday by Aaron's unexpected appearance. Of them all, only he himself had been calm. He had stood like an island eddied about by varying currents of curiosity and welcome and amazement. She had been aware of Matt's great burst of surprise and delight, of Pa's gruff greeting, of David's usual courtesy, restrained but friendly, of John Sergeant's warmth. And then, in the midst of the stir, she had discovered Myrtle standing apart with Johnny. Her black eyes were blazing. Some one must have told her, Prue had thought, and realized suddenly what a shock this must have been. That was when she heard Myrtle say, in a small, strangling voice, "Take me away, Johnny. Take me out of here."

They had slipped from the room unnoticed and had not returned until late. By then Aaron was gone. But Prue had heard Myrtle's and Matt's voices in the room behind hers long into the night.

She understood, now, Matt's feeling for his wife. She was a decoration, the loveliest flower in a field of lovely flowers that he had been able to pluck for his keeping, the living proof of his success in life, the symbol of his pride. He would humor her and spoil her. He would buy her anything she coveted, from a thoroughbred horse for her riding, to emeralds for her white throat. He would engage the most famous painter of the times, John Singleton Copley, to paint her portrait which would be hung in the most conspicuous place in his house. But she was outside of him. She was a secondary interest, for his first was, as it had always been, himself and his aims and purposes which he would not have crossed. Myrtle was not woven into the web and woof of his thoughts and his feelings as Prue was in David's and as Mary was in Alec's. And though passion there might be, it was a passion that took much and gave little and—no doubt—left Myrtle staring into the dark spiritually empty.

So thought Prue, and was not far from the truth.

They were gone. All of them had gone clattering off through a light drifting snow that was more like mist or smoke in its fluidity. Through it the trees stood dim and shadowy and the hills were lost.

It was a bad day for them to start but Matt would not wait

longer. Any time now, he said, the weather would worsen and the roads would be blocked. They would be all right once they reached Egremont and could travel in the shelter of a coach. And he was right, for that night, after they had gone, the world froze and the next day all outdoors was a scene done in black metal and clear shining glass, with the hill road a glare of smooth ice on which no horse could keep its feet.

The house seemed silent without them. Faith, helping Prudence put it to rights, said so repeatedly. And then she said something else that brought Prue's wandering thoughts to swift attention.

"Ma, what's kissing kin mean?"

"Who said that, Faith?"

"Aunt Myrtle. She said it to Uncle Johnny. She said that since he was Uncle Matt's brother, she and he were kissing kin and so he could kiss her good-by. And then he did."

"I see. Well, that's a Southern expression. And that's exactly what it means—that people closely related may be granted the privilege of kissing now and then."

"She invited him to come down there and visit her, too. I wish she'd invite me. I'd like to learn to dance."

Prue, remembering that roomful of frozen faces, thought suddenly, *"You shall."* But she said only, "Perhaps she will some day. Or, if she doesn't, Aunt Mary will."

Would Johnny accept Myrtle's invitation, Prue wondered? The guilt of his charm, which had brought him, unasked, a gift he could neither take nor refuse, lay heavily on him. She could sense that. Some people, like Andy, knew things by studying about them. Others, like Matt and Mary, knew them by doing them. But Johnny and she just knew them.

She knew, for example, when Mary wrote that Myrtle had taken a room to herself since their return and it was all because of Aaron, that it was not because of Aaron, at all, but because of Johnny. She knew, too, that Matt would not tolerate such independence long. But whether he did or not, Johnny must never visit there no matter how much he was urged.

So she told him one time, boldly invading his privacy without hint of invitation from him and expecting him to resent it. Instead, he narrowed his gray-green eyes under their odd, pointed-up lids and said, "There's no use my trying to hide from you, Prue. You've always guessed my thoughts from the time I was a little tyke. Well, I'm glad you know." He paused. "And I won't go, as I was planning. You're right. 'Twould only be putting my head into the lion's mouth. But—" A sudden savagery came into his voice and face. "Whatever I'm to do with my life now, I don't know, I'm sure. It stretches ahead of me a mortal weary waste."

The lightning had struck, indeed, Prue thought, and was astounded at the havoc it had wrought, for how little they had seen each other, after all. And then she remembered the times they had been together that last week, walking or riding, while Matt was tramping the ninety acres with Aaron, or with him at Mr. Sedgwick's law office down in Great Barrington going over the papers that were to make the property his. There had been opportunity then for them to discover each other.

She said gently, "For a man, life can be more than having—or not having—love. Think on it, Johnny."

CHAPTER 18

The Gathering Clouds

THE DAYS AND THE WEEKS and the months slipped by and it was spring again. The tremendous icicle spears hanging from the front veranda roof were gradually warmed by sun and air till they melted with a slow musical tinkle into the wooden trough below. The barberry bushes shed their transparent coats of glass and gleamed scarlet out by the roadside. The pale iridescence of the sky that had held all through March so like the lining of an egg shell, deepened to a delicate blue. The brown earth became soft and workable, and now through the still air could be heard the voices of men, the iron clang of plows, the lowing of cattle let out to pasture, while up at Aaron's house behind Martin Manor, he could be glimpsed every day, his tall, lean figure moving with swift, agile strength as he cleared his land, readying it for seeding and planting.

He had built a neat English house of two rooms with a great chimney between such as Mark had put up for his family when they first arrived. Prue was glad to have a neighbor so near her and befriended Aaron's wife, young Sara, in many thoughtful ways. Scarcely a day went by that first winter that she did not, when weather permitted, walk up there over the snow to see that all was well, for a baby was expected. And when he came it was Prue who took him and oiled him and bathed him, finally bringing him back to the silent, plain-faced girl with such a warm smile that it broke through the crust of her reserve at last.

"You're good," she whispered.

290

"Let me be your friend," Prue returned.

"I—I didn't know, Aaron being part Injun—"

"Aaron is one of us, Sara. We have always been fond of him. And he will take good care of you."

"I know."

"You were wise to marry him, I think. It has brought you back among white people again. And you can be happy with him if you want to be."

"I do want to be."

That was all Prue wanted to hear.

Spring—summer—fall—and another winter. Through them the community continued in its placid, patriarchal pattern. But the placidity lay only on the surface, for Stockbridge, now the most important town in the shire, was no longer quite as isolated as it had been formerly, and the rumbles of discontent that were being heard throughout the Colonies found echoes here. Knots of men gathered daily on the porch of the general store to voice their protests and sound their anger against the taxes being imposed by England, as men all over were doing. And the women, turning these protests into action, spun and wove as many articles as they could so as not to be dependent on British imports, so as to show the mother country that America was determined in her resentment. Prue was one of the most diligent among them, and night after night found her at her work in the keeping room with David watching her silently, a strange expression of pain on his face when she was not looking.

By now Mark was finishing at the college in Prince's Town, Luke had started to school where Faith had finished, and Johnny had become a torch to inflame laggard spirits over repeated injustices. He and Fighting Parson Allen from Pittsfield, who preached a rebellious patriotism from his pulpit, could be seen together at every meeting called anywhere in the county. Yet, in spite of the uncertainty and ferment, people continued to push out to new places and start new homes. Williamstown was established, in accordance with the will left by Ephraim Williams, Jr.; New Marlboro was filling up; Tyringham had been incorporated; South Lee was growing and enlarging its inn, and West Stockbridge was being settled with square, sturdy-built, white frame houses. (It was a place Elijah Williams soon saw offered him an opportunity to add to his prosperity, so he quickly established an iron factory there.) Stockbridge itself seemed to Prue and Pa to be overflowing, and glad they were to be living on the outskirts, protected from too close an encroachment of strangers by their own broad acreage.

In the spring of 1767, Mary wrote Prue from Charles Town asking if Faith, who was now approaching fourteen, might come and visit her? Safe travel was arranged and she departed in a flutter of excitement, her great brown eyes glowing with anticipation under her smooth pale gold hair. At the end of six months she returned with a noticeable Southern accent, a new grace, a pretty air of poise and sophistication, enamored of the South and —from all her talk of him—of a Mr. James Humphrey, as well.

Another year sped. Mark planning now to go to the first medical school in the country down in Philadelphia. Luke shooting up tall and thin. Johnny less restless now that he had found release for pent-up feelings in political activity. And Pa living happily off his land, watching it prosper in deep contentment and—though he never went to Aaron's—taking a kindly liking to his little son, Ben, and letting the small toddler dog his heels whenever Sara brought him down.

Everything seemed to be going on as usual though Prue felt a difference in the air, for the mutter of protest and rebellion continued to grow steadily through that year and into the next. It made Johnny more and more resolute and active and vocal in the cause of the Colonies but it turned David more and more silent. It was as well this was so, Prue often thought; otherwise bitter words might pass between the two of them, for David was conservative and loyal to the Crown while Johnny was heart and soul in this new interest that was taking his mind off Myrtle. It grieved her that there was this difference between the two of them, for of all Pa's family David had been fondest of Johnny.

And then came the March night at the end of the winter of 1770 when Johnny came galloping home late to fling himself from his horse and into the house with his eyes burning in excitement and anger.

"There's been a massacre in Boston! The British troops have fired on and killed five of our men! The fat's in the fire this time for fair!"

There was a shocked silence. David, who had turned quite pale, opened his mouth to speak, only to shut it again without saying a word. Faith cried, "Oh! What will happen now?" And Pa, half in reply and half to himself, said slowly, "You can't lick a man tame, that's for sure."

But Prue, heartsick, thought it seemed only yesterday since the French and Indian War had ended and peace was promised. Was the aftermath of war always to be the threat of another?

For the next two years all the country seemed to hold its breath. Mary wrote from South Carolina:

"We feel sometimes we are living on a volcano. Our governor, Lord William Campbell, is not one to take forceful action, however. He is very young and seeming irresolute and continues to lead our social life here as if nothing threatened. Indeed, I do not see how violence is possible under his rule, so if, as you say, Faith desires to visit me again, I do truly feel she will be safe. Can she reach here in time for the Governor's Ball? Young James Humphrey asks about her constantly and would like to be her escort for that affair. I hope you will let her come. I cannot help but feel those two need only another meeting to settle the question in their hearts. And since Faith must be nearing nineteen now, isn't it high time it was settled?"

Faith went—and wrote back a most glowing account of her first big ball. Prue read the letter aloud to David and when she came to the last line, "I will not do anything hasty about James, as I promised you, but I think my mind is decided on him," she looked up from the letter and spoke to her husband.

"I believe our Faith will be a married woman ere long," she said.

David made no answer. She looked across at him and realized suddenly that he was not thinking of Faith at all. Indeed, she doubted if he had more than half heard the letter. There were on his face now, as so often lately, the deep, graven lines from his nostrils to the corners of his mouth that bespoke sober thought and anxious worry. She knew he was much disturbed at Johnny's activities on behalf of the Massachusetts Colony, that the Boston Tea Party—and Johnny's exuberant approval of it— had been most upsetting to him. "I can see your reasons for resentment," he had said, with slow care. "But I can never con- done violent action taken against our King or his representa- tives." Johnny had flashed back, "And what are we to do then? Meekly submit?" It had been she who had intervened. "David simply means he believes a peaceful way can be found to settle our disputes, Johnny. Your viewpoints differ only because of the difference in your ages. And I must say I'm with David. War is dreadful." Johnny had looked at her for a moment, then he had said, "You're not with him as much as you think, Prue." And he had walked away.

Well, was David remembering all that now? Or was his frown caused by the letter Prue had read? Was he reluctant to have his daughter wed and live so far distant, no matter how happy her prospects?

Determined to know, she spoke his name. He turned his head toward her quickly, seeming to come back to her from a great distance.

"David, what troubles you?"

He said abruptly, "Prudence, will you go to England with me?"

"To England!"

"Yes. You promised you would go once. Do you remember?"

"Yes. I remember," she replied, slowly. "But why now?"

"Because—because I thought I might get a clearer view of the differences between this country and England if I went back there for a bit."

She said gently, "But the view is clear enough, isn't it? We are being put upon." She shook her head. "I truly don't see how

we can go now, David, with Faith maybe getting married soon.
And then there's Pa. Who would do for him? I'm sorry to seem—"
"Never mind."

It had been a wild idea, of course, born of his private desper-
ation and it would not really solve his problem, anyway. That
would remain no matter where he was. He got up and came toward her with the swift, limber grace that was still his despite
his added years and drew her to her feet.

"My darling, don't look so troubled," he said.

"But I *did* promise you. Couldn't we go later? Won't that do
just as well?"

"Yes. Later—perhaps."

But later might be too late, he was thinking, and he spoke
suddenly. "Listen, Prue. I want to tell you something and I want
you to remember it no matter what comes. I love you. I love you
as I always have. You are my heart and my life. Never forget."

She put her hand up to his cheek. He turned it and kissed her
palm. "I love you," he repeated, and he caught her to him and
said in a breaking voice, "God in heaven, how I love you!"

It was an unusual display of emotion after all their life together and it moved her to exaltation. At the same time her heart
felt curiously cast down into a dark misery that she could not
name or understand.

CHAPTER 19

The Cleavage

IT WAS THE YEAR 1774. Mark had opened his doctor's office in
Great Barrington; Faith, married now to James Humphrey
in Charles Town, expected her first child in the fall; and Sara's
second child, Rebecca, had come to the log cabin north of Prue.

In the village Timothy Edwards, Jonathan Edwards' son, returning to Stockbridge after years away, had built a home for
himself and his family cater-cornered to the new Red Lion Inn.

The inn was quite pretentious. Downstairs there were eight
bedrooms and the usual bar where hot toddies and punches were
served by the eminently respectable innkeeper, Captain Isaac
Marsh. Upstairs there was a great hall for important gatherings
and outside on the street hung a wooden sign with a red lion
painted on it, a red lion with a green tail.

It was to the hall upstairs that David went for an important
meeting in July. Here a Berkshire convention had been called
to discuss the grave events that had been taking place, and to it
came delegates from all the neighboring communities.

David knew all about these grave events. He knew that no
more commerce was to be permitted with the port of Boston until
that town should make its submission. He knew, further, that the
entire commonwealth was to be punished by the declaration, as
null and void, certain charter provisions granted by William III
as far back as 1692—a serious matter since it set up the doctrine
that charters proceeding from the Crown could be altered by
statue and that from now on Parliament could be all-powerful

in Colonial matters. He knew, too, of the ruling that officers and soldiers, resisting riots, were to be sent to England for trial. And finally he knew that a new measure had been passed by Parliament to provide for the quartering of soldiers upon the citizens —this to facilitate the setting up of a military government in Massachusetts.

Oh, he knew it all! His head ached with what he knew. The burden of his knowledge was no greater than that of any of the other men present, yet it weighed on him more heavily, for he had come with his mind not yet fully made up as to the side he was on, though of his prejudice there was no doubt. But now he must choose between his thinking and his feeling. He could no longer remain impartial. He could no longer stand aloof. Pressure was being put on those whose loyalties were in question. There was ostracism. There was even rough usage. No one suspected his own indecision—save, perhaps, Johnny—yet how long it had harassed him!

He knew full well all the arguments pro and con. He admitted that the British government had taken a wrong step in its legislation, but the Colonies, frenzied by their tireless leaders who saw nothing possible but secession, had taken an equally wrong one by repeated acts of violence. This was where his mind halted and his feeling stepped in, for it was at this point that all his English inheritance of orderliness, of responsibility, of compromise, cried out that the settlement of the entire dispute should have been—might have been—by the usual course of law. Only the Americans would not wait. And now matters had drifted too far. It all filled him with an anguished bitter helplessness, for one could not live with might-have-beens. One had to live with what was.

He had come alone and he was sitting alone on a hard bench far in the back of the room. Now his eyes moved thoughtfully over the assembled group. He knew them all by sight if not by name. They were a grim, resolute-appearing lot, men who had built their own homes and wrested a living from their farms, who were disciplined to a staunch self-reliance and who were accustomed to liberty of action. It seemed to him, studying them, that he could almost read what was going on in their minds now. Certainly there were men here who, like him, would have preferred not to give their presence to this gathering. He was sure of that.

Timothy Edwards, for example, who ran the store where he traded his merchandise for wheat which he was able to sell at a good profit to himself, was rightfully fearful of what a war might do to his business. He had steered a neutral course for many months—yet today here he was.

And Jahleel Woodbridge, Timothy's nephew and the leader of the community, had been openly opposed to the view of the liberal party—until he had heard that the British intended to abrogate the provincial charter. That, he had declared, swinging quickly and firmly about, was carrying things too far. Well, he was right and England was wrong on that. But could two wrongs —and rebellion *was* wrong—make a right again?

His glance found the well-dressed figure of Theodore Sedgwick —he who had poured oil on the troubled waters at Prue's party for Mary, and who, later, had acted for Matt in the transfer of his property to Aaron. He was another who stood to lose if war developed, for he was a rising young lawyer, one of the few in the state. By nature he was conservative and he had been opposed to the circular letter Johnny and his Committee of Correspondence had sent out to other Colonies asking for aid against England's aggressiveness. Why had he changed his tune today? Was it that he, like so many others in this raw land, had a spirit that could not help resenting what seemed to them high-handedness shown by the mother country? They were so fiercely independent —these Americans! Was it not possible, anyway, that all this furor was based on too great a greed on the part of the Massachusetts Colony? After all, she was a colony and as such owed something to England. He sighed heavily.

None of the Williams family was present, David reflected. Elijah Williams, sheriff of Stockbridge, had loudly deplored the Boston Massacre and the Boston Tea Party. He was undoubtedly one of many of that huge family that the British government could count on. David did not relish the thought of being on the side of the Williamses in this or any other matter. But if he eventually decided he was, it would not be because he was considering his possessions, as they were, but because he could not get away from the conviction that he owed his allegiance to the Crown, because he was less an American than an Englishman, because he had no roots in this land at all—save for Prue.

The sound of heavy boots shuffling on the hard wood floor grew louder as more men arrived. There was a scraping of benches when these were pulled nearer to the front. Several paused in passing to say to David they were glad to see him there, to which he merely nodded. Then the rumble of deep voices increased with the heat of argument and indignation, and swift gestures cut the air. Yet there was an underlying quiet in the room, too, and David could not help but recognize that a unity existed in all minds now, however divided they had been before today.

Unity. Yes. That was what the Coercive Acts had produced, he sadly told himself. They had served to show that the great bulk of this colony stood firmly together. Yet even now (he asked himself) could not the trouble be peaceably resolved? It could be if the Colonists did not rush into inconsidered deeds. Oh, surely they would not! This was his prayer and his hope. On it, he decided suddenly, he would base his own future actions. Indeed, he would take no action so long as hope lasted.

There came a hush as quick short footsteps were heard coming up the stairs. In a moment the small neat figure of Dr. West appeared. Clad in his black clerical clothes, he walked forward to the front of the room and as he lifted his arms in the signal for his listeners to bow their heads, David saw that his hands— indeed, his whole body—were a-tremble with his emotion.

"We pray Thee, oh, Lord, to guide us in this hour of danger—"

Dr. West was as conservative as any one, David's mind now went on. Wasn't his wife a former Williams? Yet today, however frighted he might be, here he was. He stirred uneasily. And John Ashley, from Sheffield, who had been a guest at Prue's party also,

was now ardently proclaiming himself a Whig by being here.
And Johnny, whose fair head topped all the others— Was he,
David, fathering a futile and unrealistic wish? But what else
could he do? He was on the rack. The choice before him was no
choice at all. It was an end.

The prayer was concluded and the meeting was called to order.
John Ashley was quickly elected president of the present congress and Theodore Sedgwick the clerk. A day of fast was pro-
claimed for July 14th, and then the assembly drew up its protest.

WHEREAS the Parliament of Great Britain have of late
undertaken to give and grant away our money without our
knowledge or consent; and in order to compel us to servile
submission to the above measures, have proceeded to block
up the harbor of Boston, we do, solemnly and in good faith
covenant and engage with each other—

1. That we will not import, purchase or consume, or suffer
any person by, or for us, to import or consume in any manner whatever, any goods, wares or merchandise which shall
arrive in America from Great Britain from and after the
first day of October, 1774, or any other such time as shall be
agreed upon by the American Congress, nor any goods which
shall be ordered from thence, after this day, until our chart-
ered and constitutional rights shall be restored."

There were other provisions. To "observe the most strict obedi-
ence to all constitutional laws and authority." To "promise and
agree that we will by every prudent method, endeavor to guard
against those inconveniences which may otherwise arise from the
foregoing agreement." To "refuse to purchase any article of
British manufacturing" from "whatever trader or shopkeeper in
the county" who was "unwilling, after forty-eight hours of consideration, to enter into a similar covenant."

These resolutions were unanimously and soberly adopted.
They—and the league that was formed by a similar covenant with
other towns in the county—were the first unconditional act of
nonintercourse with Great Britain in Massachusetts.

But before they were passed around for signatures, David had risen and quietly made his way out of the room.

The sun was pitiless that August morning but the men grouped about the court house in Great Barrington seemed unmindful of the heat. Stolidly, silently, with stern and resolute countenances they massed themselves around the building, one thousand gathered from Berkshire County and five hundred more from Litchfield, while they waited for court to open.

They were unarmed, and the leaders among them, including Johnny, who moved constantly about the outer ring, kept issuing quiet warning injunctions. "Remember! No violence. No words or arguments. Just hold your places."

It was the day for hearings in the Court of Common Pleas and Sheriff Elijah Williams with the presiding officers of the court garbed in their official robes and their white whigs were due at any moment now. Soon a bell would be heard and the cry, "Make way for the Court!" That was the signal for the mob to melt and divide, leaving a clear passageway to the front doors of the story-and-a-half frame building there on Main Street.

But court was not going to open. This had been decided by the waiting band of independent men. Weeks ago, following the convention at Red Lion Inn, a petition had been sent to Governor Gage in Boston by the county, asking that the Courts of Justice immediately cease, until all grievances were fully redressed by a final repeal of the injurious and unconstitutional acts.

This petition the governor had chosen to ignore. Instead, he had ordered the courts to act "under the new British regulation."

Johnny, moving with catlike quiet among the men, was stirred as he had never been stirred before. Here, at last, was action after weary months of letter writing. Here was something definite, something decisive, something formidable. It should wake up those stupid Britishers! His gray-green eyes under their pointed hooding lids, glinted with his pleasure. He ran a hand through his fair tumbled locks and addressed the men before him again.

"They're coming. I hear the bell. Remember now! No violence. And not a word. But stand firm and don't give an inch."

He, himself, moved toward the street. Every one could hear the bell by this time and the intoned cry, "Make way for the Court!"

Yes, here they came, a half-dozen authorities, elegantly gowned and properly bewigged, stepping briskly in their neat silver-buckled shoes, stepping confidently, and led by the stocky sheriff of Stockbridge. But as they drew nearer and saw that massed multitude they slowed a bit.

Johnny grinned to himself. He stood with his back to the crowd, his thumbs carelessly thrust through his belt, his head tossed back, his eyes on the sheriff. Here was a time when Elijah Williams would meet his come-uppance, he was thinking. Here was a moment when the lord of the hill would know what the men of the plain and the men of the meadow thought and felt. Here was a mob arrayed against him and his like that he could no more disperse than his father had been able to disperse another mob at an earlier time.

"Make way for the Court!"

The little procession came on. But no one stirred. Johnny's look met Elijah's, and Elijah barked out angrily, "These are the King's orders! Make way!"

There was no reply. If there was any movement it was only to inch closer together, to pack still tighter shoulder against shoulder, to make a more solid wall of opposition to this hated authority.

The judge spoke up, but his voice betrayed his uncertainty. His glance ran quickly over those hard faces, those still figures and then he turned to his men.

"There are too few of us. We can do nothing. We are not armed."

"Nor are we," Johnny said softly.

Elijah threw him a wrathful look. He and the judge spoke together in low voices for a moment, then the group turned and, in a discomfiture that was plainly evident, marched away again.

As the sound of their footsteps receded on the summer air, as the last swinging robe disappeared from sight, there was a low murmur from the crowd. It might have been the beginning of a roar of laughter or a cheer of triumph. But it was quickly hushed as Johnny sprang up onto the stump of a tree.

"Quiet, men! We've won! But the day is not over! They may return later! We must wait here till dark whether our hay rots in the fields or not!"

"We'll wait!" came from a thousand throats.

Pa was there at Great Barrington that day, nursing his troublesome arm that was getting more and more rheumatic. Aaron was there, too, and young Luke, who, at fourteen, was afire with patriotism. And likewise the level-headed, level-eyed Dr. Mark Martin. He had closed his office door and put out a sign saying where he could be found if needed.

All the Martin family was there—save only David. David stayed at home and toiled in the hot fields to get in his hay with the help of his two field hands. And Prue did not urge him to go. She was glad he was keeping clear. How could she help but be glad? One war was enough for a man to fight through. She would never let him take part in another. The country could not—must not—need him. He knew how she felt. It was his knowledge, doubtless, that held him aloof now, though now, as before, she could see he was torn between his desire and his conscience. She was sorry for that. But she would never weaken. Not again.

September. The First Continental Congress met in Philadelphia. That fall, too, saw the organization of minute men all over the country and groups of volunteers drilling in towns and villages everywhere. In Stockbridge two companies were raised by voluntary enlistment. Indeed, so many men sent in their names that there weren't enough arms to go around and the town had to borrow twenty pounds for their purchase and voted fifty pounds for tents. Aaron was among those who joined up, and, of course, Johnny. And Luke.

Luke. He was tall for his age and strong and easily looked sixteen or more instead of the fourteen that he was. But Prue's heart was filled with fearful foreboding each week as she watched him swing off down the hill, his black head held high with pride, to the green where the drilling took place. Luke was her youngest. Her last baby. Yet what could she say if his country needed him? She found a grain of comfort in knowing that David, anyway, would not go.

Or would he? By many he would not be considered too old. He was no older than Fighting Parson Allen of Pittsfield. At least, not much. Yet surely some one had to stay and work the farm! That was her secret argument should he and she ever have to discuss the matter. Pa was fairly hale for seventy but not able to manage everything here alone with his crippled arm and only indifferent help. Yet—oh, how unhappy David was! Did he truly want to go? She was not certain. The disjuncture made within him by the tug of his conscience and the wish of his heart—for he *could* not want to leave her again!—had harried him so that he looked as she had not seen him since the Indians murdered little Esther. Now, as then, he wore that same terrible expression that revealed better than speech his bitter anguish. Was he waiting for her to say a word that would release him to action? But she could not! She *would* not!

So the days and the weeks went by, seeming the same on the surface with the gathering in of the crops for the winter, the preserving, the canning and spinning and weaving. Yet they were not the same, for impending trouble that could not much longer be staved off was a dark threat over every moment. Even the Williamses and the Dwights saw which way the wind was blowing and they were walking carefully and talking softly lest their own townspeople turn against them and run them out—for that could easily be done! Why, over in Plymouth it was said a whole congregation left church one Sunday because they would not sit in the same place with old George Watson, a "mandamus councilor." And down in New York, where Alexander Hamilton was so ardently speaking for the cause, a judge by the name of Smith had been tarred and feathered. And in Lenox a Royalist had been strung up and only barely saved from death. Oh! One lived on a powder keg these days, for sure!

And then came the seventeenth of March and town-meeting

day. No one ever missed a town meeting in New England. Regardless of the weather men gathered from far and near to speak whatever lay in their minds, to vote for or against proposed measures, to elect new officers for town management. It was the most important day of the year, for it was then that policies and plans were set, for better or worse, for the coming year.

Prue saw David and Johnny and Pa and Luke all go off together in the sleigh through a falling snow. (Luke now felt himself man enough to attend this year.) Likely they'd have a time getting back, she thought, if the wind came up. There was nothing like the drifts that could form on this high plateau. Later Aaron passed on horseback, sitting erect and proud with his long black hair flying over his shoulders and already powdered white. She waved to him through the window, wishing Sara could come down to keep her company but knowing she would not because she would have trouble getting her little ones here safely through the storm. How confident Aaron had grown, she thought to herself, as she watched him disappear from sight, now that he owned land that no white man could ever take away from him. Surely Matt's thought of him that way was a good deed to chalk up against other deeds that might not be so good in his book of life.

She got out her loom and busied herself with weaving. The house seemed very lonely to her with the children all grown and going their different ways. She wished Mark had seen fit to settle in Stockbridge but he had said that Dr. Erastus Sergeant was enough for this town. Perhaps, though, she missed Faith more. It would have been such a pleasure to have her closer with her little girl. Think on it! She'd never seen Dulcie—and when would she if things stayed stirred up the way they were now?

The house seemed still, too. Cindy was out in her cabin back of the barn caring for old Zeke who was probably in his last illness. And Pearl had gone to help her so Prue was alone with only the whistling wind for company. Sakes! How it howled. There'd be drifts, for sure, and could be the men might not get home at all this night. Well, at least she had no savages to fear.

The minutes crept by. Darkness came early because of the storm. Over and over she went to the window to peer out but she could see nothing. Nor would she be able to hear their return, either, she thought, over this blanket of snow. Still, there was no sense to worrying. Worrying had just got to be a habit, she reckoned.

Yet the worry persisted. It was a dark cloud weighing down her spirit and she could not say why. Then, of a sudden, she did hear something. Muffled galloping hoofbeats in the drive outside. Aaron?

But it was David who came in, leaving the horse fast to the post, shaking the snow off his heavy cap, stomping it from his feet before the fire and breathing—and looking—as if he'd raced with the devil. Never had she seen him like this.

"David! What is it?"

"Prue, I have to leave you."

"Leave me? Whatever do you mean?"

He told her. They had voted today for or against a recommendation for autonomy. There had been forty votes for it and only one against.

"That man will have to flee for his life," he said.

She stared at him. "*You,* David? You voted against—?"

"I abstained. But that's as good as against the way the feeling runs here now." He dropped suddenly into a chair and put his head in his hands with a groan. All his desperate hope that time would be on his side was gone now. He must—at last—speak. He must—at last—make Prue know how he felt.

Only—how could he tell her? How could he possibly make her know of the struggle that had been going on within him for so long? But she did not give him a chance.

She was saying slowly, incredulously, "You—would run away? Hide in the mountains somewhere?"

He lifted his head as if he had not heard aright. Then he rose. "No," he told her quietly. "I'll never skulk in hiding. I am going to join the British Army."

"*David!*"

Shocked, she recoiled from him. He saw the movement and winced but he did not stir. They gazed at each other a moment, then she whispered, "You—you don't mean that."

"I do mean it," he replied in a sad, grave tone.

There was another silence while all that this portended gathered in a growing horror in her blue eyes. She put a hand to her throat through which her words came as if she were strangling.

"I never thought to hear this from you. Not this! Why—" She stopped. "But you went to the convention at Red Lion Inn! You signed the protest that day! How can you now—"

He shook his head. "I never signed it. I left before the paper reached me."

She flung out a hand toward him. "David! Do you know what this means? It will be brother against brother! You against Johnny! And Matt! And they against you!"

"We are not at war yet, Prue."

"But war will come! And when it does you will have no choice! You will kill Johnny—"

"You know I will never do that."

"—and your own son, Luke—"

"Prue! Stop!"

"I will not stop! That is how I see it and that is how it will be, since war is for killing!" Her voice steadied and her eyes turned now to blue ice. She went on in an accusing, frozen inexorability. "I could let you go to fight on our side. I could— though I had determined not to—for that would do me honor. America has given you a home. It has given you a family and made you prosperous. Yet now you say you will turn against all that—that you will murder us for what you have received. Indeed, you have already murdered me."

He cried out her name and took a step toward her with his arms out but she retreated.

"No. Do not touch me. I will not be wooed to agreement as I was once before. I say to you now—and may God bear me witness —that if you do this thing—if you turn Tory against all who have known you and loved you—then there is no longer love between us. There is nothing. And you need never come back."

The stillness was the stillness of death in the room. In it the wind wailed around the house and the snow rushed against the window glass and the horse outside whinnied his misery. Slowly

David's arms fell to his sides while the specks of fire in his brown eyes died as they met Prue's hard stare.

He said at last, "You have decided this. You have divided us. Not I. For I will never cease loving you as long as I draw breath."

He waited a moment for a flickering sign of her yielding. But none came. He spoke again, his voice ragged. "I have been over this and over it in my mind till I am torn asunder. But—I belong to England."

"You belong to me. And to America."

"I cannot make it seem so." He shook his head wearily and stood waiting for her reply to that. "It is my conscience, Prue. I must govern myself according to my conscience."

But to Prue there was no right or wrong in this matter. There was no conscience. There was only love—or no love. Oh, she had never dreamed of such dreadfulness as this! To have him go to war for the American cause would have been bad enough. But to have him side with England— She could not rightly take it in. Not yet. She was stark and stiff with shame and shock.

Once more the horse whinnied outside and once more the snow dashed against the window. David took a long breath and drew himself erect.

"I will go," he said heavily. "Tell Aaron I have left his horse in our barn."

He reached for his cap and pulled it on over his ears. He wound his thick muffler about his throat. He picked up his heavy mittens. At the door he turned toward her once more.

"Good-by, Prue."

She made no answer. He went out, closing the door quietly behind him.

```
PART FIVE

PA AND PRUE

1775-1785
```

CHAPTER 20

The War Years

THE SHOT THAT WAS HEARD around the world on April 19th did not reach the ears of the Stockbridge inhabitants until the next day. But by the early dawn of the twenty-first a full regiment, fully equipped and under the leadership of Colonel Patterson from Lenox marched out of the little village on it way to Boston. Included in this regiment were some fifty or sixty Indians commanded by their own Captain Abraham Ninham. Included also were Major Thomas Williams, Major Elnathan Curtis, and Aaron, Johnny and Luke Martin.

Prue was there to see them all go off. She stood quietly in the early morning light, her eyes going from Luke's darkly excited face to Johnny's sterner calm. She should, she knew, be feeling something as they were: some tingle of triumph, some thrill of pride, some sick dread—or all of these. But her heart was a stone within her, for she and David had quarreled and parted, and so, for her, there was no feeling left for anything. *Oh, David! David! What you have done to me!*

Yet life and the world and the war went on and flowed back

to her where she remained, frozen, and alone with Pa—save for a few slaves—there on the Martin Manor hilltop.

Luke wrote from Boston that their regiment had arrived too late (he was sorry to say) for the fighting at Lexington and Concord but at least they now had Governor Gage shut up in the city and were planning a siege to force his surrender. Their division was being reorganized (he continued), but Johnny and Major Thomas Williams and Aaron and he were still all together. The Stockbridge Indians had set up an encampment on the fringe of the city with their wives and children, for all the world as if they were on the plain and the meadow at home. There was little other news, save that he had enlisted until the war's end, though most had signed for only eight months. And would she send word, as soon as she knew, what part his cousins, Keith and Kim, were playing in the struggle?

He had not mentioned David, Prue thought. Yet she was not surprised. The boy had been too shocked and bewildered by his father's action to know what stand to take. How could he say aught against his own blood? Yet how could he see any view of this business save the one he himself took?

He is too young either to condemn or forgive, Prue told herself, so he keeps silence—as I do. But now my silence is too late. I would take back my harsh words if I could. I would, like Luke, be stunned into numbness if I might live over that night again. But it is too late. I cried out my anger in terrible words and now they are knives turning and twisting in my heart.

Mark, however, had something to say about his father. Writing the next month from Fort Ticonderoga (which, he related, he had helped Colonel Ethan Allen capture by a surprise attack), he said, "In many ways my father's decision is unaccountable to me. Yet I know his choice must have torn him as it is tearing you. We can only hope and pray that all will come out right in the end. If I may say so to you, dearest mother, I think you are wrong to harden your heart against him. After all, he was only doing what seemed right to him and no one should be blamed —or loved—the less for that."

He blamed her, Prue thought. Well, she blamed herself. But, oh! if only David could know how it was with a woman! A man spoke of duty and honor but to a woman these were only high-sounding words for something less noble—politics. She—Prue—cared not a jot or tittle for politics! She cared only for David. And she knew now that it made little difference to her what side he fought on just so he did not fight with her. How could she reach him to tell him to come back to her when the war was over? How could she let him know she was bleeding her life away until his return?

There seemed no way. The summer dragged by and the fall days came. Runners brought news of the war's progress and though it was good news for the most part, it rang dully in Prue's ears. Governor Gage was still a prisoner in Boston and Benedict Arnold was to lead a band of men north to capture Quebec. What of it? Then she heard that Luke, tired of inaction at Boston, had gone with Arnold, together with some other Stockbridge boys. Luke's first letter regarding this adventure was one Prue read aloud to Pa.

What agonies her youngest son had endured! Rough rapids in which boats capsized and provisions were lost. Long difficult portages over rough country that held dense underbrush and mosquito-filled swamps. Heavy rains, bitter cold, snow and sickness. The way unknown and the Indian guides of little help. The men utterly disheartened and badly weakened by their hardships and "reduced to eating candles for supper and a gruel made of those left for breakfast."

"Do you note that, Pa? And listen!" She read on, her voice shaking with indignation.

" 'We were thankful to eat chopped rawhide breeches from which we first singed the hair and then boiled the pieces to make a fairly palatable juice. This was after we reached our camp here at Spider Lake. Indeed, only Captain Morgan's dauntless spirit keeps us going now and the hope that Arnold, scouting ahead, may get succor from some French settlement.' "

Prue looked at Pa, her blue eyes blazing.

"If there is good to come out of such suffering and toil and heartache as this war brings, the Lord had better make it *very* good!"

Pa's black glance moved slowly toward her.

"First you tell Dr. Edwards what kind of sermons he's to preach and now you tell the Lord how He's to run His affairs. 'Tis a managing woman you are, Prudence."

Prudence folded Luke's letter with trembling fingers, a flush mantling her cheeks.

Oh, I am! I am! I tried to manage David's life and thoughts and conscience for him. It's no wonder to me any more that he left me.

It was Johnny who gave Prue her first glimmer of hope for a reconciliation with David. Faith had only echoed Mark, saying that it mattered little how beliefs differed when a loved one went forth to face death. Why had Prue not thought of that herself that unforgettable night? For he had, indeed, gone to face death, and what terrible words of hers he was carrying with him to face it! Suppose she had journeyed to England with him as he had once asked? Would she not have felt and behaved there as David had felt and behaved here? Would she not have told him she belonged to America as he had told her he belonged to England? She could hardly live with herself thinking these things. And then came Johnny's letter.

> November 29, '75
> Boston

Dear Prue,

I have recently been made an aide-de-camp to General Washington. This pleases me, as you can imagine. I did not relish being a fighting man (though I helped defend the fort at the Battle of Bunker Hill) and much prefer to bear messages, however dangerous a mission I may be sent on.

I sometimes wonder, as General Washington must, how an army can ever be made out of the men who have assembled here in this area. They take no orders unless they feel so inclined. They drink and fornicate and barter in their idle hours as if the fate of a nation did not hang on them. Their encampment has no look of the military, some tents being of sailcloth, others of board, others of stone and turf and some—Indian fashion—of withes and wreaths. And their dress is as individual. But they can shoot straight and hate well and that is something, I suppose. Anyway, the general is ever calm and undismayed and inspires confidence if not liking. He has his heart set on the success of Arnold's expedition and is rejoiced over Montgomery's capture of Montreal. We await final word of the fall of Quebec.

Prue, I have been making inquiries whenever and wherever I can as to David's whereabouts and have finally learned that he is a captain cooped up with Governor Gage in the city of Boston. If possible, I will get some word to him telling him I am here and can forward a message to you from him. But do not count on any success in this. It is only a hope.

Your devoted brother
Johnny

To this Prue made all haste to reply. She wrote:

Oh, you are a good and understanding brother! Your letter has just come to me and lifts my heart to a great height.

I would love a message from David, Johnny, but fear none will be forthcoming until I send one to him first. Can you, therefore, get word to him somehow that I deeply regret and will never forgive myself for all I said to him at our parting. That I have learned, in my loneliness, that political opinions cannot compare to life. They are, after all, only thoughts, words, ideas. But he—David—is the reality. He may be wrong in the decision he has taken—or I may be. How do I know? How could I have imagined myself so superior as to set myself up in judgment over him? Anyway, that is all beside the point. The point is I love him still and want him to come back to me whenever he can and will. Will you convey this to him, Johnny?

My love for David has made me think often of you, dear
brother, and the loneliness that will be yours unless you can
find a woman to be your companion through life. Have you
not been able to forget Myrtle by this time so that you can
turn your thoughts elsewhere? I do not mean to pry but
your fortune is dear to me, as you know.

With thanks to you again for your efforts on my behalf
and in haste and praying you may be successful, I am

Your loving sister
Prue

The end of the year brought the tragic news that the Quebec
expedition had been, in spite of a bold and successful beginning,
a failure, after all; that Arnold had been wounded, General
Montgomery (who had tried to go to Arnold's rescue) killed; Captain Morgan and his followers forced to surrender; and the
wretched little remnant of the American Army, abandoning its
attack, had retreated to Montreal where it was suffering from
smallpox, scanty provisions and frigid cold at the height of a bit-
terly cruel Canadian winter.

No word from Luke about all this. Prue did not know if he
was dead or alive, ill or captured. No word from Johnny, either,
who had doubtless been sent off on some mission or other. Had
he ever received her letter? If so, had he been able to reach
David before he left? And where was Mark now? Oh! The in-
humanity of men to women to make them suffer such tortures of
uncertainty—all for the sake of war! It was not reason enough,
Prue told herself. No fine-sounding words that seemed to justify
it would ever be reason enough. Men must just love carnage
more than they loved God, the Giver of Life, that they could so
wantonly destroy it.

The August sun burned down on Prue's back making her
gown stick like a plaster to her skin. Ahead of her the heat
danced in shimmering waves over the hot earth so that when she
looked up to rest her eyes from the glare, the hills seemed to be
dancing, too. More than once little black specks swam in the

air before her and she wanted to stop awhile and cool off. But she would not stop. Not till she was done. Those clouds rolling up in a dark heap in the west meant a thunderstorm and this hay must be got in before it broke. What was more, there was no one but herself to help Pa do it.

She was pitching great forkfuls up from the ground (Pa's bad arm wouldn't let him do such work) while he spread it around and tramped it down on the wagon. La! But her shoulders ached. Each time she lifted she thought it would be her last load; yet she kept on. Under the sunbonnet her scarlet face was covered with a layer of fine dust, down which the perspiration made small streaky tracks. Bits of hay had fallen into the neck of her dress and scratched her tender skin. She had pinned up her skirt above her knees and David's boots on her feet made them seem not her own every time she glanced down. She was certainly a sight! But she couldn't stand to go barefoot the way the boys always did and she had to be saving with her shoes. Anyway, what did she care how she looked?

It was Agrippa Hull was the cause of Pa's losing his field help. Agrippa, an outstanding Negro in Stockbridge, had enlisted and was now body servant to a general. Because of Agrippa's enviable position, Remus and Hannibal, Pa's helpers, had got it into their heads they could do as fine. Of course they couldn't. They hadn't Agrippa's character or personality. But Pa had never felt he owned his slaves body and soul and he had thought it not a bad idea that they, too, should defend the cause of freedom, since they were free themselves. And so they'd gone.

Prue stuck her pitchfork into the mound before her and bent her back to its lifting. This was hard work and she was near beat by it. But other women were doing the same. Earlier— about the time the British had evacuated Boston, thanks to the cannon sledded to that town from Fort Ticonderoga—she'd seen more than one woman driving a plow. Sara, for example, with her two children tagging at her heels, worked Aaron's farm alone. There had been no choice. She, herself, had been lucky in the spring, for John Konkapot—the old chief's son—had come back for a while and had kindly helped her.

"You all right, Prue?"

"Yes."

"One more's all she'll take."

She looked up, gave him a small stiff smile and nodded. One more. Then she'd rest riding to the barn. She gave a heave and tossed her load as high as she could. It was not quite high enough but Pa caught it before it slid off, and worked it up the rest of the way.

"You set awhile," he told her, looking down at her out of his bright, black, knowledgeable eyes. "Go over under the tree yonder and set. I can manage to shove this off in the barn all right."

"You sure?"

"Yep."

Prue watched him pick up the reins with old hands that shook a trifle, then the loaded wagon lumbered away. She walked gratefully toward the one great oak Pa had never had the heart to chop down when he was clearing this field, and dropped beneath its shade.

Over a year now since the war had started. It had ended auspiciously for the patriots with General Gage forced to retreat from Boston to New York, giving the rebel army its first real victory that had assuaged the shock and disappointment of the Quebec disaster. That success and the Declaration of Independence had put fire into the hearts of the Americans, but there was no fire in Prue's, for Johnny, coming home for a brief visit, reported he had not been able to get her message through to David who must be now either in New York or Halifax.

And a short letter from Luke had given the bare, grim facts of his terrible winter in Montreal, his decision to inoculate himself against smallpox and the confusion and wretchedness that existed in spite of the arrival (too late) of re-enforcements. "Everyone is sick or frightened to death," he finished. At least, though, Mark had come back safe from Saint John's.

And Mary had sent good news, writing jubilantly of the amazing rout of the British Navy from the shores of Charles Town. Her sons, Kim and Keith had both been in that action. Now, however (Mary wrote) the boys had chosen to be privateers and they hoped Luke would come down to Charles Town and join them as soon as ever he got back from Canada.

"Oh, Prue!" (Mary ended). "Never did I think the rumble and thunder of guns would be music in my ears! But I vow it was just that and no women are prouder than those of us here in Charles Town who witnessed our great success."

Prue closed her eyes and leaned back against the tree. Had something been left out of her nature that she could not feel, as Mary and so many others did, a great surge of patriotic fervor? Even the Declaration of Independence, fine sounding though it was, had not stirred her, for it still seemed to her that nations should settle their differences by other ways than fighting.

Yet, at the same time, she was beginning to concede that there was a nobility in men's souls if they were willing to lay aside all personal selfish desires and die for an idea which, in their minds, transcended their own importance.

Yes, David, who she had thought had wronged her, might have been more right than she. If only she could say this to him! If only Johnny would write that he had at last gotten word to him!

It was the next month that Prue heard again from Johnny. The letter held no cheer. He was in Headquarters in New York after General Washington's defeat on Long Island. Here they hoped to take a stand and successfully defend the city.

"At any rate," he wrote, "there has been a lull in military operations since the Long Island battle and I have this chance to write you of my latest efforts to locate David. In our present positions the redcoats and Yankees are drawn up so close as to be able to exchange words together. I, therefore, instructed our sentry to pass on a message to the British sentry to the effect that I would like to converse with Captain David Reynolds on a personal matter if he was in that area. The report came back, however, that he is not here, so, again, I have been frustrated. I am sorry but will keep on trying.

"Finally, in reply to your query about a life's companion for me, I will tell you that the image of the woman I want for that role continues to live clear and sharp in my mind and heart. I had thought to root it out by my preoccupation with national matters long before this, but have not been successful. My hope now is to be sent to the Southland on a mission that I may discover finally if I am cherishing to no purpose and beyond reason a young man's fancy. I suppose it has not been wise for us to correspond but it was a solace for both of us and through her letters I have discovered how lonely a life Myrtle has led these last years and that her regard for me has grown stronger because of Matt's imperious ways which alternate with indifferent neglect. I would to God she was free so that I might shower her with the love she has missed! But anyway, I must and shall talk with her.

"Tell Sara that Aaron is here in New York also. He, and in fact, all of the Indians, are used as scouts. A hazardous business but they are good at it.

"Do not work too hard, my sister, and rest assured I will continue to try to reach David for you. Johnny."

It was a gray Sunday in August, and Pa and Prue were on their way down to church. Pa was talking about the Stockbridge Indians and the willingness they had shown to help the Americans in this war.

"Folks say they're corrupted," he said. "Corrupted more'n civilized. Well, to my mind, there's plenty of whites are just as corrupted. Of course there's bad Indians. But there's good, too." He paused. "Trouble here has laid with the greed of the whites and the fact they were smarter'n the savages."

It was true, Prue thought, relieved to be brought out of the sadness of her thoughts. Yes, it was true. The Indians had taken at face value what had been told them. And they had been deceived. Simplicity was no match for shrewdness. Ignorance could not stand up against intelligence. When knowledge was power and power was not unselfish—

A musket shot in the village broke into her revery.

"What was that?"

"Dunno." Pa clucked to the horse. "But we'll soon find out."

A second shot followed the first in a few moments and Prue murmured, "Oh, I fear there's bad news!"

Hardly had she spoken the words when a distant cannonading

was heard to the north behind them. The sound was faint but unmistakable.

"Pa! It must be the British coming down!"

He nodded. He was leaning over the dashboard now urging the old mare to a gallop. As they raced down the hill others joined them, all hurrying to reach the village to find out what this summons meant. Ever since the shocking evacuation of Fort Ticonderoga without a fight the month before, the whole countryside south of that had lived in terror and dread.

"We'll head for the store," Pa said.

When they reached it a crowd had already gathered and sober faces were lifted to await the words of Jahleel Woodbridge, spokesman for the town. It was he who had fired the shots.

Jahleel stood on the store steps above them all, a short, thick-set man who held himself with the stiffness of delegated authority, his chin out, his mouth pursed, a fierce frown on his red face. Dressed for church in a long coat of fine blue broadcloth, ruffled white shirt and silk hose, with his three-cornered hat set firm on his powdered hair, he ignored the light rain that had begun to fall and waited, without moving toward shelter, for the last stragglers to come running up. Prue and Pa, driving as close as they could, sat waiting, too.

At last he spoke, his words falling into a dead silence.

"The British are marching down. A dispatch rider has brought the news. Every available man is needed all up and down this valley. Even though you've just finished your enlistment, you're needed and must go." His eyes roved over the assembly, coming to rest on Aaron, but recently returned home, then traveling on to others he knew were counting on working on their neglected farms. "You'll all have to go," he repeated. "King Solomon! Are you ready to lead your company again?"

The Indian grunted an assent. Aaron stepped forward, quickly followed by others. Jahleel turned to the dapper little figure of Dr. West who stood on the porch behind him—under its protecting roof.

"Reverend, I will ask you to lead us in prayer."

The minister, his Bible in his hand, took over the impromptu meeting.

"There will be no church service this day," he announced. "God will forgive this, I am certain, for He knows that the families of our defenders need a little time together before they part. Let us, therefore, offer up our prayers here and now for the success of our brave men, for the righteous cause they serve, and for their safe and speedy return. Oh, Lord! Hear us now, as, in humiliation and hope, with confidence in Thee, we ask for Thy protection and help in the ordeal that lies before us all."

There was gravity but little weeping as the men faced the inevitable, and before noon Indians and whites together were on their way north.

Anxious weeks followed. Daily the sound of cannonading grew clearer. Rumors and contradictory rumors were brought to the tense little village by fleet-footed Indians. At last came the news of the defeat of the redcoats at the Battle of Bennington. This was the beginning of a series of successes that finally resulted in Burgoyne's surrender to General Gates at Saratoga.

Surrender! The British had surrendered! Was David among those men? Would he be one to march with the defeated troops to the seacoast and Boston? If only Prue could know!

"You could find out," Pa told her.

"How?"

"I hear tell they're a-goin' to march through Great Barrington. Fact, they're a-goin' to stop there overnight for supplies. You could go to Mark's. If David's amongst 'em you could likely see him."

If he was amongst them! It was too much to hope. Prue would not permit herself to hope.

Nevertheless, she was in the front row of the crowd that gathered at the edge of the road that day to watch for the arrival of the Britishers. And when the first rat-a-tat-tat of the drummers was heard in the distance, she began trembling so that Mark, beside her, put his arm about her to give support.

"Oh, Mark, I'm so glad you're with me. I don't know which

will be worse—or better—to see him or not to see him!" She lifted
a face gone white with her suspense and ended in a whisper. "He
must hate me so."

"He doesn't hate you, Ma. The more a man's in battle, the
dearer are the ones he left behind."

The drum beats drew nearer. Here came the first scouts riding
ahead of the column. Here came the American troops, their faces
a-grin. Here came the drummer boys and the buglers—and the
watching crowd went suddenly wild. Cheering and yelling, it
surged forward to peer and was pushed back to leave room. Hats
and caps flew in the air. Arms waved. Voices shouted greetings.
And then a silence fell as the defeated general, heading his unarmed troops, appeared on his uneasily prancing horse. Behind
him Prue's blurred vision saw a mass of red. Presently the red
separated for her into individual shapes. How tired the foot soldiers looked. How draggled. How humbled in their pride. Now
the drums had stopped and there was only the sound of shuffling
feet and the whistles, jeers and taunts of the onlookers. As the
first group trudged past, Prue clutched Mark's arm.

"I can hardly bear it. I can hardly *see*. Suppose—suppose he's
not with them, Mark?"

"Then we'll find out where he is. Colonel Dwight is to give a
reception for General Burgoyne tonight. We'll go. We'll meet the
general and ask him David's whereabouts."

"But I didn't bring a gown suitable—" She broke off, for suddenly her seeking gaze had seen a familiar face. Familiar, yet not
familiar, so gaunt it was, so drawn and lined with fatigue and
pain, so—so hopeless and despairing. And then, as if compelled
by her look, he turned his head and their eyes met. Instantly into
his sprang the well-remembered little dancing fires.

"David!" she screamed, and flung herself forward toward him,
oblivious of the crowd, of the sudden halting of the soldiers or
the barked order that was relayed back through the crisp air.

She could never clearly recall anything that followed. Did he
speak to his men? Or did they continue their marching in understanding without a word from him? What mattered it? They

were together, clinging in a close embrace, he murmuring her name over and over, she saying—she knew not what.

And then Mark spoke. "Pa. You're wounded."

Yes. He was wounded. He was holding her with only one arm, the other hanging loose and helpless. And there was the glaze of fever in his eyes and the heat of it on his face. Why had she never noticed? How cruel, how selfish!

"David! Come to Mark's office at once! Let him—"

"Not now, my sweet. I must go with my men. Later, perhaps."

Later! How much later? Prue was beside herself.

"I must talk to you, David. I must— Oh, there's too much to say! But first—your wound. When—"

"Rest assured I'll join you at Mark's as soon as ever I can. Until then—tell me: Am I forgiven?"

His husky anxious whisper, his hope, his dread—both so clear in his eyes.

She was overwhelmed. "Are *you*—! You mean, am *I?*"

No other words were needed. How kind Providence was to her! And how little she deserved it. David returned, thin, war-weary and wounded, but without resentment in his heart for all her wild and wicked words. Loving her truly still as he had promised he would.

David was home again. Home at Martin Manor. Home in his own bed. She bent over him now, seeing him asleep there and thinking what a miracle it was.

How had it happened?

She had waited endless hours, or so it seemed, at Mark's office for David to appear. At last he had come, and Mark, seeing his brightly burning eyes, hearing his confused talk, had said to Prue, "Find Dr. Erastus Sergeant, if you can, Ma. This is serious."

Dr. Sergeant, Abigail's son, was soon found, and he and Mark examined David's wounds together. A bullet had grazed a lung. He was coughing blood. Another bullet had shattered the collar bone and infection had set in. They agreed David must not travel farther in that condition and they helped Prue arrange with the officer in command of the prisoners to take her husband home with her.

He was a parolee. She had gone bond for him and had given her word he would not escape. Now she would nurse him back to health and then—well—only God knew what would transpire but she was willing to leave the future in His hands.

CHAPTER 21

The End and the Beginning

As A PAROLEE, David was required, as soon as he was able, to take the patriot's oath. This he did without demur, for he had seen the people fighting for their land. He had come to know their spirit, and to respect it deeply. He felt, at last, a kinship with them, a sense of belonging. Yes, this was home for him, finally, and he was able to say, "I am glad to lay down arms. I shall be most thankful when all concerned can do the same, and this bloody strife reaches an end."

Prue sighed with deep relief. "I am so happy to hear that, David! But you are not saying this just for me?"

"No. Not just for you. I've changed, Prue. I've come to a new understanding of America and Americans. It is one good thing the war has done."

"I've changed too. I want to see your home in England. I'll go—anytime."

David's face lighted up. "We'll go, Prue, just as soon as it can be arranged."

With David home and slowly getting better, that winter held the first real joy Prue had known since he had left her. She was given relief in other ways, too, for Aaron was back again, on his farm, and Luke was not one of that battered, ragged army starving and dying in Valley Forge. He had returned from Canada and been transferred, as he had requested, to a ship where (he wrote) he had good treatment and good food. He was not with Keith and Kim, but that might came later.

324

Neither was Johnny at Valley Forge. Where was he? Had he ever reached the Southland as he had long wanted to do? Had he seen Myrtle? Mary never mentioned his having been there in any of her letters, though she did say that Matt, grown restless, had gone on the high seas again himself. Well, Matt could survive anything, Prue told herself. He always had.

So the winter passed with its measure of healing for David and its measure of peace for Prue. Happily she hovered over him, bundling him against the cold, bringing him nourishing snacks between meals, enfolding him in the watchful protection of her love in all the ways she could think of, and wanting, in return, only to see his smile light up his brown eyes, his thin hand reach out for hers.

Then came spring—and anxiety again, for Luke, in an engagement on the high seas, was taken prisoner and put aboard the prison ship *Jersey*.

The *Jersey*—the prison ship! Prue's heart was pinched with dread and despair, for she knew few ever escaped alive from there. And when Luke wrote that he was in the hospital "reduced to the gates of the grave from bad living and every kind of hardship," she gave up all hope of ever seeing him alive again.

"They have no bedding save one small blanket even in the coldest weather," she told David. "They are given putrid water to drink and condemned horse beef and biscuit filled with weevils to eat. Oh! I am afraid! Nothing but a miracle will save him!"

"Miracles can happen," he returned. "Are we not together again?"

His faith restored hers, and in due time the miracle occurred. Luke wrote later that he had won the interest and liking of a "physician gentlemen" who had arranged his transfer to the barracks on shore in his own service and would, as soon as he could, negotiate his release.

Luke would be home! The Lord be thanked. And Johnny would be home, too. But not rescued from the grave, as was Luke. Indeed, not for any reason Prue could ever have imagined.

She was apprised of it through Mary who, when the war swung south in 1779, wrote of the terrible threat to Charles Town and the undoubted imminent surrender of that proud city.

"Prevost's army" (she said in her letter) "is so close that thought of saving Charles Town has been abandoned, fear of a slave uprising is dreaded by all, and the populace is divided between staying and fleeing. Faith and her children—Dulcie and baby William—have moved from their plantation and are here with Alec and me in our town house, as James left orders for her to do in such an emergency. We have not heard from Matt in weeks and begin to fear disaster has overtaken him. Myrtle has been beside herself, wanting to leave and not knowing how she dared or where to go, when Johnny, in good disguise, slipped through the lines and told her he would help her and her two girls escape to the North. He has asked me to let you know that he is bringing them to you. Oh, Prue! These are terrible days and we face a frightful calamity and disgrace here! Yet we must face it, so pray for us. I do not mean by that that I blame Myrtle for leaving. She has two daughters to think of that she must protect and with no man by her side and in the house only blacks she cannot trust— Anyway, each must decide for himself."

So! Myrtle was escaping and coming North to live at Martin Manor. And Johnny was bringing her. Slowly Prue folded the letter, put it back into its envelope and lifted troubled eyes to David.

"I don't know what will come of this," she murmured.

"You could do nothing about it if you did."

"Perhaps not. But I could try."

"Yes. You could try."

She glanced at him quickly. "You think I shouldn't?"

He said gently, "Can you be a conscience for other people, Prue?"

She looked down at her hands in her lap, remembering. "No," she said, in a low tone. Then she smiled ruefully at David. "I never learn, do I? What a woman I have become!"

David nodded. "Yes. What a woman you have become," he repeated. But there was in his caressing, weary voice a note of utter contentment.

Two years later the war ended. America had bungled through to a successful conclusion in spite of Arnold's treachery and national bankruptcy.

One of the first things Stockbridge did to mark the victory was to have a great feast on Laurel Hill not far from the pass through which the defeated Burgoyne and his troops had marched (without David) on their way to Boston.

It had been ordered by George Washington in a letter to Jahleel Woodbridge, as an expression of gratitude to the Indians who had been of such service during the war. Everyone came, not only from Stockbridge but from the neighboring towns. A great fire was built close to the rocks under the trees and here, while the bullock was being roasted for the feast, the ceremony took place. John Sergeant, Jr., was in charge of the proceedings.

There was, first, a welcome by Jahleel, then a prayer by Dr. West, an address of appreciation by Theodore Sedgwick, whose importance in the community and the colony was growing, and, last, a poem written and read by Johnny. After that the war hatchet was buried with appropriate speeches by the Indians, following which the evening was given over to lighter matters. An effigy of Benedict Arnold was hung, scalped and burned. A ration of whisky for each Indian was distributed and—at last— the great ox was carved and divided among them all.

Pa sat a little apart, on a rock seat, watching the scene. There was only a handful of Indians left here now, he was thinking, compared to the numbers that had been here when he arrived. And these would not be staying much longer. Two years ago—in 1779—they had held their last office and now that they had lost all their hunting ground to the whites they were moving to New York State where the Oneidas had offered them a part of their own reservation. John Sergeant was going with them. Well, that was one good thing, Pa said to himself. Certainly there was no other. To think of all those high hopes of the first John Sergeant, all the effort and difficulties and disappointments, all the faith-

fulness and trust of the savages—their loyalty even unto death—
and then to have everything peter out to nothing in the end!
This feast was more an apology than a payment, to his thinking
—and if payment, it wasn't enough.

He said as much to Theodore Sedgwick who came up to him
just then.

"I agree," Sedgwick replied readily. "I am mindful of the same
thing. But further recompense cannot be considered now. There
are other matters our new nation must work out first. Our finances are in a dreadful state, as you know. And Massachusetts
has not as yet drawn up its own State constitution. However, give
us time. We will accomplish all we must in due season and then
our Indians will not be neglected." He glanced toward a group
of younger people and went on. "I'm glad to see David is able
to be with us tonight. Has he quite recovered from his wounds?"

"He's in fair health now."

"Good. I thought Johnny's poem a very fine expression of sen-
timent," he went on, with his usual tact.

Pa grunted. "Johnny's bound to scribble. I don't hold much
with such for a man. No livin' in it fur as I can see. But as long
as Myrtle's willin' to support him—"

"Myrtle? Ah, yes. I remember. Matt's widow. He was killed in
a skirmish at sea, wasn't he?"

Pa's face changed, and his voice roughened. "Happened a year
ago. She and Johnny got married soon after, and her and her
girls and him are all livin' in New York now." His tone said he
didn't think much of that, either.

"I should have known, I suppose, but I'm in Boston a good
deal and my mind is mostly on state and national matters."

"Hear you're plannin' to build yourself a place on the plain."

"Yes. Pamela and I decided we would make Stockbridge our
future home. Pamela wants to be near her mother, Mrs. Abigail
Dwight. Well, I'll say good night to you, Captain, and go over
to give my belated congratulations to Johnny and his wife. Then
I must be on my way back to Boston."

Pa looked up at him, his black eyes glinting with all his old command. "Whilst you're there, don't forget about the Indians," he said.

As Pa had thought, the Indians did not remain long in Stockbridge after the Great Feast. By 1785 all except a few, who refused to leave, had sadly departed to their second home which they called New Stockbridge. It was on a June morning of that year of their departure that Pa was sitting alone on the hilltop where the great white house called Martin Manor stood under its spreading protective trees.

Pa was sitting out in the sun where he could just glimpse the steeple of the new church built a year or so ago half way up the hill on land Dr. West had yielded for that purpose. Pa was eighty years old today. Before him the farm he had visioned lay stretched out in a rich fertility. He was proud of it, as well he might be. It had prospered well and had freed him from all need of the world. He had his own flax, his own wheat, his own barley. He kept horses and oxen, cows and sheep, swine, chickens, turkeys. He had the wherewithal to make his own shoes and clothes. He could cooper his own barrels. For food there were cheeses and hams, eggs and fruits and vegetables of all kinds. Oh! He lacked nothing! Nothing at all—save a son who would care about it and for it as he did. But three were dead and the fourth was gone to the city to live. Nor had he a grandson, either, with Mark a doctor and Luke off to Charles Town to go into the ship business there with his cousins, Keith and Kim.

His thoughts moved sluggishly as do the thoughts of an old man. But they were sharp and clear.

This place needed a man and he was troubled that there was none outside of hired help, for he was conscious of some intangible force rising, some change threatening, that might destroy all he had wrought. He had seen it once in a trip to the lower valley where industry had crept in that had ruined the farmland and rendered ugly the whole area. That must not happen here.

Yet was it not inevitable? Elijah Williams in West Stockbridge with his iron mines. Furniture factories in Curtisville. A paper factory in Lee. And now talk of marble quarries.

What for? To satisfy the greed of men. That was all. Yes. He could see it coming, a renewed battle between the Lord and the devil. The same battle John Sergeant had fought—yet a different one. This time it would not be over the souls of men but over the preservation of the land as the Lord had created it and meant it to be used.

And who was to fight in that battle? Who was to hold Martin Manor against the encroachments of those wishing to exploit its riches? Prue had the spirit. She alone, of all his children, had the proper feel for the land he so loved. It had done to her what it had done to him. But now she was planning to be in England with David a part of every year. And what in tarnation would happen whilst she was away? Anything could!

He shook his grizzled head and drew a sigh from within the depths of him. The cycle of his life was nearly completed. All he wanted was to live and let live. To plant and to reap. To feel an ultimate and permanent good arising from this way of life. But he was afeard. He was mighty afeard.

Prue came out now and joined him. She was a middle-aged woman, he thought suddenly, with all the gold gone out of her braids, and some sadness—Matt's death had affected her deeply—and plenty of sweetness written on the lines of her face. But her body was still slim and all her movements brisk and certain the way they had always been.

She sat down on the grass beside him and entered into his silence with him. She could do that. No needless words from Prue. But when she spoke what she said was firm and full of sense. It was he who broke their reverie.

"There's some new thing growing up here."

She nodded. "Yes. And a good thing it is, too."

"How can you say that!" —sharply.

"Because I can. It is good to have a man like Theodore Sedgwick building himself a mansion in the village."

Pa, surprised, said nothing. Prue went on.

"He is like Mr. Sergeant was—in a way. Fine things will come from his being here, I feel sure. Fine things for the village."

"What fine things?"

Prue put her elbows on her knees and, leaning forward, rested her chin on her clasped hands.

"I mean"—she said slowly— "he and his friends will bring a—a new balance to the people here. Good grows, Pa. It doesn't stay the same. It changes with the years. Mr. Sergeant brought one kind. Mr. Sedgwick will bring another."

"I don't follow."

Prue sought for clarifying words. "He'll bring the world in, is what I mean. He knows President Washington. And other great men. He—"

"Who wants the world in?" Pa interrupted. "The world's here. All that suits me of it."

Prue shook her head. "It isn't enough." She paused. "I can't say it right. I love this place, too. You know that. But—Pa! All we do here is work. Hard manual work. We need something else. Something to—to offset that. Something for our minds. I've always felt so. I've always hankered to have the time for books and such and I've never had it. If that was here—ideas, talk of ideas and the things that are being writ and said and done—Martin Manor would suit Johnny. But he couldn't stand just the body work."

Pa was silent, digesting that. So Prue thought Johnny might come back some day. It was a good thought. Still Johnny was not the one who could help Prue against what he'd meant was growing up here.

"I think," Prue went on, "that Mr. Sedgwick will bring in those things."

"Mebbe so. And mebbe 'twill be good. I wasn't thinkin' o' that, though. When I said a new thing was like to grow up here, I was thinkin' o' that rascal Williams and his plans for more mines and quarries and such like." He pounded a closed fist with sudden vigor on the arm of his chair. "I'll not have him tearin' great holes in any of *my* land! I can tell you!"

"He won't."

The vigor fell from him. "Who's to stop him? When I'm gone

—and you're off in England—who's to stop him? Who's to defend what's here? I don't see why you're goin' anyway."

Prue looked off at the hills. After a moment she said quietly, "To—heal the wounds of war."

"Wounds of war? But Dave's all right now!"

A half smile touched Prue's lips. "I can't say it any other way. I can't explain any better. It's just—I want to go. But you've no cause to fret. Aaron will be here. Aaron will defend the hill, if it needs defending."

Aaron! He had never thought of Aaron. But now—suddenly— he seemed the logical one. Aaron. Why, yes! This was his hunting ground as it had been for his people before him. Indeed, it belonged to him doubly, for it had been his father's land. He loved it as it should be loved. He would never let it be devastated or taken from him. Why had he—Pa—never thought of Aaron?

"I shall depend on him," Prue was saying. She lifted her head and looked into Pa's eyes and laid a hand gently over one of his.

"Nothing is without consequence for both good and evil in this life, Pa," she said softly. "They come out of the same root."

He knew what she meant. And it was true. But how strange that of all his children, the most troublesome, the most heart-breaking, the most selfish one of them, had left him the greatest comfort in the end.

David appeared now and Prue, seeing him, rose to meet him. Together, with their arms around each other, they stood in silence, looking out across the fields.

Pa watched them with a deep contentment on his face. Another era might be commencing, as Prue said. But the Lord was still in these hills, and Aaron would guard the land.

Epilogue

After leaving Stockbridge in 1785, the Indians remained in New Stockbridge for several years, later moving, first to Ohio and then to Wisconsin. There they set up a New England Village, a replica of the one they had known and loved in Massachusetts, with neat houses, a similar system of government, a Christian church, a free school—and with an annual stipend of fifteen hundred dollars from the national government to help them care for their old and needy. Thus the Indians were not forgotten and the good done by the little Mission at Stockbridge lived on.